This is a work of fiction. Unless otherwise indicated, all the names, characters, places, events, and incidents in this book are either the product of the author's imagination or used in a fictitious manner. Any resemblance to actual persons, living or dead, or actual events is purely coincidental. For full content warning, please see the author's note located in the back of this book, or go to www.vanessakramerauthor.com

All rights reserved. No part of this publication may be reproduced, distributed, or transmitted in any form without permission, including AI.

Copyright August 2024 Virtue Publishing
First Edition published October 2024

ISBN 979-8-9916277-0-2 (paperback)

"If I am not,
may God put me there.
And if I am,
may God keep me so."
-St. Joan of Arc,
when asked if she was in God's grace.

1

The thing I miss the most about being alive is dreaming; even the bad dreams. I miss the relief of waking up and realizing I was only asleep, lost in my subconscious. But I miss the good dreams even more. I would dream about the future and the past. I would dream about completely made-up things, or things I had seen in movies or read in books. My dreams were vivid and realistic. I would transport to another time and place. But now? There is no dreaming. There is no sleeping. My past and future no longer matter. All there is, is now.

My name is Emma. I died from cancer at the age of 21. Before I died, I had made a suicide pact with my boyfriend, Alastor. Looking back at the whole thing now, it does seem a little dramatic. I was so caught up being in love though. Well, I was caught up in the *idea* of being in love with him. It turned out that I didn't know him at all. Alastor ended up being a demon named Ankou. Ankou's area of expertise was suicides. While demons can't make humans do anything, they can trick and persuade them into doing what they want. He almost had. Fortunately, cancer got to me first. When I died, I was worried that "Alastor" had gone through with our original plan, so I teamed up with a handful of misfit angels to find him. Dumah, a death angel, quickly became my friend, despite being the most crotchety being I've ever met. Sam, one of my childhood best friends, died at a young age and became my guardian angel. Sekhmet, a dark angel who used her horrible death to become a powerful cat-like creature, and Baraqiel, a dark angel with the power to summon lightning from his body, had also joined our party.

I had entered Hell to save my boyfriend, only to discover he was a demon who had recruited my guardian angel/childhood friend to help trick me into being trapped in Hell for eternity. Dumah died saving me, his soul returning to Earth to be reincarnated into a new body. Sekhmet and Baraqiel were severely injured, but returned to their places in Limbo, or The Space Between Spaces. Sam was placed in the Sea of Anathema, or the "Cursed Sea." She is forever cursed to float helplessly with all of the other souls who can't ever go to Hell or Heaven. I took Dumah's place as a death angel. I spent my days being present when people die, so they aren't alone. I always tried to be there for suicides, although I've gotten in trouble a few times for making my job too "personal."

Some evenings, I tried to get out on my boat and look for Sam. I had only spotted her a couple of times since becoming an angel. The first time I saw her, she looked like a sleeping child, slowly gliding along under the water's surface. The second time I saw her, her cheeks looked a little more sunken in and her skin had a gray hue. I hadn't seen her since. I've visited Sekhmet several times since becoming a death angel, but Baraqiel wanted nothing to do with me; which was fair. I did almost get him and Sekhmet permanently killed. Not to mention what happened to Dumah. I carried enough guilt about it, though. I didn't need Baraqiel trying to make me feel worse. It's been 73 years, however, it feels like it happened yesterday.

Four significant events have happened since becoming an angel. Three of those events were the deaths of my mother, father, and brother. My father died first. He had had a massive stroke and was in hospice for a short amount of time. He was unable to talk, but when he saw me, he said my name and smiled. Unfortunately, my mother and brother weren't with him when he passed, which broke my mother's heart. She died shortly after he did. Simon, my brother, was there when she died. He saw her reach her hand up, not seeing it land gently on my cheek, and whisper, "Oh, my sweet girl. You've come back for me." None of it made sense to Simon until years later. He grew up, got married, and had a family of his own. I checked in with him when I could, but could never stay for very long. When he passed away, he was surrounded by his wife and four children, including his daughter, Emma Rose. As he passed from life to death, his eyes filled with tears of joy and he leapt into my arms.

"Emma!" he exclaimed. I wrapped my arms around him for a moment before he turned to look at his lifeless body in the hospital bed. His wife was sobbing. The smile faded from his face.

"It's okay," I said softly. "They're going to be okay."

"Are you- are you an angel?" Simon asked, pointing to my black wings. I nodded.

"Yeah, it's a long story," I smiled. "Come on, they've been waiting for you."

"Who?" he asked.

"Mom and Dad."

I took Simon to Processing, which despite living a long life, he wasn't in for very long. Not surprisingly, Simon chose to go on to Paradise with our parents. I'd be lying if I said I didn't have a minor case of FOMO. The idea of blissfully spending eternity with all of the best parts of your life sounds pretty good, until you realize that's all made up; like a simulation. For example, your parents and children would be in your own Paradise, but they're actually off in their own little version of Paradise with who they want there. It's real to you, but not reality. You can also choose to return to Earth and start a new life as a new person. However, you don't have a say in where you'll end up. The option I chose, becoming an angel, gave me the most freedom. I get to stay myself, and even though I have a very important job to do, I get to choose what I do with the rest of my time; which brings me to the fourth event.

When Dumah returned to Earth 73 years ago, he was born Eduardo Reyes in Medellin, Colombia. He grew up, married a woman named Elena, and they moved to the United States with their son, Diego. Over the years, I watched over him, always afraid that Ankou would somehow weasel his way into Eduardo's life and convince him to end it. I admired his courage to move his family from Colombia to the United States, where they would be happier and safer. Eduardo and Elena opened a restaurant in Chicago, Illinois. When Diego was old enough, he started working there too. Diego helped run the restaurant until he went to college, where he met a girl named Gina. Diego and Gina married and had two children; a girl named Sloane, and a boy named Gabriel. Two years ago, Eduardo had a heart attack. I thought maybe that would have been the end for him. I stayed with him while his wife called 911 and never left his side on the way to the hospital. I thought about what I might say once he died. *Hi, remember me? I got you killed. Want your old job back so I can seek revenge on an ex boyfriend?*

I had no intentions of giving up being an angel, but with so few of us left, I was being watched more closely than usual. The handful of times I tried to interact with Ankou, I was quickly pulled aside by my boss, Ankou's brother, Barachiel. I've been reminded over and over again that it's not my job to interfere with demons, even if they're breaking laws. We angels are supposed to report any wrongdoings to our superiors and let them handle it. But I wanted to confront Ankou and kill him. I've thought about it every day since becoming a death angel. I was obsessed over it. He had almost ruined my eternity. He had corrupted Sam. He killed Dumah. He was recruiting angels to help him get more souls into Hell.

I tried multiple times to tell the archangels what Ankou was doing and how he needed to be stopped.

"There are certain ways to take care of these situations," Michael had said. "We have to be careful not to break any treaties. I'm sure whatever Ankou has planned will get snuffed out by the authorities in Hell."

When I asked them to look into it more, Michael waved me away, like a gnat. I went to Sekhmet to ask for help, but she more or less agreed with the archangels.

"Best leave that stuff to them," she said. "After all, Michael is the one who threw the rebellious angels into Hell. If he's not worried, you shouldn't be."

"How did you go from being the goddess of chaos, blood thirst, and pestilence to this calm, easygoing kitty cat?"

Sekhmet shrugged and smiled.

"I don't know," she said. "I'll still go after anyone who tries to leave Hell who's supposed to stay put. And the more barbaric demons are still fun to fight. I guess I got past all the anger. Something I highly recommend you doing."

I sighed and looked out over the Sea of Anathema. I didn't have a single being on my side. I knew if Dumah had been alive still, he would agree with me. He'd fight with me. So I decided to keep quiet, keep to myself, do my job, and wait out Eduardo's remaining years. My only hope was that Eduardo was more like Dumah once he died. Deep down I knew he'd choose being an angel over Paradise though.

I walked along the beach by the hut that was once Dumah's. I had been slowly working on building a place of my own, with the help of a virtue. I tried not to disturb Dumah's hut too much, in case he remembered where he had left everything. It was more a storage shed than an actual house, with no need for a bedroom, kitchen, or bathroom. I approached the empty frame of my own little dwelling, sighing at the sight of it. Looking out at the water, I could see something in the distance. It was a ship. The ship that carried souls from Sentencing to Processing. They were the souls who did their time in the mildest part of Hell and had been granted the opportunity to go to Paradise. They would stay in Processing while guides like Hannah, who I had met when first arriving to Processing, went over their time spent on Earth and in Sentencing. That would determine how long their wait was to enter Paradise. I watched until the ship was out of sight. It would dock about a hundred miles down the shore from where I was and everyone would go straight to Processing.

I decided to visit Elijah. Elijah was a virtue who ran the front desk of what would be the world's largest hotel, if it were on Earth. He knew everyone who was brought in for Processing and where they were going. He was also how I got connected to the virtue who was building my hut. I knew all angels were pretty busy with their jobs, but waiting 73 years for a tiny home to be built seemed a little long, even if I did have eternity.

I walked towards the doors of the hotel and looked around at the new arrivals. Everyone either seemed to be smiling or in awe of their surroundings. I remembered feeling the same when Matt brought me to Processing. I wished I could find a way to feel that way again.

"I thought that was you, Emma!" I heard a tiny voice behind me exclaim. I winced at the sound and slowly turned around. Flying very close to my head was a tiny woman, no bigger than my hand. She had long black hair, light blue eyes, and wings like a giant blue morpho butterfly. Thalia was the one who promised to build me a new hut.

Sure, she was tiny, but virtues were great architects. The problem with Thalia was that she considered our relationship as more friendly than I did. It was strictly business, and my hope was that as soon as she finished my hut, I wouldn't be seeing much of her.

"Hey, Thalia," I said quickly.

"Where are you off to in such a hurry?" Thalia zipped in front of me. "You said you were free to hang out last Friday but when I came by your place, you were nowhere to be found! I checked back the next day- oh sorry!"

Thalia had flown backwards into a man's head, knocking him forward a little.

"I went back a third time and you still weren't there."

"Yeah," I mumbled. "Been real busy. Sorry."

"Oh, good. Because I was worried you were avoiding me," Thalia snorted. "But I figured that wasn't the case."

"Hey, speaking of my place," I said, "how soon do you think you'll have the hut done?"

"Well, that's why I keep trying to come over to hang out with you!" she grinned.

"You know, you can work on it when I'm not there."

"I know, I just work so much better when I have someone to chat with."

"Funny," I mumbled, "I prefer the silence."

Thalia gave me a look of hurt.

"Just kidding," I laughed awkwardly. Thalia laughed along with me.

"So, what brings you over here?" Thalia asked.

"Oh you know," I said, avoiding eye contact. "Just in the neighborhood."

"Are you here to see Elijah?" Thalia asked. "Is it about that angel that went back to Earth as a human? The one you've been waiting on to die?"

A couple of people turned to us as she said this. I gave them an awkward smile and made my way to the front desk. Elijah's face lit up as soon as he saw me.

"Emma!" he squealed. "Oh my goodness, it's been a while!"

Elijah wrapped both arms around me as he hugged me, to which I responded with a light pat. Thalia squeezed herself into the hug as well.

"Reunion hug!" Thalia exclaimed. Elijah quickly pulled away, his smile fading.

"Hello, Thalia," he said in a less excited tone.

"I was so excited when I saw Emma coming in here to visit you! I figured she was coming in here to talk to you about the ex-angel guy or her demon ex-boyfriend and-"

"Thalia!" I snapped. Thalia recoiled at the harshness of my voice.

"Sorry," she murmured.

"So why *are* you here, Emma?" Elijah asked, walking back to his desk. I leaned over the counter as he sat down.

"Will you double check to see if he's here?" I asked quietly. Elijah sighed heavily.

"And here I thought you wanted to just visit me," he rolled his eyes.

"I do!" I said quickly. "I just know that he might've slipped by without me knowing. I've been really busy lately with work so I haven't checked in on him in a couple of weeks."

"And by work you mean following Ankou?"

I didn't respond.

"Emma, you're going to get in trouble if you don't stop. You can't spend all of your time checking in on a human and a demon. You're not Eduardo's guardian angel and you're not an archangel. You're a death angel. You're supposed to be present when humans die."

"Why though?" I asked. "What's the point? There's already a greeting committee. Why can't they just do it."

"You're there for those who are scared when they're dying!" Elijah stood up. "Greeting committees are for those who pass peacefully. You're there when people die alone and afraid. They're suffering and you get to be there to comfort them."

"Yeah, I look super comforting," I said sarcastically. I extended my black wings to direct Elijah's attention to them.

"You look a lot less scary than Dumah did," Elijah smiled.

"If it makes you feel any better," Thalia spoke up. "I don't like how cute I look."

Elijah and I looked at her.

"Seriously! I wish I was a little more intimidating. Could you imagine if I ever came face to face with a demon like you have? And you did it as a human! I wouldn't stand a chance. I mean, what would I do? *Inspire* the demon?"

Elijah politely chuckled.

"Can you do that?" I asked.

"What?" Elijah and Thalia both said.

"Elijah, you're old," I turned to him.

"Gee, thanks."

"Is there a rule about that anywhere?"

Elijah thought for a moment.

"None that I can think of. But that's like saying counting cards isn't illegal, but everyone knows it's still wrong."

"You're comparing gambling to persuading demons, potentially saving human souls?" I asked.

"I'm just saying," Elijah continued, "it could have major consequences. Not to mention it's dangerous. Virtues aren't meant to be fighters. Their sole purpose is to inspire humans to do good and to use their God-given talents to spread joy. I can't imagine virtues even being able to influence demons though."

"I could try it," Thalia said, voice shaking a little. She cleared her throat before sternly repeating, "I can do it."

"Come by my shore sometime soon," I said to her. "Maybe we can talk about this some more without Elijah hovering over us."

"Okay!" Thalia exclaimed. "I'll go get a couple of jobs done now so I can have some free time. See you guys!"

Thalia quickly flew off, almost flying directly into a group of people. As she went out the door, I turned back to Elijah. He gave me a look of disapproval.

"What?" I asked. "It'll be fine. No one will get hurt, and no one will get in trouble. I'm just talking hypothetical. Plus I need her to finish my hut."

Elijah sighed and shook his head.

"By the way, no. He isn't here yet."

"Oh," I said, trying not to sound disappointed.

"What exactly are you planning on doing once he does die? He's not going to remember anything from being Dumah. He's lived an entire lifetime as someone else."

"I know."

"Emma, you didn't kill him. It's not your fault."

"You're right," I responded. "It's Ankou's fault. Just like it's his fault Sam is floating around in that sea for eternity. Ankou has ruined so many lives, not to mention all of the humans he's convinced to commit suicide. You want to talk about rule breaking? He's been doing it for years. But the archangels have so much going on, they're too busy to do anything about him. And if they're not going to do anything to stop him, I will. I can't just sit around and let him keep doing this. It's not right."

"But it's the way things are," Elijah replied. "Like it or not, angels and demons are part of the balance. You can't have good without the bad. And he's not forcing anyone to kill themselves."

"I can't believe you would say that," I scoffed.

"We can't make anyone do anything. You know that. We can persuade and influence and inspire and even manipulate. But free will will always be the number one rule, and no one gets away with breaking that rule."

I grunted in frustration and threw my hands up into the air before walking away.

"Where are you going?" Elijah called.

"Away from this conversation!" I replied.

"Very mature, Emma! Quit acting like a human!"

"I *was* a human not that long ago!" I yelled.

I looked around at the people who were gawking at me.

"Oh, mind your business!" I snapped at them before storming out the door.

As soon as I got past the doors and was clear of any people around me, I spread my wings and took off. I flew fast in anger. I wasn't angry with Elijah though. I was angry with the way things were. Angels knew that demons were cheating the system, but didn't do anything about it to avoid starting a war. But in doing so, they were allowing demons to persuade angels to help them get more souls into Hell. Instead of a war where we would most likely lose a lot of angels all at once, we were slowly losing them over a long period of time.

"Either way, we're screwed," I muttered to myself.

I flew down to shore by Dumah's hut and landed softly on the sand. I looked at the boat in front of me, remembering being on it with Sam and Dumah.

"Where have you been?" I heard a voice from behind me. I flinched.

"Heeeyyy, Barachiel," I said, turning around. "How are you doing?"

"I'd be better if you were actually working," he said sternly. "We make everything very easy for you. You have your tracker, wings, you don't need sleep or- wait. Where's your tracker?"

I put my hand over my wrist and smiled.

"It beeps non stop," I explained. "I may have put it in a drawer somewhere in the hut."

"It beeps to let you know where someone is dying," Barachiel sighed. "It beeps non stop because people are always dying. Come on, let's go get it."

We walked into the hut and started searching. After a few minutes, we heard a faint beeping sound. Barachiel pulled the watch-looking thing out of a cabinet full of books and robes. He handed it to me and I reluctantly put it on.

"It's amazing how easy we've made things for you newer angels," he smiled, tucking a strand of his long curly hair behind one ear. "All you have to do is open a location and it pulls up a world map to let you know exactly where you need to go."

"Yeah," I smiled politely. "It's really neat. Hey, while I have you here, I was wondering if we could talk about your brother."

Barachiel winced. I continued.

"It's just that I've been following him and I know for a fact that he's been selling drugs to a teenage boy *and* he's become "friends" with this man who has a gambling problem."

"Emma..."

"Just listen to me. Ankou is going to the casino with this guy three times a week and he's hundreds of thousands of dollars in debt and-"

"Emma!" Barachiel barked. "Enough. He's not killing anyone. He's not forcing anyone to kill anyone. He's not breaking any rules. I know it's upsetting. Believe me, I get it. But there isn't anything we can do about it. All we can do is hope that humans make the right choices and be there when we can for them. But you're meddling in things that don't concern you, despite your past with him. Let it go."

I stood there for a moment, brooding. I really was on my own with this. No one wanted to stop him. No one cared about anything except the rules.

"You have a really important job, Emma," he said finally. "Humans experience devastating ways of dying every day. A lot of them don't get to be surrounded by loved ones, or go peacefully in their sleep. Sometimes their guardian angels can't be there with them, or they don't have one assigned to them. I know being a death angel isn't the most glamorous job, but it's a well needed one. More so now with the way the world is. So much violence and hunger and hatred. We need you. More importantly, *they* need you. So please. Just let it go."

"Okay," I said finally. "I'll let it go."

"Thank you. What do you say? Back to work?"

I nodded.

"Good," Barachiel weakly smiled as he walked to the door. "I'll leave you to it then."

He stood in the doorway and gave me a sly smile.

"By the way, you can turn the beeping off. Just push the left button twice."

He flew away, the wind from the sea faintly whistling through the hut.

"Could've at least closed the door behind you," I muttered.

As I shut the door behind me, I looked at my tracker and pulled the world map up. It showed 361 people were about to die, all in various locations around the world. I picked one and flew there immediately. Despite my experience already, this job never got easier. Every scene I walked in on was still shocking. Still heartbreaking. I hated it every single time. Nothing about it made me feel better about myself, even though I knew I was bringing some sort of comfort to people in their last moments, when they needed it most.

I walked through the halls of the school slowly. This was one of the biggest jobs I had ever done. There were so many, I didn't know where to start. Luckily, a few guardian angels were there with their humans. They were kneeling next to them, their wings folded in as if to protect the scared teenagers. They hadn't been able to protect them from anything though. The kids were laying on the tile, some curled up in fetal positions. One girl was already gone, one side of her glasses broken from where a bullet had hit her in the eye. Many of the teens who were still alive were crying. Some were praying. A couple of them had wet themselves. A lot of the classrooms were still locked from the inside. I could hear teachers whispering to their students, trying to quietly comfort them.

    I knelt down by a young boy with curly red hair and freckles. He had been shot twice in the chest and the pool of blood around him was getting wider. I looked into his eyes and he looked back into mine. His breathing slowed, his heartbeat faded, and then as he left the world, all of the noise around us stopped. The sound of death; of nothingness. That's what this body was now. Nothing. One minute he was here, and the next he was somewhere else. His parents would never see him graduate. Never see him unpack his belongings in a college dorm. I thought momentarily of my own death and how I had gone way too young. I quickly snapped back to the present and moved onto the next victim.

    The assistant principal had tried shielding two students who were in the office with him; two girls wearing matching cheerleading outfits. One of the girls was laying underneath the man's slumped body as if he were still trying to protect her. She had blonde hair that was now partially saturated with blood. The other girl, who had braided black hair and braces, was crying. She had one hand pressed against her friend's neck, trying to stop the bleeding. She had no idea the blonde girl was already dead.

"It's okay," the girl with braids kept saying. "Shh, it's okay. Help will be here soon and we'll all be okay."

The assistant principal was looking at his cell phone, just out of reach. His wife was calling him. Silent tears ran down his face and he looked up at me.

"I'm...sorry," he gasped. I put my hand on his shoulder.

"I'm here to help you," I answered. "You're all going to be okay."

The assistant principal had been shot five times. The blonde girl had been shot once in the neck. The girl with the braids continued holding her friend's throat, sitting on the blood-soaked carpet. I waited for the assistant principal to pass and then moved on. I wish I could have told the girl with braids to get outside to safety, but I knew she wouldn't be able to hear me. I walked past several more guardian angels. One was hovering over a girl who was screaming next to a dead boy. My eyes met the angel's for just a moment before I looked away. They hated me. They hated what I stood for. No one wanted to see someone die. I was the Grim Reaper.

I heard gunfire followed by screams. I quickened my pace. A group of teenagers ran past me on the staircase. A couple of them had blood on their clothes. I couldn't tell if it was theirs or not. I reached the top of the stairs and found a discarded handgun. As I made my way down the hallway, I passed more bodies. They had died instantly, and I was too late for them. I heard a loud crash from a few classrooms away.

He must have brought more than one gun, I thought. I remembered when I was a teenager, mass shootings were a huge concern in our country. The government fought over how to handle gun laws and inevitably banned automatic weapons. But it didn't solve the problem. People like this kid started buying multiple handguns to carry out mass shootings.

"God damn it!" I heard a voice yell. "Fuck!"

I peered in to see a boy pacing back and forth. I could smell his sweat as soon as I entered the room. Then, I heard the sirens. The boy stopped pacing abruptly, ran to the window, and looked out.

"Fuck, fuck, fuck," he said while whacking himself in the side of the head with another gun in his hand. He ran to the door and shut it before pulling several desks and chairs in front of it. I knew what he was going to do, and I wanted to stop him from doing it. I tried to make myself appear to him, but wasn't able to. I knew interfering was against the rules. But I couldn't stand to see another life lost.

"Shit!" He yelled and stepped back. "What the fuck is wrong with me?"

"Lucas," I calmly took a step towards him. "I just want to talk to you. Is that okay?"

He couldn't hear me.

"Why did I kill so many of them?" he panted. "Fuuuuuuck, I'm dead. I'm dead!"

"I know what you're planning to do," I said. "Don't do it."

"I'm not going to get away with this and I can't spend the rest of my life in jail," he said to himself.

"Lucas, if you kill yourself, your soul will end up in Hell. Everyone has a chance to be saved. Spend the rest of your life repenting."

I was pleading with him, but it was useless. We heard yelling from somewhere else in the building. The police were searching for him. They would be here soon. If I could distract him at least long enough for them to find him, they would either arrest him or shoot him. Both were better outcomes than him killing himself. Lucas lifted the gun up to his temple.

"PLEASE, LUCAS!!" I screamed.

The windows in the room blew out and Lucas ducked down. *Please*, I thought. *Let that stall him long enough for the police to get in here.* He slowly stood up and glanced out the windows.

All of the sirens and yelling wailing around us grew deafening.

"I'm ready for this all to go away now," Lucas sobbed. Snot was running into his mouth, spraying as he spoke. "I'm tired of all the pain."

"No," I whispered.

"I can't do this anymore," he said as he lifted the gun again.

"Through this holy anointing, may the Lord in His love and mercy-"

And then he pulled the trigger.

I ran over to him and held his head in my hands. I looked into his eyes and he finally saw me. His face was covered in acne, sweat, snot, and tears and he smelled of the fluids his body had expelled. This was how they would find him. A pimple-faced kid with shit in his pants. A killer who died crying out to an empty room. I gently laid his head back down and looked out the window. There were a dozen police cars, ambulances, and fire trucks. Kids were hugging each other, crying. They stumbled around covered in the blood of their peers, making phone calls to their parents to tell them they were alive. Some of them already had parents showing up, holding them as they once did when they were smaller children. They had survived, for now at least. But eventually, I'd come for all of them. Hopefully much later, after they had lived long, fulfilling lives. I kept watching until something caught my eye. A young man wearing a letterman jacket was standing by the tree line, looking up at me.

"Ankou," I whispered. I looked back at Lucas' body and then back out to Ankou. He smiled, put two fingers against his temple, and mimed shooting himself. I glared at him as he waved and then casually walked away. I was going to kill him.

2

"He always seems to be one step ahead of me!" I snapped at Elijah. "I can't get a one-up on him!"

"Emma, he's centuries old," Elijah sighed. "You've been an angel for less than a hundred years. In angel terms, you're still in your first week on the job. You're a newbie."

I let out a loud, aggressive sigh and slumped over the side of Elijah's desk.

"Hello!" Elijah perked up and an elderly man walked up next to me. "Can I help you?"

"Why am I still old?" the man asked.

"I beg your pardon?" Elijah said, side-eyeing me.

"I don't want to be old!" he grumbled. "I want to be young and sexy! What if I see my wife here? She died almost twenty years ago. She's not going to want to be with an old man."

He looked over at me and then looked at my black wings. I waved.

"Oh," he muttered. "It's you again. I'm already dead. Leave me alone."

"I'm off the clock actually," I responded.

"All the same, bugger off. Unless you have my dear Midge with you."

"Nope, no Midge here."

"Please," the old man turned back to Elijah. "I can't look like this. I look like a wrinkled prune!"

I sighed and looked back at Elijah. "I'll talk to you later. Let me know if you hear anything at all."

"The minute he dies I will let you know. Although, you'll probably know before I do," he smiled.

"Ha ha ha," I said dryly before turning to leave.

I walked out the door and saw Michael, the archangel, making a beeline for the hotel. I turned to head back into the hotel but he had already seen me.

"Emma!" he called cheerfully, waving me down.

"Ugh," I grunted. Michael's smile faded as he got closer. I didn't smile or say anything.

"Well, you've certainly adopted Dumah's warm greetings. Got a moment?"

"I don't know," I said sarcastically. "I'm apparently supposed to be focusing on my job and that's it. All work and no play. Busy, busy, busy!"

Michael gave me a stern look.

"I thought you might appreciate me asking you directly if you'd like to do a little side task for me. If you're not *too busy*."

"What kind of task?" I asked.

"Well, uh, it involves taking a small trip. Down South."

He dramatically pointed a finger at the ground.

"If you know what I mean."

"You want me to go to Hell?" I asked. "Are you serious? You know how much they hate me there. You know how much *I* hate going there."

"Yes, well I thought that would make you kind of perfect for the job. I can trust you to get in and out as quickly as possible. We have a couple of angels who have gone...missing."

"Missing?"

"Yes, but please keep this between us. We have reason to believe they've been kidnapped."

"You think they've been kidnapped?" I repeated. "By? Demons?"

"We're not really sure what the details are. Only that's where they were last seen."

"So I'm allowed to take a break from my job to go do this, without getting reprimanded at all?" I asked.

"Correct," Michael replied. "We'll give you all of the information we have on the missing angels. We'll give you whatever resources you need. And in return, we'll give you some deserved time off. We don't want you getting job burnout already. Plus this will give you some experience that could be beneficial in the future."

"Sounds good," I said casually. "I can get started right away if you want."

"Oh, there's one more thing," Michael added. "We had an eager volunteer to accompany you. You know, to make sure you stay on task."

"Who?"

"A friend of yours. She should be here any minute."

"Hey, guys!" I heard Thalia's voice and immediately regretted my decision.

"Well, what did she say?" Thalia asked, flying closer to us. "She said yes, didn't she? I told you she would."

I looked from Thalia to Michael, who smiled at me.

"I'm ready to go!" Thalia said enthusiastically. I sighed.

"Fine," I finally said. "Let's go."

Thalia and I flew to my shore. She talked the whole way there, barely pausing to breathe. I stayed silent the entire time. I couldn't believe Michael had sent Thalia with me to make sure I would "stay on task." So he thought I needed a babysitter. We landed on the shore by the hut. Thalia was still babbling but I did my best to tune her out. I grabbed a few essentials for the trip and made my way out to Dumah's boat.

"And then I told them there's no way anyone is going to forget that. Setting a guitar on fire would be more effective in getting people's attention. I love music; I know what I'm talking about. You can imagine their surprise when- wait. What are you doing?"

"We're taking the boat," I answered.

"Why can't we just fly there?"

"Because I don't want to."

"Wouldn't it be faster to fly though?"

I turned and got in Thaila's face. Her light blue eyes widened.

"If I'm going to have to drag you along, we're going to do things *my* way. *I'm* making the decisions. We're taking the damn boat."

"Okay, I'm sorry," Thalia said quietly before grabbing a small bag and getting into the boat. I slung the last of our cargo in and spread my wings before pushing the boat forward, into the water. Thalia braced herself and fell back to sit. Neither of us spoke for a long time. Finally, Thalia cleared her throat.

"Was this Dumah's boat?" she asked. I nodded.

"Oh."

I caught her eye, as if she was waiting for more. I sighed.

"Well, technically it's Baraqiel's boat. But he has to stay on the other side, so Dumah would use it to travel back and forth. He found it peaceful. The boat actually wrecked on the other side," I chuckled briefly before clearing the lump in my throat. "It was the last time Dumah ever sailed. It was when, ya know, everything happened."

Thalia sat quietly, eager for me to continue.

"Uh, I felt bad about everything, so I had some angels help me restore it. Baraqiel wouldn't take it back, so I started using it. I get out on the water a lot to just think."

"With all of *them* down there?" Thalia nodded her head towards the water.

"As long as it's daytime or you have enough light on the boat, they don't bother you," I explained. "They want to be left alone as much as I do."

I looked out at the sea, placing my hands on the edge of the boat. Somewhere, Sam was floating along. Her soul was forever trapped under the glassy surface, and it was my fault. No, it was Ankou's fault. He had tricked her into working for him. She had been manipulated by him, just as I had been. I hadn't realized my grip had tightened until I heard the wood under my fingers start to splinter.

"Are you okay?" Thalia asked. "Listen, I know you're not a huge fan of mine. I'm annoying and I talk a lot. I've had enough people tell me that. But I do want to be your friend, whether you want to be mine or not. I know you like to be more of a loner, and that's okay. Just know that if you want to talk, I'm here. I know it doesn't seem like it, but I'm as good of a listener as I am a talker."

I looked at Thalia and she smiled. I smiled weakly back at her.

"Thanks," I said softly. "I guess I'm just not great at making friends anymore. And the ones I *do* make, end up hurt, dead, or betraying me."

"You don't have to worry about those things with me. I also don't seem like that good of a fighter, and that worries you, right?"

I nodded.

"Well, I'm *not* a good fighter," she laughed. "I've actually never been in a fight in my whole existence."

"Oh great," I laughed. "How are you going to defend yourself if you need to?"

"I'm hoping I can persuade, like you suggested," she flipped her hair back confidently. "That's what I do; inspire and persuade. I can't directly affect free will of course. But I can get closer to affecting it than any other celestial being."

"How?" I asked.

"It's sort of hard to explain. You know God gave humans, well everyone, free will? Meaning He can't make anyone do anything, say anything, feel anything, etc. However, He's still God. He knows everything that is happening, ever has happened, and ever will happen. For example, you're a human. You have eaten your dinner and now you want dessert. You have a choice between cookies or candy. Your choices have branched off into two separate paths. God knows these are choices you have. But it's not just these two choices. Because you could decide that you need to watch your weight and end up skipping dessert. Or you could decide to go out and buy ice cream. This has set off another group of branches. The store doesn't carry the ice cream you were wanting so you buy a different flavor. Or you get into a car wreck on the way to the store. All because you had a thought that set a number of possibilities into motion."

"And that's where you come in," I stated.

"Exactly!" she chirped. "Virtues like me push the first domino over that sets the whole thing into motion. All I have to do is whisper, 'something sweet sounds good," and it sets it all in motion. And in a blink of an eye, I've already written out all of the endless possibilities of every choice. Each human life is like a Choose Your Own Adventure Book. The whole story is in God's hands, already written out. But depending on what the human chooses, the outcome of the story changes."

"That makes sense I guess," I smiled. I caught a glimpse of red hair out of the corner of my eye and my eyes darted to the water again. It wasn't Sam.

"What's wrong?" Thalia asked.

"My guardian angel is in there somewhere."

"What exactly happened with Sam?"

"It's a long story."

"It's a long boat ride. Besides, I'd rather hear it from you than the rumor mill."

I sat down before starting the story of Sam, me, Ankou, and how he had tricked her into talking me into going to Hell in hopes my soul would become trapped there.

"Wow," she said after I finished. "No wonder you're so troubled. That's a lot."

"Yeah," I sighed. "*Troubled.*"

"There's actually been a lot of that happening recently," Thalia said. "Angels and demons working together."

"Why though? Why would they purposely help the wrong side?" I asked.

"Rumor is when the end of the world comes, we aren't going to be on the winning side. So some angels are getting bullied into working for the other side. Because if Hell does win, I can't imagine what they'll do to the remaining angels."

"What, like kill us?"

"I'd think something much worse. Enslave us or torture us. They're demons so they're going to have their fun with us."

"Good thing we're the ones on the winning side," I said.

"Yeah," Thalia sighed. "I hope so."

Thalia looked down into the water.

"Do you think there's any way to save them?" I asked.

"I don't know," she said. "1 Timothy 2:3-4 says, 'This is good and pleasing to God our savior, who wills everyone to be saved and to come to knowledge of the truth.' I honestly don't think anyone is out of reach for Him."

"That's very optimistic of you," I chuckled. "I've tried looking for a way though. I can't find anything about lost souls being recovered from the Sea of Anathema."

"Have you visited the Temple of Da'at?" Thalia asked.

"I've never even heard of it," I said, shaking my head.

"It's a huge library," she explained. "Now that I think of it, I've never seen any death angels there. But you can go with me sometime. If there's any information on the Sea of Anathema, it'll be there."

"That's great," I said. "Maybe we can go after we're finished with this job."

"Sounds like a plan!"

A few minutes went by before Thalia added, "I'm glad you decided to team up with me."

I started to correct her that she was actually teaming up with *me*, but just nodded instead. Thalia got on my nerves, but I knew deep down that it wasn't her fault. Elijah was my only friend because I knew he was safe behind his desk job. The thought of dragging another angel into my personal drama frightened me. I didn't want to hurt anyone else, especially someone so sweet like Thalia. We made small talk as we made our way to the shore. As we drew close, I could see Sekhmet waiting on the sand. She went from being on all fours to stand up, her paws turning into human hands and feet. Thalia gasped.

"It's okay," I smiled. "She's a friend."

The boat docked and Thalia hesitantly followed me off the boat, towards Sekhmet.

"Small welcoming party," I smiled. "Did Baraqiel forget the balloons?"

"You know how he feels about everything," Sekhmet sighed.

"About *me*, you mean?"

"It's just difficult for him to see you. He and Dumah were close."

"I know-"

"And we almost died."

"I know!" I snapped. "I am well aware of what happened and what almost happened and how everyone has been affected by it."

I spread my black wings out.

"If you haven't noticed, I've been affected by it too! But I am trying my hardest to get Dumah back and to make things right."

Sekhmet shook her head.

"He's not coming back, Emma," she reached her hand out and took mine in it. "You know that."

"How can you say that?" I pulled away. "It's *his* soul in that human right now! He's in there.

side of his glasses was cracked and he smelled heavily of cigarettes. Thalia didn't attempt to hide her disdain, whether it was for the man or our surroundings. A broken down couch sat in the motel lobby where a young man and woman were making out and groping each other. A cockroach ran across the desk before the man sitting behind it smashed it with a thick book. Thalia let out a groan as the man opened the book.

"Names?" he grumbled, looking us up and down. "You angels ain't plannin' on stayin' long, are ya?"

"Probably just a couple of days," I quietly replied, filling out the blank space on the book's page. "You haven't had any other angels come through here recently, have you?"

"Why? Ya misplace some angels here?" the man chuckled. "Funny place to lose angels."

"Have you or haven't you?" I frowned at him, trying to sound tougher.

"Listen, I ain't about to get myself involved in no angel/demon drama if that's what this is. You can take that shit somewhere else."

"We just have a few questions, if you don't mind," Thalia said softly.

"Piss off, fairy!"

"There's no need to be an asshole!" I snapped.

Thalia flew over the desk and whispered in the man's ear. For a moment, he moved as if he were about to swat at her, but then quickly put his hand back down. His face seemed to calm and he smiled at me.

"I haven't had any other angels come through, but I can get you a list of other local establishments you could check out."

"That would be...great," I said hesitantly before looking at Thalia.

"And if there's anything else I can do for you, you ladies let me know," the man continued to smile at us. "My name is Curtis."

"Thank you so much, Curtis," Thalia grinned. "We'll be back for that list in a little bit."

I took our room key and we headed down the narrow hallway to our room. The place smelled like mildew and was dimly lit. We reached our door and I unlocked it. I had to give it a hard push with my shoulder and we stepped inside. Thalia flipped the light switch and we both let out groans. The carpet was stained and sticky. There were no curtains on the window. The screen on the tv was busted. And the "bed" was just a mattress on the floor; not that we needed a bed anyways.

"Emma, I don't think I can stay here," Thalia frowned, looking around. "It smells like vomit."

I pulled the bed sheet back and gagged. There was a bloated dead rat.

"I found the source of the vomit smell!" Thalia called from the bathroom.

"What is it?" I asked, dropping the sheet and wiping my hand.

"Vomit," Thalia answered.

"You know what?" I shook my head quickly. "We can just hang out in a diner or something at night when we're not looking for the angels. Can't be worse than this place."

We headed back to the lobby and I handed my room key to Curtis.

"On second thought, we won't be needing a room," I smiled.

"Do you by chance know of any places with decent food around here?" Thalia asked.

"Decent food in Hell doesn't exist, I'm afraid," Curtis chuckled as he took the key. "But if you're looking for something that isn't absolutely horrendous, there's a bar a few blocks from here that serves chicken tenders that will make you second guess where you are."

Curtis wrote the address and name of the bar on a piece of paper that already had a list of places on it, and gave it to me. Thalia smiled at him cheerfully. She turned to fly out the door a man was holding open, but Curtis stopped us.

"Oh, miss?" he called. We both stopped and turned. "You might want to come up with a disguise while you're here. You look even more out of place than your friend."

"Ah, yes," Thalia landed on the floor next to me. "I almost forgot."

I watched as Thalia slowly grew to my size. Everything about her looked the exact same, just bigger, except her wings were now gone.

"I didn't know you could do that!" I exclaimed. "Is that why Elijah isn't small like you?"

"Yeah, he hasn't been virtue-size since the archangels assigned him to book keeping," Thalia nodded. "Makes his current job easier, I suppose."

As we exited the motel, I noticed that Thalia was walking rather quickly.

"Why don't you stay this size all the time?" I asked.

"It's not what I'm supposed to look like," Thalia said in a lower tone. "I like how I normally look, especially my wings. I only do this when I absolutely have to. I actually hate being this big. I don't know how you stand it."

"Why are we walking so quickly?"

"I noticed someone in the motel lobby watching us talk to Curtis. I got Curtis to tell us about that bar because if that person is following us, they'll ask him where we're going and head there. Here, this way!"

Thalia grabbed me by the shoulder and pulled me into an alley. We crouched behind a large pile of trash bags. I pinched my nose and tried to peak around but Thalia pulled me back into the shadows. I glanced behind me and noticed a group of people in the alley shooting up heroin. Some of them were slumped over a dumpster while the rest laid on the dirty ground. One woman seemed to be calling out for her mother. Thalia nudged me and stood up. I followed her to the sidewalk where we peaked out. She pointed to a person in a green hoodie walking quickly ahead of us.

"Is that who you saw?" I whispered.

Thalia nodded.

"Let's see who it is."

We kept our distance from them but still stayed close enough to not lose them. The hooded person went inside the bar Curtis had told us about.

"I knew it," Thalia said. "After we left, they probably asked Curtis where we were heading."

"I wonder who it is," I whispered.

"Let's go find out."

We walked in and it was like every generic, shitty bar you see in the movies. The place smelled like stale beer, piss, and cigarettes. Thalia and I made our way carefully through the dimly lit building. I nudged Thalia with my elbow and nodded toward the jukebox. There was our hooded figure, browsing the songs. We stood there, just watching, waiting for the reveal. Finally, "Son of a Preacher Man" started playing and the person at the jukebox started swaying their hips. Slowly, hands lifted to remove the hood, showing a scaly, bald head. The person turned to us to reveal themselves. With the body of a man and a face resembling one of those yellowish Burmese pythons, he sashayed towards us, still swaying his hips.

"Emma," he said, smiling. I looked into his bulging, reddish brown eyes that never blinked. There were two slits where a nose would normally be.

"Yes?" I hesitantly replied. The creature opened its large mouth into a smile full of needle-sharp teeth. A hand was extended out towards me.

"Abaddon," he said, shaking my hand. "Pleasure to meet you. And you are?"

He turned to Thalia.

"Thalia," she answered quietly.

"I'm sorry, but who are you exactly?" I asked. "And why are you following us?"

"Actually, you'd be the ones following *me*," Abaddon said with another wide grin. "I am the fallen angel of the bottomless pit! The prince of the Abyss!"

Thalia and I stood there, waiting for him to continue.

"You've really never heard of me?" he asked, sounding disappointed. We shook our heads while he scratched his.

"Bummer," Abaddon sighed. "I used to be an angel who judged people in God's name. But when the war against Heaven started, I sided with Lucifer. So now I take up residency in Hell and look like this. Anyway, enough about me. I've heard you're looking for two angels here."

"From who?" I asked.

"A reliable source," Abaddon beamed. "That's not really important. But I can show you where they are and get you back on your merry way, death angel."

"And I'm supposed to just trust that this isn't a trap and you're not trying to screw me over in any way?" I asked.

"I don't expect you to trust anything from a demon, knowing your history with them."

I scoffed.

"So you think you know me?" I asked.

"I know quite a bit thanks to your ex-boyfriend."

My blood immediately turned to ice.

"Alastor," I found myself saying out loud.

"Ankou," Thalia corrected.

"Alastor, Ankou, whatever he goes by," Abaddon cackled. "I just work with the guy. But if you want to get to those angels, we better get moving."

"To where?" Thalia asked.

Without saying another word, Abaddon started moving towards the bar. The bartender was a short, stocky man with a cloudy eye and a large scar that ran above and below it. Abaddon pulled something small out of his hoodie pocket and flashed it at the bartender. The man nodded at him but gave Thalia and me a dirty look. He lifted a portion of the bar top and we went through. There was very little room for the four of us and the bartender smelled like alcohol and sweat.

"This way," Abaddon nodded towards the wall behind the bar that was covered in shelves housing bottles of liquor. Before I protested, Abaddon slipped behind a gap on the far end of the wall. Unless you knew to look for it, you'd never know it was there. Behind the wall was a dark hallway lined with boxes on the floor.

"Watch your step," Abaddon warned. He grabbed a lantern that had been sitting on top of one of the boxes and attempted handing it to me. I pulled my sword out and it caught fire. Abaddon shrugged and handed the lantern to Thalia. He then grabbed a book of matches that had been by the lantern and struck one before lighting the lantern. Thalia handed it back to him and Abaddon led us down the hallway to a doorway. She gave me a concerned look.

"There's a railing that I suggest you hold onto," Abaddon said before dropping the match. We watched it fall down, down, down until it finally disappeared. "That's a long way to fall."

"I have wings," I muttered.

However, I took my time going down the large spiral staircase. Thalia seemed to keep both hands gripped tightly to the railing the whole time. The music from the bar was quiet and I could hear how quickly she was breathing. I wanted to tell her to calm down but didn't want Abaddon to hear. As we got to the bottom of the staircase, I could see something dark and big ahead of us.

"She doesn't get used too often, but she still runs well and she's faster than any car," Abaddon tapped on a clunky metal cart. He placed the lantern on a holder at the front of the cart, creating a makeshift headlight. The cart laid on a track that disappeared into the vast darkness before us.

"Where does this take us?" I asked.

"This is an underground transportation option," Abaddon explained as he looked over the cart. "Every once in a while, things get a little chaotic here and there needs to be a backup option for getting around. This little beauty can get us anywhere without running into trouble."

"A mine cart was the best you guys could come up with?" Thalia scoffed. "Inspiration and creativity run thin here, huh?"

"Says the two angels who traveled here by boat?"

"How did you know that?" I asked.

"I have eyes everywhere, my dear," he winked at me. I glared at him and reluctantly stepped into the cart, Thalia getting in after me. "And think of this as more of a very small locomotive. I know safety isn't usually a concern for us immortals, but I highly suggest fastening seat belts so you don't get launched out of the cart. It goes pretty fast."

Thalia and I fastened our harnesses as Abaddon flipped some switches beside the cart. The machine jumped to life and steam whistled out of the back. He sat in the front and got buckled in before turning around at us and smiling.

"Hold on tight," he laughed.

Abaddon pushed a large red button in front of him and the machine started lurching forward. It was like being on a rollercoaster. We sped down the track going at least 120 miles per hour. At each turn, Thalia and I were forced into each other, shoulders squeezing together. I was surprised when I glanced over to see Thalia smiling. She was actually enjoying it.

"I can't help it!" she giggled when she noticed my expression. "It's fun!"

Even as we were diving into the depths of Hell, two angels in a sea of demons and other nightmares, she was having fun. I envied how easily Thalia could see past danger and just enjoy a good time. I refused to let my guard down. Trusting demons wasn't a mistake I wanted to repeat. The cart finally began to slow down and I could see a landing come into view. There were lights everywhere, like an underground city, except I knew it wasn't electricity causing the glow from down there. It was fire.

3

"I really hate it here," I groaned as we all got out of the cart. Every man, woman, and demon around us was staring.

"Piss off!" Abaddon announced as he guided us through the crowd. "Like you all have never seen a couple of angels around here."

"Will you keep it down," I growled. "Are you trying to draw unwanted attention?"

Abaddon laughed.

"I was being sarcastic. These people see angels here often. Although, now that I think about it, you might be the first death angel here."

I kept my hand on the hilt of my sword as we headed down the street to a small building that resembled a fast food place. Six guardians stood in front of the doors. As we approached them, Abaddon waved his hand and the guardians moved to let us by.

"I won't be eating here," Thalia muttered, trying to make a joke.

"They don't serve food this far down," I said. "That's a first floor luxury."

"Yeah, we keep the real baddies hungry," Abaddon grinned at us. "Keeps them in check."

We walked through the door and there was a large room filled with small tables with four chairs around each one. In the middle of the room were several tables pushed together to create one bigger one. Several demons were seated at the table, along with the two missing angels. Both were male, however, one had light brown hair and a smaller build while the other was bigger with jet black hair. They certainly didn't look kidnapped. They were laughing and talking until they looked up and saw us. The whole place grew silent.

A familiar, gray-skinned face was grinning at me. The sight of his bull-like horns, protruding chest bones, and glowing red eyes took me back to the night I had first met him with Dumah.

"Why, hello, Emma."

"Hello, Ah Puch," I responded. "What's going on here?"

"I think introductions first would be the polite thing to do," Ah Puch clapped his hands together and stood up, smoothing out his black suit.

"This," he said pointing at us, "is Emma, the one who took Dumah's place. And it seems as though she brought a little fairy with her."

"Thalia's an angel," I interrupted. "She's just as important as the rest of us."

This last bit was aimed at the two angels sitting at the table, who weren't making eye contact with me. The four demons, including Ah Puch, were laughing. Even Abaddon was smiling. I was already starting to lose my patience.

"This is Lamashtu," Ah Puch said, pointing to a bald woman with black ram horns that curled around her head. She glared at us with bulging eyes that were almost popping out of their sockets. Next to her was a little boy with curly brown hair and rosy cheeks. He looked like a cupid baby.

"This is Ualac," Ah Puch smiled at him, his yellow, jagged teeth showing. "And under the table is Ualac's...companion, Doolas."

I peeked under the table where the boy was sitting and saw a sleeping two-headed dragon. I looked back at the boy and he smiled, showing two rows of many, small fangs. Thalia scrunched her nose and gave him a finger wiggle wave; the kind one would give a small child to show that they're friendly. Ualac hissed at Thalia, which made her recoil. That made the demons laugh again.

"And this is Orobas," Ah Puch said, pointing to the being I had been trying very hard not to stare at. At the end of the table sat something with an elongated, almost horse-like face, and two hooves instead of feet sticking out from under the table. Orobas and Ualac both wore suits, similar to Ah Puch. Lamashtu wore a sheer red dress. This made it clear that they were all elite demons.

"Don't forget our welcomed guests," Lamashtu smiled.

"Ah, yes," Ah Puch said, making his way over to the two angels. "This is Claude and Pavel, although I still don't know which one is which."

"I'm Claude," The one with the brown hair said. "He's-"

Ah Puch put his hand up to silence Claude.

"I honestly don't give a shit," he laughed with the other demons.

"Got room for three more?" Abaddon asked.

"I can tell you right now *she's* not interested," Ah Puch pointed to me. "The fairy might be a good addition though."

"Whatever this is, I'm not interested either," Thalia said to him before turning to the angels. "What are you guys doing here?"

"What are *you* doing here?" Pavel asked.

"We were sent to rescue you," Thalia explained. The whole table roared with laughter.

"So you're here by choice?" I asked, fuming. Claude and Pavel looked down, avoiding eye contact again.

"What the fuck is going on?" I pressed.

"Whoa!" Ualac giggled. "I didn't know angels cussed! What other naughty things do angels do?"

"Look, Emma, I think you know what's going on," Ah Puch said, leaning on the table with both hands. "Claude and Pavel here have decided that the current state of things aren't going so well and they'd like a....new job opportunity."

"No," Thalia whispered. Lamashtu smiled at her.

"You guys can't really be considering this," I said.

"Emma," Claude sighed. "Everyday things are getting worse and worse. When things start falling apart, we don't really want to be on the wrong side. It's either join them now or become their prisoners later."

"What do you mean 'when things start falling apart?'" I asked. "Nothing is going to happen. There are rules set in place that both sides know they have to follow."

I was now looking at each of the demons.

"Demons aren't supposed to directly interfere with humans or angels. You guys know this! You can influence or inspire or suggest, but you know you can't bully or force anyone into doing what you want them to. It affects free will."

"There's no one to regulate us," Orobas said. "The archangels are too worried about getting people into Paradise that they can't afford to waste time focusing on what we're doing. It's basically the Wild West now. We govern ourselves. God and Satan are so busy with their own little rivalry that they aren't paying attention to what we do."

"God knows *everything* though," Thalia chimed in. This made Ah Puch and Ualac chuckle again.

"Even God can turn a blind eye on some things," Abaddon said. I had almost forgotten he was here. "God knows good can't exist without bad."

"But can't the opposite be said for you guys?" I asked. "What good is it to conquer all of Earth if there's nothing left to conquer?"

"That's where your logic is flawed though," Abaddon continued. "If God gets fed up enough with people, all he has to do is wipe the slate clean. For fuck's sake, he's already done it several times. If he gets tired of all the war, greed, poverty, rape, murder, etc., he merely has to snap his fat fingers and poof! No more people. Do you know how long life existed before humans came into the picture? The bible says God created man on the sixth day. First off, God didn't create everything in a week. It took billions of years. It's not like one day there were suddenly dogs and hamsters and possums. He created single cell organisms. He watched as they grew and eventually evolved into something else. Of course, he knew they would, but he didn't just create all of the creatures we know today. He had to play around with shit like the dinosaurs and other prehistoric beings. God attempted so many things before humans. Even the Australopithecus. They had no morals. No way of even knowing what was good or evil.

Up until the first man and woman, God and Lucifer had no way of beating each other. Lucifer tried to overthrow God, was punished for it, and spent billions of years creating his domain here.

God created Heaven and Earth because He knew He had to one-up the Devil somehow. So God cheated. He put something in men that would forever change everything. He gave them a soul. This invisible organ that He added to, more or less, upgrade humans. Adam and Eve were created in His image, made with God's love in their hearts. But God knows Lucifer and His powers, so Adam and Eve came to know Lucifer as well. See, at the time, there were no rules set in place. God and Lucifer could walk the Earth as equals. There were no threats because God just didn't want the Devil in Paradise."

    Abaddon stops to laugh to himself.

    "It's so funny that as soon as God makes man, they immediately fuck it up for the rest. God gives them one rule. One! Don't eat from the tree. You have the whole goddamn planet to do what you want. To wander in ignorant, naked bliss. Just don't eat the fruit from the Tree of the Knowledge of Good and Evil. Dumb man says, 'okay, whatever you say!' He's loyal to God. Lucifer can see this. Man is the first creature with a soul. But the woman? She's weaker than Adam. She has a soul, but it's not as strong as his. She wants to know. She wants to eat; wants to be fed knowledge. She's not built as big or as strong as Adam, so she needs the knowledge to protect herself. And as soon as she does, she manipulates him into doing it too. In that moment, God's plan was foiled. These creatures with souls, who now know good and bad, well....they're fucked. And how does God punish Eve? By giving her the power of creation.

Humans now are so stupid when it comes to motherhood. They think it's a miracle or a gift. But it's a punishment! Women can do what only God can. They can create life, bear the weight of it in every sense of the meaning. They carry a fetus for nine months, are sick and in discomfort, and have horribly painful childbirth. Up until formula was created, mothers were the only way babies could be fed. They solely relied on their mothers. And then mothers watch for years as their children hopefully stay healthy and make good choices. Mothers can influence their children to be good, but they can't make them. Just like God. Eve was the first one to realize that. She had four sons. Two are widely known and two, not so much. Both sets met the same fate. The first son who slaughtered his brother became one of the most powerful demons. His brother that he murdered?"

"Oh god, we're not talking about that again, are we?"

The voice I heard from behind sent instant shivers down my spine. I slowly turned to see Ankou standing in the doorway. He was wearing a white button up shirt with dark blue dress pants and his hands were tucked in his pockets. I reached for my sword just as Thalia and Abaddon seized me from each side. I could see the whole table stand up from the corner of my eye.

"Let me go!" I cried.

"Not here," Thalia said calmly. "You'll start a war attacking demons in Hell. Use your head."

"I dream of the day when I can use this sword to kill you," I snarled at Ankou, who didn't budge. The only movement from him was a growing smile on his face.

"Aww, but you don't dream anymore, sweetie," Ankou pouted. "You don't even sleep anymore. You're dead."

"And I wasted the last months of my life with you."

"I don't know why you're still so upset. You didn't kill yourself. I lost! I should be the one who's upset, but I'm not. I'm happy for you. You get to actually make a difference in people's...last seconds of their lives. And my job helps you stay busy with yours. I get people to commit suicide, and you can be there to send them off to me."

I squirmed in Thalia and Abaddon's grip.

"You know what one of my favorite parts of my job is?" Ankou asked. "A side effect of being near me causes humans to have nightmares. The closer they get to me, the worse the nightmares become. The psychosis I cause inevitably makes people more vulnerable and to kill themselves. So at the end of your life, you couldn't even dream peacefully because of me."

Without hesitation, I violently spit in Ankou's face. All of the demons at the table started to move towards us. Ankou put a hand up at them and they slowly sat back down.

"I don't know how to explain it," he said, taking a step closer to me. "But seeing you hate me this much kind of turns me on."

I fought to break free from Thalia and Abaddon. They pulled even harder on my arms.

"Don't, Emma," Thalia whispered in my ear. "He's not worth it."

"Do you remember what it was like to have sex with me?" Ankou continued, lowering his voice. "You *loved* it. You would beg me to fuck you."

I stopped for a moment as he drew closer.

"Do you remember what it felt like?" he said softly. "To have me inside of you? To make you scream from coming so hard? Our sweaty bodies pressed against each other and me thrusting into you until you couldn't take anymore. Your human body collapsing from too much pleasure. Imagine how much you could take now."

"That's enough, Ankou," Abaddon snapped at him. "Quit causing problems."

"Oh, I'm just messing with her," Ankou said. "If she's going to be Dumah's replacement, she needs some thicker skin. She needs to learn to control that temper and not let things, or me, upset her that easily. It's not a good look."

"As soon as I get Dumah back, I *will* kill you," I found myself saying out loud.

There was a pause before Ankou grinned again.

"He's not Dumah anymore," he said. "It's not the same person. You know that. That man has lived a whole life and doesn't even know he used to be a death angel. He won't remember you."

"When he dies, I'll remind him of who he was," I explained. "I'll get him back to what he used to be and then I'll kill you. And I don't care if it's the last thing I do. But it will happen. I won't let you win."

"And what about poor Samantha?" he asked.

I recoiled at her name.

"Sekhmet and Baraqiel are fine now. You have this big, elaborate plan for Dumah and myself. But what about poor, widdle, baby Sam? Out there floating around in the water, lost forever?"

I tugged loose from Thalia and Abaddon and hung my head.

"There's nothing I can do about Sam."

"Hm," Ankou chuckled. "Yeah, you're probably right. You've probably looked everywhere for an answer. If only there were someone who knew a way to get her out of there. Oh well."

I watched as Ankou casually walked by me and towards the table.

"Is...there?" I asked. He stopped and turned.

"I beg your pardon?"

"Is there a way to free Sam?"

He smiled and walked up to me. He was so close, I could smell him. He smelled the way he always had. It wasn't fair how beautiful he was. Even now, knowing he was a demon, I couldn't help but notice how attractive he was. A few strands of hair hung on his forehead. As if he knew what I was thinking, he ran a hand through the hair, pulling them away from his face.

"Emma Rose, are you asking for my help?" he asked quietly.

"No," I replied. "But if you know a way, I'm sure someone else does."

He glanced at Abaddon. I looked at him too.

"Do you know a way?" I asked.

Abaddon shrugged.

"I might. But I don't have the book."

"What book?" I asked.

"There's apparently a book that tells you exactly how to do it."

"Where can I find the book?"

"Nowhere in Hell, that's for sure," Ankou scoffed. "Believe me, we've looked."

"There's only one place it could be and we can't go there," Abaddon added.

"Well how would you be able to find it if you don't know what it looks like?" I asked.

"Supposedly, the book is actually a scroll," Abaddon continued. "But it's called The Book.....something."

"A book that is actually a scroll that's called 'the book of something,' but you don't know where it is or what it looks like."

"I know," Abaddon said. "Demons don't have access to it and aren't supposed to know where to find it."

"Probably for a good reason," Thalia chirped.

"If it frees the lost souls in the Sea of Anathema, it's probably against the rules for angels *and* demons to use the book," Claude chimed in.

"If the book is in Paradise, then it's probably for our eyes only," I argued. "Well, those of us who are loyal to Paradise."

Claude hung his head again, but Pavel glared at me. I looked back at Abaddon and leaned in close.

"If you know how to use the book but don't have access to it; and I have access to it but don't know how to use it, maybe we could..."

I trailed off. I didn't know what I was saying.

"What?" Ankou chortled. "Work together?"

My face grew hot as he said it.

"What could you possibly offer us that would make it worth our time?"

I stood there a moment with a room full of demons and angels staring at me.

"I don't..." I started. My eyes met Thalia and she shook her head, as if to tell me to stop.

"I don't have anything to offer, at the moment," I continued. "But I can promise you that by the time we figure out how to get Sam out of there, I'll come up with something. I don't want to promise you anything just yet."

"I look forward to seeing what you come up with," Ankou said softly in my ear.

I backed away slowly from him and looked at the two angels.

"Are you two coming home with us?" I asked hesitantly. "If you turn away now, you can never come back. Everyone will know you're traitors."

"I wouldn't call them traitors," Ah Puch sighed. "They've seen the error of their ways and now their alliance is leaning in a different direction."

"You're really doing this?" Thalia asked Claude and Pavel. They didn't respond.

"Well, there you have it, ladies," Lamashtu said. "You have your answer. Abaddon, I think it's about time you send these two on their way back home. We have some important business to attend to."

"And Doolas will need to feed soon," Ualac added.

"Come on," Abaddon showed us to the door. We were silent the whole trip back on the cart. Every once in a while Thalia wiped her eyes. Once we were back out of the bar in Sentencing, Abaddon finally broke his silence.

"Look," he said. "I know you're disappointed with the outcome of your visit. But here's the thing. I like you, Emma. Ankou has told me a lot about you and I honestly respect you."

He leaned in closer to me and lowered his voice.

"And I know that Dumah got himself out of here."

"What do you mean?" I said, surprised. "Everyone knows that Dumah got himself out of Hell."

"Well, I'd be interested to know how."

I looked at Abaddon, shocked.

"Yeah," he said. "I'm kind of tired of it. The whole, deceiving people to get them trapped here. It's not rewarding. I miss working for God."

"You're shitting me."

"I'm being serious, Emma. I want to help you get your friend out of the Sea of Anathema. But I also need your help. And obviously no one can know that I'm trying to get out of here. They'd eat me alive. You're all the help I have."

"I don't know," I said. "For one, we just met. I don't know if I can trust you. Second, I don't even know what all Dumah had to do to get out of Hell."

"While you're looking for the book, maybe you'll stumble across something that could help me."

I didn't say anything.

"Well, if you change your mind, you know where to find me. And if you happen to find that book, let me know. I'd like to at least help you with your friend before the end times. Even if you don't want to help me."

He stuck his hand out. I reluctantly shook it.

"This is nice," he sighed. "angels and demons finding a way to get along."

I quickly pulled away. Thalia and I left without saying another word to him. We carefully made our way back to Baraqiel's hut as the sun was setting.

"You don't really believe him, do you?" Thalia said as we approached the hut.

"Abaddon? No."

I didn't want to at least. Anyone who worked closely with Ankou *had* to be bad. *Right?*

I knocked on the door and Sekhmet answered.

"I've got some bad news," I said as we went in.

Baraqiel quickly stood up when he saw us. I froze. Sekhmet sighed.

"You couldn't keep avoiding her forever," she said.

"You've been purposely avoiding me?" I said sarcastically, rolling my eyes. "I had no idea."

"What are you doing here?" Baraqiel asked.

"My job," I answered. "We just lost two more angels."

"Are you serious?" Sekhmet scoffed. "Fucking demons."

"One named Claude. The other is Pavel."

"Claude?" Baraqiel asked. "Scrawny French kid with brown hair?"

I nodded.

"Aw, I liked Claude," Sekhmet sighed. "He seemed sweet."

"Well now be on the lookout for him and his buddy," I said. "Don't let them back over. It's bad enough having angels double cross. But they need to stay out of Processing and Paradise as much as possible."

"We'll let the other dark angels know," Sekhmet said. "Thank you for letting us know so quickly, Emma."

She nudged Baraqiel in the arm.

"Yeah," he muttered. "Thanks."

"You're welcome," I said. "I actually had a question, and I figured you'd be the best person to ask."

"What is it, sweetheart?" Sekhmet purred.

"How did Dumah get out of Hell?"

At the sound of his name, Baraqiel immediately recoiled and sat back down.

"He became a death angel," Sekhmet said. "You know this."

"Did anyone help him figure out how to get out of Hell and become an angel?"

Sekhmet looked at Baraqiel.

"Barry?" I asked. He let out a long sigh before placing a hand on the table.

"Yeah, I helped him. He and I ran into each other a lot when I would have to check in on demons who were violating rules. Dumah pulled me aside and asked me to help him get out. He told me his story and said he'd do anything to get out of Hell, to get back to her. His love. He had to gain my trust first obviously. He had been working for demons."

"Can a demon be saved?" I asked.

Sekhmet and Baraqiel just stared at me. Thalia sighed.

"Emma, you're not talking about Ankou, are you?" Sekhmet asked.

"No!" I snapped. "Of course not!"

"You couldn't save Dumah, but you're wanting to save a demon?" Baraqiel asked coldly.

"You know what? Forget I asked. Come on, Thalia."

"Emma!" Sekhmet called.

We walked out of the door and made our way to the shore. I heard Sekhmet call my name again as we reached the sand. She was running on all fours to get to us faster.

"Just wait!" she said as she approached us. "At least stay until morning. You know how dangerous the sea is after dark."

"We'll be fine," I grunted. "Besides, it's not like you and Baraqiel actually give a shit about me."

"Don't say that. You know we care about you."

"No you don't! I'm just some stupid human who got your friend killed, then thought I could fill his shoes. You don't think I constantly think about what I did? I don't sleep so I am awake all the time, thinking about what I put you two and Dumah through! But I'm trying! I really am! I don't want to be a constant fuck up anymore. I want to help. I just don't know how. And you two seem so reluctant to help me be better."

"You're right," she sighed. "I'm sorry. You could have just moved on to Paradise or returned to Earth. But you chose the harder option of becoming a death angel. I know it's not easy. And you probably feel like you don't have anyone."

"She has me," Thalia chimed in. I smiled at her.

"She has us too," Sekhmet continued. "I really am sorry. Please, come back and wait until morning when it's safer."

I looked at Thalia and she nodded at me. We grabbed our bags and went back to the hut.

Nighttime had surrounded us and things were starting to stir in the trees.

"Thalia," I whispered. "There are a couple of blood grenades in that bag. If we're attacked, use them."

"What are they?" Thalia asked.

"Mongrels," Sekhmet said. "Basically the guard dogs of Hell. They rip people apart, wait for them to heal, and rip them apart again. They can't kill us, but they hunt in large packs so they're a bitch to take on. Even with there being three of us. We should have just gotten on the boat and left."

Thalia got closer to me. We were still too far from the hut. Creatures around started howling and growling. I drew my sword and set it ablaze. The fire from the blade provided enough light to see the first faces appear from the trees. Mongrels were a type of demon I hadn't encountered yet. I rarely visited Hell and when I did, I made sure I was out before nightfall. I had lost track of time with the elite demons and gotten Thalia and I stuck here for the night.

As five mongrels started to circle us, Thalia gasped. They had blueish white skin that hung thinly over skeletal bodies. Their legs were long and slender. They ran on all fours and had hunched backs that ended in whip-like tails. They were a Hellish mixture of human and canine, with long ears and a large mouth full of teeth.

"We can take them," I said quietly.

One of the mongrels let out a long, loud howl. The other four joined it and we heard a reply call from many other mongrels in the woods.

"Can we?" Thalia asked.

"We can try," Sekhmet said.

All at once, we were completely surrounded by more than fifty mongrels. One jumped at us and I swung my sword, slicing it in half. Next thing I knew, we were fighting all of them off. Sekhmet was fighting three at a time while I swung my sword back and forth, cutting through mongrel after mongrel, and setting them on fire. At one point, I saw Thalia throw a grenade far into the pack. There was an explosion and mongrels were sent airborne. Then, I saw her slowly approach one of them, with her hands out.

"Thalia!" I yelled. "What are you doing?"

She took a few more steps towards the mongrel and it snapped at her. She hesitated for a moment before putting her hands out again. Suddenly, three of the mongrels closest to her turned and started attacking some of the others. A couple more charged at her but as soon as they got close enough to lunge at her they turned and also began to attack other mongrels.

"Are you making them do that?" I asked Thalia as I swung my sword at an attacking mongrel. She nodded without saying a word or taking her eyes off the creatures. I had less of them to fight off since they were focusing on their own kind turning on them.

"What is going on?" Sekhmet yelled at us. "Why are they fighting each other?"

"Thalia's doing it!" I called back.

There was a blinding flash as lightning suddenly struck several of the remaining mongrels. As some of the pack cleared, we could see Baraqiel strike more of them with lightning.

"Come on!" he shouted at us.

We sprinted towards the hut while Baraqiel and Sekhmet stayed in the rear to hold off the mongrels. We all made it safely through the door and shut it behind us. The four of us were panting and I noticed Sekhmet and I were covered in mongrel blood.

"That was one of the craziest things I've ever seen," Thalia exclaimed.

"Watching what you just did was one of the craziest things *I've* ever seen!" I laughed. "That was awesome!"

Thalia blushed.

"Maybe it was a good idea to have you come along after all. You're more of a badass than I thought you were."

"You did great," Sekhmet said, wrapping her arms around Thalia, covering her in blood.

I looked at Baraqiel.

"Thanks," I muttered.

He nodded.

"I mean, I think we would have had it," I continued. "But you helped wrap things up more quickly."

"Just 'thanks' would have worked," he said. I nodded back.

"Alright," Sekhmet clapped her hands together. "I'm going to go clean up, then let Emma have a turn, and then why don't I make us all some tea and we relax until morning."

"I would love some tea," Thalia said.

Sekhmet smiled at her before washing her arms and hands off in the sink.

"I saw a ship," I said, trying to make small talk. "Crossing from Sentencing to Processing. It's been a while since I've seen one."

Sekhmet's eyes shifted towards Baraqiel and her smile faded.

"Yeah," Baraqiel stiffened. "There have been less transfers lately."

I looked from him back to Sekhmet, waiting for someone to elaborate. Sekhmet sighed as she sat down next to Barry, waiting for the kettle to heat up.

"I know you miss it," she said, patting his knee gently before turning to us. "Baraqiel built that ship. It was a beautiful upgrade from the smaller boat they had been using for transfers. Baraqiel had hoped that he'd be the one to take the transfers over to Processing."

"Nope," Barry sighed. "'Stick to the shore. Guard the entrance.' That's it."

"If it's any consolation," Sekhmet leaned in, "I'm grateful for that. You're the best friend a girl like me could ever have."

Barry smiled at Sekhmet, grabbed her hand, and gently kissed it. The kettle began to whistle and Sekhmet hopped up to prepare tea for her and Thalia.

"I know this may come as a surprise to you, but I was a shipwright," Baraqiel laughed.

"What does that mean?" I asked.

"Someone who builds and repairs boats and ships," Thalia explained.

"I loved helping my father work on boats," Baraqiel continued. "I learned so quickly that my skill surpassed his by the time I was 17. I could see he was starting to get old and slow, and he wasn't bringing as much coin home as he once did. In Ancient Greece, every male had to join the military at some point in his life. Some men stayed to fight for their country, but most of them did it just to get paid. My family was guaranteed to be taken care of while I served, and I would also get paid for my service.

It was hard leaving the boats and the water, but I wanted to make sure my family was taken care of. My parents were older and had five children, including myself. I had two older brothers who had both died in battle. They had stayed in the military to help take care of the rest of us, and now it was my turn. As much as I wanted to stay to work near the water, I knew it would kill my father to retire earlier than he was ready to; to pass the torch to me and just sit around while I worked.

We were called, 'hoplites.' Citizen-soldiers who, unlike the elite soldiers like the Spartans, were rarely given armor. My eldest brother had spent some of our family money on a bronze suit when others wore linen. Unfortunately, he was cut in the leg and bled out. My next oldest brother was given shin guards, called "greaves," by my mother so the same thing wouldn't happen to him. He took an arrow to the skull. So, once it was my turn, I had been gifted a helmet with cheek plates, along with full armor. I had a spear, a sword, and a shield with my family's emblem on it. Before I left home, my mother quoted Pericles and said, 'Remember this. What we leave behind is not engraved in stone monuments but woven into the lives of others.' So, I started training, completely protected everywhere..."

Baraqiel paused for a moment.

"Everywhere, but my heart," he said. "Our training was grueling. The first two weeks I was there, all I could focus on was how hot, tired, sore, and hungry I was. We trained all day, every day for twenty days until we finally got a day of rest. Some of the boys already knew each other. They had been sent from the same towns. I didn't know anyone, but I wasn't there to make friends so I kept to myself. On our day off, I went to the nearest body of water, which was a stream. I was desperately missing the ocean but any water would do. I stripped down and went into the water completely naked. I floated there, letting all of the sweat and dirt wash off and pictured myself as one of the boats my father and I had just worked on, drifting in the water. And that's when I saw him. A scrawny boy, about my age, sitting on the bank, watching me. I was so startled by him, I quickly went under water. I knew how to swim, of course, but I swallowed too much water and was flailing around, panicking. I came up quickly, bashing my head on an exposed tree root, and everything went black.

    I regained consciousness and realized what had happened. He had pulled me out of the water and resuscitated me. He asked if I was okay and all I could think about was being naked in front of this other boy. I covered myself and wiped my mouth. He introduced himself as Matariel and put his hand out. Without offering mine in return I asked what he was doing out there.

    'Some fresh air away from the training camp sounded good,' he said. 'I wanted to come out here for peace and quiet and to just enjoy nature.'

He looked at me, still covering myself with my hands and laughed.

'We should go get your clothes,' he said. He was very respectful and didn't look at me until I was dressed again.

We somehow ended up spending the whole day together at that stream, getting to know each other. He had noticed me at camp although I hadn't realized he existed until that day. After that, we were inseparable. We learned how to fight in the phalanx formation, which was standing shoulder to shoulder and building a wall with our shields. If done correctly, we were impenetrable. Matariel and I also got good at doing the 'in two' attack, in which I would go overhand with my spear and he would go low with his. We worked so well together that everyone else thought we were long lost brothers.

After training, we marched to battle. The Greeks were at war with the Persians, who outnumbered us greatly. For three days it poured down rain on us, so hard that if you looked up at the sky, it would drown you. We took shelter when we could but most of the time we were left to the elements. Matariel and I stayed huddled together, just talking about ourselves or telling stories. One clear night, after the rain finally stopped, I was laying under the stars, unable to sleep. Matariel came over and asked if I was okay.

'Just can't sleep,' I said. 'I keep thinking about how we'll soon be fighting Persians and all I want in the world is to be on a boat. The water stirs my soul and inspires me. It makes me feel so small and so powerful at the same time. Like I could do anything. Become anything. I've grown so fond of the ocean that my heart beats to the same rhythm as the waves. Now that I'm so far away from it, I can't seem to find my heartbeat.'

Matariel slowly took my hand in his and placed it on his chest, and then placed his hand on my chest.

'Do you feel that?' he asked. 'Now your heart can beat with mine.'

I smiled at him.

'The way you describe the ocean? I know exactly how it makes you feel. You're my ocean.'

I looked into his eyes and gently held his face. My fingertips softly traced over his cheek bones, chin, and forehead before I leaned in and kissed him. It was like a veil had been lifted. I loved Matariel almost instantly, I just hadn't realized what that love meant. We continued to march until we reached the battlefield. There were 53 of us and 700 Persians. The battle was not significant in the war, nor was it recorded. But it gave Persia a taste of just how strong Greece was. They retreated with only 40 or so men. We came away from battle with 50. However, one of the three that we lost was Matariel."

Baraqiel paused and let out a shaky sigh before wiping his face.

"After we broke the phalanx formation, we broke off into pairs for the 'in twos.' Matariel and I were killing Persian after Persian, but I could see that he was getting fatigued. Spending days out in the rain had weakened his immune system and he was fighting while sick. Any other person would have had trouble seeing it, but I could tell. He was slightly slower than usual. So when one Persian came for us, I went high and he went low. But the Persian thrust his sword at us, piercing Matariel in the neck. I had stabbed the Persian in the chest and killed him, but he had hurt me more. I watched Matariel slump to the ground, blood gushing out of the hole in his neck. I placed both hands over the wound and called out for help. But no one came. I cradled Matariel's head in my lap and fought back tears as I told him everything would be okay. He struggled to talk and all that came out was gurgling sounds. But I watched his lips move until I understood.

'I love you too,' I smiled. And then the light went out in his eyes. I whispered in his ear, 'find me on the ocean.'

I don't know why I said that. I guess I had some hope that we would find each other in the afterlife. I lived the rest of my days as a soldier, waiting for my turn to die. But it never came. After each battle, I would return home to my family, a hero. My father would tell everyone that lightning ran through my veins instead of blood. I guess that's why I was gifted with that power when I chose to become a dark angel. Being a warrior was all I knew. I stopped going out on the water and just wanted to fight. I lost my heartbeat the day Matariel died. I thought once I became an angel, I'd be able to go find him. But I'm forced to stay on the shore. My only purpose is to keep the creatures of Hell here. The worst part is, Matariel suffered the same fate."

"What do you mean?" I asked.

"After Baraqiel, Dumah, and I became friends, I was able to locate Matariel," Sekhmet said. "He was given the exact same task as Baraqiel, but on another shore."

"And neither of you can leave?" I asked. Baraqiel shook his head.

"I've tried so many times," he said. "I can only get so far into Hell or out on the water before I'm somehow teleported back to my house. When Sekhmet found Matariel, he said the same thing happened to him when he tried."

"That's so unfair!" Thalia exclaimed. "Have you tried talking to someone about it?"

"Of course I have," Baraqiel laughed. "But this is what I signed up for. This is my duty. When Emma, Sam, and I were attacked by those demons years ago, I was hoping it would kill me. I could be reincarnated back on Earth like Dumah, and maybe if Matariel heard, he'd do it too. But no. I was injured, healed, and am right back to where I was. I guess that's the main reason why I was so upset about Dumah. Not only was he killed, but he gets to start all over. Meanwhile, I'm stuck for eternity separated from my love. Deep down I know our souls would find each other in another life."

"I'm going to see if I can do something about this," I said, standing up. The sun was beginning to rise outside. "I'm going to help you get this figured out."

"Emma, there's nothing you can do that I haven't already tried," Baraqiel replied. "I appreciate it though. I just wanted you to understand why I am the way I am. I'm just a bitter angel, stuck here just like you."

I leaned over and hugged him.

"I promise you that I'll find a way."

Thalia and I left as soon as it was light outside. We boarded the boat and made our way back to the other side.

"You've been making a lot of promises lately," Thalia finally said. "I know you want to help, but maybe there are some things that just can't be done."

"I'm going to keep all of my promises," I replied.

"I think you should try focusing on your job and not worry about so much. You're a good soul, Emma. You don't have to take on so much."

"I'm going to keep all of my promises," I repeated. "I'm going to get Dumah back as a death angel, I'm going to free Sam, I'm going to save Abaddon, I'm going to help Baraqiel and Matariel, and I'm going to kill Ankou."

Thalia didn't say another word. As we crossed the water, I sang a familiar song that I once heard while traveling this very sea, years ago.

"My mother told me
Someday I would buy
Galleys with good oars and
Sails to distant shores.
My mother told me
Someday I would buy
Galleys with good oars and
Sails to distant shores.
Stand up on the prow
Noble barque I steer
Steady course to the haven
Hew many foe-men
Hew many foe-men."

I'm going to keep all of my promises, I thought again to myself.

4

As we approached the shore, I could see Dumah's hut. Every time I got within eyesight of it, I thought I would see him walk out the door, a frown on his face when he saw me using his boat. But like every other time, he didn't come out. No one did. I was reminded how alone I was. I got out and pulled the boat onto the sand and helped Thalia out. She gave me a hug, one that I reluctantly returned, and we said our goodbyes. She returned back to her normal size and flew away. I brought my stuff inside Dumah's hut and sat down at the table. I stopped to listen to the waves crash outside. I still felt tired from being in Hell for a couple of days and all I wanted was sleep. I placed my folded arms on the table and laid my head down. I closed my eyes. Minutes passed. Hours passed. But sleep didn't come. I went outside and laid down on the sand. Again, I tried closing my eyes to rest. Even if I got five minutes of sleep, I'd feel better.

After some time had passed, I slowly started to get up. I would have to report back to the archangels about my side mission. And then it was back to work; hanging around dying people. I walked around a bit, stretched my wings, and took off to find Michael. I circled around Processing to see if I could spot any archangels, but no such luck. As much as I disliked going to The Gates, I knew I'd have to if I wanted to check in with one of them. The Gates, as obvious as it seems, is the entryway into Paradise from Processing, much like The Abyss is the entryway into Hell from Sentencing. Unlike The Abyss, where anyone could go through, The Gates were heavily secured by archangels. They took turns guarding the area, making sure no one entered who wasn't allowed to.

    I hated going there because of how some of the archangels treated me. Dumah had mentioned how other angels didn't necessarily like death angels and at the time it seemed silly to me. Angels worked together for the greater good, right? Nope. Turns out, angels can still be assholes. The hierarchy of Heaven was no different than cliques in a high school. Archangels held a higher ranking than other angels, so they acted like they were better than everyone else. Michael, Raphael, Azrael, Barachiel (Ankou's brother), Uriel, Gabriel, Jerahmeel, and Sealtiel are the O.G. angels of God, with Lucifer having been the ninth. The eight of them who are left serve as sort of generals for God. Other than God Himself, the only other Heavenly beings higher than the archangels are the seraphim, who never leave God's side. The only reason why the archangels act like they're in charge of everyone else is because no one has actually seen God or the seraphim. God is like the

King of England and the archangels are the Prime Minister and Parliament. They're only in charge of us because God doesn't leave Buckingham Palace.

So there I was, at The Gates, dreading what I was about to walk into. The giant golden archway seemed to be looming over me. From the outside, it looked like nothing was past the archway. But as I stepped through, I could see a giant golden staircase, spiraling up into blinding white light, and a large white building that reminded me of the United States Capitol.

"Well, well, well," Azrael said as soon as he saw me. "If it isn't Emma, the infamous death angel."

"Hey," I said quickly. "I'm just here to report back from my little side mission."

"Side mission?" he repeated. "I was unaware you had a side mission. Aren't you supposed to be watching people die alone?"

"Yeah," I said calmly, trying to ignore his contempt. "Michael is the one who asked me to go, so if you want to check with him-"

"CAW! CAW! CAW!"

The sudden yelling in my ear made me jump as Raphael came into view, flapping his arms. He and Azrael laughed.

"Or if you could just let Michael know I stopped by with an update," I continued. I was losing patience quickly.

"Awww, what's the matter, Emma?" Raphael asked. "You don't like us?"

"I just can't spend a lot of time here," I lied. "I have other, more important things to do."

"Oh please," Azrael scoffed. "Like your job is *that* important."

"Also," Raphael added, "you're not even good at your job. Barachiel complains about how awful you are. He just feels sorry for you and doesn't say anything to your face."

"I'm doing my best," I said through gritted teeth. "I wouldn't be here if I didn't want to be a death angel."

Raphael snapped his fingers as if he just thought of something.

"Oh, actually you're only here because you killed Dumah."

Even Azrael looked slightly shocked at this comment. I glared at Raphael and walked right up to his face and whispered, "no wonder they named the mean ninja turtle after you."

"What?" Raphael asked, confused.

"Look," Azreal said. "Michael's inside the Temple of Da'at right now, looking for some book. Apparently a guardian angel accidentally broke through the veil and interacted with their human, which is forbidden. Anyways, Michael has to look up how to punish the guardian angel."

"Why? Did something bad happen to the human?" I asked.

"No, the opposite actually. He talked the human into leaving an abusive relationship she was in."

"Why would the guardian angel be punished for that?" I asked. "He helped that human!"

"None of us are supposed to mess with the divine timeline," Raphael said. "Duh."

"So what?" I snapped. "He was supposed to let her just continue to be abused, and possibly die?"

"I know you can't possibly understand this," Azrael said. "You've been an angel for what? Like a week? You're still learning how things work. We cannot, *absolutely* cannot, interfere. God has painted a specific picture for every human that ever has been and ever will be. We do not have authority to scribble over those."

"Doesn't that fuck with free will?" I asked.

"Don't use that kind of language here," Raphael spat at me.

"What about angels who are meant to influence?" I continued. "What's the difference? I mean, what if that angel talked her into leaving an abusive relationship and she, I don't know, went back to school, became a therapist, and can now help other abused women?"

"She didn't," Azrael said. "She went back and murdered her boyfriend. She's now serving a life sentence and then will go to Hell when she dies. But if she had stayed in the relationship without any interference, he would have been arrested for driving while drunk. It would have given her the time and clarity to leave in a more healthy way."

"This is such bullshit," I scoffed.

"Knock it off with the language!" Raphael seethed. "This is Heaven, for goodness sake!"

"Will you just tell Michael I need to talk to him?" I said to Azrael, ignoring Raphael.

"I'm not telling Michel anything," he said, pointing to the white building behind them. "Tell him yourself once he's done."

"Can't I just go inside the temple?"

"You don't have clearance," Raphael chuckled. "Death angels don't get the privilege. Probably because they're supposed to be working."

"How do I gain access?" I asked.

"You don't," Raphael smiled.

"Can I get in if I go with someone else? I think he was wanting to know as soon as I got back so it's kind of urgent."

"I don't see why not," Azreal shrugged. "As long as you don't take anything."

"Then why can't one of you just let me in?"

"I'm busy," Raphael answered.

"Doing what?" I asked.

"Guarding, obviously."

I grunted with frustration and looked at Azrael.

"We actually are in rotation right now. But if you want to wait here, you can. Just stay out of the way."

"Fine."

I stood there as they walked back and forth in front of the entrance. I watched as different angels came through the archway and went into the building. Death angels were the only ones who didn't have access to the Temple of Da'at. But why? We served Heaven just like the rest of them, so why were we treated as less? No wonder Dumah was always so bitter. I sat down and got lost in my own thoughts for some time before hearing a voice.

"You're waiting on Michael?" Uriel asked.

I nodded.

"I think he's almost done if you want to wait just a bit longer."

"What are you doing?" I asked.

"It's my turn for rotation. We swap out every three days."

"I've been sitting here for three days?" I grunted. "You know, if you guys would give me access to that building, I could have talked to Michael already and been back to doing my stupid job!"

"Whoa, whoa, whoa," Jarahmeel said, coming up from behind Uriel. "Why are you shouting?"

"She's been waiting for Michael," Uriel explained. "He's inside Da'at looking for something."

"And apparently I'm not allowed in there so I've been sitting here for three days," I muttered.

"You remind me of Dumah," Uriel smiled. "Same grumpy, impatient demeanor."

"Three days!" I exclaimed. "I've wasted three days just sitting here."

"Three days to us is like thirty minutes to humans," Jarahmeel said. "Time doesn't move the same for us. Perks of being immortal."

I rolled my eyes and then noticed Micahel walk out of the building. I quickly stood and rushed over to him, waving him down.

"Emma!" he said, smiling. "What are you doing here?"

"I've been waiting for you to finish up so I could give you an update."

He gave me a puzzled look.

"Claude and Pavel?"

"I'm sorry, I-"

"You made me go to Hell to find them."

"Oh yes."

"Well Thalia and I met a demon named Abaddon-"

"Thalia told me."

"And he took us to this place where the angels were meeting with some demons."

"Emma, Thalia told me."

"And they're joining them."

"Emma-"

"I know!" I yelled. "I heard you! But you asked me to do this and wanted me to report back to you. I would have done so three days sooner but you've been in that stupid building looking up how to punish an angel for trying to help someone. And since I don't have permission to enter that stupid building, I've been sitting out here for three days getting bullied by archangels and watching everyone else go in there."

"First of all, don't raise your voice at me," Michael said in a more stern voice than I was used to from him. "I haven't done anything to deserve that. Second, the angel I'm dealing with right now is none of your business and I'm not sure why you even know about it. And third, Thalia was asked to go on the mission as well. She had the decency to come straight to me instead of attempting to take a nap. She thought you would too but figured you went back to work. So she told me everything that happened."

"Yeah well she has access to Da'at," I scoffed.

"Emma, I really wish you wouldn't be like that," Michael put his hand on my shoulder. I moved away and folded my arms. He sighed and smiled at me.

"It's hard to be happy when all of your bosses make fun of you and treat you like an outcast," I retorted.

"You wouldn't be treated like an outcast if you didn't act like one."

"What is that supposed to mean?" I asked.

"You don't have to act so brooding. Do your job well, do some favors that are asked of you, maybe go out of your way to do some good, and the other archangels might start treating you better."

"*Might*. They're angels. They're supposed to treat everyone with kindness."

"And you're someone whose sole purpose is to bring comfort. Do you feel like you're a comforting individual? Or just someone who rushes to get the job done just so you can stalk an ex-boyfriend?"

My jaw dropped.

"That's extremely unfair to say," I uttered. "He's a demon who was trying to get me to commit suicide."

"But you didn't. So why are you still holding such a grudge."

"It's funny, you sound exactly like him," I laughed. "Guess demons and angels aren't that different."

"You know, I try to be patient and understanding with you, Emma. You haven't been an angel long at all. Your human life was cut short.

Also, you've experienced a lot of trauma, both in life and after. I understand that all of those things can make a person become...the way you are."

"At least I have an excuse to be an asshole," I said. "What about Raphael? Or any of them that treat me like crap?"

"You have to understand that we've been here since the very beginning. We were the ones who sent our fallen brothers to Hell. We don't leave Paradise because we're constantly paranoid that we'll be attacked. You have no idea how much you've been blessed. You're an angel who gets to go anywhere you want. You should be so much happier than what you are. But I truly think that if you focus on your job and its purpose, it could bring you some joy and peace."

I frowned at him. Michael started to say something again, but then stopped and smiled at me.

"At least tell me you'll try," he finally said.

Instead of arguing any further, I slowly nodded and said, "sure." Michael gently patted my shoulder and nodded back before starting to walk away.

"Oh!" Michael exclaimed and pointed in my direction. "Start wearing your tracker all the time from now on, please. No more hiding it."

I watched him continue on his way for a moment. My tracker kept vibrating, alerting me of new deaths. I let out a heavy sigh and checked it.

"Eeny, meeny, miny, moe," I whispered to myself.

I wound up somewhere in Colorado. The trees were dense, there was a little bit of snow on the ground, and I could hear the faint trickling of water nearby. There was another noise, however. As I made my way towards the soft whimpering, I stumbled across a makeshift campsite. There was a beat up tent, a small fire, some empty food cans and Ziploc bags, and a couple of backpacks. There was also the body of a man who, judging by the stage of decomposition, had been dead for some time. I looked up at the cliff above the campsite and then back at the dead man. The whimpering was coming from the tent and when I looked inside, I saw a black Labrador Retriever laying next to a little girl huddled in a sleeping bag.

I got closer and the dog sat up, looked at me, and laid back down, resting its head on the little girl's legs. I could see the name "Rocky" on the dog's collar. Outside the tent, the wind picked up and a bird started chirping.

"It's okay," the little girl said hoarsely. "There's no one out there."

The little girl let out a terrible-sounding wave of coughs before rolling over on her other side. Rocky waited for her to get comfortable before cuddling up to her again. I looked around the tent and noticed a coloring book with a rock holding it open to a page with a picture of a unicorn and a note written in purple crayon. Some of the words were spelled incorrectly but I could still tell what it said.

My name is Cora Bridger. I am 8 years old and am from Muskogee, Oklahoma. My daddy Luke took me on a camping trip and fell from the rocks up above. Me and Rocky wayted for someone to find us but we ran out of food and I am sick. Tell my mommy I did what she told me and stayd by Daddys side no matter what. Take care of Rocky.

Cora started coughing hard again and then began to gasp for air. I knelt down beside her and Rocky and waited. She was dirty, pale, and obviously hadn't eaten in a while. Her lips were tinted blue and she had apparently been in the sleeping bag for a long time because it smelled heavily of urine. Suddenly, Cora looked right at me. Her eyes widened and she gasped.

"It's okay," I smiled. "Just a little bit longer and then everything will be okay. I promise."

"Am I going with Daddy?" she asked softly. I nodded.

"Can Rocky come?"

Before I could say another word, Cora closed her eyes and exhaled. The wind, the bird, and everything else around us grew silent for a moment. Cora was with her daddy and wasn't cold and hungry anymore. Rocky started whining and I gently placed my hand between his ears. He flinched for a moment and then whined again.

"Good boy," I said. "Good boy."

I walked outside the tent and sighed, looking down at my tracker. I randomly selected another location and left. This time, I was in an alleyway in the Philippines. I came up on a young woman and man standing over another, much older man. The woman was obviously a prostitute and I assumed the man with her was either her boyfriend or pimp, or both. They had brutally beaten their victim and were now searching him for any jewelry and his wallet. The man on the ground tried calling for help but was unable to make any sound.

"Take any money you find!" the younger man said to the woman. "Hurry up, you dumb bitch! Before someone sees us!"

"There's nothing in his wallet!" she exclaimed. "Just a bunch of pictures of kids!"

"Where's your money?" he yelled at the older man.

All that came out of him were groans.

"We have to go," the woman said hurriedly. "Come on!"

The young man pulled a knife out of his jacket and stabbed the beaten man three times. The couple ran out of the alley and I was left alone with the dying man. I crouched down and put my face closer to his. He briefly looked back at me and the world went silent once more. The wind picked up and the photos from his wallet started blowing away from his body. I stood up and quickly selected my next location.

I was standing in a dank, dark prison cell, somewhere in Montana. The inmates were all supposed to be in bed, but the man in front of me was kneeling next to his cot. He had both hands in front of his face, gripping each other tightly as he whispered. I got closer to him and realized he was praying.

"There are so many things I'm sorry for, Lord," the man's quivering voice said softly as he wept. "I'm sorry I never made amends with my dad before he died. I'm sorry I dropped out of school and never went back. I'm sorry I started doing drugs and I'm sorry I got in with the wrong crowd. But most of all, I'm sorry that I put myself in the position I'm in right now. I know this goes against all of my beliefs, but I'm hoping- no. I'm *begging* that you'll understand. I can't spend the rest of my life in prison. I can't. I'm tired of being so scared and waking up every day to this. I've lost all of my friends and family because no one wants to be associated with a convicted murderer. I'll never see my sons and daughter again because of this. My life is over anyways. So I guess…"

The man put his forehead against his folded hands and started sobbing.

"I hope you can forgive me for what I'm about to do. Please continue to watch over my babies since I can't. I love you, Jesus. In your name, amen."

I watched him pull something out from under his pillow and climb into bed, pulling the blanket up to his neck. I leaned in over him as he made two jerking motions under his blanket. His breath quickened and a dark spot started spreading over the blanket. I knelt down beside the man and looked into his eyes. His breath slowed down and his eyes met mine. Then, he did something I wasn't expecting. He smiled at me before his eyes closed. A hand suddenly dropped out from under the blanket and dropped something onto the tile. It was a plastic spoon that had either been cut or shaved down to make the rounded end cornered and sharp. There was a light tapping sound on the floor and I noticed dark red droplets slowly start forming a puddle. The blood was coming from the man's open gash on his wrist.

I stood up and turned around. Ankou was standing outside the cell. I gasped.

"Before you say anything, this one actually wasn't mine," he said.

"How dare you," I sneered at him. "What are you doing here?"

"I got a suicide notification that wasn't mine and I was interested in checking it out."

He held up a device on his wrist similar to my own. Heaven and Hell had a lot more in common than I'd realized.

"Look familiar?" he asked.

"Wait," I said. "Is that my watch?"

"Whenever we get ahold of one of these, we reprogram them so we can use them."

"So that's how we keep running into each other," I gritted my teeth.

"Actually, he was going to you eventually, but then he pulled this."

"What do you mean?" I asked. "He was a murderer."

"No, he wasn't," Ankou let out a chuckle. "He was falsely accused of murder. He hadn't done anything except drugs and was framed by someone he knew."

"That's not true," I scoffed.

"Despite the many times I've lied to you, I can promise that I have no reason to right now," he replied.

"A demon making a promise; that's funny."

"I can prove it to you if you'd like," he said, sticking his hand through the cell bars. I looked at it and then at him.

"We can even make a bet if you want," he winked at me.

"No thanks," I said. Ankou shrugged.

"All the same, just proving I'm right is enough for me."

I stood there a moment longer and then reluctantly put my hand out to his. As soon as our hands touched, he gripped mine tightly and we were suddenly standing in front of the Sentencing building.

"After you," Ankou nodded towards the door, but I was already walking past him.

We walked inside and I looked around, remembering the last time I was here. Sam and I had come here, looking for a way to get to The Abyss, the gateway to the true Hell. At the time I thought we were on our way to rescue Alastor. But really we were on our way for Sam to deliver me to Ankou. We got on the elevator and Ankou reached in front of me to push the button for the third floor. We stood in silence as the walls of the tiny box seemed to close in on us.

"So...." Ankou started. "How are you liking the wings?"

"We're not making small talk," I glared at him. "I have nothing to say to you. And even if I did, it wouldn't be to talk about my job. It's none of your business."

"Sheesh," he put his hands up defensively. "Sorry. Just trying to be polite."

"Pff," I rolled my eyes.

The door to the elevator opened and I stepped out, not waiting for Ankou. I walked up to the desk and the same lady with permed hair was sitting in a chair on wheels. She was still wearing the same name tag that said, "HELLo, my name is Debbie." It didn't seem funny to me this time, however. Her eyes moved up at me and she sighed.

"Can I help you?" she asked, sounding a lot less cheerful than the last time I saw her.

"New arrivals?" Ankou asked from behind me.

"Well now this is a surprise!" the lady beamed. "Ankou, honey! How are you?"

"Can't complain," he smirked.

"New arrivals?" I repeated. Debbie's smile disappeared as she looked back at me.

"Through that hallway and to the left," she pointed to our right.

"Thanks," I smiled sarcastically. "Have a great day!"

I marched down the hall with Ankou closely behind me. I turned left and saw a group of people standing in line. They all looked miserable. Some were even crying. One lady was even sitting on the floor, sobbing and repeatedly yelling, "I'm sorry!"

"These are all suicides?" I whispered to Ankou.

"Yep," he answered a little too boastfully. "But again, don't get mad at me. Even though it's my area of expertise, I'm not responsible for all of them. Ah, here he is."

We walked up to the man I had just been with in the prison cell.

"Excuse me, sir?" Ankou tapped him on the shoulder. He turned to us, startled.

"Sorry to bother you," Ankou continued. "My friend and I have a little wager going on-"

I started to correct him on the term, "friend," but decided not to interrupt him.

"-And we were wondering if you could explain how you ended up here. What's your name? Tell us your story."

He looked at both of us, clearly confused.

"Uh, my name is Joseph Baird, but everyone calls me Joey. I'm 37 years old. Or I guess I *was*. Um, I was in prison for murder when I killed myself."

I smiled at Ankou.

"But I, uh, I never killed anyone."

My smile faded.

"What?" I asked. Ankou was now grinning.

"Yeah," Joey continued. "I was with a group of friends, drinking and getting high. My wife had filed for a divorce and I was feeling pretty shitty. At some point, I passed out. When I woke up, someone was banging on my door. I was on the floor next to my buddy, Rick, who was dead. I was covered in his blood and there was a knife sticking out of his stomach. I pulled the knife out and tried giving chest compressions but the police kicked the door in and arrested me before I could help him. I think he had already been dead for a while though. But I didn't lay a finger on him. My friend,

Stefon, had testified that I was already passed out when he left. But it didn't matter. My fingerprints were on the knife, I was covered in his blood, and they found too many drugs and guns in my apartment for their liking. So the jury found me guilty. My lawyer begged me to take a plea deal. But I wasn't going to admit to something I didn't do. When my last appeal was denied and my lawyer quit on me, I just couldn't take it anymore."

"But if you hadn't killed yourself, you would have gone to Heaven," I explained.

"I honestly wasn't thinking about that," Joey shook his head. "All I could think about was how alone I was, living the rest of my life labeled as a 'murderer.' I couldn't handle it."

I let out a long, heavy sigh. A man poked his head out into the hallway and called, "Next!" The line moved forward.

"I know we didn't technically bet on anything, but I won," Ankou muttered.

"Shut up!" I snapped at him before turning to Joey again. "Listen, if you do your time down here for a while, put in a request to become a death angel. You don't have to stay here forever."

"Hey!" the man at the door shouted at me. "What the fuck do you think you're doing?"

"Can I also do that?" a woman in line asked.

"How do we sign up for that?" a man added.

"Emma!" Ankou yelled and pulled on my arm. "Fuck! Come on!"

There was now a commotion as several people in line were trying to ask questions at the same time. A few people were trying to get closer to the door.

"Everyone get back in line and wait your turn!" the man at the door shouted.

Ankou held on tightly to my arm until we were in the stairwell. He pushed me hard up against the wall and pointed a finger in my face. His eyes went all black as he scolded me.

"Don't you ever fucking pull that shit around here again, you understand? You could get us both in a lot of trouble."

I tried to push against him, but he was stronger than me. He shoved me against the wall again.

"I mean it, Emma. Do you know how bad it would be if rumors spread that I was helping an angel get souls into Heaven?"

"Oh, you mean kind of like a demon manipulating angels into helping him get souls into Hell?" I snapped at him.

"That's different!"

"Bullshit!"

"It is! I don't interfere with free will!"

"No, lying to humans and making them fall in love with you so they'll want to kill themselves for you is so much better!" I shoved Ankou as I yelled.

"Jesus fucking Christ, is that what this is about?" he got close to my face again. He was so close now that his breath blew strands of my hair around.

"Get over it! You're an angel! If you hadn't met me, you would have just died sad and lonely. You got to experience love, which is something a lot of humans never get."

"But it was fake!"

"Not to you!"

"Oh please! Don't make it sound like you were doing me a favor."

"Wasn't I though?" He asked, now leaning in so that his lips grazed my neck as he spoke. "If it wasn't for me, you wouldn't have had one of the most important human life experiences. And so what if I didn't love you back? A lot of young women fall in love with men who don't love them in return. It sucks but that's also another life experience. You can't be mad at me that I tried to influence you to kill yourself. You didn't do it."

"I'm not mad about that!" I suddenly yelled. "I'm mad...."

I stopped and stared at him, trying to collect myself. "I'm mad about Sam and Dumah."

"Why though?" Ankou asked, taking a step back from me. "Seriously, think about it. Sam was a *guardian angel*. Her sole purpose was to guide people into doing the right thing, and she couldn't even do that. Doesn't a part, even if it's a very small part, make you feel a little relieved that she's gone so she can't hurt anyone else?"

"She wouldn't have tried to hurt me if it wasn't for you," I murmured.

"True. But I'm just doing my job. Too bad she couldn't do hers."

"How dare you! What aren't you getting about this? If you hadn't come along and tricked her into tricking me, none of this would have happened."

"If a kid offers another kid drugs, and that kid dies of an overdose, whose fault is it? The drug dealer's? Or the kid who should have said no in the first place and lived?"

I didn't say anything. Ankou tilted his head at me, as if he had me cornered.

"And what's your excuse for Dumah?" I asked.

"I don't have one," Ankou sighed. "He died trying to protect you. But his soul was sent back to Earth and he's living a pretty decent life from what I've heard. Sounds like I almost did him a favor. He got a second chance, and Heaven replaced him with you. Everyone wins. Everyone's happy."

I didn't respond again.

"Ahh, so that's it then."

"What?" I asked.

"You're not happy. You want Dumah to come back and take his spot so you can....what? Get *your* second chance?"

"Don't you for one second think you know what I want."

Ankou stepped towards me again and gently pushed back the strands of hair that had fallen into my face.

"If there's one thing demons know, it's the wants and desires of humans," he smiled.

"I'm not a human anymore though."

"So then why are you still acting like one?"

I scoffed and then started walking down the stairs.

"Where are you going?" Ankou asked.

"I'm leaving. I honestly don't know what I was thinking, coming here in the first place. I guess I'm so desperate to prove you wrong that I'd waste a whole day coming to Hell with you."

"I'm trying to help you. You're an angel now. Sure, you play for the opposing team, but I'd much rather you play fairly than make things harder for everyone."

"What do you mean?" I asked before reaching the main floor.

"Tap into your divine powers. Learn about the people you're dealing with. Find out what led up to the moment of their death. Don't think I don't know you haven't been trying to bless suicides before they die so they have a better chance of getting into Paradise. What if you blessed a suicide to get them into Paradise, only to find out they had killed someone else moments prior."

"Every soul deserves a chance to be saved," I said. Ankou scoffed.

We made our way to the lobby and I noticed the older man I had just seen beaten and stabbed in the Philippines.

"What in the world," I said out loud.

I walked over to the desk, confused.

"I'm telling you, there's been a mistake," the man said to the woman behind the desk.

"Sir, I've read your file," she explained. "I'm positive that you're in the right place. You need to go up to floor five and speak with someone up there. They'll explain everything in more detail and let you know where you need to go next."

"Excuse me," I said.

"Emma, don't," Ankou started. I held my hand up to him.

"Can I help you?" the woman behind the desk asked me.

"Can you tell me why this poor man is here?" I asked. "I literally just watched him get mugged, beaten, and stabbed to death."

"Thank you!" the older man said. "There's been a mistake. My name is Banoy Abalos. I was murdered."

"You also fucked little kids, didn't you?" Ankou said suddenly. We all turned to look at him.

"What?" Banoy said, sounding like all the air left his body.

"Fifth floor is for pedophiles," Ankou replied. "She said she read your file and that's the floor you need to go to."

"No," I said. "He-"

And then I remembered.

"There's nothing in his wallet!" the woman had said. *"Just a bunch of pictures of kids!"*

I looked at Banoy and took a step back. He slowly dropped to his knees and started sobbing.

"I'm sorry!" he cried. "I was a sick, lonely man."

"Who preyed on innocent children for years," Ankou said. "Including your own grandson."

"I'm so sorry!" Banoy repeated. "Please!"

He crawled over to me and grabbed one of my boots.

"Please, help me!" he cried.

"I need security down here, immediately," I heard the woman at the desk say.

"We need to get you out of here," Ankou said, touching my shoulder.

"No!" Banoy shouted. "Please don't leave me! Take me with you!"

Suddenly, he climbed up my body, holding onto me tightly. Ankou yanked him off of me and punched him in the mouth. Banoy dropped to the ground again, covering his mouth with both hands, howling in pain. Ankou grabbed my hand, there was a sudden *whoosh!* and we were both back at the prison. The guards had discovered Joey's body and were waiting for the police to arrive.

"How did no one catch the weapon he made?" I heard one of the guards whisper.

"I don't know," the other one said. "Thank the Lord Almighty that he used it on himself and not someone else."

"Bastard probably felt guilty, as he should."

"At least we don't have to waste three meals a day on a fucking scumbag murderer."

I watched as the first guard kicked Joey's cot with his boot. I turned to Ankou, who was already looking at me.

"This is awful," I said. "You're right. I'm not happy. In a single day I watched a child die alone in the woods, an innocent man take his own life and no one will ever know that he didn't do anything, and a pedophile who will never see the prison time he deserves. Why is life like this?"

"Because humans made it this way for themselves," he said. "The second Adam and Eve gained knowledge of good and evil, they chose wrong. And thousands of years later, nothing has changed."

I put my face in my hand before sighing.

"I'm going home," I said. "I need a break."

I jumped as Ankou gently took my wrists and moved my hands away.

"You're quitting already?" he asked, raising his eyebrows and smiling.

"I can't stomach anymore. It's too much."

Ankou brushed my hair away from my face and lifted my chin to meet his gaze.

"Trust me," Ankou said, smiling. "The more you do it, the easier it gets. The less you care about them."

I scoffed and pulled away from him.

"I hope you're wrong about that," I said before leaving.

I landed back in Processing and just stood there a moment. I was surrounded by people who had just died again, only this time, most of them looked happy. Some looked a little confused, but for the most part, this was much better than watching people die. And it was certainly better than Sentencing. I walked around a little bit, watching the newcomers.

"Emma!" I heard a voice yell from behind me. I turned to see Elijah running towards me.

I smiled until he got closer and I could see the serious look on his face.

"Where have you been?" he asked. "Never mind that. I have an update!"

"Dumah?" I asked. Even though my heart was no longer beating, I could feel a skip in my chest. But Elijah shook his head.

"No," he said. "It's his grandson, Gabriel. He's dying."

5

"What happened to him?" I asked.

"He was in a really bad motorcycle accident," Elijah explained to me. "A truck ran a red light and hit him. He's at Kindred Hospital."

"I know where that's at," I replied. Before Elijah could say another word, I was on my way to the hospital. That was where Eduardo stayed when he had his heart attack and needed surgery. I remember that was also the first time I had met another death angel since becoming one.

Prior to Eduardo's heart attack, I had only been present for a handful of deaths. When I first became an angel, I spent a lot of my time trying to figure out who Dumah had become, where he was, and tracking Ankou. I wasn't very concerned about my job, which pissed off a lot of other death angels. I already wasn't liked because of the whole situation with Dumah. Although I wasn't the one who killed him, they all blamed me. Add that to my "slacker" angel persona and the fact that my ex-boyfriend was a demon, it wasn't necessarily surprising that all the other death angels avoided me at all costs.

While I was staying at the hospital, watching over Eduardo, I missed a lot of deaths. I could have easily been present at about twenty deaths while there, but I never left Eduardo's side.

One night, Eduardo was asleep in his hospital bed and his wife, Elena, was trying to sleep in a recliner beside him. I decided to wander the halls for a bit. I found myself walking around the maternity ward. I thought maybe surrounding myself with brand new babies might help clear my head. I looked at their tiny fingers and their soft, little, round cheeks and all I could think was, *one day, hopefully many years from now, I'll be visiting every single one of you.* And then, an alarm went off.

"CODE BLUE, CODE BLUE, CODE BLUE," a loud automated voice announced over the speakers.

"I need a crash cart now!" I heard a woman yell as she ran past the nursery. I followed a group of doctors and nurses who were running down the hall. I peered inside Room 102 and immediately noticed how much blood there was on the floor. A pregnant woman was laying on the bed unconscious, with more blood between her legs. A doctor was standing over her doing chest compressions. I started backing away from the room when I saw her. She appeared out of thin air and was leaning over the pregnant woman, one hand on the woman's stomach. She had large black wings and was wearing a dark gray hood that covered her face as she looked down at the woman's face. Long red hair draped over her right shoulder and her skin looked like porcelain. I stood frozen in place watching as the silence engulfed us.

"She's gone," one of the doctors said. "Call it."

The doctor doing the chest compressions stopped, looked around, and sighed.

"Time of death, 1437."

The death angel standing over the woman lifted her head and looked at me. Her white eyes met mine and she began to walk towards me. As she got closer, I could see what looked like scales covering her skin.

"You," she glowered at me. "You've been at this hospital for days and you couldn't even be bothered to do your job while you've been here."

I didn't say anything.

"That woman's baby died inside of her and she almost died without one of us being present. She would have been completely alone if I hadn't shown up. I've already done three other deaths at this hospital since yesterday morning. I know Michael and Barachiel are taking it easy on you because you're still new. And they also feel sorry for you because of what happened. But I think it's crap. Most of us have been around hundreds or thousands of years. We take our job very seriously. You're a disgrace to the rest of us."

"I- I'm sorry," I stuttered.

"You should be," she said stiffly. "Because of you, we lost one of our best."

My jaw dropped.

"You will never replace Dumah. But the least you can do is *try* to do the things he no longer can."

Before I could say another word, she was gone. The next day, I found myself in the emergency room, watching as an ambulance pulled up to the doors and pulled a young woman out. They wheeled her on a gurney and rushed her into an operating room. From what the paramedics were telling the nurses, and then what the police officers added after they showed up, I gathered what had happened. This woman's boyfriend was abusive. He had beaten her pretty badly, breaking her collar bone and two of her ribs. When she tried to leave to go to the hospital, he pulled out a gun and shot her in the stomach. One of the doctors had her hands over the gunshot wound, yelling to one of the other doctors that the woman needed to be sedated. She was flailing around on the gurney, screaming in pain.

I stood next to the doctor who was still yelling orders at everyone. She knew time was running out. I looked down at the woman and she looked right back at me. I glanced away, feeling uncomfortable. She stopped screaming, gasped, and then was dead.

"You need to hold eye contact until they pass," I heard a voice say from behind me. I turned and saw the death angel from the day before. She was leaning against the wall, watching. Her hood hung low, revealing only her mouth.

"I felt like I scared her," I explained. "I wish we didn't look so horrifying."

"It's not that bad," she smirked. "Once you get used to how you look, you start to like it. It becomes a new normal. You don't even miss how you used to look. There's not anything I miss, actually."

"You don't miss being human?"

"Nah. My life wasn't that great. Besides, I'm more powerful and I'm immortal now. I don't need to sleep or eat."

"How long have you been an angel?" I asked.

"I became an angel after my death in 1594. I was burned at the stake after being accused of being a witch. When I ended up in Hell, I was a little confused. I had just been unlawfully murdered. But then they explained that you can't kill over ten men and not go to Hell for it."

I looked at her, bewildered, and she smiled.

"My name is Isla. I was an innkeeper in Scotland. I served a lot of men who were married but came in with women who were not their wives. Then, the wives would come in and sit with me, crying that their husbands were running around on them. Some of them were even being abused by their husbands! One day, a woman offered me a lot of money, and I mean *a lot*, to kill her husband.

Women couldn't just freely leave their spouses just because they were being cheated on. So when she suggested that, obviously my initial reaction was to reject her offer. But over the next few days, I had a few more women come in who offered the same deal. They were friends of mine, or so I thought. The extra money sounded good, but I mostly wanted to help them.

So the married men who came in with mistresses and prostitutes got a 'special drink,' made with foxglove. More mild symptoms of being poisoned by foxglove are mostly vomiting and lethargy. But I had figured out a perfect amount that caused a heart attack hours later. It worked out in a way that my business and the women who came in with the men were never connected to the deaths.

Eventually suspicions grew that men were getting ill and dying, and soon the wives were being accused. Although there was an agreement not to mention my name, one woman got scared and told authorities that I had been luring men into my establishment with witchcraft and giving them some sort of witch's brew. Of course when they raided my inn, they found the foxglove, glasses with traces of it in them, belongings of the men were found in my basement, a large sum of money was discovered under my mattress, and some of the prostitutes and mistresses came forward saying the men were fine when they arrived at the inn, only to become ill afterwards. While imprisoned, my inn was burned to the ground. It was deemed unholy grounds so they 'cleansed it.' 38 women came forward saying that I had murdered their husbands. I had only killed eleven men. I knew that for a fact because I had been paid by nine women; one of the women had been raped by two men and asked me to take care of them both for her. The other murders were not my doing. But of course there was no point in arguing. Whether it was 11 or 38, they had come to their own conclusions about me and sentenced me to death. They had a witch pricker come to my cell, strip me down naked, and search my body for a 'witch's mark.' Of course he found one."

    Isla pulled her sleeve up and showed me a dark brown oval right below her elbow.

    "But that's just a birthmark," I said. "My brother Simon had one on his ankle."

    "Well, that was scientific facts back then," Isla smiled, shaking her head. "That was all the proof they needed to deem me a witch. They tortured me with sleep deprivation. Guards took shifts to make sure I stayed awake; dumping cold water on me or hitting me every time I started to nod off. They tortured me until I confessed."

    Isla removed her hood and revealed horrific burn scars all along her neck and the left side of her face and head. She was missing a fair amount of hair on that side and she gently rubbed the bald part as she continued.

"I don't remember much about the day I died. It was cold and I remembered making a joke to 'hurry up and get the fire started.' All 38 women who accused me of murdering their husbands were there, along with the rest of the town. They cursed me, calling me a demon and a witch. I remember the smoke choked me. The heat was excruciating and I held back my screaming by biting down on my tongue. And then suddenly, I saw him. He walked up from the crowd, right up to my face. He looked into my eyes, and then I woke up in Hell. Eventually, the death angel found me and told me that I could get out faster if I became like him. I accepted immediately."

"It was Dumah, wasn't it?" I asked.

"Yes. And you got him killed. And for what? A demon! Dumah should have just let Ankou have you. You don't deserve to be an angel; to carry his sword!"

"I know, and I'm sorry! I know he should be here instead of me. If I could bring him back, I would."

"He's gone," Isla said. "Dumah will never return."

"Barachiel said he returned to Earth. I've been watching over him. His name is Eduardo now, but it's Dumah. I asked around until I finally found out where his soul went. He had a heart attack and is here-"

"Emma," Isla interrupted. "It's not *him* though. He's lived a whole life as Eduardo. He doesn't remember anything as Dumah."

"Then what's the point?" I yelled. "It's the same as him being dead then?"

"Not necessarily. Dumah only lived to be in his forties. The end of his life was sad so he chose to end it. He spent centuries in Hell, and even then, couldn't go to Paradise. He had to become a death angel just to get out of Hell. Now, he has lived a much longer, happier life. He has a chance to go to Paradise; something he didn't have before. As much as I selfishly want Dumah back, knowing that his soul might actually be at peace makes me feel better about him being gone. Lord knows I would choose Paradise if I could."

Her face hardened as she looked back at me.

"But I still don't like you," she said, narrowing her eyes. "You're lazy, inconsiderate of others, and you have a terrible judgment of character."

"I didn't become a death angel to make friends," I explained. "I couldn't care less if you like me. All I can say is I'm doing my best with all of this."

"It's so strange," Isla smiled slightly.

"What?"

"You almost remind me of him. Hm. Well, Emma, I have to get back to work. You probably should too. See you around."

Isla gave me a nod and then was gone. That was two years ago.

There I was again, in the same hospital. Except I wasn't there for Eduardo. I was there to check on Gabriel, his grandson. Watching them over the years, I knew how close the two of them were. Gabriel even resembled Eduardo, with his curly dark brown hair and slightly hooked nose. However, Gabriel had fuller lips and green eyes like his mom. I walked into Gabriel's hospital room and could hear all of the machines working to keep him alive. In the corner, Eduardo was leaning back in a recliner sleeping. I moved over to Gabriel and inspected him. His shoulder-length hair was brushed back, away from his cut up face. A tube was in his mouth and I watched as his chest rose and fell, breathing with the assistance of the ventilator.

"I know you're here," I heard a soft voice say from the corner. Eduardo was sitting up and looking around the room. "I felt your presence when I had my heart attack. You were here to take me. I wasn't ready then, and my Gabe isn't ready now. So you get the hell out of here."

I didn't say anything or move. Eduardo placed his elbows on his knees and then rested his face into his hands. He didn't make a sound as he cried, but his shoulders convulsed as he did.

"At least wait for his mother and father to come back," Eduardo continued, his voice cracking. "They should be back any minute. They would never forgive themselves if they weren't here. But please....I'm begging you. Please don't take our baby. He's a good boy who never hurt anyone. He has the biggest heart and is always making us laugh."

Now Eduardo was slowly getting onto his knees, looking around the room for me.

"Please, take me instead. I've lived a full life. Gabe's has only begun. He still has so much to see and do."

The door opened and a man and woman walked in.

"*Papi?*" the man said. It was Diego, Eduardo's son. "What's wrong?"

"Nothing, *mijo*. I was just praying."

Diego and his wife, Gina, helped Eduardo back into the chair.

"Where is Sloane?" Eduardo asked.

"Mom's getting ready to bring her in," Gina explained. "She's prepping Sloane for what he looks like."

Gina's face contorted as she started crying. The door opened again and Elena walked in with Sloane, Gabriel's 19 year old sister. Gabe was nine years older than her, but cared for her as a child when Diego and Gina were busy helping run the restaurant. Sloane put a hand up to her mouth and gasped.

"Gabe," she whispered as she got close to him. I moved out of the way, although it didn't matter. She wouldn't have been able to feel me. Still, I did so out of respect. Sloane gently touched Gabriel's upper arm before turning back to Gina and Diego.

"Can he hear us?" Sloane asked.

"We don't know," Diego said.

"I think he can," Eduardo smiled. "You say whatever you need to, *mi cielo*. He's listening."

"Gabe," Sloane whispered, her voice cracking. "You're the strongest person I know. I know you want to just sit up and pull that stupid tube out of your mouth."

She stood there a moment, tears falling into the hairs on Gabriel's arm. There were no sounds except the beeping of the heart monitor, the whooshing of the ventilator, and the soft sniffling of people crying.

"Gabe, please wake up," Sloane cried. "Please!"

"It's okay, honey," Diego said, putting a hand on Sloane's shoulder. She turned and buried her face into his chest, sobbing. Elena comforted Gina while Eduardo sat and stared in my direction. I moved over to the other side of Gabriel and was relieved that Eduardo's eyes didn't follow me.

There was a knock on the door and a young Asian man walked in.

"Hello," he said with a fake cheerfulness. "I'm Dr. Chen. It looks like all of the paperwork is signed."

"What paperwork?" Eduardo asked.

"Dad," Diego said as Eduardo rose to his feet. "The machines are keeping Gabe alive. And they won't be able to do it much longer. There's no brain activity so his body is slowly shutting down."

"What are you saying?" Eduardo asked.

"Ed-" Elena started. Sloane started crying again.

"You all are ready to give up on our boy?" Eduardo asked. "It's only been three days, and you're ready to just give up on your child?"

"Dad, they've run every test they can," Gina said shakily. "He's not going to make it."

"You just said it yourself that the machines are keeping him alive!"

"The machines are prolonging the inevitable," Dr. Chen said. "Gabriel's organs are shutting down and if we're going to harvest any viable ones for donation-"

"*What?*" Eduardo hissed. "What did you say?"

"Gabriel is listed as an organ donor," Diego explained. "He can still help save other people."

"I want them to save *him*, god damn it!"

Eduardo slammed his fist down on the little table next to the recliner.

"Dad, please don't do this," Gina cried. "Diego and I have talked about this a lot and we just can't see Gabe like this. He's going to either die slowly on life support, or quickly without pain if we take him off of it. At least this way, we can see his face and hold him."

Eduardo slowly sat back in the chair in disbelief.

"I'm going to have to ask you all to step out of the room while we unhook everything," Dr. Chen explained. "There will be some unpleasant sounds that may seem like Gabriel trying to breathe and regain consciousness. It's just the body's reflexes, but it can be alarming for loved ones. Once everything is removed, you all can come back in and be with him."

"How long will it take to- to-?" Diego tried asking.

"To pass?" Dr. Chen asked. Diego nodded. "It varies from person to person. It could take hours."

"But, we *can* hold him?" Gina asked.

"Absolutely. Make him as comfortable as possible. If he seems to be in pain, we can give something to take that away. I will tell you though that once oxygen levels start dropping, Gabriel might start turning blue and towards the very end he may start convulsing. That's just the brain trying to send messages to the body that it's running out of oxygen."

Elena placed her fingertips quickly against her forehead, chest, and both shoulders, signing the cross. She then pulled a rosary out of her pocket and took Sloane's hand. One by one, the family stepped out into the hallway while staff came in to take Gabriel off of life support. First, they removed the breathing tube to the ventilator. Then, they removed his feeding tube. Lastly, they removed the IV lines. After everything was taken away, he looked so much smaller. So frail. Dr. Chen ushered the family back in, and everyone except Eduardo started crying again.

"Gabriel isn't able to breath on his own at all without the ventilator," Dr. Chen explained. "So he'll pass sooner than later without the help of the machine. If anyone would like to say anything to him, now would be the time."

Dr. Chen took a step back so the family could get closer to Gabriel. Elena and Sloane came up first.

"I love you," Sloane cried. "I love you so much. I don't want you to go but I know you're hurting. I don't know how I'm going to get through anything without you though. I-"

She started sobbing and couldn't continue. Elena leaned forward and kissed Gabriel on the forehead. She smiled at him and took his hand in hers.

"You go be with God, *mijo*. You don't belong in this bed. You go run and be healthy again."

Elena put her rosary in Gabriel's hand, kissed and hugged Diego and Gina, and ushered Sloane to the door.

"We'll be in the chapel praying," she smiled weakly to Eduardo. He nodded as they walked out.

Gina got up on the hospital bed next to Gabriel and leaned in towards him. She smelled his head and started rubbing above his right eyebrow with her thumb. Diego sat on the other side of the bed and took Gabriel's hand in his.

"You are my sunshine," Elena whispered. "My only sunshine."

She wasn't really singing to him, maybe because she was fighting back tears. Instead it came out like someone trying to talk while running. Gabriel started jerking mildly. Elena, Diego, and Eduardo looked at Dr. Chen.

"It's okay," he said softly. "This is the convulsing I was telling you about. His brain is trying to send signals for oxygen. Just be here for him."

"You make me happy, when skies are gray," Elena continued, her voice cracking. "You'll never know dear-"

"How much we love you," Diego joined in, kissing the top of Gabriel's hand. Gabriel's convulsions grew more intense.

"Please don't take...."Elena gasped. "My sunshine....."

"It's okay, *mijo*," Diego smiled weakly.

"*Mami* and *Papi* are here. It's okay. You can let go. We'll be okay."

Gabriel stopped convulsing, and then went very still. Dr. Chen walked up to the heart monitor that was now barely beeping.

"I love you so much, my baby," Elena cried into Gabriel's ear. "I love you."

There was a long beep on the heart monitor and Dr. Chen turned it off as a nurse came in beside him.

"Time of death, 1307," Dr. Chen announced.

Elena let out an agonizing wail and Eduardo stood up slowly before walking over to Diego. He placed his hand on Diego's shoulder and watched as his son sobbed over the body of his now dead grandson. Diego leaned into Eduardo but still held onto Gabriel's hand. Eduardo was looking straight at me again, scowling. I suddenly felt like I was impeding on a very personal situation.

"I'm so sorry," I muttered. "I'm so, so sorry."

I left immediately and went straight to Processing. I found Elijah behind his desk and sighed heavily.

"That bad, huh?" he asked as he jotted something down in his book.

"I think he saw me," I said.

"Who?"

"Dumah."

Elijah gave me a look.

"I mean, Eduardo," I corrected myself.

Elijah's expression didn't change.

"He for sure talked to me. He knew I was there. Or at least he knew *something* was there."

"To be fair, a lot of humans attempt to communicate with us when something distressing is happening. I don't think he actually knew you were there."

"He said he remembers me being at the hospital when he had his heart attack."

At this, Elijah stopped writing and looked at me. I nodded.

"How?" he asked.

"No idea," I answered. "But my theory is, the part of Dumah that's still in there remembers me or recognizes me or something."

"Emma...not this again."

"How else would you explain it? There's still a part of Dumah in there. And as soon as he dies and gets here, I'm going to help remind him who he was before he became Eduardo."

Elijah looked behind me and quickly went back to writing. I turned to see Barachiel and Michael standing there.

"Shit," I murmured.

6

"Emma, what were you doing at the hospital?" Michael asked sternly.

"Do I really need to answer when you already know?"

He raised an eyebrow at me.

"Sorry," I sighed. "I was just curious. I've been around this family for years and-"

"Yes, that is the issue," Barachiel chimed in. "You're too obsessed with that family when you should be focusing on your job."

"My job isn't even that important!" I snapped. "Yes it's a kind gesture to be with someone when they die but in the long run, does it really matter that much? Seriously. No one gives a shit if we're there when they die. We're not guardian angels. We're not virtues. We're certainly not archangels. No one likes death angels. Death angels don't even seem to like other death angels! And when people die, they either end up here in Processing or over in Sentencing so really what's the point?"

"I'd like you to meet someone," Barachiel smiled. A man and a little girl appeared from behind him and grinned at me. I didn't say anything.

"This is Luke Bridger and his daughter, Cora," Michael said.

"Hi," I waved awkwardly. Suddenly, Luke leaped forward and hugged me, his arms wrapping around my wings.

"Oookay," I said, patting his shoulder.

"Thank you so much," Luke beamed as he took a step back.

"You're welcome?"

It came out more as a question, but I was so confused I didn't know what to say.

"Cora was a recent mission of yours," Barachiel explained.

I looked at the little girl and she smiled at me.

"I don't-"

"Me and Daddy stayed long enough to make sure Rocky was okay until someone found us," she said.

"He's a good boy," Luke smiled at her. "He stayed right by our side until park rangers found us."

And then I remembered the little girl's face had been pale and dirty. She was thin and her hair was matted. Now, her cheeks were rosy and plump. Her eyes sparkled and her hair was clean and shiny. Her dad, who had been a heap of mangled limbs and broken bones, now stood strong and tall.

"Thank you for staying with Cora in her final moments," Luke said.

"I was scared until I saw you," Cora told me. "But when I saw you, I didn't feel scared anymore."

Michael and Barachiel both smiled at me. I sighed heavily.

"I get it," I said. "I get it."

"We just want you to understand that your job *is* important," Barachiel explained. "I know it may not seem like it to you but people really do appreciate what you do."

"As do we," Michael added. "We have found that humans who die completely alone are less likely to move on. Processing isn't a perfect system by any means, but we try to do what we can to help as many people as possible."

"It was nice to meet you," Luke nodded. "And thanks again."

"Bye!" Cora waved.

I watched Luke take Cora's hand as they walked away.

"Little Cora would have been all alone in that forest if it weren't for you," Barachiel said.

"Not completely alone," I retorted. "Rocky was there too."

"Pets don't count," Michael sighed. "Unlike family members. Gabe had family with him when he died. There was no reason for you to be there."

"You guys didn't have any issues with me being present at Simon's death. Or my mom's death. Or my dad's. Or even Whitney's death!"

"Those were your family members and a close friend; people you knew as a human. And Whitney was a bonus one we gave you because you seem to be having a hard time adjusting to all of this. But you have no connection to Gabe."

I started to argue but decided it was best to remain silent as Michael continued.

"Look, we have agreed to let you meet Gabe. You can introduce yourself to him, but then you need to let him move on."

"Really?" I asked enthusiastically.

"And we would prefer you not mention Dumah being reincarnated as his grandfather," Barachiel said. "It will only confuse him."

"That's fine," I said. "I would love to meet him."

"On one condition," Barachiel held up a finger at me. "You leave that family alone and focus on your job."

"Fine," I sighed.

"I mean it, Emma. You do what you said you would do and be a death angel to those who don't have anybody else."

"I said fine!" I snapped.

Michael and Barachiel turned from me and began to walk. I looked back at Elijah and smiled. He smiled back but it was more of a wince. I followed the archangels outside to a bench.

"We'll be right back with him," Michael said.

"Before you go," I said. "I have a question. Why do I have to be present for people who go to Hell? I just saw a child molester die and I can't help but wonder why he would get the same treatment as a little girl dying alone in the wilderness."

"It's not our place to judge," Barachiel smiled. "You treat everyone equally, despite where they end up. Their souls aren't your burden."

I nodded slowly, showing them that I understood, and then they walked away. I sat on the bench, watching the people around me. This was what truly made me happy as an angel. Sitting in the courtyard just inside the welcoming gates, surrounded by all the people coming and realizing where they are. The garden beds everywhere were full of beautiful flowers and the sun was shining. Hearing laughter and singing, I had a sudden flashback of what life was like in my little Missouri town I grew up in, realizing that the courtyard reminded me of it. I felt at peace for the first time in a long time.

I should make it a point to come here more often, I thought to myself. Maybe the hut on the shore, away from everyone, wasn't the best for me. Maybe being alone so much wasn't good after all.

"Look, mama!" a little boy shouted and pointed at me. He was wearing a dark blue and white kurta pajama set and looked around five years old. His mother, a woman in a burgundy saree dress, glanced over at me and gasped. She pulled her son in closer as they both continued to stare.

"She's looking at us," he said more quietly. "She's scary, like a monster. Do you see her white eyes and black wings?"

"Stop staring at it!" the mother hissed as they hurried along.

I looked away and pulled the hood of my cloak up around my face. I noticed a few other people either staring at me or completely avoiding my gaze. I supposed spending more time at the entrance wasn't such a great idea.

"Emma?" I heard a voice to my left say. I turned and looked up to see Gabriel standing there with Michael. I stood up and Gabriel put his hand out to me, smiling.

"It's nice to meet you," he said.

"Gabriel," I replied, taking his hand in mine. "I'm Emma."

"You can call me Gabe."

I looked down at our hands that were still slowly shaking. I finally pulled away and looked him over. He was tall like Dumah, but other than that bore no resemblance. Not that I was surprised really. There was a slight familiarity about Gabe though.

"Well, I will let you two get acquainted," Michael said. "He'll need to get set up in his room soon. I trust you can show him the way?"

I nodded.

"Good. Gabe, it was very nice meeting you and I wish you well."

"Thanks," Gabe responded. "It was really great meeting you. My *abuela* will be so excited to meet you someday. You're her favorite angel."

I fought the urge to roll my eyes. Michael laughed.

"I'm very flattered. You take care, Gabe."

As Michael walked off, Gabe turned back to face me.

"You're a lot taller than I remember," I said.

"Oh, yeah I get my height from my mom's dad. He's- wait. You remember me? Have we met before?"

"Not exactly," I muttered. "Come on. We have a lot to discuss."

I led Gabe back to the hotel and went up to the desk.

"Gabriel Reyes," I said. Elijah looked up at me, looked at Gabe, dropped his mouth open, and looked back at me. I lifted my eyebrows and pursed my lips at him as if to silently say, "Don't make it weird!"

"Uhh yeah," Elijah finally managed to say. "Let me just...."

He flipped a couple of pages of his book, ran a pointed finger down a list of names, and gently tapped the book.

"Right," he continued. "Room 238A5213."

"Wow," Gabe laughed.

"Yeah, that's a common reaction we get," Elijah smirked. "Enjoy your stay."

"I have a question," Gabe said. "Could I by chance get a 7:00 a.m. wake up call and some extra towels?"

Elijah laughed politely while I gently tugged on Gabe's shirt.

"Come on," I murmured.

"I thought it was funny!" Elijah called as we headed towards the elevator. Gabe jokingly saluted at him.

"Hilarious," I said dryly as we stepped onto the platform.

"Can I ask you something?" Gabe asked.

"If it's for more towels, no."

"No," he chuckled. "You obviously didn't enjoy that joke. How come you…look the way you do."

I sighed.

"Sorry, I'm not trying to be rude or anything."

"Then don't be."

"It's just, I don't know. You're an angel, right?"

"Yep."

"Then why the all black outfit and wings, and white eyes? Is it a choice or were you made that way?"

"No, it's not a choice," I explained. "And I wasn't made this way. I was born a human."

"How long ago?"

"I was born in 1989."

"Oh wow!" Gabe exclaimed. "You don't look that old."

"I died when I was only 21."

"Oh. I'm sorry."

"It's fine. I- I'm sorry too. That you died so young."

"Thanks. I have mixed feelings about it actually. I feel like I didn't get to do nearly as much as I wanted to. But I really wasn't doing much with my life anyways."

"You were only 25 years old," I explained. "You still had plenty of life left to accomplish things. Well, at least you thought you did. Which, I get it. I thought I had more time too. When you're in your twenties you think you still have a whole lifetime to figure shit out."

Gabe chuckled. I noticed how his green eyes sparkled when he laughed.

"What?" I asked.

"I didn't know angels cussed."

The corners of my mouth raised ever so slightly into a smile. The elevator slowed to a stop and opened its doors.

"I'm a death angel," I said as we stepped off the platform. "There are different types of angels. The archangels like Michael mostly stay in

Paradise, but sometimes they'll go to Processing to check in on things. Guardian angels look over humans, usually starting with people they knew when they were alive. Virtues make up the smallest group of angels, but they're some of the oldest. Before guardian angels really started taking off, virtues were the ones who persuaded humans in a positive way and inspired them to create and love and have passions and hobbies. Although there are a lot more humans alive now, there are far less virtues. There doesn't seem to be a need for inspiration anymore."

"That's really sad," Gabe sighed. "I remember when I was in high school, I really enjoyed painting. Watercolors, specifically. My art teacher wanted me to take a more advanced class my senior year."

"You made that beautiful painting of the woman surrounded by all of the flowers."

"Yeah," Gabe smiled.

"It was your grandma when she was young."

Gabe wouldn't stop smiling or staring at me until we approached the door of his room.

"You didn't take the advanced class though," I said. "You graduated at semester so you could help the family out at the restaurant."

"Yeah," he shrugged. "Family always comes first. Then, I became too busy to start it back up. Then, I was just too tired. You always think you're going to give yourself more time for hobbies. But then the car needs to be worked on or your mom asks you to come over and fix a faucet or something. Or most of the time you feel so stuck in your mundane life that you need to decompress from real shit so you play a video game or watch crappy television shows. I can't tell you how many times I sat down to relax for 5 minutes and start scrolling social media. Next thing you know, an hour has passed. I could have used a virtue."

Gabe opened the door to his room and gasped. There's a bed and dresser against one wall. Against another wall were hundreds of vinyl records and a record player. But the thing Gabe noticed immediately was an art easel in the middle of the room with a canvas resting on it. There was a cart next to it with paints of all types and colors, and brushes of all sizes.

"Wow!" Gabe breathed. "Is this for me?"

I nodded.

"To tie you over until your processing is complete. You'll also be able to eat and sleep until your body adjusts to being here."

"Adjusts to being dead," Gabe corrected me.

He ran his fingertips gingerly along each brush head.

"Archangels, guardian angels, virtues, and death angels. Who knew there were so many different kinds?"

"There are also dark angels," I continued. "They seem to be more important than ever lately.

They patrol the borders of Sentencing to make sure everyone stays in Hell that's supposed to. They also keep track of demons to make sure they're not breaking any rules."

"That sounds pretty cool. So what exactly do you do?"

"My job is to be present for those who die alone or in particularly tragic ways. If someone doesn't have a guardian angel or doesn't have anyone with them when they die, I'm supposed to be there to guide them."

"So then why were you there when I died?" Gabe asked. This was my chance.

"Your grandfather was very important to me," I started slowly. "Although when I knew him, he wasn't Eduardo Reyes. He was a death angel named Dumah."

Gabe sat down on the bed and stayed completely silent while I told him about meeting Alastor, getting sick and dying, and going on my adventure with angels into Hell in hopes of rescuing my boyfriend who ended up being a demon. I told him about Dumah being killed and his soul getting sent back to Earth as a new person, and in my guilt took his place as a death angel. After I finished, I watched Gabe process everything I had told him, waiting for him to say anything. When he still didn't, I decided to speak again.

"Has your grandfather ever....I don't know, mentioned anything weird or said anything about memories or dreams that would coincide with what I just told you?"

Gabe slowly shook his head.

"Shit," I muttered.

"Wait," Gabe said. "A couple years ago, he had a heart attack. He said he saw a dark hooded figure that was trying to take him away."

"I wasn't-"

"My grandma thought he had been dreaming, or was heavily drugged and imagined it. But it was you, wasn't it? You came to take him from us. And now you've brought me here."

"No!" I exclaimed. "I don't *take* anyone! If you're already dying, *then* I show up, but I don't ever kill anyone."

"Why were you at the hospital then?" Gabe asked, sounding a little angry. "What, are you trying to get your friend back? Didn't you say his soul was sent back to become someone else?"

"It's still Dumah's soul though!"

"And whose soul was it before that?"

I stopped.

"If my grandfather was someone else before, then that means Dumah was someone else before he was Dumah. So why have you spent so many years obsessing over my grandfather, waiting for him to die? And what, you thought, 'if I can't get the real thing, I'll settle for the grandson?'"

"That's not it at all," I explained. "I just wanted you to know how great he was."

"He *is* great!" Gabe yelled. "What the hell is wrong with you? He grew up in the slums of Columbia, met the love of his life, married her, and got her out of there so their son, my dad, wouldn't grow up in a country full of crime and poverty. My grandparents arrived in the United States with nothing but the clothes on their backs, and my *abuela* did it pregnant! My grandfather, Eduardo Reyes, worked two and sometimes three jobs to take care of his family. He raised my father to work just as hard, so when he went to college and got a degree in business, my dad was able to help my grandfather open two more restaurants. And sure, we're not a rich family. We're not considered famous unless you live in the Chicago area. We didn't have a pool or a boat or go on fancy vacations. But my grandparents have been married 52 years. They learned English but also made sure my dad knew Spanish. They paid off their house and helped pay for my dad's college education. To go from poverty in one country and start off in another country just as poor, that's huge. So no, he's not your death angel. He's not your friend. And he's not your hero. But he is mine."

I let Gabe finish his rant and stared at him. He sighed, staring at the floor, looking as defeated as I felt. Neither of us had anything else to say. It was time for me to go. As I reached the door, I turned back to Gabe once more.

"You know," I said softly. "A person's soul is the part of a person that houses their personality, emotions, and will. In life and in death, Dumah did great things. He was brave and caring. He put others first, no matter what. I wasn't Eduardo's guardian angel, but I still watched over him his whole life. He's never ceased to amaze me. He gave free food to the homeless. He volunteered a lot of his free time to help immigrants get settled in and made sure Chicago became their new home. One time he was working at the restaurant alone and a man came in and robbed him at gunpoint. He stayed perfectly calm. Because seven-year-old you was sitting at a table in the back room and he didn't want you to be afraid. And the only thing he was afraid of was something happening to you. So he calmly gave the man all of the money in the register and the wedding ring your grandma gave him. It made him sad but he knew it wasn't as important as your life or his. That kind of greatness can't be killed. It can't die or go away. It was passed on to your grandfather. And he passed it on to your dad. And to you."

Gabe looked up at me. I nodded at him and left. The elevator ride felt extra long and the smiling faces around me seemed blurred. As soon as Elijah saw me walk through the lobby, he stood up, trying to get my attention. I ignored him and kept going. And I didn't stop.

    The next thing I knew, I was standing on a beach. This wasn't mine and Dumah's beach though. Camps Bay Beach of Cape Town, South Africa, was listed as one of the world's most beautiful beaches. It was on my bucket list of places to visit when I was human. The scenery, the culture, and the wildlife would have given me so much to photograph. I loved the idea of going out on a boat and catching a great white shark breaching the water. But like every dream I had, it was snuffed out when I died.

    I stood there, listening to the waves. I was the only one around, although no humans would be able to see me anyways. Still, it was nice to have a moment of privacy. I took my boots and socks off. I looked down and watched my toes wiggle around in the sand, unable to feel it at all. Holding my hand up to my face like a visor, I looked up at the sun, unable to sweat or sunburn in the African heat. I slowly began to take off all of my clothes, looking around as I did so.

    My pants, shirt, and cloak laid in a heap on the shore as I took one step at a time towards the water. I stopped briefly as the water creeped up to my feet, smacking my skin before retreating back to the ocean. I continued until the water was up to my hips. I stretched my black wings out as far as they would go, lifting them out of the water. The gentle waves rolled towards me, hitting me just at my breasts, and then making their way towards the shore. There I was, standing in the way of the waves, but not stopping them at all. No matter where I stood, the waves would always make their way to the shore. No matter what I did, it didn't change anything. So instead of trying to stop or slow the process, I needed to accept the fact that I was a part of the process.

"Okay," I said out loud, my voice cracking. "I surrender. I'll let go of my human body for once and for all. I'll let go of my human thoughts and emotions. I'm a death angel."

Tears began to roll down my cheeks. I lifted both of my arms up, reaching towards the sky.

"I'm a death angel," I repeated. "I'm here to serve God in any way that's needed of me. I'll let go of my obsessions with Ankou and Sam and Dumah. I want to be freed from these things that are keeping me from moving forward."

I lowered my arms, letting them fall to my sides. I stood there, gently bobbing with the tide. Suddenly, something dark swam quickly in my direction and circled around me. A seal was darting through the water. I took a step forward and the seal reacted to my movement, startled by something it couldn't see. In the same instant it appeared, it was gone. I walked back up to the beach and dressed myself. Then, I made my way over to some large rocks and picked one to sit on. The sun was setting, making it look like the whole sky was on fire. Vivid reds and oranges spread over the dark blue water. I knew what my real problem was. It wasn't anger or revenge or guilt. There was something else eating away at me. I was lonely.

My human life had been somewhat boring, but I was always surrounded by people who loved and cared for me. When I died, I thought I had made friends with Sam, Dumah, Sekhmet, Baraqiel, and Elijah. But each of them are either gone or are committed to their duties. Not that I expected it any other way. I had so much respect for those who give every moment of their time to their roles. But a part of me still craved company. Someone to talk to. Someone who would listen to me. I was an angel, but at my core, human. And no matter how hard I tried, I couldn't shake it.

"What is wrong with me?" I muttered.

"Well, talking to yourself isn't a good sign, that's for sure."

I turned around, startled. A man in all black clothing was walking up to me. He had large black wings, short black hair, and a mustache. When I stood up to greet him, his white eyes met mine.

"You're a death angel," I said. "Like me."

"I am," he smiled. "My name is Otomatsu."

"Where did you come from?" I asked, looking around.

"I was born on May 8th, 1847 in Nagano, Japan. My mother gave birth to me during an earthquake. She was convinced that I was the cause of the earthquake. She thought a giant underground catfish named Namazu, put a part of its soul into her womb and was born human; me. Namazu was blamed for earthquakes, which caused destruction and death, but also was perceived as an avenger of injustice. There was always a myth that the rich buried their treasures either in the ground or in various hiding places, and earthquakes would unearth them. As I was growing up, the Edo period was ending and the Meji period began in 1867. An American naval officer forced Japan to open its ports, which also forced Japan to end its isolationism. I witnessed the Western influence swarm my country.

The Industrial Revolution in Japan happened and suddenly there were railroads, steel, and textile factories everywhere you looked. My mother was a well-known seamstress. She made the most beautiful hand-woven kimonos. Growing up around her, I learned a thing or two. So when the opportunity presented itself years later, I opened a textile factory that made silk clothing. In the time it took my mother to make a kimono, my factory could produce anywhere from ten to fifty. And once Japanese culture started influencing artists and aristocrats of the West, the world was suddenly intrigued and in love with our clothing, art, and culture. My mother no longer had customers. I tried to convince her that it was a good thing! She was old and could rest; enjoy her remaining years relaxing. She didn't want to though. She loved her work. She continued to make clothes although no one would buy them. She began to resent me, telling me that factory owners like me were putting hard working people like her out of business. I told her that it was good for the economy but she didn't understand.

'You are Namazu,' she said. 'You came into this world through destruction and you are destroying Japan now with your factory. You choke the air and water with the poison your factory breathes out. That poison is breathed in by people who think they need more of what you make. More, more, more. More things to buy so the factory can breathe out more poison. You destroy everything because you are Namazu.'

And maybe she was right. I know now how much pollution the Industrial Revolution caused. I know that the mass production of kimonos made them available to anyone; whereas when my mom made them, they were more for the upper class. I saw that as a good thing at the time because I thought I was helping people. But I was also hurting people like my mother.

When I died, I wanted my existence to have meaning. And when I discovered death angels, beings of both light and darkness, I knew I wanted to become one. We see people die horrible, lonely deaths. But we help them by being with them. Both destroyer and avenger. Like Namazu. So here I am. And here you are. A beautiful and horrible creature. Always surrounded by others but so lonely."

When he finally stopped talking, I awkwardly stuck my hand out to shake his.

"Uh, hi," I said. "I'm Emma."

7

Otomatsu and I sat on the beach late into the night talking about ourselves. Although he had heard of Dumah, he didn't know him personally, which helped me open up to him. He listened intently to my entire story, from start to finish. Once I was done, he sat there and shook his head slowly.

"So?" I asked. "What do you think?"

Otomatsu tilted his head.

"Of?" he asked.

"Me," I answered.

"Oh!" he laughed. "I think you're a wonderful person who has spent her existence trying her best to do the right thing. Unfortunately, things don't turn out the way you think they will sometimes."

I smiled at him before looking out at the crescent moon and stars.

"I'll admit that I've been lonely for some time now," Otomatsu finally said. "I never had a family when I was alive. I focused too much on growing my business and making money. And after I died, I secluded myself and focused on work again. But it would be nice to have a friend."

"I would like that very much. Where do you stay?"

"What do you mean?"

"Dumah has a hut along a beach that takes you into Hell. I started building one for myself on the same beach. Although I tend to stay in Dumah's hut most of the time since mine is still just a frame."

"Oh. I don't have a home."

I froze except for my raised eyebrows. Otomatsu shrugged.

"I have no need for it," he explained. "I don't sleep or eat or need a bathroom. I wear the same thing every day and don't need to shower. What's the point?"

"Just a place to rest and reflect," I said. He laughed.

"What are we doing here, right now?"

I looked around, listening to the ocean.

"Where do you keep your belongings?" I asked.

"This is the only thing I own."

Otomatsu moved his robe away and slowly pulled a thin, curved sword from a wooden sheath at his side.

"Is that a katana?" I asked. He nodded.

"I know most angels carry longswords. But I had always wanted a katana. Now that I have one, I don't need anything else."

"Well, don't you *want* a home?"

"I'm not human anymore," he went on. "I do not want to be contained to a box. The world is my home now. The beach is my living room. The mountains are my bedroom. The desert is my study. The rainforest is more beautiful than any mansion I've ever seen. Why be surrounded by four walls when you could be surrounded by all of this?"

Otomatsu raised his hands and glanced around.

"You make a good point."

"I'm older and wiser," he winked. I chuckled.

"How would you feel about having a partner?" I asked. "We don't have to do every job together, and we can take breaks when needed. But I hate not having someone to talk to. Someone who knows what it's like being us. And you're the first death angel I've come across who didn't immediately dislike me."

Otomatsu leaned back on his hands, thinking. I instantly regretted saying anything. I worried that I looked pathetic, begging for someone to hang out with me so I wouldn't have to do this alone.

"Okay," he said.

"Really?"

"Sure. As long as you don't think of me as a replacement for your father or your other death angel."

"Of course not," I said. "I would just like a friend."

"I think I could do that."

We decided to take turns, choosing where our next mission would be. I chose an old woman who was dying in a nursing home. She was laying in her bed, alone and scared. She had been sick for years and now her body was shutting down. I sat down on the bed beside her and placed my hand on hers as she passed. She looked up at me and smiled before closing her eyes. Otomatsu nodded in approval as the silence swept over everything. I looked over at a picture on a shelf. The woman who had just passed sat in a chair, smiling. Surrounding her were seven adults and nineteen children, infants to teenagers. She had a big family.Her Paradise would be full of so much love.

    Otomatsu chose a young man who had hung himself. As he tended to the man, I read a note left to be found with him. The man had gambled his money away. He had accumulated thousands of dollars in debt and when his wife found out, she left him. The note apologized to her and to his parents. I wondered if Ankou had anything to do with this. Before I could give it much thought, Otomatsu told me to pick our next person.

    I chose a teenage boy who had accidentally overdosed. He had bought Adderall to help him study for his finals. And this was a kid who seemed like he didn't even like taking Nyquil. His room didn't look like a teenage boy's room. It was extremely clean and organized. There were no posters of bands or women on his walls. There wasn't any sign of video games, or even a television in the room. The bed was made and the color-coordinated closet was full of polos and button-up dress shirts. The only things out of place was the boy's cold body on the floor and the desk chair tipped over beside him. He just wanted to get his GPA up for his dream college. Again, I thought of Ankou.

"You can't blame him for every suicide," Otomatsu said, as if he had been reading my mind. "Sometimes humans make mistakes."

"Do you think they would have still made those mistakes if angels were allowed to interact with humans the way demons do?"

"We're rule-followers though. We don't interact with them."

"And it's bullshit!"

"I know it is," he smiled weakly. "All we can do is what we were sent to do. My turn."

He chose a woman who had been trying to cross the street when she was suddenly hit by a speeding car. She was walking home from work and had been about halfway across the street when a man looking down at his phone struck her. Instead of getting out to check on the woman, he drove off. I'm sure he was scared, but so was the woman dying in the middle of the street. I ran over to her, noticing how dark the street was where she was laying. I knelt down next to her and waited for her to pass. I looked around and saw a car coming. I glanced up at the street lamp that seemed too dim for the oncoming driver to see the woman laying there. Panicked, I screamed for the car to stop and the light quickly grew brighter and then exploded just as the car approached us. It screeched to a halt and two older men got out of the car and rushed to the woman. They called 911 and waited with her until an ambulance showed up.

"We weren't here for her," Otomtaus sighed before flying away.

"What?" I asked before taking off after him.

I followed him down the road until we came across the wreckage.

"The driver of the vehicle crashed, hitting a concrete barrier at 80 miles per hour," Otomatsu said.

The impact of hitting the barrier split the car almost completely in half. The front driver's side was smashed all the way to where the seat should have been. Otomatsu told me that the man had died instantly so we weren't able to be there for him when he passed.

"It was him we were here for," I breathed.

"The woman will be okay. She'll get to the hospital in time. We need to move on."

There were two things I noticed almost instantly. First, seeing these horrible deaths wasn't nearly as bad with someone else there. We could talk about it, how we were feeling, and ask each other if we were okay afterwards. The other thing I noticed was time went by a lot more quickly with Otomatsu. Next thing I knew, a year had passed since meeting him. We spent every single day together except Fridays. For some reason, he chose Fridays as his one day of the week to take time to himself. He would go off and do his own thing while I chose one new place in the world to visit for the day. Otomatsu never told me where he had been on his day away from me, but it didn't seem to affect his mood either way. He was always calm and caring, and always made me laugh. And that was probably the most surprising thing about our friendship. Since becoming an angel, I hardly ever laughed. I didn't have much to laugh about when I was on my own. But Otomatsu always had a story or a joke to tell that would at least put a smile on my face. I was finally enjoying my new life.

    That is until one Friday when Otomatsu was preparing to leave for his one day off. I had read that a solar eclipse was going to happen that day and neither of us had ever seen one, but had always wanted to.

    "Can't you just switch your day off from me this week?" I asked.

    "Fridays are my one day," he explained. "I'll catch it from wherever I'm at and we'll compare notes later."

"It's just that you said we'd watch the next one together so I was kind of looking forward to it. I even picked the perfect spot in-"

"Sorry, not this time."

His tone wasn't mean, but it did have some bite to it. Disappointed, I let it go. The next day, I told him all about sitting in Recife, Brazil, watching the totality of the eclipse. Otomatsu told me that he had been in San Francisco when he had seen the totality. However, I had looked at the cities that would be in the path of the solar eclipse, and San Francisco wasn't one of them. Why had Otomatsu lied to me? I didn't say anything, but the rest of the week it stayed in the back of my mind. The following Friday, I told him I would be visiting Iguaza Falls.

"After seeing the solar eclipse in Brazil, I want to check out more places there," I explained to him. "It's supposed to be the largest broken waterfall in the world."

"That sounds amazing!" Otomatsu said. "I can't wait to hear all about it."

Once again, he refrained from telling me where he planned on spending his day. I normally didn't ask where he went, but gave it a shot.

"So what will you be doing?" I asked casually.

"What?"

"Any specific plans for your day off?"

"You don't normally ask me where I go," he chuckled. "But if you must know, I am going to spend the day walking the streets of Rome. I haven't been there in many years and thought I'd visit again."

"That sounds lovely," I smiled. "I look forward to hearing all about it."

As soon as we parted ways, I headed for Processing. Elijah was at his desk, scribbling away in his books, checking people in and out of the hotel. He gasped when he saw me.

"Emma! Where have you been?"

"What do you mean?" I asked. "I've been doing my job."

"You haven't shown your face around here in over a year and you honestly expect me to believe you've been working this whole time?"

"Is it that hard to believe?" I laughed. "Listen, I need a favor."

"Of course you do," he raised his eyebrows. "Why else would you grace me with your presence?"

I frowned at him and he winked at me.

"Do you know a death angel named Otomatsu?" I asked.

"Uh huh," Elijah nodded slowly.

"Could you let me know if he's currently in Rome?"

"Why?"

"Can you just check please?"

"Emma, if he did anything to you-"

"What! Why would he have?" I asked.

"He's not very well-liked by the other angels," Elijah explained.

"Yeah, well, we have that in common," I muttered.

"That's probably the only thing you have in common. Let me go check the map to see where he's at," Elijah said, getting up from his seat. "If anyone comes up to the desk needing anything, tell them I'll be right back."

I nodded as he went into a room behind the desk. I waited around a couple of minutes before Elijah came back out.

"He's definitely not in Rome," he said, sitting back down.

"He's not?" I asked. "Where is he then?"

"Let me see your arm."

I put my arm out and Elijah grabbed my tracker on my wrist. He zoomed in on a location and tapped it.

"Russia!" I said, shocked.

"Magadan, to be exact. Emma, what do you want with Otomatsu?"

"He's who I've been with for the past year. He's become my closest friend."

"You can't be serious."

"Why?" I asked. "He's who finally got me to start doing my job consistently. I thought you'd be happy about that. What's your problem with him?"

"Do you know what landed him in Hell to begin with?"

"Suicide?" I asked. "I'm assuming that was it since he didn't want to tell me."

"Suicide after he murdered a woman and a child," Elijah said. "An infant girl and the woman he was in love with were both killed before he took his own life."

"What?" I questioned. "Why?"

"Ask him," Elijah shrugged. "He's your new best friend so I'm sure he will tell you."

"Thanks for your help," I said dryly. "I'll touch base with you after I pay a visit to Russia."

"By the way, Gabe's training to be a dark angel," Elijah added as I started to walk away. I stopped and turned.

"What?"

"Yeah," Elijah continued. "Told the archangels you inspired him to become one."

"Really?"

"Yep, he's going to be a dark angel because of you," Elijah nodded. "In a couple of weeks they'll have his assignment figured out."

"I'll check back in then to see where they put him. And to update you on Otomatsu."

"Just be careful until then, okay?"

"Okay," I said. "See you then."

I stretched my wings and took off for Magadan, Russia. When I arrived, the temperature was -26 degrees and I was very thankful I couldn't feel how cold it was. I walked around for a while, trying to find Otomatsu. A church bell rang in the distance and I started to follow the sound. I turned a street corner and saw him. Otomatsu had his face covered with a black scarf, but it was definitely him. A satchel was slung over his shoulder and he was looking around, as if he were worried he was being followed.

"What are you up to?" I whispered.

I kept my distance but made sure I could still see him. Otomatsu approached the cathedral where the bells were ringing. It was a large, white building. Three golden onion domes sat on top of the tall church. The bells continued to ring out in the otherwise silent, cold morning. Completely dismissing the front door, Otomatsu made his way to the side of the building. I thought about following him around but instead went in through the front. I phased through the door slowly, making sure to look around. There was no one inside the vestibule; just a pair of wooden doors. There were statues paying tribute to Jesus, his mother, Mary, and various saints.

I heard voices from inside the chapel. It sounded like all male voices but I couldn't make out what anyone was saying. One of the voices is undoubtedly Otomatsu. Without hesitation, I went right through the wooden doors, and stopped dead in my tracks.

"What are you doing here?"

I couldn't fully focus on what Otomatsu asked me because I was concentrating on the three figures in suits standing between us. The familiar stench of rotting meat and earth filled my nostrils. Demons.

"Emma, you need to leave now," he said sternly.

"Rome, huh?" I said shakily. "Just like you were in San Francisco for the eclipse?"

"Emma, please go."

"Why did you lie to me?" I asked. "What are you keeping from me?"

"Emma-"

"No!" I snapped. "This seems like some super shady shit. I just talked to Elijah about spending the last year with you and he seemed concerned for me. Who are you, really?"

"I promise I will explain everything to you. But I need you to leave now."

I crossed my arms, holding my stance. Otomatsu sighed.

"What the fuck, Otto?" one of the demons scoffed. "What is this?"

"My apologies, gentlemen," Otomatsu laughed. "Can I have just one moment?"

He walked past the three demons and up to me, grabbing my shoulder roughly. We walked to a corner so he could talk to me more privately.

"Fine," he whispered. "But you have to swear you won't tell anyone about this."

I nodded.

"I mean it, Emma! Swear you won't say a word. The less who knows, the better."

"Fine!"

"Just stay quiet and let me handle this. I promise that everything is okay though."

"Okay?"

It came out more as a question than a statement. *What the hell have I gotten myself into?* I thought. Otomatsu straightened up, smiled, and guided me back to the main area of the cathedral. There was a golden chandelier above us in the center of the high ceiling. I took a moment to look around. The walls matched the chandelier, all golden. Paintings of saints and other religious figures covered them from top to bottom. The candles along the left wall flickered as I heard heavy footsteps moving towards us. As the demons got closer, I recognized one of them as Pavel, the former angel. I glared at him but all he did was glare right back.

"You said you'd be coming alone," the demon in the middle smiled.

"You said you'd be alone too," Otomatsu said in an overly friendly tone.

"Guess we're both liars."

"You still outnumber us by one though," Otomatsu replied. "Why don't you have one of your buddies step outside while we discuss business?"

"Not a chance," the demon grinned before turning to me. "I'm sorry, I don't think we've met before. You are?"

"Why don't you go first?" I asked.

"Very well," he said. "My name is Nav. *Now*, you tell me who you are."

"I'm Emma."

There was a flash in Nav's eyes. He must have recognized me by name.

"Emma? *The* Emma? The one who killed Dumah?"

I felt my body tense up.

"Don't get too excited," Otomatsu said. "She's not part of the bargain."

"Aw man!" Nav clapped his hands together. "I *so* got my hopes up! Well, what do you have for me then? And maybe we can revisit Emma later."

"I know of three guardian angels and a virtue who are interested."

"A virtue?" Nav repeated, rubbing his chin. "No shit."

I looked at Otomatsu, stunned. He wouldn't look back at me, but instead, continued to talk.

"Do you have names for me?" Otomatsu asked.

"Ah, ah, ah" Nav wagged a finger at him. "You didn't give us names."

Otomatsu sighed.

"Robert, Caitlyn, Alina, and Nikau. Nikau is a virtue."

"Thank you," Nav grinned. "I look forward to meeting them. Now, let's have a drink. Did you bring it?"

"Names, Nav," Otomatsu said.

"Over drinks," Nav repeated. "Where's the bottle?"

Otomatsu reluctantly pulled a bottle out of his satchel and handed it to Nav, who laughed abruptly.

"A list of names in exchange for a list of names and a 1.3 million dollar bottle of vodka!"

The other two demons laughed along with him while Otomatsu pulled three shot glasses out of his bag.

"Only three glasses?" Nav asked. "I planned on sharing."

"I don't drink," I said sharply.

"Now, Emma," Otomatsu said, sitting down in the first pew. Nav poured a shot into the glass and watched him drink it. "No need to be rude."

Otomatsu handed me a shot glass and Nav poured the alcohol into it. I took a quick drink, not tasting or feeling anything. I knew what this was. They were bragging about being able to taste, because we couldn't.

"We're wasting expensive vodka on angels!" Pavel grunted.

"You can have some next, don't worry."

I watched as the three of them poured their drinks. But instead of throwing them back quickly like we did, the demons sipped and purred over the drinks. Otomatsu stood back up, one hand inside his satchel.

"When I say so, run," he whispered to me. I gave him a look of confusion.

"Names?" Otomatsu asked, in a louder tone.

"You know," Nav sighed. "I'm so sorry. I know I promised you five names in exchange for your four and the vodka, but I can only remember one. And unfortunately, I already knew about Alina and Robert. So I'm contemplating whether or not I want to give you the one name."

"Nav, don't do this," Otomatsu said softly. "Don't waste my time."

"All we have is time, baby!" Nav chuckled, putting his hands up in the air. "Don't worry, if you bring me two new names, I'll be sure to give you the one plus a bonus."

Nav cleared his throat and then coughed. The smile faded from his face and the other two demons started coughing. Pavel doubled over and started gasping.

"Now," Otomatsu said to me. I shook my head at him.

"Emma, go now!" he yelled. I stayed put.

He let out a yell of frustration and charged towards the demons. I watched Otomatsu pull out what looked like a large hook on a rope, but looking more closely, I saw that it was actually a small, metal clawed hand. Otomatsu whipped it towards the third demon whose name I never learned. The metal claw dug into the demon's neck, the fingers curling in, to "grab" him. Otomatsu pulled the demon in as he held his other arm out with an opened hand. His katana seemed to appear out of thin air in his hand and he swung it fiercely. The demon's eyes bugged out as his torso slowly slid away from the lower half of his body. When the two halves of the body fell to the floor, Pavel and Nav weakly ran at Otomatsu.

"I've got Pavel," I said, pulling my own sword from its sheath.

I stepped closer to Pavel as he took his jacket off and put his fists up. He had steel bracers covering his forearms and the tops of his hands.

"You made me look like a fool in front of those demons!" he grimaced. "I was there to prove myself a worthy ally and you show up with that virtue to...what? Rescue me? I've been wanting to knock your teeth in since I met you that day in Hell!"

"Trust me, the feeling is mutual," I said, placing both hands on the handle of the sword. "I stuck my neck out to help you and you're just another fallen angel loser. I bet you're living it up in Hell now, huh?"

"Eating, drinking, sleeping, fucking," he smiled. "It's pretty much all the best parts of being human. Except now I'm invincible."

I swung my sword at him and he dodged, punching me hard in the stomach. I gasped from the wind being knocked out of me. One of the most bullshit Heaven/Hell rules; I was dead but could still be hurt by demons. I swung again and hit one of Pavel's bracers as he lifted an arm up. He counteracted with another punch; this time right to my mouth. My head snapped back from the force and I saw stars. Pavel chuckled and went back to a fighting stance. I wiped my mouth and held my sword up again.

"You hit like a bitch," I panted.

Pavel charged at me and I lunged towards him with my blade again, cutting his left bicep. I slashed at him again and nicked his right leg.

"I'm going to kill you, angel!" he snarled at me.

I backed up to the front door of the church, next to the holy water stoup, a large stone basin on a stand. As Pavel dove at me, I pivoted, causing him to go straight into the water. He let out a yelp as his skin burned, blistering from where it made contact with the water.

"You know," Pavel breathed heavily, "After you and the other angel left Hell that day, Ankou shared some funny stories about you."

He took a step forward and I took one back. He took another step towards me and I retreated.

"You were one dumb human," he laughed. "Wanting to kill yourself over some guy you barely knew."

"Yeah well, joke's on him, right?" I said. "I'm sure since he's still talking about it, it really chapped his ass knowing he didn't get me *and* I became an angel."

"Sure, but he killed two angels in the process, and one of them was supposedly a powerful one. Heard he took Dumah down pretty easily though."

I could feel the anger start to heat up my body again.

"Not to mention all of the demons he has now helping with suicides."

As Pavel stepped forwards again, I backed into a pew and lost my balance. Pavel pushed me down onto the bench, his huge hands around my throat. My sword was on the ground next to me. I reached my arm out to it. Pavel hit me in the face, his fist striking me in the right eye and cheek. I felt him grab my shoulders and slam my head into the bench seat again, disorienting me. Before I could move again, he headbutted me in the face. Everything slowed down and I closed my eyes as I started losing consciousness.

"Also, Ankou told us he killed your cat," I heard Pavel say softly into my ear as he started choking me again. His voice sounded muffled as everything started to close in on me.

"Cheeseball, I think he said? What a fucking stupid name for a cat!"

Suddenly, I felt rage build up inside me and screamed at him. Pavel stumbled back and grabbed his ears as I sat up.

"It's not...a stupid...name."

I reached out blindly for my sword and stood up, stumbling. I swung a couple of times, not making contact with anything but pews. I heard a shrill scream but wasn't able to tell who it had come from. My vision began to clear and I could see what was going on. Otomatsu was tying Pavel to Nav with the rope he had the claw on. The two demons were sitting back to back on the floor and their hands had been cut off. Their bloody stumps were tied against their chests with the rope and Otomatsu was in the process of wrapping bandanas around their mouths to quiet them.

"I just need the names, Nav," Otomatsu sighed as he tightened the mouth gag around Pavel's head. "And then we can be done with all of this."

"Fuck you," Nav spat. "I'm not telling you shit."

Otomatsu rubbed his eyes with a thumb and index finger, clearly fed up by this excursion.

"Alright then," he said before tightening Nav's mouth gag.

Otomatsu stood up and placed a finger on his forehead, chest, and each shoulder, making the sign of the cross. Next, he pulled out a vial of dark liquid and spread his hands out over Nav and Pavel.

"Thanks be the merciful heart of our God!" he exclaimed. "To shine upon those who sit in darkness and in the shadowland of death!"

Pavel and Nav both reacted to this, their eyes widening and starting to squirm where they were sitting.

"May Thy mercy, Lord, descend upon us, as great as our hope in Thee. We drive you from us, whoever you may be, unclean spirits, all satanic powers, all infernal invaders, and all wicked legions!"

Through muffled cries, Pavel tried saying something that sounded like, "please, stop!" Nav glared at Otomatsu.

"Did you want to say something, Pavel?" Otomatsu asked, removing the cloth from around his mouth.

"Don't do this!" Pavel begged. "I'd rather be reborn as another human! Please don't do this!"

"Names," Otomatsu said calmly.

"I don't know!" Pavel cried.

"You can't give me any locations or names of any other demons?"

"I just go where I'm told and stay out of other people's business! You can respect that, can't you? I honestly don't know why I'm here other than to make sure nothing went wrong. If you let me go, I swear I won't say a word!"

"No, you'll just continue to possess humans, which is the number one rule you're not allowed to break!"

"What!" I said, shocked.

"Yeah!" Otomatsu turned to me. "You want to know what I do on my Fridays? I hunt demons who have been known to possess humans. And usually, they'll snitch on others who are doing it."

"I haven't possessed anybody!" Pavel shrieked. "I've only seen Nav do it but I haven't, I swear!"

"You've been watching Nav do it so you can learn how to do it!" Otomatsu yelled. "A more skilled demon taking on a couple of apprentices to teach them how it's done!"

"No, no! I promise if you let me go, I'll find out some names for you! I'll work for you!"

"What makes you think he would trust you?" I asked. "You're a former angel who, up until about ten minutes ago, was helping demons. You were going to kill me!"

"She does make a good point," Otomatsu nodded as he removed Nav's gag. "What about you? Are you ready to talk? Pavel's sure been doing a lot of it."

"Unlike my partner here, I refuse to rat out any of my colleagues," Nav explained. "Turn me into one of those mindless monsters. I don't care."

"*Partner*, huh?" Otomatsu glared at Pavel. "Sounds like a little more than just watching Nav, eh?"

"Okay so maybe at one point I thought about possession!" Pavel laughed nervously. "But thinking about it and actually doing it are two different things! Turn Nav into a mongrel, but please! Don't do it to me!"

"You are so weak," Nav snarled at Pavel. "You were a weak angel and you're a weak demon. You disgust me. And to think, I saw potential in you at one point. You don't deserve to be turned into dog shit."

"Well, if no one wants to provide any useful information," Otomatsu said, "let's continue."

Otomatsu took the vial of liquid and dabbed some on his index finger. He made a small red cross on Pavel's forehead, which caused him to scream in agony. Then, he did the same to Nav, who just breathed heavily, obviously holding back his reaction to what was happening to him.

"God wants all to be saved and to come to the knowledge of the truth! Begone, Satan, master of all deceit, enemy of man's salvation! Stop deceiving human creatures and pouring out to them the poison of eternal damnation!"

Pavel and Nav writhed against the rope that bound them. Pavel repeated, "please," over and over.

"Most glorious God on high!" continued Otomatsu. "Defend us in our battle against the rulers of this world of darkness and against the spirits of wickedness!"

"I have names!" Pavel cried out. "Christ on the cross, I have names! Just please stop!"

"Don't, Pavel!" Nav snapped. "He'll kill us whether we tell him or not."

"That's a risk I'm willing to take! I can't become one of those....*things*."

Otomatsu knelt down beside Pavel, whose forehead and now scalp was beginning to pustule and ooze pus onto his face.

"I'm listening," he said quietly.

"Pruflas, Vassago, and Sut," he panted.

"Pruflas, Vassago, and Sut," Otomatsu repeated. Pavel nodded slowly.

"You stupid fuck," Nav sighed.

"Thank you, Pavel," Otomatsu smiled before tightening their mouth gags once again. Then, he stood up and stretched his arms out again.

"Cast out any evil spirits! In the name of the Father-!"

The two demons started squirming violently, trying to yell through muffled cries.

"-and The Son-!"

Otomatsu pulled his katana back out.

"-and The Holy Spirit."

Otomatsu swung the blade at Pavel and Nav, slicing their heads clean off. The yelling stopped immediately and the church was quiet, except for Otomatsu's final word.

"Amen."

8

I watched in both horror and wonder as all three of the demons' headless bodies started squirming.

"Oh no," I whispered, holding my sword defensively. Otomatsu gently put his hand on my wrist.

The bodies began to ball up, their limbs fusing to the torsos, and hardened.

"What's happening?" I asked. Otomatsu didn't answer.

Then, there was a cracking sound, like an egg on the edge of a pan. The large, chrysalis-looking pods were an amber color, and the things inside moved and started breaking through the shell. A slimy, opaque substance began seeping out of the cracks.

"Back up," Otomatsu said, pulling me a few steps away from the grotesque scene.

As the pods opened, large maggot-like creatures emerged, screeching and whipping their repulsive bodies around. Some of the slime flinged off of one of them and landed on my right shoe.

"Ugh!" I exclaimed.

The three creatures stopped at the sound of my voice. They started shrieking again and wriggled across the floor towards us.

"Oh god!" I said, backing up.

The gruesome creatures halted three feet from us and began melting into the floor. I stared as they seemed to disappear, leaving behind a trail of the slime and a foul smell.

"Where did they go?"

"Back to Hell, where they'll stay. Are you all right? Your face is already starting to heal but it still looks a little rough."

He raised a hand to my cheek but I recoiled. He knew I didn't trust him.

"I will explain everything, but we need to go somewhere else. How about that beach hut you were telling me about?"

I gave him a doubtful look.

"Emma, I will tell you everything. I promise."

I reluctantly took his hand and we teleported to Dumah's hut. It was weird to be back after so long, and it no longer felt like my home.

"Is that one yours?" Otomatsu pointed behind me. I turned to see what he was talking about and gasped.

My hut was now fully built, only it wasn't a hut anymore. It was an actual house, and it was even bigger and more beautifully constructed than anything I could have imagined. It reminded me of something from a fairytale. There was even a newly built pier that the boat was tied to. I walked over to peer into the windows of the house, but someone had put curtains up, blocking my view of the inside. I made my way over to the front door and opened it slowly.

"Hello?"

No answer.

We walked in cautiously, but the house was completely empty. The decor of the house was as if I had picked it myself. There was beautiful art and photography from all of my favorite places in the world. There was a photo of me with my parents and brother on the fireplace mantle. It was from when I had come in fourth place at a school talent show in ninth grade. I was so nervous to sing, "A Thousand Miles" by Vanessa Carlton. My grandparents, parents, and brother came to support me. After they announced first, second, and third place, they gave me a runner-up award for my performance and I was so disappointed. My grandma wanted to take our picture even though I tried to make it obvious that I wasn't in the mood. Right before she snapped the photo, Simon held up a piece of notebook paper in front of me that said, "1st place." I saw it and laughed, and that's what my grandma captured.

Next to it, was another photograph. This one used to sit on the dresser in my bedroom. It was a picture of Whitney, Maddi, and me. We were seniors in high school and had gone to an end-of-the-year foam party. The school hosted the event for seniors only, and they filled the school's courtyard with foam, a DJ, and all kinds of lights and decorations celebrating our graduation. In the photo, we're wearing neon shirts, bracelets, and even had paint on our faces. The three of us are laughing and have our arms wrapped around each other.

"Who do you think did all of this?" Otomatsu asked.

"I don't know," I answered. "But they did a great job. It's like they took all the best things about my life and brought them here to me."

I sat down on a soft, deep couch and leaned my elbow on the armrest.

"Okay," I said. "Explain."

"Where to start?" Otomatsu asked, pacing the room. "After I became a death angel, I kept to myself. I didn't even report back to Processing for a whole decade. I did my job and didn't care what anyone else was doing. And then one day, I came across a village in Peru that was experiencing a strange 'illness' that made the people violent. Men were killing their neighbors, mothers were killing their babies, and no one knew why. A demon had been possessing people, making them murder each other, and then those people would end up in Hell. It was blatant cheating. Those poor people didn't have a chance. And I guess…"

Otomatsu trailed off.

"Something came over me," he continued. "I became so enraged, I had to find a way to stop him. So I went to the Temple of Da'at. I spent months trying to find something that would help. When I finally came across the exorcism instructions, I couldn't believe it. I returned to the village and found the demon inhabiting an old woman. I cornered the demon and tried to get him to give up names of other demons who were possessing humans. He wasn't willing to give me much, and the exorcism did not go smoothly. I ended up breaking the woman's wrist when I tied her up. But I did get the demon out of her and then I killed him. That's when I found out that when elite demons 'die,' they become mongrels. Mindless, deformed creatures that run wild through Hell. They're dangerous if you run into a pack on your own, but they're nowhere near as dangerous as they were when they were elites."

"Because elite demons are the only demons who can walk the Earth?" I asked.

"Yes," Otomatsu nodded. "They're Satan-made to go where he can't. That's why it's so imperative to send them back as mongrels. Mongrels aren't able to leave Hell."

"Aren't all demons Satan-made though?"

"Runts come from corrupt human souls and are used to torment other human souls in Sentencing and Hell. Tanks and wasps are Hell spawn made by elite demons for their own personal armies."

"And guardians?" I asked. "Are they Hell-made also?"

"No," Otomatsu said solemnly. "If you're 'lucky,' you get hand-picked by an elite to become a guardian. While you wait in Sentencing, you have plenty of time to get yourself into all kinds of trouble. The only humans who skip Sentencing and go straight to Hell are top offenders. Everyone else waits in Sentencing until they decide what to do with you. The elite demons try to turn as many people into runts as possible because then they have no chance of ever leaving Hell. But if the elite demons see...potential in you, then they make you an offer to become a guardian. Your buddy back at the cathedral was training to become one for Nav."

"I think Dumah almost became a guardian."

"I know Ah Puch was very angry when he left, so that would make sense."

"What about you?" I asked. "Did any elites try to recruit you while you were there?"

"Astaroth is the demon I was working for before I fled Hell to become a death angel. I spent my first years as an angel constantly looking over my shoulder. I was worried Astaroth would find me and try to lure me back to Hell or have me killed. Which is why I was so thrilled to learn how to perform exorcisms. I needed *something* that would help me defeat them more easily."

Otomatsu chuckled.

"It's a pain in the ass getting them to stay still long enough to perform the whole thing though. The hardest part was memorizing the whole exorcism prayer. Not to mention anointing them with holy blood."

I gave him a look of confusion.

"You need either first, second, or third generation blood."

"Of?"

"Jesus!" he exclaimed.

Another look of confusion.

"You don't know?"

"Know what?" I asked.

"My dear Emma. A man who lived til his mid 30s and spent his whole adult life preaching nothing but love and kindness. You don't seriously think he didn't love anyone?"

"Oh my goodness," I smiled. "I read a novel about this once. You don't actually mean Jesus was married. There's no evidence that he was."

"There's no evidence that he wasn't," Otomatsu replied.

"Why keep it secret? What's the big deal?"

"I'm trying to think of a good example you can relate to," Otomatsu rubbed his chin. "Ah! Do you remember Princess Diana?"

"Of course," I answered.

"Do you remember how obsessed everyone became with her children after she died? Can you imagine how people would have reacted to the children of Jesus Christ? They would have been mobbed, both in a positive way and a negative way. And by the way, Jesus wasn't just a man."

"What do you mean?" I asked.

"Emma! In all the years you've been an angel, have you not read a single thing of importance? Ever been to the Temple of Da'at?"

"We're not allowed inside. Which reminds me, how did you get in there?"

"You're asking an awful lot of questions all at once. How about I just take you to the temple."

"I already told you, we're not allowed in!"

"And I already told you, I've been inside. Trust me."

"Before we go," I said. "There's one question you have to answer now."

"What?"

"Who were the woman and baby you killed?"

Otomatsu looked stunned.

"How did-?"

"Please just tell me," I asked. "For the first time in a long time, I thought I found someone I could fully trust."

"Haven't you?" he asked, hurt.

"I don't know! Elijah said that you're an outcast like me and he's worried that I've been spending too much time with you."

"So someone says something about me and you immediately change your opinion of me?"

"I'm trying to give you a chance to explain yourself," I said, trying to sound more understanding.

"I don't talk about my past."

"Because you killed a woman and a baby before killing yourself?"

"It's complicated."

"Then explain."

Otomatsu looked down at the floor.

"Look," I sighed. "I don't want to push you to tell me something you don't want to. But you are my friend. So I'm giving you the opportunity to tell me, if you want to. I have trust issues, and you obviously do too. So why don't we help each other with that?"

Otomatsu looked back at me and smiled.

"Okay. Before I start, I just want you to know that who I was as a human is not who I am now. And I hope you know me well enough to know that for yourself."

I nodded.

"I met Hanako when I was 43 years old. She was a geisha, and she was the most beautiful woman I had ever seen. Geishas were performers in Japan who sang and danced, or just talked with clients who paid them. A lot of people perceive them as exploited women, who were taken advantage of for being beautiful. But in fact, geishas were very successful businesswomen. Most used their talents and profession to pay off family debts or to become independent without the need of a husband for financial needs.

I was considered an old man when I met Hanako. She was only twenty years old. I was technically old enough to be her father. But the night I met her, the entire world stopped. There were no stars in the sky because they knew none of them would shine as bright as her. The whole room was silent when she walked in. It was as if every man in that place saw her, inhaled, and didn't exhale until her performance was over. Of course, after her performance, everyone wanted to talk to her. I knew I didn't have a chance. Who would talk to me when there were younger, more interesting men there. But then, by some miracle, she walked right up to me.

'Hello,' she said.

I looked around, wondering who she was trying to talk to. I thought I was in her way.

'Do you not wish to speak to me?' she asked. 'You're the only man here who hasn't come up to introduce himself to me.'

'I- I- I didn't think you would want to talk to me,' I stammered. 'I'm not interesting enough for you.'

'The owner of Japan's most successful silk factory,' she said, tilting her head. 'I happen to think that is very interesting. Come. Let's find somewhere more private.'

Just like that. She dismissed everyone, and spent the rest of the evening with me. We walked through the gardens of the geisha house, sharing stories. By that point, I knew she would be looking for a large payment for her company. If she knew who I was, she knew how rich I was."

"You never mentioned you were rich," I stopped him.

"I was extremely wealthy and successful with my business," Otomatsu said. "I spent many years building my business, but didn't make time for my personal life. So having Hanako's attention, even just for a night, was a very special gift. When it got late, I pulled my wallet out and she gently placed a hand on mine.

'No,' she smiled. 'Just promise you'll be back soon.'

I couldn't believe it.

'Please, I insist,' I offered. 'I don't want you to think you've wasted your evening with me.'

'I haven't. Just promise me that you will return.'

'When?' I asked.

'A week from today?'

'Absolutely,' I said.

'Bring some of your friends,' she suggested. 'I'll bring some of mine to keep them company.'

The next week, I returned to the geisha house with a group of eight men. All of them were accompanied by geishas. The men threw money at the women like they couldn't get rid of it fast enough. I brought three of my best silk prints as gifts for Hanako plus three matching parasols. She was so happy, which made me happy. And that was how our relationship began. Once a week, I brought her lavish gifts and hosted parties. I helped the girls make money and I kept Hanako happy. And in return, she kept me...happy."

Otomatsu cleared his throat.

"Oh," I smirked awkwardly. "Right."

"Months went by and Hanako told me she was pregnant. I asked her to marry me right away. She said no. She wanted to be a geisha, not a wife. I told her that she didn't have to spend her time entertaining men anymore. She could have whatever she wanted. Suddenly, she grew cold with me.

'The only thing I want is my freedom,' she said.

I tried to understand her. She was an independent woman who only knew one way of life. I started buying her more things and giving her money whenever I could. When she had the baby, a girl, I knew all I wanted to be from then on was her father. While she was still on bed rest after giving birth, I decided to drop in unexpectedly. I was planning to propose properly. When I arrived at the geisha house, the women looked at me wearily and spoke in hushed tones. When I got to Hanako's room, there was a man standing outside the door. He was wearing a suit, a hat, and glasses that seemed a little too big for his face. He looked me up and down and frowned.

'Can I help you?' I asked.

'No,' he said. 'Just here to see my child.'

'I think you have the wrong room,' I smiled politely.

'Hanako has been in this same room since I've known her.'

'Hanako?'

'The mother of my child.'

The door opened and the smile on Hanako's face faded when she saw me. She looked at the man with the glasses and she frowned, wrapping her robe around herself a little tighter.

'What are you doing here?' she asked.

'Who is this?' the other man asked.

'Who is he?' I pointed a finger in his face. 'He's saying you're the mother of his child!'

'Excuse me?' a deep voice from her room said.

Another man came out, buttoning up his shirt. He had messy shoulder-length hair and was barefoot. He looked at both of us and laughed. Hanako put her hand up to her head and sighed heavily.

'You could have stayed in there while I handled this!' she snapped at him.

'What?' he laughed again. 'Am I the only one who knows?'

'Only one who knows *what*?' I asked.

'My friend,' he said, putting a hand on my shoulder. 'Hanako has been living quite lavishly, between the gifts, the geisha money, and her....*business* on the side.'

'Business on the side?' the man with the glasses asked.

'You must be a Jorogumo,' the barefoot man smiled at Hanako. 'Preying on lonely men and trapping them in your web like flies.'

She scoffed at him.

'I'm sorry to be the one to inform you of this,' he said to us. 'But your darling Hanako has deceived you, along with other men, I'm sure. She's been prostituting to make extra money.'

'No!' the man with the glasses exclaimed. 'Geishas aren't allowed to!'

'We're not allowed?' Hanako crossed her arms. 'We can do whatever we want. We don't have to ask any man for permission.'

'As fun as this has been, I have to get to work,' the barefoot man said, grabbing his shoes. 'Until next time.'

After he disappeared down the hall, the three of us stood there, not saying anything for a while.

'I want my mother's necklace back,' the man with the glasses said, sounding hurt.

'You can have it,' Hanako said coldly. 'I wasn't going to ever wear it anyways.'

'Do you know who the father is?' I asked.

'No,' she answered. 'But don't worry, I won't expect either of you to support us any longer. I'll raise her as my apprentice and teach her everything I know.'

'As a whore?' I asked.

'As a *geisha*,' Hanako narrowed her eyes.

'As I understand, there's no difference,' I retaliated. 'She'll be learning from the best, though. I'm sure she'll make you plenty of money.'

'And I thought you were the kindest out of all of them.'

'I was kind when I thought you loved me as much as I love you!' I yelled. 'I wanted to marry you! I was being patient, trying to give you the time and freedom you needed. I thought at least that made you love me.'

'I never loved you,' Hanako said softly. 'I only love myself.'

'What about the baby?' the man with glasses asked.

'I *only* love myself,' she repeated.

'You don't have a heart in your chest,' I sneered.

'At least I don't have to worry about it getting broken then,' she retorted.

At that, I left. I went to a nearby bar where American men normally went to drink. I found myself surrounded by a bunch of drunks who were laughing and celebrating. But I was angry and full of hate. The man with glasses sat down beside me. He told me that we should get our revenge; that Hanako wasn't human. She was a monster that needed to be slain. I needed to make an example of her. I was so drunk by the end of the night..."

Otomatsu stopped for a moment, rubbing his temples with his thumb and fingers.

"I agreed. My heart was broken and I had been made a fool. We went back to the geisha house with a bowie knife one of the Americans sold us."

I gasped.

"We snuck into Hanako's room while she and the baby slept," Otomatsu continued, his voice shaking. "I watched as he placed his hand over her mouth and slit her throat. And unlike it is now, there was no silence. The world didn't go quiet when he took her life. Hanako made a strange gurgling sound and her arms swung around, trying to fight him. Instead, she knocked a vase off the table by her bed. When it shattered, her baby started screaming. I was so drunk....and he said the baby had to be quiet so no one would catch us."

Otomastu started sobbing.

"I blacked out. When I woke up, there was blood everywhere. I was horrified by what he had done to them. I just let him kill them, and I was disgusted with myself for allowing it to happen. I didn't deserve to live. So I picked up the bloody knife off the floor, plunged it into my chest, and I woke up in Hell."

He looked at me, waiting for me to say something. When I didn't, he continued.

"I didn't spend a long time in Hell."

'How long?" I asked.

"80 years," he said quietly. "I died in 1891 when I was 44 years old. I became a death angel in 1971 when Dumah helped me become one."

My head snapped in his direction.

"You said you had only heard of him," I said.

"I had. I never actually met him. But as soon as I heard of a man sent to Hell after committing suicide and then becoming an angel, I swore that I would do whatever it took to become one as well. I would alert the dark angels whenever I heard someone was planning to escape. People were always trying to sneak onto the ship that went to Processing. So, I quickly became a very unlikeable person in Hell, which quickly helped me become a very unlikable angel in Heaven."

"Elijah said you were the one who killed Hanako and the baby."

"Most other angels know I was involved in a double murder and then killed myself. Rumors spread more quickly than the truth. And I never cared to stand up for myself and correct them. I wasn't the one who slit their throats, but I didn't stop the one who *did* have the knife. I'm just as guilty."

"You're not a murderer," I said.

"No," Otomatsu looked away. "Just a coward."

"Was it Baraqiel who helped you?" I asked. "That's who helped Dumah become a death angel."

"No. No, it was a dark angel named Matariel."

"Matariel helped you?" I beamed.

"Do you know him?"

"No, but I know of him."

"He saved me," Otomatsu smiled. "I ran all the way to the shoreline and found him trying to build a boat. His presence startled me as much as mine startled him. I told him I wanted out of Hell and would do whatever I could. He told me the only option was to become a death angel. He described the work and said I would have to do it until the end of time. Without hesitation, I accepted.

'So now what?' I asked him. 'Is there some sort of training or ceremony that needs to be done?'

Matariel laughed and shook his head.

'All you need to do,' he said, 'is hold your arms out in front of you, close your eyes, and swear your servitude to God.'

I did as he said and closed my eyes while holding my hands out in front of me.

'I swear.'

And then it happened. I felt a sudden weight in my hands and when my eyes opened, my katana was there. My clothes had changed to this all black uniform. I had massive jet black wings.

And I did what I promised I would do. While also exorcising some demons here and there."

Otomatsu shrugged.

"That's it," he said. "That's my story. And I'm really sorry I didn't tell you sooner. It's not a past that I'm proud of. I know I can never take back what I did, and I'll never forgive myself for it either, but I've spent every day since trying to make up for all of it."

I sat there for a moment, thinking. Otomatsu stopped talking and waited patiently for me.

"How many demons have you killed?"

"Hundreds," he answered. "I don't think there's a number of guilty demon lives that will ever make up the two innocent human lives I took but if there is, I'm willing to reach that number. It's just been harder lately because demons aren't possessing people as often these days. They seem to be only targeting people who have higher worldly status. People who have amassed a large number of followers."

"Really?" I asked. "And you learned how to exorcise them by reading a book in the Temple of Da'at?"

"Yeah, it's really simple once you memorize all of the words. Getting ahold of the blood is a bit tricky so I've learned to dilute it with holy water. Also, demons are strong so I've resorted to doing things like poisoning vodka with holy water to weaken them. But all there is to it is reciting the words correctly while the demon is weak, and you have to perform it on Earth. Which can also be challenging."

"How did you get inside the temple?" I asked. "I was told death angels were the only ones not allowed inside."

"I befriended the virtue that oversees the library," Otomatsu explained. "I also promised to kill any demon of his choosing if he let me in and learn how to do it."

"Do you know why death angels aren't allowed in?"

"My guess is we're bottom of the barrel and don't get any of the perks of being an angel other than being one?" Otomatsu shrugged again. "Most of us start off in Hell for being bad people. It's kind of like any other business. Janitors are technically employees of the same company as the CEO, but they certainly don't associate with one another."

"Don't you think that's kind of bullshit though?"

"Nah," he said, swiping a hand playfully in the air. "It's better than anything in Hell."

Otomatsu glanced at me.

"So...still friends?"

I met his eyes and sighed.

"I've done a lot of growing recently," I said. "I've been letting go of negativity and have been embracing this new life I've been given. I've been enjoying helping people, even though what we do is sad and morbid. But being there for people when they need someone is important. And you've been there for me. We've made mistakes and even though yours hurt other people, I know you must have been hurting pretty badly yourself. So I don't need to make you feel worse by judging you. I know you're not that same person anymore, and *this* is the Otomatsu I want to be friends with."

He smiled and opened his arms. I stood up and hugged him.

"I know I wasn't a good person when I was alive, and that I did terrible things to people who didn't deserve it, but I'm willing to spend the rest of eternity making up for those things. And I'm glad I'll have you right by my side."

I quickly brushed a tear that ran down my cheek and pulled away, smiling at him.

"So speaking of friends," I said, "are you still buddies with the virtue?"

"As a matter of fact, I am. Wanna pay him a visit?"

"Absolutely!" I exclaimed. "But one more thing. You *have* to tell me all about Jesus."

Otomatsu beamed.

"Deal," he said.

9

There once was a man named Joseph. He married a woman named Mary. Joseph was 20 years old and Mary was only 16 years old. As soon as they were married, they both had the same dream. An angel appeared to each of them saying Mary would have a baby who they would name Jesus. The angel told them the baby would be the son of God and change the world. When they both woke up the next day, they shared their dreams. Surprised, they agreed it was merely an odd coincidence. That night, they both had the same dream again.

Many people believe that Mary was much younger when she became pregnant, and that she was a virgin. Being married to Joseph, this logic was very wrong. The couple consummated their marriage like normal. They both continued having the same dream every single night. The angel would visit them individually and tell them about the son God had promised them. He would be called the "king of kings." Jesus would be the light of the world that ended pain and suffering. There would be no more war, poverty, hunger, or illnesses. Their son would be humanity's savior. Every morning, Mary and Joseph would tell each other about their similar dreams.

Mary and Joseph were waiting for a sign while they were awake that their dreams would become reality. Then, Mary found out that she was pregnant. The couple thought it was a very strange coincidence, but not completely shocking since they had been together. Throughout Mary's pregnancy, they both continued having dreams of the angel visiting them. As time went on, they both agreed to try and communicate with the angel, asking it questions. Joseph suggested they ask the same questions to compare notes. The first question they asked was the angel's name. They both were told Gabriel.

The next question Mary asked was, "How is this baby the son of God when Joseph is clearly the biological father?" The angel answered, "The son of God has lived many past lives. Every time he has lived, his heart has been the same. He had spent every life helping people and putting others before himself. God has watched this soul be reborn for hundreds of years and now it is the person growing in your womb. God has blessed this baby with His divine gifts to fulfill the prophecy that the son will save humanity."

When Mary spoke to Joseph the following morning, he had received the same answer from the angel, Gabriel.

"What do you think he meant by, 'the son of God has lived many past lives?" Joseph asked.

"I don't know," Mary replied. "As far as I know, we only live one life."

Joseph and Mary didn't know when a person dies, they sometimes have the choice to go back to Earth as a new person. God was allowing only a select few who were exceptionally good people to do this. Everyone else just went straight to Paradise. This person, who would become Jesus, had been reborn multiple times, choosing to go back every time they died to make the world a better place. God saw this and thought it was the most selfless thing any human had ever done. So He rewarded this soul with special abilities, but only for this one life. Jesus would have one lifetime to make a difference in the world. God couldn't directly fight Satan because one was stuck in Paradise while the other was stuck in Hell. And the archangels couldn't leave Paradise unprotected. However, demons were free to roam the Earth, tempting and tricking humans. Jesus would be the one to stop them and set man on the righteous path.

Jesus was born and everything Gabriel had prophesied, came to be. The night he made his entrance into the world, the dreams stopped for Mary and Joseph. Jesus grew up a seemingly normal child. However, at a young age, he showed interest in world affairs, philosophy, and culture. When other children were playing, Jesus wanted to learn. He sat with the teachers and elders who were all astonished by his eagerness to know things. Mary grew concerned as Jesus became a pariah, being teased by other children and whispered about by other adults. She urged him to spend time with kids his own age. One day while pleading with him, Jesus turned to her and gently said, "let the children play. I am learning from my elders and I am teaching them. I cannot become stronger or wiser from playing children's games." Joseph reminded Mary of the great plans God had for Jesus and she kept her worries to herself.

    As Jesus grew older, unexpected things began to happen. Once, Joseph brought Jesus with him to deliver some furniture to a neighbor. Jesus had been Joseph's apprentice, learning carpentry. They passed a farm along the way and noticed a farmer in a field who seemed distressed. His cow had given birth to a calf. The calf was dead and the cow was dying. Joseph watched as Jesus went over to observe what was happening. He laid next to the cow and rested his head on her side. The farmer and Joseph were amazed to see that the cow's breathing returned to normal and she slowly stood up. The farmer asked Jesus to also save the calf. He simply replied that he had not saved the cow, only comforted her.

    Joseph and Mary raised Jesus without telling him anything about his destiny or Mary's pregnancy with him. However, he seemed to know exactly what he was meant to be. He taught love, grace, kindness, and forgiveness. He taught people to love each other, even the people we want to hate; and in fact, love those people even more. As time passed, more people began to follow Jesus, believing he was nothing more than a very wise teacher. It wasn't until one day, when his friend's mother-in-law was in bed with a fever, that Jesus started to question his existence. Jesus had been over to visit his friend, but when he heard of the sick woman, he asked if he could go see her. The family seemed grim, believing the woman would not get better. Jesus sat beside her and talked, making her laugh and keeping her company. When it was time to leave, she asked if she could try to sit up. Jesus helped his friend prop her up. As soon as Jesus touched her, she jolted. Suddenly, she felt better than she had since becoming sick. She then asked to sit in the chair next to her bed. Before even reaching the chair, the color seemed to come back in her face. The woman stood up straight and let go of Jesus and his friend, able to stand on her own. The family was in complete shock. They thought she was about to die, and then she was suddenly up and walking around, laughing and conversing with everyone. She told them all that Jesus had healed her.

  Jesus immediately denied it, just as confused as everyone else. He said that he had only wanted to give the woman some company and make her smile. Still, she insisted he had done something else to heal her. His kindness towards her healed her, even if he did it unintentionally. Word spread quickly of the incident and people started coming to Jesus with their ailments. Most of the time, he couldn't do anything about it. He wasn't a doctor; he was a carpenter. But sometimes, someone would come to him with debilitating pain or agonizing sores, and Jesus would simply spend some time with them. They would return in a day or two completely healed. No one could explain it. Not even Jesus.

One day, Jesus was with his friends at the shore when a man approached him. Jesus could see that the man had cuts all over his body, and his bare feet were blistered and bleeding.

"Are you Jesus?" the man asked. "Jesus, born to Mary and Joseph, but son of God?"

Jesus turned to the man and said, "I *am* Jesus, and Mary and Joseph are my parents. But we are all children of God. What is your name, friend?"

"I do not know the name of the man I possess," the man said. "And my name is of no importance to you. I am a demon, and I come with a message from Satan himself. He wants to know what you have done to make it where he cannot see what you are doing."

"I'm sorry but I don't understand," Jesus replied. "Satan told you this?"

"Yes," the demon continued. "How have you made it impossible for the devil himself to see you? He can see everything that God can. That's always been part of the rules. They both have the ability to see every human soul on Earth. But Satan says he cannot see you. Why is this?"

"I'm afraid I don't know what you're talking about."

The possessed man lunged at Jesus, screaming suddenly with rage. Jesus' friends grabbed the man by the arms and legs and pinned him down to the ground.

"WHAT ARE YOU?" the man shouted. "NOT HUMAN! NOT GOD! BUT BOTH!"

"If you really are a demon possessing this innocent man," Jesus said, placing his hand on the man's forehead, "you need to leave him at once. You're hurting his soul and he did not do anything to deserve your punishment."

The man howled in pain when Jesus touched him.

"WE WILL COME BACK FOR YOU, SON OF GOD!" the man screamed. "WE WILL-!"

"BEGONE!" Jesus' voice boomed.

There was silence.

The man stopped thrashing around and went still, his eyes rolling back white before closing. Jesus' friends gasped and let go of him. They all ran to the water, washing themselves and praying. Jesus, exhausted and exasperated, kneeled next to the man and began to pray. Eventually, the man's eyes slowly opened. He looked up at Jesus, frightened and confused.

"Everything is all right," Jesus sighed. "You're okay. Go home and tell your family what happened and that you are healed."

The man got to his feet and left. Jesus sat on the shore and watched his friends murmur to one another in the distance. He knew they were discussing what had just happened. He knew he was different. And he knew he would not be able to live an ordinary life.

"Um, hello," Jesus said out loud. "I know I've prayed to you before, but it feels a little different now. I don't normally ask for anything for myself. I don't want to be selfish. I feel like big things are planned for me, and that's fine, but is that the only reason I was born?"

Silence.

"If you won't, or *can't*, talk to me, how will I know if I'm doing the right thing? What if no one listens to me?"

Peter Simon, John, and James started walking back over to Jesus. He smiled wearily at them.

"Are you all right?" James asked. Jesus nodded.

"We were talking about things we've seen you do," John said. "For quite some time now, I've known there was something very special about you. And after what we just witnessed, I think more people will come to see how special you are. But there will also be plenty of enemies. We will follow you and spread news of your greatness. God has spoken to me about the great things you will do for generations to come."

"God spoke to you?" Jesus asked. John nodded.

"Yes, God has spoken to me as well," Peter Simon smiled. "He said I should follow you and share stories of the things you do."

Jesus turned to James. He nodded.

"So, God can speak?" he asked, more to himself than to him.

"Of course!" James said. "Doesn't He speak to you?"

"Yes," Jesus lied. "I just didn't know He spoke to anyone else."

Jesus stood up and placed a hand on Peter Simon's shoulder.

"Go and get your brother, Andrew," Jesus smiled. "We need to get started."

While Jesus did perform minor miracles and gave excellent sermons, some of the things he "did" in the Bible, didn't actually happen. He never turned water into wine. He never fed 5,000 people with five loaves and two fish. He couldn't control the weather. The truth was, Jesus relied solely on people's faith. If he had actually performed all of the miracles the bible listed, it would have been much easier for onlookers to believe he was the son of God. However, God wanted them to believe because they believed, not because of some parlor tricks Jesus was able to do to convince them.

When John the Baptist was beheaded, Jesus fled to solitude. Not only was John a loyal disciple, but he was also Jesus' closest friend. After hearing of John's brutal killing, Jesus took some time away from crowds and even from the apostles. While Jesus was taking a public break from being the Messiah, the apostles were writing about and sharing stories of the miracles Jesus performed that simply weren't true. They were trying to protect Jesus, making him seem even more divine and powerful than he was. But at his core, Jesus was a man. And hearing of his loved one being beheaded made him realize that he was mortal, and maybe not in the safest position.

So, Jesus went away for a while. The Bible only states that Jesus sought privacy for reflection on the progress of his kingdom. Believers think this was him thinking about the kingdom of God. However, he was talking about his own personal kingdom. When Jesus retreated after John's death, he found a place where no one had heard of him. No one wanted to kiss his feet or sing praise of him. No one bowed down to him or offered him gifts for merely existing. He was free to be only a man in a foreign land.

Jesus was able to walk around, listening and watching in the background; he was completely invisible. At one point, he stopped a while to watch a group of musicians and dancers who were performing for the passing crowds. Jesus took a bite of the fig he had. He wiped the juice from the corner of his mouth when a pair of dark eyes met him. She was a whirlwind of movement, colorful scarves and long, black hair swaying around to the music. She was beating a tambourine and wore a long green dress. She turned to the musicians and laughed as she continued to dance. Her laughter sounded more beautiful than anything that came out of the instruments. Jesus almost dropped the fig in his hand, and as he tried to catch it before it hit the ground, he ran into a man who was standing in front of him.

"Watch it!" he growled.

"I'm so sorry," Jesus said.

The man moved away as the music stopped and everyone cheered for the performers. The woman Jesus had been watching bowed and hugged one of the musicians; a young man who had been playing a flute. She tousled his hair, and then took one more bow before walking away. The musicians started playing a slower song and she made her way over to an older woman who handed her a drink. Jesus approached her, unsure of what to say. But he was good with words, so he thought whatever came out would impress her.

"I've never seen a woman sweat like that," Jesus said abruptly. The woman turned, startled.

"I just mean-" Jesus started. She laughed awkwardly and handed the cup back to the older woman, who was watching the interaction.

"I mean, you work hard, like a donkey."

"You're calling me a donkey?" she scrunched her nose.

"No! Of course not! I only meant that..."

Someone who usually had such a way with words suddenly found himself at a loss for them.

"I never knew such a beautiful desert could grow in a flower," Jesus smiled sheepishly.

"What?" the woman said, puzzled.

"Uh, I mean *flower*, in the desert. Beautiful flower."

"Okay," the woman giggled. "Well, I have to get back to the performance. If your tongue starts working correctly, maybe you can stay afterwards. We're having a huge party for my father's birthday."

Without getting a chance to say another word, she sprinted back to the musicians as the next song started. She picked up her tambourine and began to dance again. A couple of times, Jesus caught her smiling at him.

"Her name is Zemira," a voice said. The woman who had given her the drink was smirking at Jesus.

"Zemira," Jesus sighed. "I've never seen anything like her before in all my life."

"Sometimes the best things come to us when we are not looking for them," she smiled. "That's how I met Zemira's father."

Jesus turned to the woman and she chuckled.

"Yes, I am Zemira's mother," she said. "And that darling boy playing the flute is my son, Abiah."

Zemira's mother watched Jesus watch her daughter dance and smiled. After the performance was over, Zemira seemed to disappear. Then, people put tables together and brought out plates and plates of food. Jesus socialized with people all evening, but could not find Zemira anywhere. The man that he had bumped into earlier came up to him and crossed his arms.

"Did you lose something?" he asked.

"Yes," Jesus laughed. "A precious flower that needs to be tended to. Excuse me."

As Jesus turned, the man grabbed his arm and swung him around.

"That precious flower happens to be my daughter, Zemira," the man grumbled. "My wife tells me you took quite a liking to her. Who are you?"

"I am nobody," Jesus said. "Just someone who wishes to spend his evening with the best company here. Happy birthday."

"If you are nobody, then you don't need to speak with Zemira," the man frowned.

"Stop it!" Zemira's mother said from behind Jesus. "Leave him alone. He just wants to talk to her. There's no harm in that."

"Hmph," the man grunted.

"She's down by the water," the woman smiled at Jesus. "All of the noise and excitement was starting to give her a headache."

"Is she all right?" the man asked.

"She's fine," she said to him before turning back to Jesus. "Go on. I'll keep this one busy."

"It was nice to meet you," Jesus nodded to them.

He walked down to the water, away from the water and found Zemira standing alone with her hands wrapped around her arms.

"Are you cold, Zemira?" Jesus asked. Zemira jumped at the sound of his voice.

"I'm sorry, I didn't mean to startle you."

"It's fine," she said. "And no, I'm not cold. I like holding myself like this sometimes to make sure I'm still here."

"Where else would you be?" he asked.

"Somewhere this body can't go," she smiled. "You know, it's not fair that you know my name but I don't know yours."

"My name is Jesus."

"Are you enjoying yourself, Jesus?"

"Everyone seems very nice and welcoming," Jesus said. "And then I met your father."

Zemira started laughing.

"He's a little protective of me," she explained. "I have a disease that gives me headaches and seizures. None of the healers thought I would live to this age because of how sick I was as a child. Sometimes I'm in so much pain I can't walk, let alone dance. I'm very thankful today was a good day for my father's birthday."

Zemira sighed and rubbed her head.

"I think I might have overdone it a little though. I just didn't want my parents to see I was hurting and end the party early."

Jesus raised his hands towards Zemira's head and she took a step backwards.

"What are you doing?" she asked.

"I'm asking you to trust me," Jesus replied. "Have a little faith."

She stood still as Jesus placed a hand on each side of her head. He closed his eyes and concentrated. He could almost feel the disease in her head. He prayed to have her healed and to not let the disease return. Suddenly, Zemira gasped and moved away from him. She touched her head and gaped at Jesus.

"What did you just do?" she asked.

"I healed you."

"No one can heal me."

"I can, and I did. And I was able to do so because you believed in me. I've been gifted with special abilities by God himself. He sent me to heal people and teach them about Him. I am the Messiah that was prophesied."

Zemira frowned.

"How dare you take advantage of a sick woman!" she snapped. "I don't know what you just did to my head but I'm sure the pain will come back at some point. It always does. But I think you should go."

"Did I do something wrong?" Jesus asked.

"Yes! You're clearly ill to say such blasphemous things. I want you to leave!"

"But Zemira-"

"Leave!"

Feeling hurt, Jesus left. He wandered away from the town, further into the desert. After several days without food and water, Jesus began to feel weak. He was looking for some sort of sign from God, but he wasn't getting any. Finally, he saw something in the distance ahead. A very tall figure was standing in the middle of the desert, as if they were waiting for Jesus. This was his sign! As he approached the person, Jesus realized that she wasn't abnormally tall, but she was floating. The woman was about five feet off the ground with her arms outstretched. Jesus tripped over a stone and fell down.

"Jesus, son of God," the floating woman said, pouting her lips. "You look tired and hungry."

"I am, demon," Jesus breathed heavily. "Leave me alone."

"Ah, your powers are getting a little stronger. I am Lilith. One of Satan's strongest demons. He has sent me to make a deal with you."

"I'm not interested," Jesus said, wiping sweat from his forehead.

He watched Lilith lower herself to the ground to pick up a stone. She ran her hand across it. The stone turned into a big red apple. She slowly took a bite of it, moaning as she did so. Jesus turned his head away.

"What's the matter?" Lilith said. "If you're hungry and you're the son of God, turn one of these stones into an apple as I did."

"Food isn't the only thing that feeds men," Jesus spat. "Having faith that I will eat again keeps me fed. Believing a stone is bread does not change the fact that it is still a stone."

Lilith slowly leaned in close to Jesus and grabbed the front of his cloak. Suddenly, they were back in the city, standing on top of the highest temple. Lilith still had a hold of his clothes, but Jesus' feet were on the very edge of the roof.

"If you are the son of God, jump from this building. It is said that angels will swoop down from heaven and catch you. Do you not think God will save you?"

"Do not test God!" Jesus yelled. "Having faith that God will save you in times of need does not mean you put yourself in a position to force God to save you!"

Lilith snarled at him and then they were standing on a mountain. Lilith once again outstretched her arms.

"If you swear allegiance to my master and promise to follow him, this will all be yours. Satan will continue to rule Hell while you can rule Earth. God cannot promise you such power."

"Begone, demon!" Jesus shouted. "God is the only one people shall worship! In this, they will only find love and goodness. And in doing so, will enter Paradise for eternity!"

Jesus shoved Lilith away from him and she disappeared. Jesus stumbled a bit before leaning against a rock.

"Please...." Jesus murmured. "Let me find a way home."

Jesus collapsed and lost consciousness.

When he awoke, his mother and father were sitting next to him.

"Joseph, he's waking up!" his mother said.

"How- how did I get here?" Jesus asked.

"I went outside and you were laying on the ground in front of our door," Joseph explained. "I brought you inside and your mother has been giving you water."

"I'm so hungry," Jesus cried.

"Here," Mary said, holding up a spoon to his mouth. "It may not be hot anymore, but this bone broth will help you regain your strength."

"My father brought me home," Jesus smiled wearily. "I needed his help and he gave it to me."

"Yes, son," Joseph replied. "You're home and safe now."

After Jesus healed, he went to find his disciples. They had written and shared stories of the miracles they thought would make people believe in him more. Jesus was upset that they had lied, but when they told him how many people were awaiting a sermon from him, he could hardly believe it.

"Hundreds of people will come," Thomas said excitedly.

"Maybe even thousands," Matthew added. "All to hear what you have to say."

And so, with the help of his friends, Jesus prepared for the famous "Sermon on the Mount." The parables and moral teachings he spoke changed the hearts of many that day. But there was one person in the crowd that he did not expect. After he finished speaking and personally addressed several sick people, Zemira approached him.

"Hello," she said softly. "May I speak with you in private?"

"You may speak with us all if you wish to speak to Jesus," Judas declared.

"No," Jesus stopped him. "It's all right. I'll be back in a little while."

Jesus walked with Zemira for a while until she finally spoke.

"I'm sorry for the way I treated you," she said. "After you left, all of my symptoms completely went away. No more headaches, no more seizures, no more pain."

"That makes me very glad," Jesus smiled.

"And I'm sorry I didn't believe you. Or maybe I thought I did believe and that idea scared me. But coming here today, seeing how many people look up to you and listen to you-"

"I'm only a vessel for God," Jesus said. "He is working through me, not the other way around."

"I understand," Zemira continued. "Last night, I had a dream that I was visited by an angel."

"Really?"

"Yes. He told me that you were sent to do great things. And that I am to be your companion through it all."

Jesus stopped and listened more intently.

"He also said that it would not be safe for either of us to be publicly married, so we have to do so in private. I will live in a separate house with our children-"

"Children?" Jesus asked, astonished. She nodded.

"Your disciples may know about us, to help keep us safe. But we can't let anyone know because it could put your bloodline in danger."

"Of course," Jesus replied. "I understand. So then, that leaves one question."

"Which is?"

"When can we get married?"

Jesus and Zemira were wed the following evening. The only ones in attendance were Jesus' parents, Zemira's parents and brother, and the disciples. There was no grand party or loud music, but instead, a quiet dinner while Abiah played his flute. Afterwards, Zemira moved into Joseph and Mary's house, as their "servant." Joseph worked night and day to build her own house on their land. Jesus visited her often when he had down time. Before the house was completed, Zemira became pregnant. Joseph had just finished the house when Zemira gave birth to a son.

This happened during a time when Jesus grew very popular. People started referring to him as "lord," which did not set right with those in power. Jesus asked people not to call him that, but they did anyway, saying he was the "king of kings!" Zemira, Joseph, and Mary became worried for Jesus' safety. The day Jesus rode into Jerusalem on a donkey, Zemira found out that she was pregnant with a second child. When she came to visit him secretly that night, she told him that she had wonderful news.

"I have wonderful news too!" Jesus exclaimed. "You should have seen how much love and joy was all around as I rode in. They laid down palm branches for my donkey to walk on. People were cheering, 'Hosanna! Blessed is he! He comes in the name of the Lord! The king of Israel!' It was incredible!"

"But you are not the king of Israel, Jesus," Zemira said. "You"ll get in a lot of trouble with the king if people call you that."

"God always protects me," Jesus assured her, kissing her forehead. "Everything will be fine. Now, what was it you wanted to tell me?"

"Jesus," Matthew said, walking in with Judas. "I'm sorry to interrupt, but you need to come now. The Pharisees are asking you to calm the crowds down and to tell them to stop their praising."

Zemira looked worried.

"Trust me," Jesus said. "It's all right. I want you to stay with my good friend, Martha, while you're in town. I don't want you to be close to the crowds in case things get too chaotic."

"Chaotic?" Zemira repeated. "Will you be safe?"

"We will keep him safe," Judas said. "Don't worry."

"I'll come find you tomorrow evening," Jesus said before kissing Zemira. "I'll sneak away to Martha's after dark. We'll talk more then."

They never got a chance to talk again, for that week was when Jesus was betrayed by Judas and later arrested. Everything about the story of Jesus' arrest and crucifixion is accurate in the Bible, other than mentioning Zemira being present at his death. After Jesus died and was buried, Zemira wept over her deceased husband. Her family urged her to flee from the area, afraid that the authorities would come after her. Heeding their advice, she took her son and left. She never knew that Jesus returned three days later.

When Jesus died, he went straight to Paradise without spending any time in Processing. God apologized to him for everything. When God put some of His powers into Jesus, it made him unable to see him or interact with him at all. All He knew was that something extraordinary would happen because of Jesus. God thought it would be Jesus' life that changed people forever, however, it was his death that would. God told Jesus that he was never allowed to choose to be reborn again. God was hurting too much from Jesus' crucifixion and the fact that He had sent this amazing human as a gift to mankind just to see them kill him. When God told him this, Jesus protested.

"Father, I have to go back," Jesus said. "They need me."

God told him no once more.

"Can I go back long enough to show them that I'm with you and I'm okay and to tell them to keep faith that there is a Paradise waiting for them? At least give me that. And then I promise I will stay here in Heaven with you forever."

God accepted this bargain. Jesus returned to Earth to tell his apostles where he was going and promised them that if they lived their lives spreading the teachings of Jesus and strived to be like him, they would all be in Paradise with him someday. He asked about Zemira and his son and the apostles told him that they were both in a secret, safe place that not even they knew about. After the apostles promised to fulfill Jesus' wishes, Jesus returned to Paradise. Jesus suggested to God to let humans become angels.

"What if we allow humans to become angels who protect humans? Like guardians? We have archangels, but they can only stay in Paradise to protect *only* Paradise. Virtues inspire humans creatively, but they can't really interfere with demons. Dark angels *can* interfere with Demons, but stay only in Hell with them to keep them at bay. The guardians can be assigned to certain humans to watch over them their whole lives, and then we could have angels be there for humans when they're dying. Because, although I was surrounded by people when I died, I felt very alone and scared. I think having someone there to comfort them as they're leaving the world would help them a lot."

So, with Jesus' influence, God created the other angels. As time went on, humans didn't become as good as He had hoped they would be. Jesus' life and death became a new reason for them to treat each other poorly. People saw other religions as a threat, people killed each other because they had different beliefs, and used the Bible and God to rise to power over others. God became so weary from this that it caused him to become more reclusive and reallocate authority over all other angels to the archangels. To this day, Jesus has stayed right by God's side, in Paradise. And that's where he shall stay for all time.

10

"So Jesus is the reason we get to be angels," Otomatsu concluded.

"Wow," was all I could manage to say.

"I know," he smirked. "It's a lot to take in,"

"Wait," I said. "If Jesus has to stay in Heaven, what about-"

But we were interrupted by the front door suddenly opening. Otomatsu and I both drew our swords when Gabriel Reyes walked in. He was wearing white and silver armor with a white cape. We all froze for a moment before Otomatsu and I lowered our swords.

"Well, it's about time," Gabe scoffed at me. "I only finished building this for you 16 months ago."

"You...you did this?" I asked, looking around. He nodded, grinning.

"Why?" I asked.

"I figured you would need somewhere to live in case my grandpa wanted to go back to being an angel," Gabe answered. "Or if he didn't, you could have this one and I could take his. Either way, I thought you'd want something a little more, *you*. A small hut didn't really suit you, so I researched different styles and decided on a Carribean-style beach cottage. And Thalia agreed and helped me do this for you instead."

"It's really nice," I smiled. "Thank you."

"You're welcome."

Otomatsu cleared his throat.

"Oh!" I exclaimed. "Gabe, this is Otomatsu. He's also a death angel. Otomatsu, this is Gabe. Who I heard is becoming a dark angel because of me."

"Don't get too cocky," Gabe laughed. "You were only *part* of the decision, but I thought it sounded pretty cool anyways."

"Do you know where you'll be posted?" I asked.

"Not yet, but they said I can pretty much pick any available outer edge of Sentencing. They're trying to really buckle down on demons, especially mongrels. There seems to be more and more of them every day."

Otomatsu chuckled to himself at that. Suddenly, I had an epiphone and gasped.

"I think I have an idea!" I said excitedly. "You're not picky about your placement, are you?"

Gabe shook his head. I turned back to Otomatsu.

"Would you mind if we postpone going to the temple?" I asked. "We need to take a short trip across the water. But it shouldn't take too long."

"And you want me to, what? House sit?"

"Just wait here, will you?" I asked more gently.

"Hurry up," Otomatsu said, crossing his arms. "Make sure you keep Lancelot and yourself safe."

Gabe frowned at him.

"Come on," I said. "We'll have to take the boat so we better get going."

"Since you don't have wings," Otomatsu added. I gave him a stern look.

We got into the boat and made our way across the Sea of Anathema. Neither of us spoke much. I didn't know what to say to Gabe, and he obviously didn't have much to say to me. He mostly sat across from me, smiling like an idiot.

"You look nice," I finally said. I regretted it immediately.

"Thanks," he replied.

"What made you decide to go with that look?"

"My grandma had this huge book of angels and I remember my favorite being Gabriel."

"Go figure," I chuckled.

"But the armor he wore in the picture looked like this. I thought it was so cool. A warrior angel. After you left my room, it was the first thing I painted. And then I went to Elijah and asked if I could meet the real Gabriel. I was disappointed when he told me the archangel Gabriel watched over Jesus. I always thought the archangels were the only fighters. But they just patrol Paradise. Dark angels are the real fighters though. It was like

I was destined to be the angel Gabriel from my grandma's book."

"What do you think she'd say if you saw you like this?" I asked.

"She'd probably cry hysterically and pray to God, thanking him for his blessings on me. And then go to the closest church and light every single damn candle in the place."

We both started laughing.

"You know, I said you were only part of the reason I decided to become an angel. But I have to be honest with you. Something keeps pulling me to you."

My cheeks started to burn.

"I don't know what it is," he continued. "But something about you feels so familiar. It feels like home."

Our eyes locked for a moment. The sunlight on his green eyes made them look like crystals. I suddenly remembered what my eyes looked like and could only imagine what Gabe was thinking about my appearance. I stood up as we neared the shore.

"When we dock, stay close to me," I explained. "The hut isn't too far from the shore, but I don't need you wandering off and getting into trouble."

"I don't need you to protect me," Gabe smirked. "I've been training the whole time you've been away. But I appreciate the concern."

"How many demons have you seen up close?" I asked.

"Well, none. *Yet*, at least."

I put my hands on my hips and pursed my lips.

"I can handle it," Gabe continued. "I wouldn't have agreed to become an angel if I didn't think I could do it."

"Did they tell you if you die, like truly die as an angel, you have to go back to Earth and start all over?"

"Yeah....yeah, they did."

"Does that freak you at all?" I asked

"Not really."

"Seriously?"

"If you think about it, unless you go to Paradise, you get to live forever. Even if you die as an angel and live an entire life as a different human, when you die, you can just become an angel again and keep going."

The boat slowed as it approached the dock. I hopped off the deck to tie the mooring line to the pier. Gabe clumsily jumped off the boat and steadied himself. He put his hand up to his head.

"Weird," he breathed. "I feel a little dizzy. I haven't felt *anything* since I died."

"Welcome to Hell!" I announced cheerfully, lifting my arms up.

"Even angels are affected by being here?" Gabe asked.

"Unfortunately," I sighed.

"Emma!" I heard a voice call.

I turned from Gabe and saw Baraqiel walking up the shore to us, waving. I waved back.

"Oh good," I said. "The quicker we can get this done, the better."

As Baraqiel came closer, I noticed that his arm was wrapped in a bandage. He smiled at me and then looked at Gabe.

"Who is this?" Barry asked.

"What happened to your arm?" I ignored his question.

"Oh, a pack of mongrels got to me pretty good," he smiled tiredly. "Sekhmet's been stretched a little thin lately, running back and forth between shores. I had to take them on alone. But I'll be good here in a day or so."

"Do you know where Sekhmet is right now?"

"She was supposed to be back by now," Barry answered. "She's probably exhausted. I wish I could make clones of myself to be able to do more."

"That's actually why I'm here," I explained. "This is Gabriel Reyes. He's almost done with his training to become a dark angel."

"Oh, thank goodness," Baraqiel laughed. "We could use all the help we can get."

"I was thinking," I said, "maybe he could take Matariel's shore."

This caught Baraqiel's attention.

"And then maybe Sekhmet wouldn't have as much land to scout on her own if Matariel was able to come further out this way."

"Really?" Barry asked, looking at Gabe.

"I really don't mind where I get assigned," Gabe said. "And if it means helping another angel in the process, that makes it even better."

Baraqiel suddenly wrapped his huge arms around Gabe and me, squeezing us in tightly. Gabe and I glanced at each other and chuckled.

"I'll have Gabe let the archangels know right away so they can get the details worked out," I explained as we pulled away from the hug.

"You won't come with me?" Gabe asked me.

"Uh, you better go on your own. I need to get back to work anyways. And if the archangels knew it was my idea, there's a good chance they wouldn't like it."

"That's a good point," Baraqiel agreed. "Actually, don't mention Emma at all. Make them think it was all your idea. I'll let Sekhmet know what the plan is when I see her and she can let Matariel know. That way everyone is on the same page."

"Well, I guess we should head back," I said. "I'll have Gabe update me on what they say and let you know."

"As soon as possible!" Baraqiel shook a finger at me. "Don't even bother with the boat. Use the wings to get here faster."

"Okay," I laughed.

Baraqiel hugged me again.

"Thank you, Emma," he said softly in my ear.

"Don't thank me yet," I replied. "We have to see what the archangels say first."

"But thank you for wanting to do this for me," he said, looking at me. "It means a lot."

"No problem. I'll talk to you soon."

Gabe and I made our way back over to my side of the sea, making small talk the entire ride back. The more I learned about Gabe, the more I liked him. As we approached the shore, I saw a small, familiar figure waiting for us on the pier with Otomatsu. I docked the boat and helped Gabe out.

"Thalia?" I said. "What are you doing here?"

"Oh," she said, looking at Gabe. "You're here too. Um, well, 'two birds with one stone' and such. Uh, there's something...."

"What is it?" I asked.

"You two need to go see Elijah," Thalia said. "Immediately."

Gabe and I looked at each other before I turned to Otomatsu. He sighed.

"I'll plan to meet you at Camps Bay Beach in three days," he said sharply. "I have some things

I need to take care of and I can't sit around waiting for you to do whatever this is."

"I just need to help some friends," I explained. "I'll meet you at our spot in three days. I promise."

We parted ways and Thalia took Gabe and me to Elijah. As soon as he saw us walk through the doors of the hotel, he stood up quickly and rushed over to us.

"It's Eduardo," Elijah breathed. "He's been put into hospice care. He doesn't have much time. I thought you both would want to know."

Gabe gasped and gently placed his hand in mine. I glanced at him and could see the hurt in his eyes.

"You go ahead and go be with him," I told him, squeezing his hand. "He'll no doubt be with family so there's no reason for me to go."

"What about the archangels?" Gabe asked.

"That can wait. Go be with your grandpa. He'll need a familiar face when he gets here. I'll come back when it's time."

"Are you sure?"

"Yes. Elijah can let you know where I'm at. Come find me once your grandpa passes. I'd like to meet him."

Gabe smiled wearily at me and kissed the top of my hand. I felt my cheeks get warm and said goodbye before he left.

"I'm proud of you," Thalia beamed.

"I'm surprised you didn't want to go," Elijah said. "You've been waiting for this since you became an angel."

"Whether I'm there or not doesn't change when he dies. I'm trying to be respectful to Gabe and let him be with his grandpa in his final moments. Because Eduardo may be dying, but who knows who is going to show up when he dies."

"Emma-" Elijah started.

"I know," I stopped him. "It might not be Dumah. But, it might be."

I looked at my tracker and sighed heavily.

"When Gabe comes back, tell him where I'm at so I can return immediately."

"What are you going to be doing?" Elijah asked.

"My job," I shrugged. "What else?"

I picked a location and left. I stayed busy with work, trying to not think about Gabe and his dying grandfather. It was hard to focus when I constantly wondered how soon Eduardo would die. The third day came and I met up with Otomatsu. It was Saturday, so I knew what he had been up to the day before. He was already at the beach when I arrived, and he looked somber. He didn't even look at me when I walked up to him.

"Hey," I said.

"Hi."

"Everything okay?"

Otomatsu looked down at his feet before slowly looking at me.

"What's wrong?" I asked. "Did something happen?"

"I caught a demon possessing a human and he attacked me while still inside."

My eyes widened as he continued.

"I tried to exorcise the demon out of the woman so I wouldn't hurt her, but he seemed to know every move I was going to make. I just couldn't keep up with him."

Otomatsu sat down in the sand and covered his face with his hands. I sat down next to him and touched his shoulder gently. He winced, but still kept his face covered.

"What happened?" I asked, my voice was barely a whisper.

"It happened at the woman's home," he finally said. "Apparently she was some internet celebrity and had a huge following on social media. Unfortunately, the type of content she posted was unrealistic beauty standards. At first, her intentions were to share fashion and makeup tips. But after a few hateful comments, her makeup became more extreme and her outfits became more revealing, which was something she hadn't wanted to do in the beginning. She went as far as getting multiple cosmetic surgeries and went on a very strict diet. She promoted it as, 'natural beauty.' Men would tell her she had the perfect body. Women looked at her photos and wondered what was wrong with theirs."

"What does this have to do with a demon?" I asked.

"What started off as an innocent, inspirational thing ended up being a vain, narcissist way of making others idolize her and feel bad about themselves. She would have never let things get like that if she wasn't heavily influenced by someone herself."

"She was being possessed by a demon to post pictures of herself on social media?" I questioned. "Isn't vanity kind of a silly thing to send a human to Hell over?"

"Vanity leads people to believe that they are almost at the same level as God," Otomatsu explained. "They want people to worship them and praise them. They're not doing anything to help others. They just want their audience to tell them how beautiful or special they are. Also, vanity leads to other sins such as envy, pride, and rage. Do you realize there are humans who end up hurting themselves or even killing themselves because they can not be someone else who is prettier, more handsome, more successful, richer, or happier?"

I sat there and thought about what he was saying.

"Astaroth, my former boss, has been on my list of scumbags to get rid of. He works closely with Ankou since vanity causes a lot of suicides.

But I saw an opportunity and went for it. He had been working on this woman for months, but I was so certain that I could get him since he was alone. She was in her backyard by the pool, taking selfie after selfie. The woman fluffed up her hair, arched her back, and took a photo. She grabbed her glass full of iced tea, pretended to laugh, and took a photo. She got on her stomach, pulled a little bit of her bikini bottom inward to show her cheeks, propped her feet up in the air, and took a photo.

I took one step into the backyard and her head whipped around. As soon as she saw me, I knew for sure he was inside of her. I told him to release her and face me himself. He refused to. Instead, he lunged at me in her body. I fought her off of me as gently as I could but she tried scratching out my eyes. I pushed her off and she fell backwards, smacking her head on the concrete. I hadn't pushed her that hard, and she had landed on her bottom first. But her head went back so hard. As if...as if he purposely hit her head harder. She went still and blood started coming out the back of her head. The puddle of blood grew larger and I stood there, unsure of what to do. I had been able to physically touch a human because of that demon being inside of her. Suddenly, the woman's eyes opened and she looked at me, diabolically grinning. She rolled into the pool and started sinking, a faint red cloud forming around her head.

'You did this,' I heard from behind me. I turned and saw Astaroth standing there, grinning the same grin that had been on the woman's face. And then he disappeared.

I jumped into the water, already knowing what would happen. I tried so hard to pull her out of the pool. But I couldn't. I couldn't touch her anymore. And I had to watch her die in that pool. Finally, in that final moment, she looked at me and saw me. And then she was gone. I got out of the pool and prayed for a moment. It was interrupted by a bunch of ringing sounds. I looked at her phone and saw as notifications popped up. Like reactions, hearts, and comments appeared on the lock screen.

You are so hot!
You're the most beautiful woman I've ever seen.
I'd give anything to take you out.
Perfect body.
I'd go skinny dipping with you.
Why aren't there more women like you out there?
Let me spoil you, baby.
I wish my face was between those!
OMG yes, this just made my day!
You are perfect.

She was dead, and no one knew. The notifications kept coming as I heard a voice call out.

I then saw a young teenage boy come out the sliding back door. He kept calling, "mom, mom" over and over. I watched him get closer and closer to the pool. And then he found her. He screamed and called out for help. A neighbor came over and tried to get her out of the pool while her son dialed 911. I felt compelled to stay with him until the ambulance showed up. She was pronounced dead. I already knew she was, but hearing someone say it out loud made it concrete. I had killed her."

"No!" I said. "No, you didn't. You didn't mean to hurt her, let alone kill her. That demon shouldn't have been in her to begin with. You were trying to help her. This is so fucking unfair! How can they get away with this?"

"Because there's not enough of us to keep them at bay," Otomatsu sighed. "You can only put so many fingers in the holes of a boat to keep water from coming in. But if there's eleven holes, you're screwed. The boat's sinking anyways."

"Have you talked to the archangels about any of this?" I asked. "You know, about what you do on Fridays and the things you've seen?"

"Who do you think told me to start doing it?" he asked.

"What?"

"Yeah, it's a side job I was assigned," he scoffed. "And as far as I knew, Dumah was the only other angel who was exorcising demons. That's probably why they're so concerned with you following orders and doing their minor side missions they've given."

"Dumah did it too?"

"Yes. I think because he also worked closely with elite demons. We have intel that other death angels don't. Although it puts a target on our backs that the others don't have to worry about."

"But I don't have to worry about it because I didn't start off in Hell."

"But they still need a replacement for Dumah. I wouldn't be surprised if they eventually tell you to start performing exorcisms once you get good at your regular job. Once you become more acquainted with demons and more in tune with your divine powers."

I thought about what Ankou had said back at the jail.

"I don't think I have divine powers," I explained.

"Sure you do," Otomatsu smiled. "We all do. It's how we know where to find demons or know what a person is thinking as they're dying. Or what kind of person they were like. We can see the soul more clearly than the physical body."

I hung my head.

"When you first became an angel, you flew everywhere, right?" he asked.

"Yeah."

"And now, you see a location on your tracker, think about it, and then you're there. You're becoming more in tune with your divine powers. You're becoming a true angel."

He beamed at me proudly and I smiled back. Otomatsu gave me a pat on the shoulder and then stood up.

"Come on," he sighed.

"What?" I asked, rising to my feet.

"Back to work," Otomatsu winked.

We resumed taking turns picking dying humans. Otomatsu made being an angel seem so easy and normal. I felt like I finally had a place; a purpose. He taught me how to appreciate my job. It was anything but fun, and that would never change, but once I started opening up to what people were like during their lives, it was easier to be there for them when they died.

I watched a man in New Jersey leave a gym, get into his car, and roll down his window. I looked at the empty seat next to him and suddenly was sitting in the seat as he flipped through the radio stations. I concentrated hard and saw the man's life in flashes of memories. He had been obese since his father died when he was twelve years old. His mom let him eat whatever he wanted, and however much he wanted. He was bullied in school for his weight, so he began to work out. Eventually, he changed his eating habits and became a personal trainer. After graduating college with a business degree, he opened a nonprofit gym just for kids. It was a place where overweight children could learn about healthy eating and exercise, and where troubled kids could deal with their anger issues in a safe setting.

He had just opened his second gym where he was the instructor for kickboxing on Saturdays and yoga on Sundays. It was Monday. He had stopped by to print off some flyers and grab the money out of the lockbox to take to the bank. His finger pushed through the radio stations one by one until he reached a song he wanted to listen to. I knew it was happening before it happened. A figure appeared on the driver's side of the car.

"Give me the money!" a voice shouted. The man in the car jolted at the sound and looked up.

I knew the person outside the car was a 14-year-old boy, even though his face was covered with a ski mask. His voice cracked when he yelled and the gun in his hands shook with fear. I also knew that his older friends who had talked him into mugging the man were in a parked car on the side of the building. Any minute they would be pulling up beside this boy to take off with the cash the man had. Behind the boy, stood his guardian angel; an elderly woman, who had her hands resting on the boy's shoulder. She gave me a sad look.

"I'm really sorry about this," the angel said. "I was his second grade teacher. I passed away the year he went into fourth grade. I watch over all of my former students."

"Something's about to happen," I explained.

"I figured as much since you're here," the angel sighed. "What a shame. His mother has been trying so hard with him. He really is a good kid. Just scared and lost."

"Listen," the man in the car said. "You don't want to do this."

"Shut the fuck up!" the boy cried, shoving the gun into the man's face. "You don't know what I want. You don't know anything about me!"

"Shhhhh," the angel whispered in his ear as a tear ran down the boy's face. "It's okay, honey."

"Your mom works two jobs to make ends meet since your dad left," the man said. "You see how much she's struggling and you would do anything for her."

"How did-?"

"You told me she had to work an extra shift to get those shoes for your birthday."

The boy glanced down at his feet.

"I get it," the man continued. "I watched my dad walk out on my mom and saw how much she struggled taking care of me by herself. I would have done anything to make things easier for her. Listen, I'm going to give you the money. But I want this to be the only time you steal. I'll give you a job if you want one. You can do odds and ends jobs around the gym for me. But I don't want you to become a criminal, J.J."

"Please, baby, don't do it," the angel pleaded. "Don't hurt this man. I know you don't want to."

The boy dropped the gun and looked at him with wide eyes. The man held out the envelope to the kid and waited for him to take it. Just then, a car squealed as it pulled up behind J.J. There were two older boys in the front.

"Come on!" the boy in the passenger seat yelled. "Grab the money and let's get the hell out of here!"

J.J. slowly took the envelope from the man in the car and backed up.

"He knows who I am," J.J. said softly.

"What?"

"He knows who I am!" J.J. repeated louder.

"WHAT!" the driver screamed.

"It's okay," the man in the car lifted his hands in defense. I placed my hand on his shoulder.

There was a *Pop! Pop! Pop!* as the boy in the passenger seat shot the man.

"GET IN NOW!" the driver yelled.

J.J. frantically picked up the gun and got in the backseat before the car peeled away. The man in the car looked around, holding his chest. His eyes met mine, they closed, and the world went silent for a moment.

"Better," Otomatsu smiled. "Much better."

"He helped so many kids," I shook my head. "What a shame."

"But what a life to have lived where he took something horrible that happened to him and made the lives of others better."

I looked at the angel, who had her hands up to her heart.

"It wasn't him," she smiled.

"There's still hope," I told her.

"We should probably get going," Otomatsu said.

We said our goodbyes to the guardian angel and carried on with our tasks. A few days later, we came across a woman in her 40s who was standing on the roof of a building, about to jump. It was night time, so I was certain no one from the lit streets below could see her.

"I can take this one if you-" Otomatsu started.

"No," I said. "It's fine. It's my turn anyway. So do I go down there and wait for her or stay up here with her?"

"Is this your first jumper?"

I nodded.

"Stay up here with her for as long as possible. Chances are that she'll die on impact. So be here with her while she still needs someone."

"She doesn't know we're here," I scoffed.

"But she's hoping that we are. Listen."

I approached the woman, who was sobbing, and I stood right beside as she talked.

"Please, God," she cried. "I'm sorry for what I'm about to do. But I'm just so lost without him. He was the only good thing in my life and with him gone, I can't go on anymore. I don't want to be here. I can't live without Rocco. I hope you can forgive me for what I'm about to do."

I looked down at the pavement and knew that if I had still been human, it would have immediately made me dizzy. As the crowds passed, one figure stood completely still. He was looking up at her. My eyes widened in horror.

"*It's him*," I gasped. "Ankou."

I looked back frantically at the woman as she began to recite the Lord's Prayer.

"Through this holy anointing, may the Lord in His love and mercy help you with the grace of the Holy Spirit!" I blurted as she ended her prayer. "May the Lord who frees you from sin save you-!"

She jumped.

"-And raise you."

I heard screams as the woman fell. People rushed over to help her, although she was already dead. A man called for an ambulance while another one tried to shield the woman's body with his coat. Ankou glared at me, his eyes all black and his mouth twisted in a snarl.

"Did that actually work?" Otomatsu asked.

"There's no way of telling unless we check in with Elijah," I shrugged.

"But has it worked before?"

"One other time," I answered. "I usually can't get to them in time to save them."

"Holy shit, Emma," Otomatsu said. "How did you even know to do that?"

"Dumah had some books and scrolls in his hut that I went through one time. There was one book that had a chapter titled, 'Blessing a Suicide.' I figured if I was going to follow Ankou, I could also try and sabotage his job."

"Let's go see Elijah."

I nodded in agreement and we went back to Processing. Elijah was in his usual spot, flipping through pages and jotting things down. He didn't even look up when we approached the desk.

"Hey," I said, urgently.

"Oh!" Elijah started. "Emma, hi."

He glanced at Otomatsu.

"Otomatsu," he added. "What can I do for you both?"

"Did a woman just arrive?" I asked.

"You'll have to be more specific than that," he teased. "I just had 1,023 females arrive."

"She was in Milan, Italy."

Elijah started looking through names.

"She jumped off a building."

Elijah slowly looked up at me.

"I just need you to check for me," I said impatiently.

I watched Elijah look through names and then stop on one. I peered over the side of the desk at where his finger pointed.

"Bianca Rossi," he read. "She should be here by now."

"Thank you!" I exclaimed as Otomatsu and I ran out the door.

The courtyard was busy as usual. People surrounded us, unsure of where to go, looking either confused or blissfully happy. There were so many faces, I couldn't focus.

"Bianca!" I called out. "Bianca Rossi!"

A few people looked in my direction, but none were the woman I saw on the roof.

"Bianca Rossi!" I called again.

And then, our eyes met. The woman who had jumped, Bianca, looked right at me through the moving crowds with an almost bewildered look. We got closer and she started to smile at me.

"It's you," she said softly. "The one who saved me."

I stood there, unable to speak.

"What exactly happened when you died?" Otomatsu asked.

"I woke up in my childhood home," she recalled. "I sat up in my bed, surrounded by my pink comforter and all of my stuffed animals. I could smell food being cooked and could hear a woman's voice. It was my mother's voice, and she was singing. I tiptoed down the hallway in my nightgown and peered into the kitchen. There she was, just as I remembered her. Before I could say anything, she turned around and smiled this huge smile.

'Good morning, my little ray of sunshine!' she said to me. 'Are you hungry? Want some breakfast?'

I crept closer to her and stared, and she started laughing.

'It's okay, sweetheart,' she said. 'It's me. You're not dreaming.'

'If I'm not dreaming, then am I dead?' I asked.

My mom's smile faded and she nodded. My mom passed away from breast cancer when I was a child. I probably should have been a little sadder to be dead, but seeing my mom again, and after all of the sorrow I had felt when I was alive, I was a little relieved. You see, my boyfriend, Rocco, had just died in a car accident. They found an engagement ring and a handwritten note to me in his car. He said how I had been the only thing worth living for and that the only thing he wanted was to spend the rest of his life with me. I had-"

"Listen," I cut her off. "I hate to break it to you, but that was not a human."

"What are you talking about?" Bianca asked.

"That was a demon named Ankou, trying to get you to kill yourself. But I saved you. Well, I saved your soul. You're still dead. But you get to go to Paradise now instead of Hell."

"Emma," Otomatsu muttered.

"I'm sorry," Bianca chuckled. "You're not making any sense. What are you talking about? A demon?"

"He tried doing the same thing to me when I was a human. He tries to get people to commit suicide to get more souls into Hell. But I figured out a way-"

I reached a hand out to her, but she recoiled from me. I put my hand back down at my side.

"-I figured out a way to help," I continued.

"Rocco is here somewhere," Bianca barked. "He died in a car accident a week ago. He was a good person; kind and gentle. He wrote poetry and gave to charities. He was anything but a demon."

"He's a liar."

"*You* are the liar!"

Bianca stuck her finger in my face and raised her voice. People were watching us now.

"Calm down," Otomatsu said.

"Leave me alone!" Bianca snapped. "Get away from me!"

She stormed off towards the hotel and we stood there in shock. I looked at Otomatsu, and he shrugged.

"She'll thank you one day," he smiled.

"At least we know it worked," I sighed.

"That's right," Otomatsu gasped. "This changes everything. We can save suicides."

I should have felt happier, but seeing Ankou and what he had done to Bianca made me angry. We went back inside the hotel after a while. Elijah told me that Bianca would be in Processing for 17,520 hours. Two years. I had saved her from an eternity in Hell. But with that long of a waiting period, who knew what kind of trouble she could potentially get herself into. Would she go looking for Rocco? Would she make the same mistake I had? One thing was for certain. I was not taking that ungrateful woman to Hell to look for her boyfriend.

11

I was in Ontario, Canada with Otomatsu, checking out the Bruce Peninsula National Park. We were visiting Flowerpot Island when Gabe found me. As soon as I saw him, he slowly nodded and had a somber look on his face. I nodded in return. He didn't have to say a thing. I knew.

Otomatsu declined going with us, and told me that he would meet me at "our spot" when I was done. I went with Gabe back to Processing and Elijah told us which room Eduardo was staying in. I wasn't sure what to expect, but I was trying not to get my hopes up. I fidgeted with my cloak the whole way up on the elevator. Gabe was obviously anxious as well because he wasn't his usual, talkative self. The elevator slowed to a stop and the door opened. I froze for a moment.

"Emma?" I heard Gabe say. "You okay?"

"What? Yeah, sorry."

I stepped off the platform and peered down the hallway. The walk to the door felt like it took hours, although it was a mere eighteen seconds. Gabe knocked.

"Come in!" We heard a cheerful voice call from the other side.

Gabe let out a long, deep breath, smiled at me, and then opened the door. We walked in and saw Eduardo shimmying around his room. Music was playing and there were vibrant flowers all over the room, mostly orchids. There was a long table against the wall filled with various foods and drinks. Eduardo turned around and yelled out in excitement as soon as he saw Gabe.

"Ah! Gabriel!" He exclaimed, holding his arms out. "Look at you, *mijo*! You look fantastic!"

Eduardo embraced Gabe and lifted him a few inches off the ground. Gabe let out a boyish laugh and hugged his grandpa back.

"I don't remember the last time I was able to pick you up," Eduardo chuckled. "And I'm able to salsa without my hip giving me trouble! Isn't this wonderful?"

He scurried over to the table of food and grabbed a round piece of bread.

"You want an *arepa*?" Eduardo asked. "Or *ajiaco*? Some *cholado*?"

"No," Gabe smiled. "I'm fine."

"Want some *lulada* to drink?"

"No, it's okay."

"These are all of my favorite foods from Colombia. Oh, and these flowers? Do you know how many times I tried to buy your *abuela* orchids and we never could keep them alive. But look at these! They're absolutely beautiful. But look at you! You're beautiful too!"

Eduardo beamed at Gabe, and then glanced at me.

"Oh! Hello. I'm sorry, I didn't see you there."

I stared, unable to speak. Gabe nudged me with his elbow.

"Uh, um, hi," was all I managed to say. Years of waiting for this moment; it was finally here, and I was locking up.

"This is Emma," Gabe explained. "She's a death angel."

The smile on Eduardo's face began to fade. "Death angel?"

I nodded. *Did that sound familiar to him?*

"You..." he said. I smiled, hopeful that the Dumah part of him recognized me.

"You were there when Gabriel was in the hospital," he pointed at me.

I nodded again and stopped smiling.

"Why are you still following him around?" Eduardo asked, looking at Gabe.

"She's not following me around," Gabe said. "She's a friend of mine."

"Ah," Eduardo grunted. "You hungry, Emma? We have plenty of food."

"We don't eat," I blurted. "You know, us angels, we don't need food."

"*Angels?*" Eduardo repeated. "Gabriel?"

"Yeah," Gabe laughed. "I'm a dark angel. That's why I'm wearing all of this armor."

"Dark angel?"

"I'm kind of like a soldier. Emma's job is to be there for people who die alone or in especially terrible ways. And I-"

"You weren't alone when you died," Eduardo sniffed. "And you died peacefully; not terribly."

"And I help to make sure demons stay in Hell as much as possible," Gabe continued.

"You know, we never learned about death angels and dark angels in church," Eduardo said.

"I know," Gabe replied. "It's going to take some getting used to."

"So you can just leave Heaven whenever you want to?"

Gabe and I exchanged looks.

"What?" Eduardo asked.

"This isn't Heaven, *abuelo*. I'm sure a greeter explained this to you already. This is called Processing. It's the place you go to before you go to Heaven, or Paradise."

"Purgatory?" Eduardo spouted.

"No!" I scoffed. "That's Sentencing. Processing is more like Limbo because you are going to go to Paradise."

"Sentencing?" he implored.

"Do you not remember any of this?" I asked.

Eduardo gave me a puzzled look.

"You know, from before?"

"Emma," Gabe mumbled.

"You were an angel before!" I ignored him. Eduardo looked even more confused now.

"Dumah," I pleaded. "Please. Please, remember."

"I'm sorry," Eduardo said. "I think you have mistaken me for someone else. I've never been an angel before. I've always been, well, me."

"No! I promise, you were this powerful death angel. Look!"

I took out my sword and it started blazing with flames. Eduardo looked bewildered.

"Emma, stop it!" Gabe snapped at me. "He doesn't remember! You're just confusing him."

"*You're* the one who's confusing him! If you weren't here, maybe he would remember more easily!"

"Don't talk to my grandson like that!" Eduardo shouted.

"Oh my god," I scoffed, putting my hand to my forehead in disbelief. "He's not even really your grandson. This life you've lived wasn't even your life. This is crazy. You were an entirely different person before."

Suddenly, there was a knock at the door. The three of us stopped and looked. There was another knock.

"Hello?" a man's voice called out lightly. "Is everything okay in there? You're being a little loud and I was wondering if you could maybe keep it down a little. Thank you!"

Once the footsteps faded and we heard a door gently shut, we all turned to each other again. I sighed.

"How long is your waiting time?" I asked Eduardo. He looked at his wrist.

"About a month, give or take," he answered shortly. "Why?"

I walked up to Eduardo and looked him in the eyes.

"I'll stop by your hut off and on for the next month. Gabe knows where it is. If you would like more answers about who you were, I'll meet you there. I'll wait a month. If I haven't heard from you by then, I'll know you made your decision."

I then turned to Gabe and gave him a stern look.

"If he decides he wants to know more-"

"I will," he sighed. "I'll bring him to you."

I nodded and without saying another word, left. I didn't stop to talk to Elijah on my way out of the hotel. When I was back on my beach, standing in front of my house, I started pacing back and forth on the sand. I could feel something rising inside of me, like a pot about to boil over. I shot up and through the air, flying as hard as I could over the water. I flew until I couldn't hold it in anymore, and I let out a scream. The water around me pushed out suddenly, like a sonic boom, causing huge waves. I saw as a giant wave made its way right at the shore; and the boat. I flew at full speed trying to beat the wave, but I wasn't quick enough. The water hit the boat and sent it rolling into some large rocks on the beach. Splinters flew in all directions.

"No," I whispered. "No, no, no, no!"

Dumah's boat was gone. There was no repairing it this time. Hundreds of pieces, some too small to do anything with, were all over the rocks and sand. Some were even floating away in the sea.

"DAMMIT!" I screamed, kicking the closest chunk of wood into the water.

"Oh no," a voice murmured behind me.

I whipped around and saw Thalia standing there.

"What are you doing here?" I asked sharply.

"Elijah told me about Eduardo and that you left pretty upset," she said. "I wanted to come check on you. I haven't seen you in a while."

"And yet, it feels like I just saw you yesterday."

"I heard you've been hanging out with Otomatsu."

"Oh my god, Thalia," I scoffed. "Are you going to lecture me about that too? Because Elijah-"

"Not at all," she replied calmly. "I actually like him. And he seems like the type you'd like too. He kind of reminds me of Dumah."

"He's nothing like Dumah."

"I'm just saying, Otomatsu is a really good choice since you lost Dumah."

"Are you saying I'm trying to replace Dumah with Otomatsu?" I asked, picking up pieces of wood along the shore.

"No, that's not what I'm saying at all."

"Then what the fuck are you trying to say, Thalia? Because as far as I can tell, you're running your mouth just for the sake of making noise, like always."

When she didn't respond, I looked at Thalia. Tears were welling up in her eyes. I let out a long sigh.

"Thalia, I'm sorry."

"I know you're hurting right now," she said. "I know you're only being mean so you won't feel as hurt. I know you don't see me as a friend like I see you as one, and that's okay. You only want to push me away because you have trust issues. You also don't want anymore losses after Sam and Dumah. I was happy to hear that you were becoming such good friends with Otomatsu because I thought maybe that meant you were letting some of those walls down. No one can change what happened to you. And no one can change how you feel from it. But I hope one day you can do that for yourself. And for your sake, I hope that day is soon."

When I dropped the pieces into a pile and turned to grab more wood, Thalia shook her head at me.

"Goodbye, Emma."

The pieces of wood I had been holding fell out of my arms and dropped to my knees. I put my face in my hands and began to cry. All I wanted was to fix the things I had broken.

As the sun began to set, I used my flaming sword to set the pile of the broken boat on fire. I sat on the beach, watching the flames dance over the wood. Once nighttime finally set, I stood up and walked down to the water. I waded in, about to my thighs, and let the gentle water move around me. I wondered if Sam felt lonely out in the pitch black waters. I wondered if she felt anything, or if she was just a mindless creature, floating in nothingness.

"Sam?" I called out weakly.

I heard a small splash in the darkness and turned, drawing my sword. In the blade's flame, a grotesque, rotting face suddenly backed away from the light. Several other faces I could barely make out in the water retreated under the glassy surface. I carefully made my way back onto the shore and sat back down next to the fire.

In the early morning light, the fire was dying. The pieces of wood were mostly ash now. A small plume of smoke rose from the blackened chunks. I threw sand on it, putting the fire completely out.

"Did you stay out here all night?" I heard Gabe say from behind me.

I turned and saw him and Eduardo walking up. I stood up and brushed some of the sand off my cloak.

"I went through the trouble of building you a house and you spent the night on the beach?" he smiled weakly.

"It was more roomy out here," I joked before looking at Eduardo.

"We talked for a bit," Gabe said. "I explained everything to my grandpa. I told him how important all of this is to you."

Eduardo glanced at Gabe.

"And how important you are to me," Gabe continued. "So he's agreed to give you the chance to show him."

Gabe gestured towards Dumah's hut.

"I'll wait for you guys next door," he added. "Take your time."

I nodded and led Eduardo up to the door. Gabe watched us as he went to my house. He gave a reassuring smile before going inside. I opened the door and we went in. At first, I let Eduardo walk around. Neither of us said anything as he put his hands behind his back. He reminded me of a teacher, pacing a classroom. He looked at items, but seemed too timid (or uninterested) in picking any of them up. I tried with all my might not to say anything or do anything. I just watched him from the doorway. Finally, he saw something on the floor that was out of my view, bent down slowly, and picked it up. When he stood back up, he held it out to me. It was a black feather. I got closer to him to look at it, but when I did, he put it next to my wings. While the feather he held was black like mine, the one in his hand had almost a bluish sheen to it. Mine were jet black. Eduardo gently sat the feather on the table closest to him and leaned on it with both hands. He stood there a moment before running his hand along a dent in the table and chuckling to himself. Then, he started moving a stack of papers around and looking at them. He looked back at me.

"I..." he breathed. "I think I....remember these."

I glanced at the papers. They were maps.

"Did I know someone named Barry?" Eduardo asked. I gasped and fell into the nearest chair.

Eduardo rubbed his head and furrowed his brows.

"Dumah?" I finally said.

Eduardo looked at me, a little sadly.

"It's so strange because I remember everything about my life," he murmured, "but when I see this place, I get little flashes of something else."

If I still had a working heart, it would have been beating out of my chest. This was working. I was going to get Dumah back. He would just look a little different.

"Do you mind if I have a moment here alone?" Eduardo asked.

"Oh," I stood up quickly. "Yeah, that's totally fine. I'll, uh, just be next door with Gabe. You, um, yeah. I'll be there."

I hurried out the door, closing it behind me and made my way next door. I practically skipped through the door and Gabe looked up at me from the couch.

"I think this is the happiest I've ever seen you," Gabe smirked. "A smile looks good on you."

"He remembers!" I exclaimed as I sat next to Gabe. "He brought up Baraqiel."

I suddenly wrapped my arms around Gabe and squeezed. He let out a noise of surprise and hugged me back.

"I'm happy for you, Emma."

"I don't know how to thank you," I said, pulling back and looking at him. "This is just the first step. He'll regain his memory, help me free Sam, I can finally kill Ankou, and then I can go back to Earth and get my second chance at life."

Gabe's smile faded.

"And Dumah can go back to being a death angel!"

"Emma," Gabe said. I stopped and looked at him.

"Please, listen to me," he pleaded. "My grandpa and I had a talk before he agreed to come here."

"Okay, and?"

"The only reason he agreed to come here is because he's already made his decision."

"What do you mean?"

"He's not going to become a death angel. Or go back to Earth. He's going to Paradise."

"I don't understand," I laughed.

"He's going to Paradise, Emma," Gabe repeated.

"And I'm sure now that everything is coming back to him, he'll change his mind."

"I don't think so."

"You didn't see him just now, Gabe!" I snapped.

"I'm just saying, don't get your hopes up."

"I don't get you," I scoffed. "You keep saying how you do all of these things for me to make me happy and to help me, but then you come at me with this bullshit."

"I just want you to understand the truth. I know this is your last effort to try to convince him, but the only reason he finally said okay to the idea is to get into Paradise. And sooner than later."

"What do you mean?" I asked.

"He asked if there was anything I could do to get his time sped up. That was part of the deal."

"What? That's not allowed, *is it*?"

"Didn't your guardian angel do the same thing?"

"That was different!"

"I'm just saying-"

"Quit *just saying*!" I yelled. "I think you should start preparing yourself for the possibility he wants to go back to being a death angel. And I think that freaks you out because even though he looks like your grandpa, he was someone else before that."

Gabe started to say something and then stopped himself. I leaned back on the couch and folded my arms. I stared at the floor, noticing bits of sand that had trailed in from our shoes. Even after death, messes are still made. We sat in silence for a few minutes before Gabe spoke.

"I know I'm not Dumah or a reincarnation of Dumah. But like you said, a part of Dumah could be in me. I'm his grandson. I became an angel, and partially for you."

"Why for me?" I asked. "Who am I to you?"

"Obviously someone very important; and to my entire family, not just me. You watched over my grandparents, my parents, my sister, and me. I know you're not a guardian angel, but you still acted like one for us. You stayed close to make sure no demons influenced or tempted us. Now that I'm here, I realize how important that is. My whole family is safe- *is saved*- because of you. You protected our souls. That makes you the most important person to me, in my opinion."

I looked at Gabe. He was staring at me a little too intensely, so I looked back at the floor.

"I'm aware that this might change my *abuelo's* mind. But do me a favor. Have the same mentality. If you expect the worst and hope for the best, you can't be disappointed."

I rolled my eyes and Gabe laughed at me.

"Were you this much of a pain in the ass when you were alive?" he asked.

"Excuse me?"

"It's too bad we didn't know each other when we were both alive."

"I would have been old enough to be your grandma," I smirked. Gabe laughed again at that.

"What you must have been like as a young woman," he shook his head.

"I definitely didn't look like this," I said, raising my wings slightly.

"I know," Gabe said, pointing to some of the pictures around the room. "I think you're still pretty though."

It was my turn to laugh.

"Please!" I said, standing up. "I will say though, I don't miss feeling sick all the time."

"I'm sorry you suffered so long."

"Yeah, you're lucky you died pretty quickly."

"Yeah."

I looked at Gabe. He hung his head slightly and had a somber look on his face. *Shit*, I thought. I grabbed his hand and tugged on it. He looked up at me. I pulled again and he slowly got to his feet. I raised his chin with my index finger and thumb. His eyes met mine and I smiled at him.

"Sorry," I said softly. "I just mean, it seems better to get it done and over with quickly than what I had to go through. Neither of us are really lucky. We both died too young. I wish I could have known you as a human too. You're a good guy. You're going to make a great angel. We're lucky to have you. *I'm* lucky to have you."

Suddenly, Gabe closed his eyes and leaned in towards me. His lips touched mine and I felt a sudden shockwave through my body. I pressed my lips into his before I realized what I was doing. I let go of his chin and moved back quickly.

"I'm sorry-"

"Sorry!"

We both paused and then laughed. Gabe shifted uncomfortably on the couch and started fiddling with his fingers while I paced around the living room. *What was that?* I thought. *I can't believe he just kissed me. And I kissed him back.*

"So...." Gabe started. "Now that I've made things awkward..."

"No," I giggled politely. "You're fine. Like, really fine. Well, I mean, it's okay."

"I had no idea I could still feel so embarrassed after death," he chuckled. "Let's change the subject."

"Please do."

"So, um, is there anyone still alive from when you were alive?"

This question caught me off guard. It was something I thought about often but tried not to.

"Yeah," I said. "My best friend, Maddi, is still alive. She lives in Washington D.C."

"Wow, really? How old is she?"

"She's 95," I answered. "Her health has actually started declining pretty rapidly."

"Have you visited her since you died?"

"Oh yeah, plenty of times. I haven't been recently though. It's getting harder and harder to see her the older she gets."

Gabe suddenly took my hand and held it tightly.

"You know, you don't have to do the hard things alone," he said. I held my breath as I looked at him. "I mean it, Emma. Don't feel like you have to be strong all the time. I'll be there for the times when you can't be. If you let me."

There was a knock on the door and Edurado walked in. We stood up and when I realized we were still holding hands, I dropped Gabe's.

"Hi," Eduardo said uncomfortably, walking towards us. "I think I've seen all there is to see."

"Are you okay?" Gabe asked.

"Yes, I'm fine," Eduardo smiled, patting Gabe on the shoulder. He looked at me.

"I can't remember everything," Eduardo said.

"That's okay," I said. "I'm sure everything will eventually come back."

Eduardo put his hand up gently to hush me.

"What I was going to say was, I can't remember everything. But I do remember you."

Eduardo handed me a folded up piece of paper. I took it and started to unfold it. He placed his hand on mine.

"Not right now," he smiled again. "Wait until after I'm gone."

"Gone?" I asked. "Where are you going?"

"I'm going to finally go rest," he sighed. "I think after two lifetimes and thousands of years of work, I deserve it."

"You haven't changed your mind?" I asked.

"No, and I know you must be disappointed to hear that. But I think I'm done. I've lived a short, sad life and I've lived a long, very happy life. I feel fulfilled."

He looked at Gabe.

"And I am so proud of you for making the decision you have made. You have an opportunity to do something great."

Gabe smiled at him and Eduardo turned back to me.

"You both do. And I'm proud of both of you."

I felt my cheeks get hot.

"Emma, I know you think I blame you for what happened to me. I don't. None of it was your fault."

"I'm still really sorry," I teared up. "I never wanted anyone to die for me. That was the whole point of everything. I didn't want to be the reason for anyone getting hurt."

"I've already forgiven you," he said, placing a hand on my cheek. "Now all that's left is for you to forgive yourself."

"I'll kill him," I said. "I'll kill Ankou."

"Will that change what happened?" Eduardo asked.

"No, but he deserves justice!"

"He's a demon," Eduardo said. "Don't you think that's enough punishment? He'll never know what Paradise is like."

Eduardo removed his hand from my cheek.

"As for me? I'm about to start an eternity of blissful happiness."

"Doesn't it bother you to know it won't really be real though?" I asked. "Like, if you want Gabe there, he won't really be there. It'll all just be an illusion."

"I won't know any better though," Eduardo shrugged. "If the illusion becomes reality, it's no longer an illusion, right?"

I didn't respond.

"I'll be fine," he added. "And so will you."

"I'm happy for you," I found myself saying. "Dumah would have never been able to go to Paradise. But you can for the both of you."

Eduardo gave me his biggest smile yet.

"Well, *mijo*," he said, slapping Gabe on his shoulder. "We should head out. There are still a few things I want to do before it's time to move on."

"Are you going to be okay?" Gabe asked me. I nodded.

"Emma," Eduardo said. "Thanks for everything."

"Uh, yeah," I replied coyly.

"Take care."

As they both walked out the door, I fought the urge to beg Eduardo to reconsider. But I knew it was pointless. I slumped down onto the couch and curled up, tucking my knees up to my chest. I closed my eyes and didn't open them until the next day. I didn't sleep, obviously. But I laid there with my eyes closed, using the waves outside as white noise. I thought about my short, but very impactful time with Dumah. I thought about meeting Matt Kinsley, lead singer of my favorite band, when I first died. I thought about how happy I was with Alastor before I knew what he really was. I thought about my mom, my dad, and Simon, who had all chosen to go to Paradise. I thought about Whitney and Maddi.

When I finally opened my eyes, I looked around the room and my eyes landed on a photo of me with Whitney and Maddi. I got up off the couch and walked over to the picture. I picked it up and traced Maddi's hair with my fingertip.

"I need you," I whispered. "You're all I have left."

I looked down at the tracker on my wrist. The world map on it lit up with thousands of tiny dots. People who were dying. People who needed me. There was only one person out there who I cared about. But she didn't need me. Not yet, at least. However, I needed her desperately.

I walked out of the house and made my way to Washington D.C.

12

Right before I died, Whitney moved in with Maddi and her then-girlfriend, Colbie. Shortly after moving in, Whitney found out that she was pregnant. She had just broken up with her boyfriend, Sam, after she found out he had been cheating on her. Not being able to provide for a baby at the time, Whitney wanted to get an abortion. Maddi and Colbi drove her out of state to get one. As Whitney sat in the backseat, thinking about her life and the choices she had made, she ultimately decided to keep the baby. The drive ended up being a last-minute "girls trip" in my honor. All three of them thought the trip would bring them closer than ever. At one point, Maddi even said, "It'll be the three of us forever."

She gently rubbed Whitney's stomach.

"Well, the *four* of us soon."

Whitney decided to become a server at a high-end restaurant while she looked for a more steady job. However, she quickly found out that companies don't hire pregnant women, and pregnant servers make really good tips. A man nine years older than Whitney, named Charlie, was a regular at the restaurant. He frequently went for business lunches with colleagues and clients. After the first time Whitney served him, he requested her area every time. Charlie, a software developer, wasn't Whitney's usual type. He was wealthy, successful, smart, and not very attractive. But that didn't stop her from dating him throughout her pregnancy.

    Maddi and Colbie threw Whitney a baby shower at the restaurant, with the help of her coworkers and Charlie. The three girls spent hours trying to put together a crib that was crammed into the corner of Whitney's room. She swore that she could tell the baby was a girl. She decided to name the baby, Emma Rose. She didn't even have a boy name in mind. But after nine months of a healthy pregnancy, Emmett Ross (the closest to my name Whitney could come with) was born weighing ten pounds and had a head full of dark hair. Charlie was the only person Whitney wanted in the delivery room with her. After the nurses got Emmett and Whitney cleaned up, Charlie told her that he had brought gifts for her and the baby. He pulled out a brown, floppy, plush puppy for Emmett. Then, he held out a small, white box. When Whitney opened it to reveal the ring inside, she gasped. Before Charlie's knee settled on the hospital floor, she squealed, "yes!"

    Six months later, Whitney and Charlie were married. They would have done it sooner, but Whitney wanted to make sure she lost all of her pregnancy weight. Her parents chipped in as much as they could, but Charlie insisted on covering most of the costs; so Whitney became an instant "bridezilla." Maddi was her maid of honor and there were several heated discussions leading up to the wedding. Neither of them realized it was the beginning of the end. Whitney and baby Emmett moved out of the apartment, which allowed Maddi and Colbie to have the whole place to themselves. But without a third person chipping in for rent, finances became a constant stress.

    Maddi was always great at money management and had built herself a nice little savings. When Colbie found out about the extra money, she asked Maddi to chip in more since she made more. Maddi didn't think it was fair to put more of her money towards bills when they initially agreed to go in half and half. Eventually, the topic ended their relationship. Maddi was completely torn up about the break up, which made it hard for her to be at Whitney's beck and call for all of her bridal needs. When Maddi didn't seem as enthusiastic about wedding details as Whitney wanted, they fought. In Maddi's opinion, Whitney was acting like a diva. In Whitney's opinion, Maddi was just being bitter and jealous.

    By the time the wedding day came, Maddi had a new roommate (a friend from school who was also going for an art degree) and was thinking about moving out of state. Whitney was embracing her new life of luxury, no longer having to work, and spent most days shopping or gossiping with other moms during play dates. Nothing really happened to officially end their friendship. One day, they were friends who knew everything about each other. Next, they were strangers with nothing in common. Their friendship became likes on social media and a yearly, "Happy birthday!"

Whitney was married to Charlie for six years. They had two kids together; another boy and a girl. Whitney's second son was named Grayson and her daughter was named Violet. Whitney was barely recognizable when the divorce was finalized. She had gotten a boob job, a tummy tuck, a nose job, lip fillers, and Botox. She was also part of the trend of taking prescribed medication to lose weight, even though she was already fairly thin. Along with the cosmetic surgery, she also earned the house, one of their three cars, and a nice chunk of change monthly from Charlie. She was constantly told that she looked younger than she was and as her children got older, they hated hearing that. Men asked if she was their older sister and then were shocked when she revealed she was their mom.

After years of dating, Whitney remarried. Money once again played a big role in her new husband, Marco, although he was much more handsome than Charlie; and Marco knew it too. Marco was in real estate and made most of his money on the properties he rented out to tenants. He took Whitney on lavish vacations, and although reluctant, he took the kids with them too occasionally. He bought Whitney expensive clothes, shoes, purses, and pretty much anything else she pointed a finger at. He did whatever he could to make up for his drinking. Marco was an alcoholic, and a mean one at that. Whitney began to drink a lot more than usual and also started smoking. She became a pro at covering her bruises with makeup and coming up with excuses for Marco's behavior. One night, however, Emmett got between his mom and step dad, trying to protect her. Marco beat Emmett up, leaving him with a black eye and cut lip. But Emmett did some damage as well, knocking a couple of Marco's teeth out. Scared, Grayson called 911. When the police showed up, Marco was put in handcuffs, despite Whitney's crying and pleading.

"It was my fault!" she sobbed. "I was running my stupid mouth and pissed him off. Emmett shouldn't have gotten involved! He's just a teenage boy with hormones! Please don't arrest him!"

After that, Emmett made the decision to live with his dad, Sam, and his stepmom and stepsister. His relationship with Whitney was never the same. Grayson and Violet begged Whitney to leave Marco while he spent a couple of days in jail. Whitney refused to leave him, but when Marco came home from jail, he packed his bags and left. Whitney was devastated. Needing a new start, Whitney moved to Florida with Violet and Grayson. She took a trip back to Missouri at Christmas to see her parents and Emmett. Meanwhile, Violet and Grayson stayed with Charlie. After that Christmas, Whitney wouldn't see Emmett again until he was an adult.

Florida suited Whitney and her nonstop lifestyle. Violet and Grayson became the popular kids at school who hosted multiple house parties. Whitney was present for all of them, saying, "I'd rather you kids drink in the safety of our home under adult supervision," but really it was so she could be a part of the fun. When Grayson was a senior and Violet was a junior, they confronted Whitney about how embarrassing she was. Neither of them went to college, which devastated Charlie. Grayson went into construction, making a good living. Violet became a social media influencer. Whitney was proud of her. She even had her own impressive following online. Whitney and Violet had men send them money and gifts in exchange for "special photos."

Once, when Violet was out clubbing with her friends, she was mugged while trying to find a ride home. The man cut her face with a knife and stole her purse. She needed stitches that went from her forehead to her cheek. After that happened, Violet's recovery journey made her briefly more famous online, but once her followers saw how her face would permanently look, her days as an influencer were over. Violet became depressed and unfortunately, Whitney was not as comforting as she should have been. Violet moved back to Missouri to live with her dad. Charlie taught her about software design and Violet decided to go back to school. She earned a degree and started working with her dad. She spent her summers with Whitney in Florida, although while Whitney was trying to hit on as many men as possible, Violet enjoyed reading on the beach most days.

    Whitney's third marriage was to a man named Henry. He had a decent job that he enjoyed but barely made a living wage. He was handsome, but in an average way. He was level-headed, which paired well with Whitney's quirkiness. Henry didn't smoke or drink, and was usually in bed by 10:00. Because of Henry, Whitney quit smoking and drinking (other than an occasional glass of red wine.) Also, Whitney was madly in love with him. He was good to her, and he made her see what she was needing her whole life. Henry always made Whitney laugh, and even taught her how to cook. Whitney was never good at cooking, but Henry made it fun. Henry helped mend Whitney's relationships with all three of her children, and convinced her to start going to therapy.

    Henry died of a heart attack when he and Whitney were in their early seventies. Whitney never married again. She spent her remaining years alone, living in an assisted living center and calling her kids and grandkids as often as possible. Whitney died of an aneurysm in her sleep when she was 78. She was always scared of getting old, but in her final years, she was scared of dying too young. Most of Whitney's life was sad and full of heartbreak. But I am happy that she died peacefully in her sleep, and with most of her relationships mended. When she died, Emmett sent Maddi an email about the funeral details. Maddi appreciated the invitation, but after years of not talking to Whitney, didn't feel comfortable attending. She did, however, send a beautiful bouquet of flowers and a sympathy card to the kids.

A week after Whitney and Charlie's wedding, while they were still on their honeymoon, Maddi was planning her next steps in life. She transferred to Georgetown University in Washington D.C. where she majored in art with a minor in art history. While at Georgetown, she met Cecilia, who was also going for art history. Cecilia was originally from New Orleans and came from a Creole family of musicians and artists. Maddi was in complete awe of Cecilia from the beginning, but the feeling wasn't mutual at first. Cecilia, or as her friends and family called her, "Cece," was two years ahead of Maddi and was the unofficial leader of her group of friends. If Cece said something or someone was cool, everyone also thought it was cool.

When a mutual friend of Maddi's and Cece introduced Maddi to the group, all she got was a slight nod from Cece before she continued telling a story. It wasn't until Thanksgiving when Maddi had her first full conversation with Cece. Everyone was leaving school for the holiday, but Maddi decided to stay behind. With her grandma and me dead, Maddi didn't have a family to spend Thanksgiving with. The lounge room was buzzing with people saying goodbyes and wheeling luggage out. Maddi was reading a book in a chair, sitting with her legs dangling over the arm, when Cece's thigh bumped into her sneaker.

"Oh!" Cece exclaimed. "I'm sorry!"

"No, that was my fault," Maddi replied, sitting up and crossing her legs. "I shouldn't have had my legs out like that."

"It's fine," Cece smiled. "You're Maddi, right?"

"Yeah," Maddi said shyly.

"You excited to be going home for Thanksgiving?"

"Oh," Maddi said, brushing her bangs off her forehead, "I, uh, I'm staying here with the queen of dragons."

"Huh?"

Maddi waved her book and chuckled.

"Oh," Cece giggled.

"My family isn't-" Maddi started. "I don't have anyone to visit."

"You're not really staying on campus for a holiday, are you?"

"I mean, I was going to take the opportunity to get familiar with the city. I figured it'd be less busy with everyone gone."

Cece stood there, looking at Maddi for a moment.

"What?" Maddi asked.

"Hold on," Cece said, starting to walk away. "I'll be right back. I need to make a phone call."

Maddi nodded and watched Cece walk out of the room, holding her breath. She let out a long sigh once Cece was out of view and hurried over to the long mirror hung on the wall. Wishing she had put even the slightest effort into her appearance, she ran her fingers through her hair and parted her bangs to the side they were supposed to be on. A piece fell back straight onto her forehead and Maddi grunted, pushing the strands back over. She rushed back over to the chair and pretended to read.

"Okay," Cece sighed, coming back in. "Hurry up and go pack. I changed my flight to a cheaper ticket so I could get one for you too. But the flight starts boarding in two hours so you need to move your ass."

"What?" Maddi asked, whipping around.

"You're coming with me to New Orleans and you're going to have Thanksgiving with my family."

"No, no, Cece. I can't impose on you like that."

"You're not imposing. I invited you. And your plane ticket is already bought so I'm not giving you the option to say no."

Cece walked up to Maddi, smiled, and brushed the rouge hairs off her forehead.

"No one deserves to be alone during the holidays. My family is super welcoming so don't worry."

After a little more convincing, Maddi agreed to go. From the moment the two of them got into the taxi to go to the airport, they talked and laughed nonstop. Cece was right about her family. They welcomed Maddi with open arms. She met Cece's parents, her grandparents, her great-grandma, her older brother, her older sister, three uncles, two aunts, and her nine cousins. Maddi was used to her house being small and quiet, just her parents and herself. This was something else entirely. The roaring laughter, playful banter, and singing made Maddi almost dizzy. Cece led Maddi away from her loud family and down the hallway to a bedroom.

"This is where we'll be," she said, opening the door. "Please do not judge anything you see in my room."

Noticing the full size bed, Maddi's heart began to race. The two of them brought their luggage into the room and Maddi quickly grabbed one of the pillows and dropped it on the floor. As she reached for one of the blankets, Cece put her hand on it.

"What are you doing?"

"Making my bed," Maddi said coyly. "That way it's ready when we go to bed."

Cece laughed and picked the pillow up.

"It's a full-sized bed and we're both tiny enough to fit," she said, tossing the pillow back on the bed. "I'm not making you sleep on the cold floor."

Throughout dinner that night, all of the women went over the game plan for the next day. Cece's mom told Maddi that she would be put to work in the kitchen and asked if she cooked at all. When Maddi joked that she was a pro at microwavable meals, the whole table laughed.

"Tomorrow, you're going to get a real good lesson on cookin'!" Cece's grandma chuckled. "You're part of the family now and women in this family cook!"

"Yes, ma'am, they do!" Cece's grandpa slapped his belly.

"The men ain't too bad at it either!" Cece's dad pointed a finger.

"And who taught you how to cook?" her grandma retorted.

"Who taught *you* how to cook?" Cece's great-grandma chimed in. "Don't no one in this house know how to do nothin' if it weren't for me!"

"Maddi, you got a boyfriend?" Cece's aunt asked, changing the subject.

"No," Maddi blushed. "No boyfriend."

"What's the point of college if you're not looking for one of those smart D.C. guys?" Cece's dad asked. "I keep trying to tell Cece that she focuses on art and her little group of friends too much. I would like to be a pop pop before I get too old to enjoy some grandbabies running around."

"Oh my god, Dad," Cece sighed. "Please stop."

After dinner, everyone formed an assembly line in the kitchen to help make cleaning up easier. Maddi rushed to the bathroom afterwards to brush her teeth and change into her pajamas. She decided to leave her bra on under her shirt for modesty, which Cece pointed out immediately.

"You sleep in a bra?" she asked.

"Yeah," Maddi lied. "I grew up in a really religious family so I was always taught to be modest."

"I was taught comfort over modesty," Cece laughed, reaching her hand up under her shirt. She wiggled and squirmed her way out of her bra and threw it into the corner of the room. As soon as Maddi saw Cece's nipples under her shirt, her face got hot. She looked every way but at Cece until the lights went out. Maddi took the side of the bed that was against the wall. She tried to press her body as close to the wall as possible, smashing her nose against it.

"I don't need that much room," Cece said. "Also, fair warning, my parents keep the house cold so don't be surprised if I cuddle. I'm a cuddler."

Maddi suddenly turned over.

"Listen, Cece, I need to tell you something," Maddi said quietly. "And this probably isn't the best time but I just want to be open and honest with you."

"Okay," Cece said, sounding concerned.

"I, uh, like girls," Maddi admitted.

"I know that," Cece smiled.

"You do?" Maddi asked. "Is it obvious? I didn't think I gave off lesbian vibes."

"We have the same friends. I've asked about you, and I've found some things out."

"You've asked about me? I didn't know you even knew I existed."

"Are you kidding me?" Cece scoffed. "Of course I know you exist. You're pretty hard to miss."

"Is your family cool about it? I didn't know what to say when your aunt asked about having a boyfriend."

"Maddi, they're completely cool with it. They're fully supportive of me. And my cousin, Reece."

Maddi gave her a puzzled look.

"Reece is trans," Cece grinned. "Oh my god, you didn't notice! She would absolutely love to hear that! She was so scared when she transitioned because she thought she would look too much like a guy still."

"I had no idea! But honestly, I don't really look too much into that sort of stuff. I just noticed her amazing fingernails."

"She did them herself," Cece said. "Reece is a nail technician. She-"

"Cece," Maddi interrupted.

"Yeah?"

"Did you say your parents are supportive of you too?"

"Yeah."

"Didn't your dad mention you finding a 'smart D.C. guy' at dinner?"

"I've dated both."

Maddi didn't say anything.

"As in guys and girls."

Maddi still didn't say anything.

"Does that surprise you?" Cece asked.

"I guess not," Maddi said.

Cece scooted a couple of inches closer to Maddi.

"I have noticed you, by the way," she continued. "I've just tried really hard not to make it obvious."

"What do you mean?" Maddi asked.

"Well, every time I would glance in your direction, you'd immediately look away. I didn't think you were a fan."

"Are you kidding me? I'm a fan. Huge fan."

Cece smiled.

"I just mean-"

Cece put her index finger up to Maddi's lips and quieted her. As her touch lingered on Maddi's lips, she reached up and lightly ran her hand from Cece's shoulder, down to her elbow. Cece slowly moved from Maddi's mouth to her hair. Then, she leaned in and kissed her. Cece's grip on Maddi's hair tightened as they pressed their bodies against each other.

"I have to admit something else," Maddi giggled as they finally pulled away. "I don't usually sleep in a bra. I made that up."

"I didn't make up the part about being a cuddler," Cece said, putting her arm around Maddi's waist.

The rest of the weekend was spent either with Cece's family or the two of them going out, showing Maddi all the best things about New Orleans. When they went back to school, they didn't tell their friends about what had happened at first. Instead, Maddi and Cece began dating, taking their time to get to know each other, and then acting casual around their group of friends. When they decided to become exclusive with each other, they told everyone. And everyone was both happy and not at all surprised. All of their mutual friends had picked up on the vibes and knew they had crushes on each other. Maddi and Cece laughed every time someone reacted with, "it's about time!"

Cece graduated from Georgetown and started her internship at the National Museum of Women in the Arts while Maddi continued going to school. The night Maddi graduated, Cece proposed. Maddi laughed hysterically before revealing that she was planning on proposing to Cece and had a ring for her also. Despite calling D.C. their home, they decided to get married in New Orleans, surrounded by Cece's family. There was a table left empty other than a group of framed pictures and candles. There was a photo of Cece's other grandparents, one of her great-grandma, one of Maddi's father (he had died from alcoholism), and one of me. It was the same picture my parent's used for my funeral. Maddi had invited my family to the wedding, but they were unable to afford the trip. They did send a congratulatory card with a check inside.

Maddi and Cece were both hired full time at the museum; Cece as an archivist and Maddi as a curator. They didn't work directly with each other, but passed each other throughout the day and had lunch together every single afternoon. After being married for four years, Maddi and Cece made a surprise visit to New Orlean; Cece's parents were thrilled to have them over for the weekend. In fact, they were so excited, they didn't even notice that Maddi said no to a glass of wine at dinner time the first night. After some bread pudding for dessert, Cece excused herself a moment while Maddi continued to talk about the vacation the two of them had taken to Maine three weeks prior to the visit. When Cece came back, she was carrying two gift bags. She handed one to her mom and the other to her dad.

"On the count of three, I want you guys to pull your gifts out at the same time," Cece smiled before grabbing Maddi's hand.

Her parents both pulled out white baby onesies that read, "The best things come in twos!"

Confused, Cece's parents looked at them. Maddi rubbed her belly.

"We're having twins!" Cece cried.

Her mom and dad jumped up and yelled in excitement. Cece's mom jumped up and down, thanking God, while her dad ran over and hugged the two of them tightly.

"I'm going to be a pop pop?" he asked, tears welling up.

"You're going to be a pop pop," Maddi reassured.

Arlo and Alexandria (Alex, she would later go by) were conceived via sperm donor. Cece insisted on having the donor be the same race as she so their babies would be biracial. They were born prematurely and spent a month in the NICU. It was a scary month for Maddi and Cece, but it was especially hard on Cece. Maddi went to the hospital every day of her maternity leave to be with the girls, but Cece had to go back to work immediately. Since she wasn't the father, there was no paternity leave allowed. And she hadn't been the one to give birth to the twins, so she wasn't able to have maternity leave either. Every day after work, Cece would rush to see her wife and babies, taking Maddi dinner. After four very long weeks, the twins were able to go home.

    Maddi and Cece were amazing moms to the twins. Growing up in Washington D.C. they were able to get so many firsthand experiences on government and social issues. Once the twins were old enough, they all went to protests and marches together as a family. They visited Cece's parents as often as possible so the twins could also get a good helping of their New Orleans roots. Maddi reached out to her mom a few times, letting her know about the twins, but there were never any responses. Eventually, Maddi stopped trying and accepted the fact that her mother was no longer a part of her life. But Cece's family more than made up for it. So many aunts, uncles, and cousins loved her and the twins, that there was no feeling of loss anymore.

    Maddi lived a long, adventurous life. She was able to travel a lot, both within and outside of the country. Maddi always seemed her happiest in European countries, appreciating art from other moments in time. She was never a huge fan of beaches or mountains. But in cities, bustling with movement and excitement, she was in her element. Even as they began to age, Maddi and Cece were always on the go. After they both retired, the two of them filled their days with hobbies and classes. Until one day when Maddi was driving home, and suddenly found herself lost.

 She was gone for six hours and was scared out of her mind. When Cece finally called the police, they connected Maddi's car to one that was pulled off at a burger place in Philadelphia. Maddi had forgotten to charge her cellphone so she neither had access to a map or any contacts. When she pulled over to the diner, she asked to use their phone to call her wife. But when the waitress behind the counter handed her a phone, Maddi couldn't remember Cece's number. Frantic, Maddi started crying. The servers gave her some hot coffee and a piece of pie while they called the authorities. The police in Philadelphia didn't have any missing persons reports with Maddi's description, so they began to call other counties. Arlo and his wife made the drive to get Maddi and the car. Maddi apologized over and over to her son and didn't understand how she had gotten so confused.

A few doctor appointments later confirmed what everyone was worried about. Maddi was diagnosed with dementia at age 80. Refusing to put her in a nursing home, Cece promised to care for her until she no longer could. When Cece passed away, Maddi wasn't fully aware of what happened; only that her wife had left and she didn't know when she'd be back. Arlo and Alex made the difficult decision to put Maddie in a home, both unable to take care of her. They visited Maddi as often as possible, but between their jobs and having families of their own, sometimes weeks would go by without anyone visiting her. Not that she really noticed.

    I stood in the doorway of Maddi's room, looking in. It was dark except for a small bedside lamp and the glow from the television. Maddi was sleeping in a recliner, her head tilted back and her feet propped up. I made my way through the room, looking at all of the pictures everywhere. There had to be about fifty either on the walls or on shelves. A larger one of her and Cece from their wedding was on the nightstand by the lamp. They both had beautiful dresses for their wedding; Maddi's was a more form-fitting, mermaid cut, while Cece's was full at the bottom, like a princess ball gown. They were both smiling lovingly at each other, like they were the only two people in the world.

I looked at places Maddi had traveled to, marathons she had run, protests she had participated in, and all of the most important people in her life. One picture caught my eye. It was the same photo of Maddi, Whitney, and me from the senior foam party that I had back at my house. Either it was a crazy coincidence, or Gabe put in a great deal of effort. I went over to Maddi and knelt beside her. I watched her chest rise and fall as she breathed slowly. Although she was a 95-year-old woman, she somehow looked child-like in her sleep.

"I know you can't hear me, but you were always my person I could come talk to about anything. I know you visited me in the hospital, but they had me so drugged up I wasn't aware of it. So the last memory I have of you was our huge fight in your car. I shouldn't have acted that way towards you or Colbie. And I can sit here and say it was because I wasn't feeling well. I mean, I *was* dying. But that doesn't excuse a shitty attitude. I do know a part of it was Alast- I mean, Ankou. I was dating a demon who was trying to get my soul, for crying out loud."

I laughed to myself and then shook my head.

"I don't know what to do anymore," I said. "I feel like no matter what I do, it's the wrong thing. I really thought Paradise wasn't the answer for me. And going back to Earth as a new human

"Can you see me?" I asked.

"Not talking, huh?" Maddi snorted. "That's okay. You and I got into a pretty bad fight right before you got really sick. We'd never gotten into a fight like that before. I'm sorry. I wish I could have told you sorry sooner."

"I'm sorry too," I said softly. Maddi didn't react to the sound of my voice. Instead, she closed her eyes again and sighed. A nurse came in with a cup of water and some pills.

"Time for your medicine, Miss Maddi!" she said cheerfully.

"I'm tired, Emma," Maddi mumbled.

"My name is Sasha," the nurse said loudly, "but I can help you into bed after you take your medicine, okay?"

Maddi opened her eyes again and looked up at the nurse.

"Where's Emma?" she asked, looking around.

"Is that your daughter's name?" the nurse asked, handing Maddi the pills and water. "You had some visitors this morning. Was that your family?"

"I want Emma."

"Okay, Miss Maddi. Let's not get ourselves worked up now. Just relax and take your medicine."

Maddi dropped the pills into her mouth, took a couple gulps of water, and winced a little before coughing. I watched the nurse help Maddi stand, pivot her to the bed, and lay her down gently. The nurse pulled her socks off and there was a small plume of dead skin that came off as she did so. She pulled the blankets up to cover Maddi and propped her up on her pillow more comfortably.

"Is that good?" the nurse asked. Maddi nodded.

"If you see Emma, tell her I'm ready to go," Maddi smiled.

"Okay," the nurse said, almost as if she were speaking to a child. "If I see Emma, I'll let her know."

"It's not time for you yet," I said. "I'll be back for you, I promise. Just be patient for a little bit longer. I have some things to take care of first."

13

I had a plan. It was a stupid plan, but it was a plan at least. But first, I needed to meet up with Otomatsu. I needed to get into the Temple of Da'at and get that scroll, and I knew Otomatsu would help me. I approached the beach where we had first met and looked around. No sign of him anywhere. I walked up to the water and looked out. The beaches on Earth were so much prettier than mine.

"I'm surprised you came," I heard Otomatsu's voice from behind me.

I looked as he came up beside me, looking at the water.

"I told you I would," I said.

"I figured you'd stay with your long-lost friend a while longer."

"Oh," I muttered. "He, uh, is moving on."

"To Paradise?" Otomatsu asked. "Good for him."

I didn't reply.

"So, you're stuck with me then."

"What?"

"We both know you would have ditched me in a heartbeat if Dumah or whatever his name is now decided to become a death angel again."

"That's not true!" I snapped. "You're my friend."

Otomatsu kept his eyes on the ocean.

"You *are* my friend, Otomatsu," I repeated.

"Your friend who you need to help you get inside the Temple of Da'at."

I looked at him wide-eyed.

"My friend who I need to be my friend," I corrected. "I don't just need your help. I need your support. Look, I'm sorry if I made you feel left out or 'second best" or whatever. Even if Eduardo had decided to become a death angel again, that wouldn't change anything between us."

"I didn't think you were coming back," Otomatsu admitted. "I thought once you convinced him to take his place again, you would go back to Earth as a human...or do something stupider."

"Such as?" I asked.

"Continue seeking revenge on Ankou."

"Oh."

"You don't sound surprised by that idea, like you *have* been thinking about it."

"I have a new plan," I explained. "And I could do it without your help but it would be easier with it. I don't want you to think I'm taking advantage of you though so it's completely up to you."

Otomastu looked at me, clearly interested. I smiled before motioning for him to sit down. As we rested on the sand, I began to explain my idea. The whole time I talked, Otomatsu stared at me;

not nodding, frowning or anything else that would give away what he was thinking. I finished and let out a sigh, relieved to get it out. I leaned forward, placing my elbows on my knees, and waited for Otomatsu to say something. Finally, he shifted where he sat. I fought the urge to say anything as he sat and thought.

"Well," he said at last. "It needs some cleaning up a bit, but overall it seems like a solid plan."

I grinned.

"You know we'll have to move very quickly. If we take too much time away from our jobs, we'll get in trouble."

"We're going to get in trouble regardless," I shrugged. "But if we can save Sam, and maybe take down some demons along the way, it's worth it."

"There's only one real problem though."

"Which is?" I asked.

"The ending."

"We'll worry about that if we get that far." I smiled weakly. "But first, we need to get a few jobs done so the archangels aren't on our asses right away."

"Good idea," Otomatsu agreed.

"Meet me at my house in five days," I said. "We'll get more jobs done separately. And no exorcisms for now. We need to keep a low profile for now."

Otomatsu reluctantly agreed and we went our separate ways. I went on autopilot as I witnessed death after death, keeping my mind focused on what was to come. I was on my second day, watching a woman sitting in her car. She was parked inside her garage and the engine was running. She was typing something out on her phone, sobbing as she did so. I lifted my hands up as I walked closer to the car.

"Through this holy anointing-"

"Stop it, Emma!"

Ankou came up from behind me and grabbed my right arm.

"Stop doing this!" he snarled in my face.

"Why?" I asked, yanking my hand away. "Because you're the only one allowed to cheat? I saw you when that woman jumped off that building."

"Yeah and you ended up saving her," Ankou retorted. "Congratulations. Did you know that she was a thief?"

"Seriously?" I scoffed. "You're going to justify taking her soul because she was a shoplifter? What, did she steal a couple of sweaters from a store?"

"I said a thief, not a shoplifter. God, how are you this bad at your job still? She was a caregiver for elderly patients. She went to people's houses to bathe them, feed them, clean house, do laundry, and steal apparently. She took money, jewelry, and even medication."

"And you knew this because you were, what, dating her?"

"I know because I'm good at being a demon," Ankou scoffed. "Fuck, Emma, you sound like a jealous ex-girlfriend. But no, she never even told me she was doing any of that. Or the fact that she sometimes hit the ones who couldn't talk. One guy who had suffered from a stroke accidentally knocked over his orange juice and she smacked him in the mouth."

I didn't say anything.

"Not that any of that shit even matters now because you saved her."

"And what about her?" I asked, pointing to the car. The woman had her head tilted back and her eyes closed.

"No!"

"She took a sleeping pill," Ankou sighed. "She's not dead yet. I'll tell you a bit about her though, since you're too lazy to do so. She's a mother who just lost a custody battle over her infant son. She chose to leave her abusive boyfriend and because she has no job and no home, he was granted full custody of their son. She didn't have a job because her boyfriend wanted her to stay home, but then used it against her in court. And since this is his house, she has nowhere to go. So, she's escaping."

"By killing herself?" I asked. "She should-"

A sudden shrill cry came from the car. I looked at the backseat and there, strapped into his carseat, was the woman's infant son.

I glanced back at Ankou. He just stood there.

"Oh god. No, no, no."

I was suddenly sitting in the backseat next to the screaming baby. He started coughing and I desperately tried to grab the buckles of the carseat.

"Just be there for him, Emma," I heard Ankou say.

"Shut up!" I yelled. "I can do this!"

"It's not your job to save anyone!"

The infant started making strange squeaky sounds. I concentrated with all of my might and still couldn't grab the restraints. In the front seat, I heard the woman gurgling. Then, there was a sound of liquid splatting, so she must have thrown up. The baby was no longer making any noise. I lowered my head so my eyes could meet his. He looked right at me, gave me a big gummy grin, and then closed his eyes. I got out of the car and stood there, watching the woman through the driver side window. Ankou was standing behind me, watching. After the woman passed, he spoke.

"Decided not to save her after all?" he asked, casually picking at his teeth with his fingernails.

"*Shut up!*" I snapped, gripping the handle of my sheathed sword.

"Oh, you really don't want to do that," Ankou scolded. "How else are you going to get little Samantha out of that sea?"

"I don't need your help," I muttered.

"But you do," he dramatically pouted his lips. "You see, the scroll is in Paradise for a reason. Only demons can read it. I just don't know what exactly is written on the scroll."

"What's in it for you?" I asked. "If I free Sam, there's no way you're getting her."

"Oh, no," Ankou smiled. "I don't want Sam."

"What *do* you want then?"

He stared at me.

"Me? Why?"

"Because I have collected every soul I've gone after. That bitch on the roof doesn't count because you interfered. And I thought I had a second chance at getting you, but Dumah interfered with *that*! You death angels really are a pain in the ass. But, I'll make a deal with you. If I help you free Sam's soul, and wait until her little prepubescent body is nestled safely in Paradise, then you're mine."

"I'm already dead though, stupid," I scoffed. "You can't just take an angel's soul. It's not yours to take."

"No, but I still want you."

Without warning, Ankou leaned in and kissed me, wrapping his hand around my throat. I shoved him away from me and smacked him as hard as I could. Ankou started for me again. I reached out to push him away, but he grabbed my wrists so tightly that it hurt a little. He kissed me again and suddenly, I was kissing him back. He pushed me against the wall and I grabbed his hair with both hands. His tongue danced with mine and I was immediately transported back in time, to when I was still alive. I let out a soft moan as the passion and excitement filled my entire body. For the first time since I died, I felt alive.

This unexpected encounter didn't throw a wrench in my plan at all. In fact, this made things so much easier. There was just one thing missing. I put my hand on his chest and backed my head away.

"On one condition," I said. "We each bring someone with us, that the other chooses, to make sure each end of the bargain is held up."

"Who did you have in mind?" he asked, panting. "Dark angels don't count."

"No," I said as I ran my fingers along his collarbone, acting like I was thinking really hard about it. "What about...hm...Abaddon? Not that I would ever trust a demon, but he seems like one I would consider trusting."

"Okay then," Ankou nodded. "I'll see if he'll consider it. Then, I'm choosing the little fairy gal you had with you in Hell."

"Thalia?" I asked. "We're not exactly on the best terms right now."

"Not my problem."

"Would you consider picking someone else?"

"What, like another death angel? Or a dark angel? Not a chance. You're bringing someone I know I can take in case shit hits the fan."

"And if Thalia refuses?" I asked.

"Again, not my problem. But I doubt she'll say no. Last time I saw her, she was following you around like a lost puppy."

I thought about it for a minute. Ankou leaned in to kiss me again but I stopped him. Thinking about it, I paced back and forth before speaking again.

"Fine. I'll see what I can do."

"Good," Ankou said, stepping closer to me. "Because I'd really love to help you get Sam out of that water."

"Only because you get me in exchange for her."

"You're absolutely right."

Ankou brushed my cheek with the back of his fingers. I wanted to pull away, but I also wanted him to take me. I still hated him but I also wanted him so badly.

"I'm going to have a lot of fun playing with you for eternity," he chuckled. "All those nightmares you had before you died? That was just child's play compared to what I'm going to do to you. You're not human anymore so I can be as rough as I want to, with both the pleasure and the pain. No holding back."

"You have to get Sam out first," I reminded him.

"I'll keep my end of the bargain. Don't you worry about that. Once you get the scroll, come find me."

"I'm not taking that scroll anywhere near Hell. I'm not stupid."

"Fair enough," Ankou said, putting his hands up in defense. "Keep it in a safe place until we meet up. I should get back to work. Duty calls."

He pointed a finger at the woman in the car and smiled at me. I decided it was best to go before things got too heated. I went onto my next job feeling mildly confident that my plan was going to work. It would have been easier to have Otomatsu with me when I saved Sam, but I could still figure out a way to keep him close by. I would just need to make amends with Thalia and convince her to come with me instead. Not just because I needed her for my mission; but I realized that she was indeed my friend, and I had to make things right with her. I also realized I would need to somehow get a new boat.

After three days of working extra hard, with no breaks at all, I met Otomatsu at my house. I told him about my encounter with Ankou (minus the kissing), and the newest updates on my little scheme. He didn't like the idea of Thalia being there instead of him, but I assured him that we could still make it work.

"I need to ask Baraqiel to make me a new boat," I sighed heavily. "Otherwise, I don't know how easy it'll be to get Sam out of the water without the other Restless pulling me in."

"I think getting another boat is smart," Otomatsu agreed. "Do you want company?"

"Sure!" I smiled. "I'm not a very fast flier."

"I'll be sure to go slow so you can keep up," he said, taking off.

I watched him dart around in the sky, clearly not trying to fly slowly at all. I gave Otomatsu a mischievous grin and took off after him. Although I enjoyed taking the boat across the sea, flying was much faster. Also, it was a bit more fun. Otomatsu would fly in zig zags and circle around me as I tried to keep up with him. He flew up really high, and I followed him. As soon as I reached the same height as him, he free-fell back down towards the water. I let myself fall too, showing him I could do whatever he could. As the sea quickly got closer, I looked at Otomatsu. His eyes were closed!

"Hey!" I yelled.

I could see my reflection in the water growing as I got closer. I spread my wings and stopped. Otomatsu had stopped himself too, with the tip of one boot touching the water. It looked like he was standing on the glassy surface of the sea. We both laughed and continued flying towards the shore on the other side. As soon as we landed on the black sand, the mood completely changed.

"Where is everyone?" Otomatsu asked. "I thought you said there's always someone around when you show up?"

"There usually is," I said.

We cautiously made our way towards Baraqiel's hut, our hands on our weapons. Everything was eerily quiet.

"I hate it here," Otomatsu said softly.

I nodded in agreement as the hut came into view. Suddenly, the door swung open and Gabe came running out.

"Emma!" He yelled, opening his arms.

Even in his armor, he ran so gracefully. He scooped me up in a big hug, lifting me off the ground. I smiled until I caught Otomatsu's eye and then gently pushed away from Gabe.

"What are you doing here?" I asked. "I thought you were staying with Eduardo until he moved on."

"He told me to go ahead and start 'the new job,' as he called it."

"Where's Baraqiel?"

"At his new post," Gabe replied. "I have this beach, Sekhmet has the surrounding woods until it goes into Baraqiel's territory. And then he has the woods on that side until it meets the beach over there where Matariel is posted."

"Damn," I said. "I had something to ask Barry."

"If you want to come hang out for a bit, Sekhmet should be done running the perimeter soon. She can take you right to him."

"We can chill for a while," I smiled. I caught Otomatsu glaring at Gabe but didn't say anything.

"So what's been new with you?" Gabe asked as we made our way into the hut.

"It's only been a few days since you've seen her last," Otomatsu sighed.

"We've just been working," I answered, glaring at Otomatsu.

"Does anyone want any tea?" Gabe asked. "I even have some Jasmine tea."

"Just because I lived in Japan doesn't mean I like Jasmine tea," Otomatsu said. "Besides, we don't eat or drink."

"When you're here, and especially when you get more into Hell, you start feeling things like hunger," Gabe replied.

"I'm aware. We just have no need for it. If your will is strong enough, you can push past the feeling of hunger. You can push past any human needs or...urges."

"Emma?" Gabe turned to me, blushing.

"I'll take some chamomile," I smiled politely.

"Got it!"

I leaned into Otomatsu.

"Why are you being so rude to him?" I asked quietly. "He's just being nice."

"Yeah well, I think he's a little *too* nice towards you."

"Oh please!" I laughed. "It's not like that. We're just friends."

"I think he wishes you were more though."

"That's ridiculous. Look at me."

"Emma, believe it or not, some people fall in love with personalities more than looks. Also, you're not as hideous as you think you are."

"Angels don't have crushes."

"Look at Baraqiel. After all these years, he's still in love with the same man he was in love as a human. It's the most powerful emotion, and you certainly can continue to feel it, even after you die."

I sat there, suddenly feeling a little awkward. Did Otomastu pick on something that I didn't? Did Gabe have feelings for me? When he came back into the room, he handed me the cup of tea, grinning. As I took the cup, our hands overlapped. Was I imagining things or had Gabe's hand lingered a moment longer than normal? I pulled my hand away and looked down as I thanked him.

"Careful, it's hot," he warned.

I nodded and took a cautious sip. I glanced at Otomatsu, who sat there staring at Gabe. Once Gabe got his cup of tea, he sat down across from me and smiled.

"It's crazy about my grandpa," Gabe shook his head. "He was always superstitious, you know?"

"What do you mean?" I asked.

"He always seemed to know when someone was about to die. He'd just get this....feeling. He never knew who, how, or when, but he'd tell my grandma he felt it. I always thought it was a silly coincidence, but my grandma would get worried. She believed that my grandpa had some sort of gift. I guess she was right since he was a death angel in another afterlife."

"Yeah," I said awkwardly.

The three of us sat in deafening silence for a while.

"Man, this is when having television would really come in handy," Gabe chuckled.

"Yeah," I giggled.

"That's what's wrong with these younger generations," Otomatsu grumbled. "I went through my entire life without needing a screen to entertain me. Reading or storytelling was enough for us."

"Tell us a story to help pass the time then," Gabe said.

"Yeah," I smiled mischievously. "Entertain us."

Otomatsu sighed and then adjusted himself into a more comfortable position.

"Alright," he breathed. "I'll tell you the myth of the Kuchisake-onna."

"Oh, I know this one!" Gabe exclaimed. "The slit-mouth woman who asks victims if she's beautiful and if they say no, she kills them. If they say yes, she slits their mouth!"

Otomatsu gave Gabe a look of astonishment, with slight annoyance.

"I watched a lot of anime and read manga," Gabe said coyly.

"Well, do you know about the jorogumo?" Otomatsu asked.

"Doesn't sound familiar," Gabe murmured.

"Then do you think I can tell the story without any interruptions?"

"Go ahead."

"Thank you," Otomatsu said shortly.

"There was a logger working in the woods one day. This was before the invention of chainsaws, so the work was laborious and tiring. After working the whole morning, the logger decided to rest and eat his lunch. He could hear a waterfall nearby and thought that would be the perfect spot to eat and relax before going back to work. When he reached the waterfall, the logger laid out his food on the rocks by the water. While eating, the logger could see something covering the bushes nearby. Setting his wrapped food down, he walked over to the bushes. It looked like soft white clouds had covered them. When the logger touched the white substance, it stuck to his hands instantly. He wiped it off on his pants and turned back towards the water as he heard a splash.

    A woman, a very beautiful woman, stood on the other side of the water, by the waterfall. She was the prettiest woman the logger had ever seen, and she was motioning for him to go to her. The logger froze in place, unsure of what to do. He was almost sure she wasn't real. He cautiously took two steps forward. The woman smiled and giggled and took two steps backwards. The logger took three more steps towards her as she stepped back. Her back was now against the rock wall beside the waterfall. As the logger stood at the water's edge, the woman disappeared behind the cascading water. The logger, now sure she was real, took his shoes, shirt, and pants off."

    "Is this going to get weird?" I asked.

    "Just listen," Otomatsu smiled. "The logger waded through the water, trying not to splash around too much. He didn't want to startle the beautiful woman. As soon as he was a little more than halfway to the waterfall, something shot out at him. It landed on his chest, sticking to his skin. It was the same substance that had covered the bushes, and there was a long line of it coming from inside the waterfall. Suddenly, something pulled him forward with great force. Water slapped his face as he went through the waterfall and into the opening of a cave. The logger was hanging upside down by the thick white rope. Then, from the shadows, came the woman. From the waist up, she was still the same beautiful creature he had laid eyes on. But from the waist down, she now had the body of a spider.

Before he could let out a scream, the jorogumo scurried up to him and shot some of her silk on his mouth. As he lifted his hands to remove it, the monster spun him quickly, wrapping him in her silky trap. The logger looked around the cave, where he could see the skeletons and carcasses of dead men. The jorogumo's smile was the last thing he saw before she bit, releasing her venom into his blood. The logger stopped wriggling and went still."

"We come back to Hell and *that's* the story you wanted to tell?" I asked. "That's fucked up."

Otomatsu laughed abruptly, which startled Gabe. That made us all start laughing. Suddenly, the door swung open and the three of us were on our feet. Otomtaus and I had our sword drawn and

Gabe raised his fists. Sekhmet casually walked in and stared at me.

"Quite the greeting committee you all are," she smiled. "Gabe, you might want to get yourself a weapon, sooner than later."

"I have something I can bring you," I said. He grinned at me.

"Emma," Sekhmet breathed. "Good to see you."

We hugged, but as I squeezed, Sekhmet winced a little. I looked at her back and saw a large gash under her shoulder blade. It was so deep that I could see muscle tissue.

"Oh shit!" I gasped. "You're hurt!"

"Yeah well, you should see the other guys," she laughed weakly. "I'll be fine. It'll heal up. I had my throat slit once and came back from that, remember?"

Sekhmet slowly made her way over to a chaise lounge sofa and laid on her stomach, her arms resting on the raised side of it.

"I actually came here looking for Barry," I said. "I didn't realize he had already been moved to his new post."

"Oh yes," Sekhmet chuckled. "He wasted no time going. But it was very sweet to see him and Matariel reunite after so long. Was there something either I or Gabe could help you with?"

"I need a new boat," I muttered.

"What happened to Dumah's?"

"Had a little accident," I admitted. "Against some rocks."

"Oh, Emma," Sekhmet scolded. "He's going to be so upset with you."

"I know. I didn't mean for it to happen."

"Why don't I talk to him? Soften him up a bit first."

"It's a little urgent," I sighed. "I don't even need you to go with me. Otomatsu and I will go while you rest."

"Nonsense," Sekhmet said, standing back up. "I feel fine."

"No," Otomatsu argued, holding his hand up. "Emma and I can handle it."

"And one more will make it easier for you," Sekhmet smiled.

"Fine," he muttered. "Don't slow us down, though."

"You're the one who's going to need to keep up with me," she winked.

What the hell, I thought. *They're not flirting, are they?*

"Keep an eye on things while I'm gone," Sekhmet said to Gabe. "Don't let those demon bastards push you around."

"I'll be all right," Gabe gulped. "You take care of yourselves."

"We will," I replied.

The three of us headed outside and made a plan.

"I think the fastest way would be through the city," Otomatsu said.

"But the easiest way would be through the woods along the northern coast," Sekhmet argued.

"I'll take my chances with damned souls if it means avoiding mongrels," Otomatsu grumbled.

"If we get moving, we can avoid them altogether until we reach the other shore," Sekhmet explained. "I run this route every day. I think I know what I'm talking about."

"And I think if we move quickly and go directly across the island, we can reach the other side sooner than going the long way around."

"And there will still be demons in the city, including elites!"

"Will you two stop arguing?" I cut in.

"You decide then," Otomatsu crossed his arms.

I looked at Otomatsu, then Sekhmet, and back to Otomatsu.

"I think..." I hesitated, glancing at Sekhmet.

"Just choose," Otomatsu sighed.

"I think we should listen to Sekhmet," I said. Otomatsu frowned.

"Good," Sekhmet smiled. "Let's get going, shall we?"

As we made our way through the woods, I lost sight of the house. Something about being completely surrounded by the trees, not being able to see anything around us besides foliage, scared me a little. I remembered how many mongrels surrounded us when Thalia was with me, and how they just appeared out of nowhere. Not to mention Sekhmet had to walk on two legs. Getting on all fours hurt her back too much so she was forced to stand up straight. I wondered if the three of us would be enough with her being in the state she was in.

"We'll be fine," Sekhmet said, as if reading my mind. "We'll meet up with Hutriel and she'll help us reach Baraqiel."

"Hutriel?" I asked.

"You'll love her. She's pretty fierce. She once stood up to Satan himself."

"Really?"

"Oh yes. Hutriel was originally an archangel. She is the one who confronted Satan about tempting Adam and Eve. She was pretty pissed, so she turned him into a snake and made him writhe in pain. That is, until he was able to get away and return back to Hell."

I chuckled at that.

"And what good did it do?" Otomatsu interrupted. "Centuries later and we're still dealing with Satan, demons, and all of their bullshit."

"She was the first angel to make it known that we weren't just going to stay in Paradise and let him roam Earth to influence people," Sekhmet continued. "She's also the only dark angel who didn't *choose* to become one. She broke the rules and was sent to Hell as punishment. She became the first one to patrol Sentencing to make sure everyone stayed where they were supposed to. Well, as much as she could. Being the only one for so long was hard. Things...slipped through the cracks."

"How many dark angels patrol Sentencing?" I asked. "I thought it was just you, Barqiel, Matariel, and now Gabe."

"Gabe watches the shore directly across the sea from your shore," Sekhmet explained. "I patrol the northwestern area while Baraqiel patrols the northeastern area until it hits Matariel's shore. He's located near The Abyss; the opening into true Hell. Hutriel covers the area south of where Baraqiel and I go, until the city starts. Ananiel patrols the southwestern area. Zihrun takes the southeastern and the area directly south of the city. If we get another dark angel here, hopefully they'll take one of the areas Zihrun patrols."

"Do the other dark angels have special powers like Barry?" I asked.

"I beg your pardon?" Sekhmet laughed. "I have special powers too, you know. I'm like a lion on steroids! I can run extraordinarily fast and I'm incredibly strong. Not to mention I have built-in demon-killing weapons with my claws and teeth."

Sekhmet raised her hands to show her large nails, and smiled to show her razor-sharp canines.

"Matariel is known as the 'angel of rain.' His powers feed the Sea of Anathema. He can also use water as a weapon when fighting. He can make it rain, and because he's an angel, he can bless it. He can turn the rain into holy water....which is like acid rain to demons."

"That's pretty cool!" I exclaimed.

"Hutriel is the angel of punishment," Sekhmet continued. "Her name means, 'rod of God.' She can induce pain with her mind. It's not necessarily the *nicest* power for an angel, but when people in the city start wandering along the outskirts, it can come in handy. Not to mention it works on all demons; *including* elites."

"Seriously?" Otomatsu asked.

Sekhmet nodded.

"After Dumah was killed, she got herself in a bit of trouble."

"With Ankou?" I asked.

"Yeah, she went after him. Destroyed several of his outposts while trying to find him."

I smiled.

"She had to keep a low profile for a while after that. He had half the island looking for her to 'teach her a lesson.' He sent two tanks to destroy her home. Things have calmed down a little since."

I remembered running into a tank in Sentencing with Baraqiel and Sam and being absolutely terrified. Being a death angel with a flaming sword made me slightly less afraid of them.

"Ananiel is the angel of wind," she went on. "He can cause destructive gusts and even tornadoes. Zihrun is the angel of light. She can control and manipulate light and darkness. She carries the Sword of Divine Light, which is the most powerful weapon against demons."

"This isn't?" I asked, touching Dumah's sword.

"No, love. It is, however, the second most powerful. Well, depending on who's wielding it. No offense."

"Thanks," I said sarcastically. "You know, I've been carrying this sword around for over seventy years."

"Once you've carried that thing around for a few centuries, then we'll talk," she chuckled. "Some of these angels have been around since before Jesus."

She winked at me.

"You'll earn your wings. Don't worry."

I noticed the light through the trees was starting to change a little.

"What time is it?" I asked. "It looks like the sun is going to set soon."

"We may need to pick up the pace a bit," Sekhmet said, looking around. "I won't be able to run as quickly with my back all torn up, but it'll be faster than walking."

"Yeah, I don't really want to get stuck out here after dark," Otomatsu added.

"You two go ahead and fly in that direction."

Sekhmet pointed into the woods.

"I'll try and keep up as best as I can, but don't let me slow you down."

She slowly got down in her lioness pose, wincing while she did so.

"Are you sure you're up for this?" Otomatsu asked.

"If I have to tell someone that I'm fine one more time, I'm biting that person's head clean off," she said sharply. "Besides, Hutriel should be just up ahead. We'll be much safer with her. Come on."

Sekhmet took off running in the direction she had pointed to. Otomatsu and I stretched out our wings and flew after her. I didn't feel comfortable flying ahead and leaving Sekhmet behind in her condition, but before long, Otomatsu got far enough in front of me that I started to lose him in the trees.

"Go, Emma!" Sekhmet panted. "I'll be fine!"

I picked up speed to catch up with Otomatsu. I caught glimpses of his black wings through the thick forest and glanced back at Sekhmet. She was nowhere in sight. As I turned back around, a branch caught me right in the face. I gasped as a second branch clotheslined me and I fell to the ground, landing hard on my back. I looked up, my vision slightly blurred, at the orange sky peaking between the green leaves. The wind picked up and the branches of trees almost seemed to be waving at me, saying, "nighty night."

No, I was *not* going to lose consciousness alone in the outskirts of Hell. I sat up slowly, wiping my cheek. It stung as the back of my hand scraped against the open cut. It had been a while since I saw my own blood. I stood up and braced myself with the trunk of the closest tree. I tenderly rubbed the back of my pounding head and momentarily I felt like I was going to vomit.

I looked around, wondering which direction I had been flying in.

"Fuck," I muttered.

Finally, I made a decision and started walking. I reached the wall and eventually came to the archway that led into the desert. Something moving across the sand caught my attention. I focused on the little girl with red hair and blinked hard. She turned her head towards me and I realized it was Sam; only she was rotting. The skin on one side of her face was gone, revealing her teeth. One eyeball dangled from its socket. I rubbed my own eyes and shook my head. When I looked again, there was no one there. I held my head and continued walking in the opposite of the archway, still too dizzy to fly.

"Otomatsu?" I called out. "Sekhmet?"

I could hear low growling and chittering coming from somewhere in the woods. A twig snapped and I whipped around quickly. A scream somewhere up ahead made my hair stand on end. I pulled my sword out, being careful not to let the flames get too close to the nearby foliage. I kept moving at a steady pace along the wall, moving silently and quickly. I suddenly came across a small hole in the wall where several rocks had been pushed away. I looked to the left of the hole and noticed a dark red streak along the grass. I reluctantly followed the blood-soaked ground, not paying attention to how dark it was getting. I made my way into a clearing and saw a woman, or what was left of her, laying on the ground. She had one leg ripped off at the knee and her stomach was shredded open, exposing her intestines. The bloody stump at her knee looked like it had been through a wood chipper. Ribbons of tissue hung from its end. I got a little closer to the woman. Her eyes were closed and her mouth gaped open, as if she had been screaming. I looked around, still holding my sword out. Something grabbed my ankle and my wings fluffed up from being startled. I looked down as the woman opened her eyes, gripping me with a bloody hand.

"He-" she tried to say, but it came out gurgled, as if she were trying to speak with a mouthful of water. Blood sprayed as she choked on her word.

"Hel-Help."

"What did this to you?" I asked, pulling away from her.

She looked past me, towards the trees, and gasped. I looked up, seeing over a dozen mongrels looking down at us. Their long, spindly arms and legs wrapped around branches as they watched, not moving. I raised my sword in defense and a couple of mongrels began growling intensely.

"Oh, come on," I said.

They all dropped down and surrounded me. The one closest to me had blood smeared all over its face and it was drooling as it snarled at me.

"What are you ugly bastards waiting for?" I yelled. My sword lit up with fire.

"Come on!"

They all charged at me at once. I swung at the closest two mongrels, slicing one's leg off and decapitating the other. I plunged my sword into another one, setting it on fire. The pierced mongrel let out howls of agony as it pulled away, flailing around. I turned around to face the group on my other side. As I did so, the mongrel missing a leg pulled on my foot from the ground. I lost my balance, but as I did, I drove the blade into its skull. The handle of the sword slipped out of my grip and I fell back onto my bottom. Instead of crawling after my weapon, I reached into a pouch on my belt, pulled my fist out, opened my hand, and blew a huge clump of cabbage palm right into the faces of three mongrels about to make a meal out of me. They all gasped and started choking immediately. While they convulsed on the ground, I took the opportunity to somersault to my sword. I grabbed the handle and placed a foot on the dead mongrel's head.

Suddenly, a mongrel bit down on my free arm and I let out a scream of pain. I used all of my strength to swing my sword into the side of the mongrel. It hacked into its stomach. The mongrel growled in anger but continued to saw its sharp teeth into my forearm. I hit it again and again, my sword slinging blood everywhere as I finally cut the monster in half. The pressure of its jaws lessened and the bottom half dropped in a heap of gore. The mongrel's eyes rolled back white and I pulled the upper part off of me. I looked at the damage done to my arm. It looked like raw hamburger meat. Blood dripped off of my wrist. I tried to grip my sword with both hands but my injured arm made it hard to hold. Seven more mongrels were slowly closing in on me. I grabbed a vial of blood without losing eye contact with the monsters getting closer. At this range, I had no idea of how hurt I would get from a blood grenade. However, I did know the outcome if I didn't throw it. I raised the vial above my head, getting ready to launch it.

The mongrels stopped. I paused. They began twisting in pain and screeching. Their bodies writhed around on the ground, being tortured by something unseen. I placed the vial back onto my belt and grabbed my torn arm. I saw a figure appear from behind the mongrels with its hands raised above its head. By this time, the sun had almost set, but dusk in the forest was already dark. The mongrels got up and ran off into the forest. I looked up to see the tallest woman I've ever seen. She had to easily be over six feet tall, maybe even seven feet. She had porcelain skin and short blonde hair. There was black paint smeared around her eyes and a line of it on her chin. She knelt next to me and I saw that her eyes were bright green and glowing.

"We've been looking for you," she smiled. She spoke in a soothing voice.

She reached her hands out to me and I noticed they looked like they were covered in black tar. I recoiled and she laughed.

"It's okay," she said softly. "I can do more than cause pain. Here."

She touched the large gash on my arm and the pain immediately abated. I looked as her black hands gently rubbed the lacerations, which seemed to disappear right before my eyes.

"I found her!" the woman yelled unexpectedly. I jumped at the sound.

"Sorry, just trying to get Sekhmet and the death angel over here before anyone else gets lost."

"Hutriel?" I asked. She smiled again.

"Oh, thank the gods!" I heard Sekhmet from behind Hutriel. She and Otomatsu ran into the clearing and looked around.

"Are you okay?" Otomatsu asked me.

"I'm fine," I answered.

"Just finishing her arm and she'll be good as new," Hutriel winked at me.

She helped me stand up as Otomatsu marched up to me and pointed a finger in my face.

"All you had to do was keep up with me. I turned around and you were nowhere in sight. And instead of going straight, you ended up over here! Do you know how worried I was?"

"I'm sorry," I sighed. "I flew into a branch and almost knocked myself out. I guess I just got turned around."

"You're lucky we found you when we did!" Sekhmet added.

"Sorry," I repeated, a little more sharply this time.

"Can you guys give her a break?" Hutriel said, helping me sheath my sword. "Come on, we need to keep moving. I'm sure once night falls, there'll be more mongrels. We might as well stay by the wall. That way there's one less side for them to sneak up on us."

"Good idea," Sekhmet nodded, looking around.

"Your back!" I pointed. "It looks so much better!"

"Thanks to Hutriel," Sekhmet said. "As soon as we realized you were missing, I pushed myself to get to her so she could heal me. And then asked her to double back with us until we found you."

I looked at my arm, and besides the dried blood caked on the skin, it was back to normal.

"Thanks," I said, holding my arm up.

"You're welcome," Hutriel gestured. I followed behind Otomatsu and Sekhmet with her behind me. We walked on and occasionally paused to hear things moving around us in the woods. Every time, I looked back at Hutriel. She would hold her hand out into the darkness, her green eyes glowing fiercely, and the sounds would stop. Luckily, nothing bothered us the whole way to the other shore. Hutriel seemed to keep the monsters at bay.

14

As we came out of the forest and onto the shore, I saw a quaint little house on the beach and a bonfire going on the sand. Baraqiel stood up next to the fire with open arms. The fire light made his pale skin look like it was glowing.

"Hol-y shit! You all look like a group of superheroes, slow motion-walking out like that!" He chuckled.

Baraqiel sprinted at me with his bald head lowered.

"Hey, Bar- OOF!"

He wrapped his arms around me, picked me up, and spun me around.

"Emma, I love you so much!" Baraqiel laughed as he kept spinning me. "Thank you!"

"You're welcome," I said awkwardly. "Can you please put me down now?"

He let go of me and grabbed my shoulders.

"I owe you big time," he beamed. "Thousands of years away from each other and now we can see each other all the time. Oh, I almost forgot! Come here."

Barry grabbed my hand and yanked me across the beach towards the young man sitting by the fire. I tried to hide my shock.

"Emma, this is Matariel," Baraqiel grinned.

"Nice to finally meet you," he said, sticking his hand out. "Thank you for helping make this happen."

"It's nice to meet you too," I said.

"You probably don't remember me," Otomatsu stuck his hand out.

"Of course I do," Matariel beamed, shaking his hand. "How are you, Otomatsu?"

"Doing very well, thank you."

Matariel looked younger than me; maybe eighteen or nineteen. Baraqiel was easily in his forties so the age difference between them was a little shocking. Matariel had curly black hair, prominent eyebrows, and thick eyelashes. When he spoke, he had a shy, boyish smile that made a dimple appear on his left cheek.

"I know what you're thinking," Barry said.

"I'm not thinking about anything!" I said quickly.

"Just don't make any cradle-robbing jokes," he muttered. "We were the same age when he died and now we're both thousands of years old."

"Well, technically we're both dead so we're not any age," Matariel smirked. "But yeah, he was pretty shocked when he saw me. I guess he forgot how young we were when we met."

"I wasn't so much shocked as I was embarrassed," Baraqiel chuckled. "I thought, 'great. He's not going to want this old man.'"

"Stop it," Matariel smiled as he wrapped his arm around Barry. "You look amazing, and I am so lucky to have found you again. My soul feels complete once more."

"And it's all thanks to Emma," Baraqiel raised a hand to me. "You've made us both so happy."

"Well, Gabe agreed to it," I said shyly. "Also, you're about to be not-so-happy with me."

"Why, what's wrong?"

"I need a new boat."

"What happened to Dumah's boat?"

"I- uh..."

"Emma, what happened to the boat?" he repeated.

"I'm sorry," I teared up. "I lost my temper and made these huge waves on accident and the boat sort of...crashed against some rocks."

Baraqiel's smile faded.

"I'm so sorry!" I added. "I didn't mean to. I've felt pretty shitty about it."

"Well, I'd be lying if I said I wasn't upset about it," Baraqiel sighed. "But accidents happen. And I know you'd never purposely ruin anything of Dumah's."

"Of course not," I insisted. "So...would you be able to make a new one?"

"Why do you need a boat?" Baraqiel asked. "You could just fly back and forth."

"You let Dumah use the boat," I said.

"Dumah liked the peace and quiet of sailing," Barry laughed. "He was okay with taking the boat sometimes to get some solitude. You don't seem like the sailing type."

"I liked using the boat too," I admitted. "I've gone out on it quite a few times. Mostly to look for Sam. But it is lovely to get out there on the water."

I looked at Otomatsu. He raised his eyebrows. Everyone stared at me.

"I thought Gabe could use it to come visit me," I looked down, lightly kicking the sand with my toes.

"I knew there was some chemistry going on between you two," Sekhmet smiled. "He hasn't stopped talking about you since he arrived."

"Aw, Emma, I love that for you," Baraqiel added. "I always told Dumah that just because he was a death angel didn't mean he had to spend eternity alone. I'm glad I don't have to worry about that with you."

"We're just friends, you guys!" I said, blushing.

"Sure," Baraqiel said. "Sometimes the greatest loves start as friendships. I'll have the boat ready in a few weeks. Think you can wait that long?"

"Definitely," I said. "Oh! Also, I want this to be a surprise so I'd appreciate it if no one told Gabe about the boat. Okay?"

"I stay here all the time so you know I won't be saying anything," Matariel smiled.

"Yeah, I stay over here as much as possible too," Baraqiel said. "But I wouldn't say anything anyways."

"You know I'm not going to ruin the surprise," Sekhmet chimed in. "I think this is all very sweet and he will love it."

"Again," I reassured her, "just friends."

A howl in the forest made me and Otomatsu both grab the handles of our swords.

"We better head in," Matariel motioned towards the house. "We'll stay inside until morning."

"I'll stay out here," Hutriel smiled. "I don't run from demons."

"I think I'll go with her," Sekhmet said. "I don't want to spend all night cooped up."

"We'll come back in the morning and see that you two get back to the shore safely," Hutriel added. Otomatsu nodded.

The two of them ran back into the darkness of the woods. Matariel, Baraqiel, Otomatsu, and I went inside and saw that everywhere, from floor to ceiling, were watercolor paintings. There were multiple beach scenes, a couple of mongrels, some of what I assumed were of Ancient Greece, but most were of Baraqiel. His face, his body, and his features were everywhere. There were even some nude paintings of the two of them.

"Yeah, I know," Matariel smirked while rubbing the back of his hair. "Now that we've found each other, I might need to branch out a bit in my art."

One of the paintings caught my attention and I moved closer to it. It was from the viewpoint of someone on the ground looking up at Baraqiel. Baraqiel's face was blotchy and his eyebrows furrowed. The veins in his forehead showed and there were tears streaming from both eyes. One tear ran all the way into Baraqiel's pouty lips. A hand in the foreground of the painting shows him reaching towards something. Towards Matariel. I looked at him and he smiled weakly.

"Is this...?" I started.

"When I died, yeah. Baraqiel doesn't want to keep this one but I feel like it captured raw emotion so well. Grief is a very powerful, all-consuming thing to go through. It's when we love someone so much who can't love us back because they're no longer around. And it doesn't have to be a romantic love or even an immediate family member. Grief can be felt for someone who moved you; changed your life for the better. But to have someone that important to you suddenly not exist in the same realm as you is a special kind of pain. That's how I knew Baraqiel was the one. To see someone grieve over me like he did. I would have waited a thousand eternities for the chance to see him again."

Baraqiel embraced Matariel and kissed him gently on the forehead. Matariel smiled and wrapped his arms around Baraqiel's neck. I started crying and felt out of breath as my emotions overwhelmed me. I hated it there, in Sentencing. I hated feeling again. It was excruciating after going so long being numb. Snot ran from my nose and I crossed my arms in front of my stomach. Otomatsu came over and put his hands on my shoulders.

"Are you okay?" he asked.

Without hesitating, I fell into his chest. All of the strength in my body left and Otomatsu held me. I sobbed uncontrollably, not really caring that everyone was watching me lose my shit. Everything hit me all at once. Losing Dumah one last time did me in. And the realization that the person I cared about most in all of existence, the person I was now scared most of losing, was holding me. I squeezed Otomatsu around the torso and held on like he would blow away in the wind.

"I love you," I whispered. "I can't lose you."

"Shhh," Otomatsu comforted me as he ran his fingers through my hair. "My sweet darling, Emma. It's okay. I never once wanted you to feel like I wanted to replace Dumah, or more importantly, your father. But I feel like you are my second chance at having a daughter. And it's okay if you don't feel the same."

"I do," I smiled up at him. "We're similar and different in all the best ways. We're two broken people who aren't well-liked by most people."

"Two broken parts that make a whole," he returned a smile. "I'm so glad Michael led me to you."

"Michael?" I pulled away. "What do you mean?"

"He knew we were both miserable and lonely. He said he thought it would be good for us. Because, unlike other death angels, you and I *hate* solitude."

"I sort of prayed for you," I said.

"What?"

"Right before you showed up on that beach. I honestly was just praying out loud. I didn't think anyone was listening to me."

"I had been working nonstop and out of nowhere received a notification from Michael," Otomatsu explained. "Which was very odd because the archangels had always left me completely alone. When I showed up in Processing, Michael invited me to sit on a bench in the courtyard with him. He asked how I was doing and it honestly confused the hell out of me."

Otomatsu chuckled lightly.

"I told him that I was fine and then he asked me again, and to tell the truth. I told him I didn't know what he was wanting to hear and that

I needed to get back to work. Then, he went on to tell me about you. Everything about you. Your life, your death, and how things were going for you as a death angel. Michael said our personalities were very similar, except you had no motivation and I put my *everything* into my duties. When he told me where you were, I went right away."

I smiled, unable to respond.

"I've got your back no matter what. And I'm very proud of you."

I paused a moment before saying, "there's a pretty decent house right next door to mine. I know you said you don't have enough stuff to need a house, but it can be a start. If you're interested."

"You know," Otomatsu said, rubbing his chin, "I think having somewhere to go to, to just hang out with someone, sounds pretty nice."

I looked at the painting again before turning to Baraqiel and Matariel.

"Could I, by chance, have this one?" I asked.

"Please!" Baraqiel said abruptly. "Then I won't have to look at it anymore."

"That's fine," Matariel said. "Besides, now that I actually have Baraqiel here with me, I don't need so many paintings of him."

"Did you want to take this one too?" Baraqiel asked, pulling a painting out from behind another one.

I caught a glimpse of a large penis taking up the canvas and then covered my eyes.

"Oh god!" I exclaimed. "No!"

"What?" he laughed. "It's art, Emma. Besides, I'm pretty proud of it; even if it is a little exaggerated on the size."

"It's actually not," Matariel smirked.

"Gross!" I groaned.

"Please stop," Otomatsu added in a serious tone that made me laugh.

At first daylight, Hutriel and Sekhmet came back. Hutriel and Baraqiel went with us as backup. I took Matariel's painting and told him goodbye. Once we reached the end of Baraqiel's territory, I said goodbye to him as well.

"Once the boat is done, I'll have Sekhmet help me hide it somewhere so Gabe doesn't find it. She'll keep it safe for you until you return."

"Thank you," I hugged him. "You don't know what this means to me."

Baraqiel looked behind in him, in the direction of Matariel's shore.

"Trust me, he said. "I know."

Baraqiel walked away as we kept going forward. Soon, Hutirel had to leave the group too.

"Emma, it was an absolute pleasure meeting you," she said. "I hope to see you again soon. And with les mongrels next time."

"Deal," I laughed. "Thanks for everything. Keep everyone safe."

"Absolutely," she winked before disappearing into the forest.

As we got closer to the shore, Sekhmet asked if we wanted to stop by the hut again, obviously trying to get me to visit Gabe before returning home. We explained that we needed to get back to work and after a couple of pleas, she finally gave up and went back to the forest. The sun was low as we reached the water.

"Are you okay carrying that?" Otomatsu asked, pointing to the painting in my hands.

"Yeah, I'll be fine," I answered. "Let's go."

As we flew back to Processing, I kept my eyes on the sea. From this far above the water, I could occasionally catch glimpses of Restless under the surface. I was one step closer to getting Sam out of there and saving her soul. When we arrived back on the beach, I put the painting in my house before going over to Dumah's hut; which was now Otomatsu's. I stocked up on vials and pouches, placing them on my belt, and then looked over the weapons hanging on the wall.

"I'm going to pick something out for Gabe," I told Otomatsu. "You go ahead and get a few jobs done while I head back to Sentencing for just a bit."

"Can't that wait?" he asked.

"I want to take it to him now so we can go to the Temple without any more side quests. Besides, it won't take long."

"Fine," Otomatsu grunted. "Take that one to him."

I looked to where he was pointing. There was a two-handed hammer with a long handle propped against the wall. One side of the hammer had a big metal mallet while the other side had an ax. I reached down with both hands and carefully brought the cumbersome weapon up to study it.

"Are you sure you don't want me to fly back with you?" Otomatsu asked. "Just to make sure you're safe."

"I'm sure," I smiled. "I'll be fine. I'll drop this off and come right back."

I parted ways with Otomatsu and made the journey back to the other shore. By the time I got there, it was very dark out. The moon was covered by clouds, leaving me with no light as I made my way to Gabe. As I got to the house, I realized no one was there. There were no lights or movement, so I carefully opened the door and went in. I laid the huge war hammer on the table and left just as quickly as I had come. Once back outside, I paused for a moment to listen to my surroundings. Everything was so quiet and eerie. In the silence, there came a hypnotic buzzing sound, like bees in a hive. I felt lightheaded and my feet started moving without my command. I went on autopilot, and I suddenly found myself standing in front of the bar Thalia and I met Abaddon in.

"What the-" I gasped, looking around.

People walked up and down the sidewalk, not paying any attention to me. A man bumped into me and I caught the ripe smell of vomit that was cascading down the front of his shirt. I went inside the bar, still confused as to how I wound up there. The stink of the bar almost choked me. The cigarette smoke was so thick that it made the dim lights even darker. Abaddon sat at a small table right next to the jukebox. He sipped on a martini and waved me over.

"Emma," he gestured to the chair opposite of his.

"What the fuck just happened?" I asked. "I was standing at the shore and then suddenly-"

"You're here with me," he smiled. "I summoned you."

"You...summoned me?"

"Yes."

"Did you possess me?"

Abaddon chuckled and took a sip.

"Emma, I can't possess you. Angels can't be possessed. I called for you and you answered."

"I didn't do anything!" I exclaimed.

"Trust me," he smiled. "You wouldn't have come if you didn't want to. Oh, my song!"

Abaddon hushed me and directed my attention to the jukebox.

"'Sea of Love' by The Honeydrippers," he sighed. "Do you know it?"

I shook my head.

"I just love music. You listen to the lyrics along with the melody and you can just picture the story. Feel what the singer is feeling. Music makes everything better."

"Was there something you needed?" I asked. "I really wasn't planning-"

"Just sit in the moment for once, will you?"

We sat there, listening to the song, while Abaddon continued to work on his martini. Abaddon kept smiling at me, which made me feel uneasy, so my eyes darted around the place. He finished his drink and slipped the green olive off its toothpick. He popped it into his mouth and waved at the bartender for another. As the song ended, Abaddon slid his hand across the table at me.

"Your turn," he said.

When he moved his hand away, there was a quarter sitting there.

"Go pick a song. Any song you want. But you better pick that up quickly. Even quarters get stolen here."

I picked up the coin and made my way to the machine. There was a country song playing that talked about being in prison and how his mama tried with him but he ended up being bad anyways. I flipped through pages and pages of songs. Finally, I settled on one and sat back down. As the country song ended and mine began, Abaddon grinned so wide, I could see all of his thin, sharp teeth.

"'Heart-Shaped Box' by Nirvana," he nodded in approval. "Very nice."

"I really should be getting back," I said. "I have a book or scroll or whatever to find. Remember?"

"Ankou said you asked for me to be his plus one. Does this mean you've thought about helping me?"

"I have thought about it, yes. I think helping me will prove that I can trust you. I know that Baraqiel helped Dumah get out of Hell, although I don't think he'll be as eager to help a demon. However, I have a friend who got out of Hell with the help of another dark angel named Matariel."

"The one that guards the shore by the lighthouse?" Abaddon asked.

"Yes," I answered. "He seems more open to helping. I'll get in touch with him after you help me get Sam out."

"I think you'll come to see that demons really aren't all that bad."

"Uh huh," I rolled my eyes. "Sure."

"Even Ankou," he winked. I scoffed.

"Emma, you have to understand that we're just trying to do our jobs here, just like you. There are some jobs that make people very unlikable, but they're jobs that need to be done."

"Influencing humans to commit murder and suicide isn't needed."

"We help maintain the balance of good and evil. If nothing bad ever happened, no one would notice the good!"

"That's such a lame answer."

"Lame, but true."

The bartender brought Abaddon another martini and he thanked him.

"Do you want anything?" Abaddon asked me.

"No," I snapped.

"Okay, okay," he put his hands up defensively. "Just asking."

The bartender glared at me and then went back to behind the counter.

"I'm working on getting a boat," I continued. "I'll come back with the scroll and Thalia, find you and Alastor, and we'll head out to sea to find Sam."

"We won't be able to go very far on the water."

"What do you mean?" I asked.

"We're demons," he explained. "We can't get too close to Processing. I'm not even sure how you'll get us past the shore since it's guarded."

"We'll have to figure out a way to distract Gabe and Sekhmet."

"I think I can come up with something."

Abaddon picked his glass up to take a drink, paused, and then laughed.

"What?" I asked.

Abaddon stood up, still laughing. He made his way back over to the jukebox and I abruptly followed him.

"What's so funny?" I asked.

You called him 'Alastor' instead of Ankou."

"I- oh."

"I think you still have a thing for him," Abaddon said as he selected a song. "You're the Only One" by The Broken Chandeliers started playing.

"I'm leaving," I snapped. "Next time you sense me nearby, it'll be because I have the scroll. Come find me but don't ever summon me again. Got it?"

Abaddon nodded once. I turned to leave and then looked back at him.

"You're wrong by the way," I said.

"About?" he smirked.

Without answering, I left the bar. Back out on the sidewalk, I exhaled deeply.

"Hey," a voice whispered from behind me. I turned quickly and saw Ankou leaning against the building, smiling. I let out an annoyed grunt and frowned.

"Get everything sorted out with Abaddon?" he grinned.

"What do you want?" I asked.

"I was taking a walk and thought that was you in there," he said. "Been visiting your new boyfriend on the coast?"

"Gabe isn't my boyfriend," I explained, walking away.

"That's good," he said, following me.

"Why's that?" I asked. Ankou pulled me into an alley

"Because you can't afford to have any distractions right now. You're supposed to be figuring out a way to get me to Sam."

"I found a way," I said. "I'm having a boat made. It should be done in a few weeks."

"A boat?" Ankou asked.

"Yes, a boat. I'm going to take you and Abaddon out on the water with Thalia. We're going to look for Sam, and you're going to get her out of that sea. Then, Thalia is going to take Sam to Paradise and I'll go with you."

"That sounds like a pretty decent plan," Ankou said, pushing his hair back. "And you'll go willingly with me? No tricks?"

"No tricks," I repeated. "I won't put up a fight at all."

Ankou clicked his tongue and sighed.

"Come on, you have to put up a little bit of a fight," he smirked. "Otherwise, where's the fun in that?"

"What exactly do you plan on doing with me for eternity?" I asked, crossing my arms.

"Remember how I said you were one of the most boring people I've ever fucked?"

I didn't say anything, although I felt myself clench my fists.

"Maybe that's the problem. Maybe humans just aren't enough for me anymore. They don't...quench my thirst, so to speak."

Ankou leaned in close to me.

"But I think a demon and an angel could have some real fucking fun."

Without hesitation, I drew back and punched Ankou as hard as I could in the face. He yelled out in pain, bending over and grabbing his cheek. Then, he slowly lifted his head, his hair flopping down on his forehead, and showed me his devilish smile.

"Yeah," he breathed. "Just like that."

I screamed as I lunged for him, wrapping my hands around his throat. Ankou put his hands around mine as we fell to the ground, me pinning him and then him pinning me. He gritted his teeth and winced as we laid there, locked on each other. People continued to walk by us as if we weren't even there.

"I...hate...you," I managed to get out between breaths.

"I...hate you...too," Ankou gasped.

He kissed me hard, pushing his body into mine. I let a moan escape as I let his tongue slip into my mouth. Somehow being with Ankou, even though I knew he was a demon and I was an angel, made me feel human again. A part of me ached to feel him again, even though he was the reason for all of the worst things in my existence. His hand cupped my breast and I gently pushed it away. He lowered his hand to the zipper of my pants and pushed it away again. I wanted him to know I was in control for once.

"You can keep fighting me and telling yourself you don't want to, but I can read you like a book, Emma Rose."

Hearing him using my name like that was like ice in my veins. Snapping back to reality, I kicked him off of me and got up quickly. Ankou grunted in disappointment.

"It's incredibly unfair that you know me so well but I never knew anything about you!"

"Besides a few minor lies and the fact that I'm a demon, you basically got to know the real me. All of my fun little quirks, my mannerisms-"

"Don't give me that bullshit," I scoffed. "You made yourself desirable so you could lure me in."

"When I found out you were dying, I almost left."

I stared at him.

"Yeah," he said, sitting up and resting his elbows on his knees. "I really thought about giving up on you and just letting you die. But I would have my ass chewed out for not trying to follow through with orders. Punishment for demons who don't fulfill their duties suffer horrible consequences. That's why I'm so good at my job. I have to be or I endure about fifty years of nonstop, agonizing torture."

"Is that supposed to make me feel sorry for you?" I asked.

"No, which is what makes us so similar," he grinned.

"I don't feel sorry for you because you don't deserve my sympathy. What you would have done to me-"

"I didn't do anything to you other than cause some 'first love' heartbreak. You would have experienced it at some point anyway if you had lived longer. Also, you forget that I was once human too. I might have been one of the very first ones, and it was thousands of years ago. But I *was* human. And being one of God's precious angels, you don't have the fucking right to tell me what I do and don't deserve. You think for one second I would have chosen any of this if I knew this was what was waiting for me?"

"You're meaning to tell me that you, an elite demon with so much power, would change your choices as a human if you had known you'd spend eternity in Hell? You're actually willing to admit that?"

"Fuck, Emma. You've been an angel for less than a hundred years but you act so self-righteous. I'm just saying...it's not exactly going how I thought it would. It's..."

"What?" I asked.

He didn't say anything as he stood up and paced.

"It's..." he started again.

"What!" I repeated.

"Lonely!" he snapped. "It's lonely. I'm constantly surrounded by demons and humans and it doesn't fucking matter. The loneliness is sometimes unbearable. And it's not exactly something I can talk about to anyone here. If I told other elites how lonely I was, they'd pin me down and shove a hot poker up my ass and laugh about it. But you...you get it."

"I'm not lonely," I replied quickly. "I have plenty of friends."

"That's the worst kind of loneliness. All those friends and you still feel like it's not enough. The constant itch that nothing is ever enough. You always feel unsatisfied."

Ankou walked up to me and got close to my face.

"But once all of this stuff with Sam is over with," he said, brushing my cheek, "I won't ever be lonely again."

I started breathing heavily through my nose and fought the urge to punch him (or kiss him) again. He gently tucked a strand of hair behind my ear and leaned closer to whisper.

"As long as you're a good girl and do as I say."

I didn't say anything as I stared into his eyes. The moment seemed to last forever. I didn't want to be the first to look away, but a part of me hoped he'd never take his eyes off of me.

"I'll let you run along now," he pulled away and winked. "I know you have lots of work to get done."

It was like a trance was broken. I walked out of the dingey alley and back out onto the sidewalk, a little embarrassed of myself and what I had just done. But a small voice in the back of my mind was saying, *turn around and take him.*

"See you around, Emma Rose."

Not able to stand it there another minute, I flew away. It's not a rule as an angel that you can't fly in Sentencing, but everyone knows that it draws unwanted attention. I didn't care. I needed to get away from Ankou as quickly as possible. As I flew out of the city and into the desert, the hot wind whipped at my face. I felt a huge mix of emotions that all conflicted with each other. I hated Ankou; there was no doubt about that. But I also still felt a yearning for him and didn't know why. I still didn't *want* to want him. The further out of Sentencing I got, the better I started to feel. I wasn't as fatigued. In fact, I had a renewed energy. I flew even faster until I was back at the shore. I landed hard on my feet and ran to the house. I swung the door open hard and it bounced off the wall. Gabe had been sitting at the table, but stood abruptly when I walked in.

"Emma?"

I ran and jumped into his arms, kissing him passionately. He wrapped his arms around me and kissed me back. We ran into the table and knocked a chair over. He carried me over to the kitchen counter and pulled away briefly.

"I didn't think-" he started.

"Shut up," I whispered before leaning in to kiss him again.

I helped him take layers of his armor off until he was naked. He stood before me, letting me just look at him for a moment. Then, I took my boots and clothes off. As a human, I would have felt vulnerable and self-conscious being naked in front of such an attractive man. But as an angel, even one that wasn't considered pretty, I felt powerful.

"You're so beautiful," Gabe said, softly placing his hand on my cheek.

"You don't have to be gentle with me," I whispered in his ear. "I won't break."

"I don't think you're fragile," Gabe said. "But you are very precious to me."

Gabe gently parted my lips with his tongue. We kissed as he laid me down on the floor. Then, he kissed my forehead, each cheek, and my chin. As he started kissing my neck, I grabbed his hair and sighed, partially with pleasure but also with impatience. I watched Gabe kiss my shoulder and collarbone, between my breasts, and down to my stomach.

"Gabe," I finally said. He looked up at me. "Just do it already."

He smiled and kissed my inner thigh.

"Let me admire all of you," he said before kissing my other thigh. "Besides, the buildup makes it better."

I looked down at Gabe and remembered looking down at Alastor the same way when he would show me ways he could please me with his mouth. Gabe delicately ran his index finger down to my knee and then slid his way back up towards my face. I wrapped my fingers around a tuft of his hair and pushed him back down. Gabe gasped in surprise but knew what I wanted him to do. As much as I wanted Gabe, a part of me couldn't help but think of Alastor.

Alastor's hazel eyes and his ashy blonde hair appeared in my mind. I thought about his full lips and the way they felt when I kissed them. He was tall enough that when I wrapped my arms around his neck to kiss him, the heels of my feet came off the ground slightly. I remembered when I ran my bike into the door of his car and how he looked when he asked if I was okay. The way his body blocked the sun, standing over me, but in a way that made it look like sunlight was coming off of him. I thought about the heart he drew on my bandaid and the way he insisted on using my middle name. I remembered what it was like being with him, and let out a loud moan as I climaxed.

Gabe smiled at me and crawled up to kiss me again. I let my knees relax and pulled him in. Gabe started grunting along to the rhythm of his thrusting. Although I would never judge someone for the noises they naturally make during sex, something about it was more distracting than arousing. I pulled his head down to mine and kissed him, hoping that would make him stop. I bit Gabe's lower lip forcefully, but not too hard. This made Gabe speed up a little. I buried my face into his neck and wrapped my legs around his waist.

"Harder," I breathed.

"Emma, I don't think-" Gabe panted.

"Please," I begged.

He did as I asked and my fingernails dug deep into the skin on his back.

"Oh, Emma!"

"Call me 'Emma Rose,'" I moaned.

"Emma...Rose."

I let out a scream as my body convulsed. As I tightened up, Gabe arched his back and then collapsed next to me, breathing heavily. He had one arm resting on his forehead and the other on his chest. I wasn't looking at him but I could see him smiling at me out of the corner of my eye. I was developing feelings for Gabe, but knew it was pointless. Once Sam was freed, I belonged to

Ankou. I wanted to love Gabe but couldn't.

Without saying a word, I stood up and got dressed.

"Are you leaving?" Gabe asked.

"Uh, yeah. I have to get back to work."

"I wish you could stay."

I forced a smile and put my boots on. Gabe stood up, not bothering to get dressed right away.

"Is everything okay?" he asked.

"Yeah," I said a little too quickly. "I just really need to be heading back."

I gave him a peck on the cheek and another smile. As I reached the door, Gabe grabbed my other hand. I turned to him.

"Thank you," he said. "That was amazing."

"Yeah," was all I could manage to say again as I let go.

I wasn't sure how long Gabe watched me as I flew away because I couldn't bring myself to look back at him. I knew why I had done what I did, and I knew how much it would hurt Gabe if he knew. And I hated myself for it.

15

Otomatsu was waiting for me when I got back to the shore. His arms were crossed and he had an extremely stern look on his face. I noticed a satchel slung over his shoulder. The flap was fastened shut so I couldn't see its contents.

"What took you so long?" he asked as soon as I landed.

"Sorry," I said, walking past him.

"That doesn't answer my question."

"I stayed longer than planned," I spat. "I don't know what else you want me to say."

"I want you to explain yourself."

"I'm not a child. I don't have a curfew."

"I was worried about you."

Otomatsu grabbed me by the shoulder and turned me around.

"Emma, stop!"

I looked at him and narrowed my eyes.

"Did you go to Sentencing?"

Yes.

"No," I said.

"Did something happen with Gabe?"

Yes.

"No."

"Are you okay?" he asked.

No.

"Yes," I lied.

Otomatsu slowly let go of my shoulders and sighed.

"Look, I'm not going to push this anymore. If you wanted me to know, you'd tell me. I trust you to make good choices. I was just worried."

"I appreciate that," I said, sticking my chin up. "I'm sorry that I worried you. I just lost track of time."

"Well, I took the liberty of tracking Thalia down for you," Otomatasu said.

"What?" I asked. "Why?"

"She's supposed to be your 'plus one.' If we're going to move forward with this grand plan of yours, we should probably get her on board with everything since she's a part of it."

"Where is she?" I asked, rubbing the inner corners of my eyes with my index finger and thumb. Otomatsu pointed at my house. I looked at him and sighed.

"No time like the present," he smiled.

"Yeah. Thanks."

I walked in and saw Thalia's tiny body sitting on the couch. She looked at us as we walked in and then looked away.

"Hey, Thalia," I smiled.

"Hello, Emma," she replied, still not looking at me.

I sat down on the couch next to her, causing her to bounce a little from the sudden weight added to the cushion. She scooted away from me and cleared her throat.

"I'm sorry I haven't been a good friend to you," I said. "I know I can be grumpy and difficult to get along with. I'm sorry for that."

"I hope you're apologizing because you really mean it and not because you need a favor," Thalia said shortly. I looked at Otomatsu.

"No!" I said. "I really am sorry. I was really shitty to you and I feel bad about the way I treated you. You've always been nothing but kind towards me and you didn't deserve the way I was in return. But I promise you that I'll be a better friend from now on. I think I just needed to move past the whole Dumah thing-"

Thalia scoffed at that.

"I know," I continued. "You were right. Everyone was right. What can I say? I'm stubborn. But I'm trying to be better. And all I can ask is for you to be a little patient with me while I try."

Thalia looked at me and smiled.

"Thank you for apologizing," she said. "Also, Otomatsu already explained everything and of course I'll help you."

"Wait, seriously?" I asked, looking from him to her. "I don't want you to do anything you don't want to do."

"We talked while we waited for you to come back from whatever it was you were doing," Otomatsu explained.

"I don't trust Ankou and Abaddon," Thalia said. "I think having both of us there is a good idea. But I think we should also tell Sekhmet and Gabe."

"No!" I exclaimed. "I think the less angels who know about this, the better."

"But it would be safer to have backup," Thalia said.

"If we have too many angels involved, Abaddon and Ankou won't trust me," I explained. "We need to keep things fair."

"We're talking about demons," she scoffed. "They don't play fair."

"I just don't want to do anything that will jeopardize the situation," I sighed. "It'll be fine. Trust me."

"We need to find that scroll," Otomatsu said. "We should probably get going sooner than later."

"Don't you need someone to let you into the temple?" Thalia asked.

"I have a way in," Otomatsu smiled.

"How?" Thalia asked. "Death angels usually aren't allowed in."

"It's a secret," he winked.

"Fine," she said, hopping off the couch and flying towards the door. "Just keep out of trouble."

"Of course," I said.

"Always," Otomatsu replied at the same time. Thalia gave us a weary look and left.

"Shall we?" I grinned.

"Let's go find that scroll," Otomatsu nodded.

I was both nervous and excited as we made our way to The Gates. I hoped I looked as calm and collected as Otomatsu did. We walked through the entrance and Raphael and Jarahmeel were standing guard.

"Crap," I whispered.

"What's wrong?" Otomatsu asked. I didn't respond as I discreetly pulled my hood up and lowered my head.

"I'm just saying," I heard Raphael say, "it's one of the most famous paintings in the world and no one has yet to confirm that it's really a man dressed as a woman and not an actual woman."

"There are conspiracy theorists who believe it to be true though," Jarahmeel responded. "Maybe no one cares enough to know the truth."

"Humans love that sort of thing though. They make movies about historical theories all the time. If they took the time to- hey!"

I kept walking, hoping Rapheal wasn't talking to us.

"If you wanted to look conspicuous, you shouldn't have put the hood up, Emma."

Raphael and Jarahmeel laughed. I pulled my hood back, gave a sarcastic smile, and kept walking. Raphael ran up to us and stood in front of me.

"What are you two up to?" he asked.

"None of your business," Otomatsu answered.

"That's not very nice," Raphael pouted.

"Why do you feel like you need to bother me every time you see me?" I asked. "What did I ever do to you?"

"Nothing!" Raphael snickered. "I just think it's funny how sensitive you all are. Lighten up."

"Let's go, Emma," Otomatsu said.

I walked around Raphael and followed Otomatsu to the marble path that led to the temple.

"Good luck with that," Raphael called. "You two aren't allowed in there unless someone with access lets you in!"

Ignoring him, I picked up my pace to get closer to Otomatsu. I looked down at the satchel, bouncing slightly against his thigh.

"What is that?"

"Secret weapon," he winked.

"Are you sure about this?" I asked quietly.

"Everything will be fine," he muttered. "I've been here before, remember?"

"How though?" I asked.

We approached the large wooden doors and Otomatsu grabbed a giant rope to the right. He gave one hard tug and a loud bell rang from overhead. We waited a moment before a sliding peephole in the door moved, revealing a pair of eyes.

"Yes?" the person on the other side said.

"Hello there, old friend," Otomatsu smiled.

"Ahhh!" the voice shrieked and the peephole slid shut, making me jump.

I looked at Otomatsu and he grinned. There was a loud banging sound and then the huge doors creaked as they slowly opened. A short, round man with a long beard stepped out with his arms extended. He was wearing a blue satin robe that was tied just above his sphere-shaped belly. Otomatsu hugged him and patted him on the back.

"It's been too long!" the man chuckled. "How are you?"

"I'm good," Otomatsu replied. "I'd like you to meet someone very special to me. This is Emma."

Otomatsu gestured towards me and the man beamed. I waved my hand awkwardly and the man squeezed me in a strong hug.

"Oh!" I exclaimed. This made Otomtasu laugh.

"Emma, this is Zhongli Quan."

"Please, call me Quan," the man patted my shoulders hard. "Emma, it is a pleasure to meet you."

"Likewise," I smirked.

"Quan is the keeper of the temple," Otomatsu explained. "And he was my very first friend when I became an angel."

"As far as I know, I was your only friend until Emma!" Quan laughed.

"Hilarious," Otomatsu said sarcastically. Quan jabbed him in the bicep.

"Where have you been? You haven't visited me in centuries!"

"I have a job I have to do!" Otomatsu said. "I don't get vacations."

"And here you are now," Quan put his hands on his hips and nodded towards me. "So should I thank you for bringing him here?"

"He actually brought me here," I smiled.

"Normally, death angels do need to come with someone who has clearance. However, Otomatsu has…special privileges."

"She knows I exorcise demons."

Quan looked wide-eyed from me to him.

"She also knows Dumah used to."

"Secret missions are called secret for a reason!"

"Oh please. She'll probably get recruited to do it anyways. She's got some natural talent."

"Oh yeah?" Quan asked, crossing his arms. "Such as?"

"I don't-" I started.

"She can save suicides," Otomatsu interrupted. I immediately blushed.

"How do you know how to do that?" Quan asked me.

"Oh, I just stumbled across something I found in Dumah's hut and tried it out. I honestly never knew if it worked until recently."

"That damned thieving death angel," Quan said through gritted teeth.

"I'm sorry?" I looked at Otomatsu, who shrugged.

"That book went missing years ago and I knew someone stole it!"

"Oh," I said. "I'm sorry. If I had known it was taken-"

"*Stolen*," Quan repeated.

"-stolen," I sighed, "I would have returned it. I can bring it back to you if you'd like."

"I would greatly appreciate that," Quan beamed at me.

"So are you going to let us come in or are we going to just stand out here?" Otomatsu said.

"Yes, yes," Quan waved us into the building. "Please, come in!"

As we walked into the temple, I was immediately in awe. Everywhere I looked, there were books and papers. Rows upon rows of shelves stacked full. There were three floors above us filled with more. People were seated at tables reading or climbing up on ladders to reach books placed on higher shelves. I couldn't stop looking around. I glanced at Otomatsu and he was smiling, watching me.

"Impressive, isn't it?" he asked.

"If I breathed still, I think this would take my breath away," I said.

Quan let out a loud chuckle, making his belly jiggle.

"Quan, may I ask you a question?"

"Of course!" He smiled at me.

"You're a virtue, right?" I asked.

"Mmhmm."

"Why are you big then?"

Quan laughed again.

"I've honestly never liked being small. Even when I was inspiring humans, I hated flying around like a silly little bird. I volunteered immediately when the archangels asked for someone to oversee the temple. I quickly found out that it's nearly impossible to tend to a place this big when you're so little. I stay this size all the time now."

I nodded, looking around as he spoke.

"So, Emma, how did you came to know Dumah?"

Quan gave me a puzzling look before turning to Otomatsu.

"It's a long story," I said.

"Ah," Quan beamed. "I love long stories. Perhaps you can indulge me over some tea."

Always tea.

"We really don't have time," I explained. "We came for something specific and then have to get going."

"We're already here," Otomatsu winked. "We can stay for a little while."

"Okay," I said wearily. "Like three hours tops."

"Right," Otomatsu smiled sheepishly. "Three hours."

As we walked through the aisles, I didn't know where to look.

"Is this all literature?" I asked.

"Literature, historical moments, the answers that everyone wants to know."

"Like Jesus' real origin story?" I looked at Otomatsu.

"He told you?" Quan asked. "Well did he tell you about Ananiel?"

"The dark angel who patrols Sentencing?" I asked. "What about him?"

"Ahh, that is an interesting story," Quan waved a finger at me. "Ananiel was not his name when he was human. He changed his name when he became a dark angel to conceal his true identity. Are you familiar with the Bible or the Quran?"

"The Bible, yes," I answered.

"He's in both, but is widely known for a coat his father gifted him."

I didn't respond.

"A coat of *many colors*."

My mouth dropped.

"Joseph?" I asked excitedly.

Quan laughed.

"Joseph is a Bible *and* Quran all star. He was envied by his brothers, who sold him to Egypt. There, he eventually became imprisoned on false charges of trying to seduce his master's wife. Joseph used his unique abilities to interpret dreams to get him out of trouble. When the Pharaoh heard of his gifts, he asked Joseph to interpret his dreams. When Joseph told him to prepare for years of famine, the Pharaoh appointed Joseph as his viceroy, ruler over the land. He oversaw the maintenance of the Nile and its surrounding fields, ensuring they would withstand a drought. Joseph died and was sent to Processing, just like everyone else. When he arrived though, he let the archangels know that he had an important job to do and would not be entering Paradise. The archangels were of course confused about this and reluctantly made Joseph a greeter. Being such a widely known and popular man, it was a good job for him. He enjoyed it. But he told the archangels that he was meant for something more important."

"He was the first human to become a dark angel," Otomatsu added. "Joseph went straight to Hutriel and asked her if he could help by becoming a dark angel. She was reluctant at first because

Joseph was such an important person in life. She didn't want him getting hurt. But Joseph said that he would pray, asking God to grant him a special power to protect himself. If God blessed him, he would change his name to protect his identity. God favored Joseph, so He gave him the powers of destructive wind. And he's been patrolling and guarding Sentencing ever since."

"Wow," was all I could say.

"And thanks to him, we have Sekhmet, Baraqiel, and the rest of the dark angels to help Hutriel."

"Why don't you have a look around while Quan and I catch up?" Otomatsu suggested.

"That's quite all right," Quan said. "I don't mind showing her around."

Otomatsu leaned in closely to Quan and tapped his satchel.

"I brought the good stuff," he whispered. "We can skip the tea."

Quan's eyes widened and he grinned from ear to ear.

"Ha ha! You were always my favorite!"

Quan and Otomatsu walked away like I had suddenly turned invisible. I stood there, not sure of what to do or where to go. Otomatsu peaked around the corner.

"This might take me a while," he whispered. "Explore the temple for a bit and then meet us down on the bottom floor."

I nodded quickly and he disappeared again. I breathed heavily, not sure of where to go. I wandered around, looking at the shelves and the people that filled the temple. Everyone looked so happy and excited, obviously getting new information or reading a story they've always wanted to read. I found myself in a section playfully called, "Commonly Asked Questions." There were books and pamphlets on shelves, and a row of computers at tables. One man was sitting in a chair, reading a pamphlet called, "Who Were Adam and Eve?"

"Can I help you?" a small, elderly woman asked me. She had short white hair and piercing blue eyes behind cat-eye glasses.

"Oh, uh, I-" I stammered. "I don't know."

She smiled up at me.

"That's why this is here, dear," she said, gently taking my hand in hers and patting it. "It's okay to not know, as long as you're willing to learn. My name is Marianne."

"You're not scared of me?" I asked. She laughed.

"I've been here a while. You're not the first death angel I've ever seen. Besides, I saw much scarier things when I was alive."

When I didn't respond, she continued.

"I was sent to Auschwitz and never left. I was a well-educated Jewish woman who had a lifelong love of books and knowledge, and I died in a gas chamber alongside hundreds of other Jews because I was too old to work. Never mind that I was valuable because of my intelligence. All I can say is I'm glad I never married or had children, and my parents had been dead long before we were all sent to camps and ghettos. I never had to worry or wonder about loved ones. It was horrible hearing the others sob and pray for their family members. They all had so much hope that we would be saved. I knew when I arrived at Auschwitz that I would die there. But I'm fortunate that I get to spend forever here. Every day I learn something new, and I get to help someone learn something new."

"I'm so sorry for what happened to you," I said.

"I am very grateful for you and other death angels though," she smiled. "We all saw you there with us in our final moments. So thank you for being there."

I hadn't personally been there when she died, but I knew better than to say so. I nodded, accepting her thanks. Taking my hand again, she led me to a computer.

"I don't do much with these things as I prefer books," she chuckled. "But I hear they're faster. Although, where's the fun in that? All any of us have now is time."

I walked up to the screen and placed my hands on the keyboard. It had been so long since I had used a computer. There was a standard search bar on the screen and a small line that was flashing, waiting for me to start typing.

"And I can ask anything?"

"Anything," she grinned. "The knowledge of the universe is at your fingertips, dear."

She patted me on the shoulder and walked away to help someone else. I stood there, frozen with my fingers on the keys. And then a question came.

"Did dinosaurs really exist?" I typed and hit the enter key. The answer was yes. I glanced around, smiling at no one in particular. I cleared the search bar.

"Did a meteor kill the dinosaurs?" The answer was yes. Satisfied, I cleared the search bar.

"Are we alone in the universe?" I typed. The answer was no. I gasped. I heard Marianne giggle from behind me like a little girl.

"I know," she said. "That's a popular question that always gets quite the reaction! But it makes so much sense. So many galaxies out there, and we're the only ones? Not even close."

"I kind of always thought that was the case," I said, "but we've never made contact with them so it seemed like such a far-fetched idea."

"No one has made the technology yet to find each other," Marianne shrugged.

"How come none of them are here?" I asked, turning back to the computer.

"None of them know this exists."

"But then-"

"I'm sorry, dear. I'd love to stay and chat but I really do need to get back to work. Try asking something other than yes and no questions. Have fun!"

I turned back to Marianne and she was gone. A little girl was standing behind me instead.

"Are you almost done?" she asked in her tiny voice. She looked to be about five or six years old.

"Huh?" I said, not registering what she had said.

"Are you almost done?" she repeated. "I have a lot of questions."

"Oh, um, sure."

I stepped aside and let her by. I watched her stand on tiptoes, reaching for the mouse and keyboard. I looked around and found an unused chair and brought it to her.

"No thanks," she said as I placed the chair beside her. "I've been in a wheelchair almost my whole life. I'm tired of sitting."

I smiled and nodded. She looked me up and down.

"You're weird looking."

I didn't say anything. She smiled.

"I like it."

I smiled back.

"Thanks."

She turned back to the screen and I read as she typed in the search bar, "Do parents know kids with cerebral palsy love them even though they can't talk?"

"Have fun learning," I said before walking away.

I walked around for a bit longer before finally finding the staircase. There was a landing and then an option to up or down. I started making my way up when a man I passed grumbled to himself.

"What, they couldn't afford to put an elevator in this place?"

"I know, right?" I agreed.

He looked at me and his eyes widened. He picked up the pace and moved closer to the railing. It was a reminder that not everyone was as accepting of how I looked like Marianne and the little girl at the computer were. I sighed and kept going. The upper level was just as impressive as the main floor. There was one whole section that veered off to the left that was all film. Movies, tv shows, and important moments in world history were organized on shelves. There were private viewing rooms on the right side of the level. There were lights above each room lit up either green or red. Green meant the room was empty and ready to use. Red meant that someone was using it and not to disturb them. I walked around for what seemed like hours until finally circling back to the staircase. *Back down I go*, I thought.

I went all the way to the bottom floor. There were only a couple of people down there, and they were all concentrating heavily on the books they had. As I passed them, they all looked up at me, smiled, and nodded. I somehow knew without asking that they were guardian angels. My "divine powers" seemed to be improving. The lowest level was full of books specifically for angels. "How To" books and training books lined shelf after shelf, and I again wondered why death angels weren't allowed in the temple if there could be useful information for their jobs. One bright yellow spine caught my eye and I read the title, tilting my head to read it. "How to Be a Virtue in a World of Technology." I pulled the book out and the cover had a small, fairy-like woman flying between two children in front front of a television. The children were playing a video game while the virtue had her hands on her hips. I placed the book carefully back on the shelf and kept walking.

I arrived at a caged off area that was locked. *If I were something that wasn't meant to be read by just anyone*, I thought, *I'd be in there*. I just had to figure out how to get inside. I frowned at the sign that said, "Restricted Area," and hit the metal fence with the palm of my hand.

"There's a call button over there," I heard a voice say.

I turned to a man in thick black glasses who was pointing to the far right wall.

"It lets them know someone is requesting access to that area," he smiled before going back to his book.

"Oh, thank you," I replied. I watched him continue to read his book, which was titled, "Guarding Humans Who Don't Believe in Angels (Or God, For That Matter!)" and I wondered if Sam had ever read it. I wondered how many times she had been to the temple, what she learned while she was there, and what made her decide to betray God. When you have all of the knowledge of the universe at your fingertips, why would you risk that kind of privilege? I couldn't understand it. Did Sam truly want to go against Paradise and the other angels, or had she been manipulated so well by Ankou that she thought she was making the best choice?

I pushed the call button for assistance. It made a loud buzzing sound and lit up.

"Sorry," I said through gritted teeth. "I didn't realize it would be that loud.

"It's fine," the angel smiled and pushed his glasses up.

"So," I pointed to his book, "are you, uh, having some issues?"

The guardian angel looked up at me and sighed.

"My wife is an atheist. I've always considered myself more agnostic. I just worry about her, ya know? She doesn't believe in God, Heaven, angels, or Hell for that matter. I'm hoping that I'll be a good enough guardian angel that by the time she dies, her mind will change pretty quickly. I still can't see her choosing Paradise though. Maybe she'll want to become an angel with me."

"Yeah, Paradise didn't seem like the right choice to me at the time either," I shrugged. "You never know though. People can surprise you."

"Right," the angel chuckled softly. "That definitely describes my wife. Surprising. She went through what can only be described as a 'midlife crisis' right before she turned forty. She cut her hair really short, colored it pink, and then got this huge bicep tattoo of a phoenix. Said it was symbolic for new beginnings or something like that. Then, she got really into tarot cards, crystals, and astrology. She was never that kind of person. In fact, she used to make fun of those people like she did with people who believed in God. She said it was the same, just a different imaginary thing to believe in. But then she became one of those people! I decided to let her be. I had just started chemo when she started going through all of that and I was too tired to say anything."

"You died from cancer?" I asked. "Sorry, I know that's rude. It's just that that's what I died from too."

"Yeah, there's quite a few of us," the angel chuckled again. "It's like a special club. I had prostate cancer. It was very aggressive. Chemotherapy just prolonged my death instead of preventing it. But Clara, my wife, insisted on me eating all organic foods. She replaced all of our cleaning supplies with 'clean' ones. The amount of homeopathic remedies she made me try was exhausting. Of course none of them helped."

"I'm sorry," I said. "I know what it's like to have family members try desperately to keep you alive."

"How old are you?" he asked. "I mean, how old were you when you died?"

"Only 21," I answered.

"Damn. That's awfully young."

"I think that's partially why I felt the need to become an angel. I hadn't done much with my life."

"That's how I feel too," he sighed. "I was older than you but I wasted years and years of just working and coming home. I didn't have any hobbies or interests. I watched movies and played video games. A mid-forties gamer. My legacy."

The man suddenly snapped the book with more force than I was expecting. It made a loud snap before he put it back on the shelf.

"You know she started seeing someone else before I died," he added. "They met at yoga. His wife had died from cancer two years prior. How messed up is that? I mean, I expected her to eventually move on after I died. I didn't want her to be alone the rest of her life. But they were sleeping together while I was pissing blood."

He knocked on the book he had placed on the shelf and sighed.

"And here I am, still worried about her."

"You're a good person," I said. "Don't let anyone take that from you. Let the bad decisions of others be theirs to carry, okay?"

Just then, the door in the back of the fenced off area opened. Quan and Otomatsu appeared out of an elevator and I quickly turned back towards the guardian angel.

"Good luck with everything," I said.

"You too. It was nice meeting you...?"

"Oh, I'm Emma," I smiled.

"I'm Mark. It was nice meeting you, Emma."

I heard the gate behind me unlock and I turned back to see Quan and Otomatsu. Quan's face was flushed and he was smiling even wider than he had been before.

"There you are, Emma!" he bellowed as he opened the gate. "Otomatsu and I have been having the best time. He told me you might be down here, and here you are! Otomatsu is one smart fellow!"

He laughed loudly as I walked inside. I glanced at Otomatsu, who just shook his head. Quan locked the gate behind me and I could smell alcohol on him.

"Normally only archangels and temple staff are allowed back here, but you two are my friends so it's fine!"

"Do you mind keeping your voice down?" Otomatsu muttered. "You're going to draw unwanted attention and get us in trouble."

"Don't be such a worrier!" Quan exclaimed through slurred speech. "We're just fine!"

I started looking around at the shelves, not having the slightest idea of what I was looking for.

"I can't read some of these," I said. Quan looked over my shoulder.

"Some of those are in the word of the devil," Quan said, his smile fading as he sat down in a wooden chair. His eyes were glossy and he seemed to be having a difficult time focusing on his surroundings. "Only a handful of people can translate them because they were scripted in a secret language by Satan himself."

"How many things here are in that language?" I asked.

"Not very many. Most of them are failed attempts to overthrow Heaven and Earth."

"Do you know if there's a scroll called 'The Book of...something?' I'm not really sure what we're looking for."

"I don't know," Quan rubbed his head. "I don't mess with those too much since I can't fully translate them. I've asked before if I could learn the language and..."

I looked at Quan and he was swaying in his seat.

"Are you okay?" I asked.

"Right as rain, my dear!" he perked up. "Right as rain!"

"Will he be okay?" I asked quietly.

"He'll be fine," Otomatsu muttered.

I kept searching through scrolls, books, and papers, hoping to find some hint as to what we needed. The worst part was not knowing what we were looking for. Elite demons could read the translations but didn't have the access we did. Technically, we weren't allowed there either. I glanced at Quan slumped over and I felt a twinge of guilt.

"Emma."

I looked over at Otomatsu, who was looking curiously at something. I put down the book I was flipping through and walked over to him. He had pulled a tattered scroll out and spread it amongst the piles of books. The scroll was made of heavy cloth instead of paper and was light brown in color. It had the unknown language written all over in reddish-brown ink. The drawing was of a figure levitating above water with its arms out. On one side of the figure was a white, winged creature. On the other, was a darker, horned creature. An angel and a demon.

"Is this it?" I whispered.

"Look at this picture down here," Otomatsu pointed at the bottom of the page. "There are two lands under the figures with water between them, and the land under the demon is black. There's a light coming out of the water and it looks similar to-"

"Anathema," I gasped. "This has to be it!"

I ran the scroll over to Quan and put it in front of him.

"Can you translate this?"

Quan squinted at the scroll, bugged his eyes, and then squinted again.

"Uh, only...a few words," he mumbled. "Light, dark, sea-"

"Does it say anything about saving someone from the Sea of Anathema?"

Quan squinted again.

"I...I think...so."

I looked back at Otomatsu.

"This is it!" I exclaimed. "It has to be!"

There was a thud and I turned to see Quan with his head down on the table in front of him. Otomatsu quickly rolled up the scroll and grabbed my cloak. He stuffed the scroll into the interior pocket and then pulled it closed.

"Button that up," he snapped. "We need to go now."

"What about him?" I asked, pointing to Quan.

"He'll be fine. But we need to leave before he wakes up and even suspects that we took something."

I wanted to ask a dozen questions but knew there wasn't time. I followed Otomatsu closely as we got into the elevator behind the fenced off area. At the top was a door that led to a room. There was a fireplace with two leather chairs in front of it. I noticed four bottles of wine; two of them were open and laying on the floor.

"What did you do to him?" I asked.

"I brought him some special wine," Otomatsu explained. "I didn't think he'd drink that much *that* quickly."

"You got him drunk?"

Otomatsu grabbed my hand and pulled me along.

"Come on, Emma!"

I started to run again as we came out of the room and out into a long hallway but Otomatsu halted me.

"We need to act calm," he said softly. "Move quickly, but calmly. If anyone stops us, just act like we need to get back to work."

I nodded and followed him through the temple, not looking around at anyone. As soon as we were to the front doors, I exhaled. We had made it without being stopped. We walked down the path, towards the entrance of The Gates. We were almost in the clear.

"Hey!"

Shit.

I turned, bumping clumsily into Otomatsu, before shuffling around him to see Michael and Raphael walking towards us.

"Be calm and get them off our backs quickly," Otomatsu whispered.

I forced a cheerful grin as the two archangels approached us.

"Hey, guys!" I said, a little too enthusiastically. Michael gave me a puzzled look.

"Where have you been?" he asked.

"I hadn't had a chance to visit the temple," I explained. "I figured, there's no time like the present!"

Raphael raised an eyebrow.

"Zhongli Quan is an old friend of mine," Otomatsu added.

"Death angels don't have friends," Raphael grumbled.

"Well, I think you two have spent enough time slacking off, visiting friends," Michael said.

"Learning the secrets of the universe is hardly slacking off," I crossed my arms.

"Did you take anything?" Raphael asked.

"Are you serious?" I glared.

"Raphael, don't be accusatory," Michael said. "Emma has been working very hard lately and even helped us recruit a new dark angel to help patrol Sentencing. She's more than welcome to check out the temple, as long as Zhongli Quan keeps a close eye on her and it doesn't interfere with her work too much."

"Which is why we need to get going," I said. "Like you said, we spent enough time there and now we need to get back to work."

"So you wouldn't mind if I searched you real quick?" Raphael asked, getting closer to me.

"Raphael," Michael scolded.

"Excuse me?" I asked.

"If you're not hiding anything, it won't be a problem," he smiled.

I scoffed and looked at Michael and Otomatsu. Panic began to rise from my belly to my throat.

"This is bullsh-"

"Emma!" Michael cut me off. "Listen. Raphael is right. If you don't have anything to hide, we can get this done quickly and you two can be on your way."

Otomatsu and I held eye contact while Raphael checked my pockets. As he pulled my cloak away, I held my breath. He searched the interior pockets before stepping back.

"Can we go now?" Otomatsu asked.

"You're next," Raphael said, walking towards him.

"I think we've wasted enough of everyone's time," Michael said. "Let them go."

We walked out of The Gates and Otomatsu grabbed my wrist. He pushed something on the tracker's map and we were suddenly on the streets of Mumbai, India, in the middle of Dharavi, one of the largest slums in the world. I looked around, confused.

"What-?"

"Not yet," Otomatsu said, quickly moving into one of the shacks.

The sound of flies buzzing was almost deafening. As we turned the corner, I saw an older man laying on a dirty mattress. There was vomit on the floor next to him and he was shivering, even though it was hot outside. The skin on his ankle was swollen and red.

"He was bitten by a cobra," I said softly. "The snake was in his home and when the man rolled over in his sleep, it startled the snake, causing it to bite him. It woke him up but he didn't have time to get to a hospital. He has a heart condition and asthma so the venom is already killing him."

I knelt down next to the mattress on the floor. The man was shaking so badly, it looked like he was having a seizure. I placed my hand gently on his shoulder. He looked up and saw me. His shivering stopped and he slowly raised his hand to my face. As soon as his dirty palm reached my cheek, it fell next to him. Everything went silent for a moment. I stood up and faced Otomatsu.

"You're getting better," he said.

"Thanks."

We left the man's shack and walked down the road.

"There's another one just up ahead," Otomatsu pointed. "This is actually a frequent place for us death angels. This many people in such a small area, and with so many diseases. Not to mention starvation and crime."

"Are you going to tell me what's going on?" I asked.

"I knew they'd track us to see where we went," he explained. "We needed to get back to work immediately to take the attention off of us. We need to lay low for a little bit before we move forward with the plan."

"What about the scroll? I don't have it."

Otomatsu unbuttoned the flap on his satchel and opened it. I peaked in and didn't see anything. He pulled back the lining of the inside of the bag to reveal the scroll.

"How?" I asked.

"As soon as I saw the archangels, I knew we were going to have some problems. When you bumped into me, I grabbed it."

"What if they would have searched you?"

"Then I guess I would have been caught with the scroll and you'd be in the clear."

I stared at him for a while, half in shock, half in admiration.

"This is important to you," Otomatsu said. "You're important to me. That's all there is to it."

"I would have felt horrible if you would have gotten caught with that though."

"Let's not worry about what could have been," he smiled. "We have another job to do."

We passed a tiny stream of water and there were several people, including children, drinking from it. One woman was washing her baby in the same water.

"How can people live like this?" I asked.

"This is all they know. They don't have the means to leave."

A couple of kids ran in front of us with a scraggly dog, laughing and chasing each other. The dog paused for a moment, looked at us, and then ran along to catch up with the kids.

"They seem happy," Otomatsu shrugged.

As we followed the stream, we saw more people either drinking or bathing. The water became shallower the further we walked, and then I was mortified by what I saw.

"Oh my god," I whispered.

"Cholera outbreak," Otomatsu sighed. "There are about three dozen sick people. And without access to clean water or medicine, it's just going to get worse."

We made our way through the quarantined area, where all of the severely sick people were. This part of the slum was vastly different from the front. Instead of laughter, we heard babies crying and people screaming out in pain. There were dead bodies wrapped in sheets lining the streets and people knelt down praying in front of them.

"Most of the population here is Muslim," Otomatsu explained. "They believe that pain, sickness, and dying are all tests from God. Illness is a reminder of how vulnerable they are as humans."

"But this could be prevented with clean water and good hygiene."

"Easier said than done, Emma. This isn't Midwest America. You grew up with air conditioning and television. You always had plenty of food and clean clothes. Their water pipes are constantly cracking and breaking, which mixes their clean water with sewage. There's one toilet per 500 people so most of them go wherever they can."

I looked at a pregnant woman sitting in the doorway of her little home. She was holding an emaciated toddler on one knee while she sang softly. She was so skinny that the child in her lap looked like it was sitting on a twig. Her baby bump was so large and round, it reminded me of when children would put beach balls under their shirts and pretend to be pregnant.

"They're all sick," I murmured. "They're all going to die."

"Yes," Otomatsu replied in a low, solemn voice.

We approached one of the shacks where a group of people crowded around outside of it. Inside were four beds in a row, each one with a very ill person laying on it. There was an elderly man, an elderly woman, a middle-aged man, and a young man; all of them were laying on their backs with sheets tucked tightly around them.

"A whole family," I said. "The parents and two sons are all sick and dying."

Otomatsu nodded. I knelt beside the youngest man, who was mumbling to himself, praying. I gently placed my hand on his sunken cheek. He jolted at the touch and looked at me. He smiled at me and lifted his head slightly to meet my gaze. Everyone who was outside grew quiet as they watched. The man's head fell and a single tear ran from his eye into the black hair next to his temple. The silence of death enveloped us and then I stood up. A couple of men with shirts wrapped around their noses and mouths came in to check the man who had just passed. Once they confirmed that he was dead, the elderly woman wailed loudly. The elderly man next to her started convulsing. Otomatsu was already standing next to him.

"He's having a seizure. He's not getting enough oxygen and is about to pass."

"This woman is about to lose her son and husband at the same time?" I asked.

Otomatsu didn't answer me as he knelt next to the flailing man. The woman was crying for someone to help him but no one else wanted to go into their home. The man finally went still and passed away. Otomatsu stood up and headed for the doorway.

"Let's move on."

He picked our next location. We walked into the living room of a duplex and saw a young man and woman kneeling over another woman who was lying on the floor.

"Fuck!" The man yelled. "She's not breathing!"

"Call 911!" the woman cried.

"No!" he snapped. "We'll go to jail!"

"She'll die if we don't! We didn't do anything to her, she took the pills herself!"

"We'll still go to jail for drug possesion, you fucking idiot! And you're the one who gave them to her!"

"Fentanyl again," Otomatsu growled. "I hate that shit."

"What if I flush the rest of the pills and you call 911?" the girl sobbed.

"Kennedy, I spent all of my money on those!"

"Josh, she's fucking dying!" Kennedy screamed. "I can't go to jail for murder!"

Josh blinked a couple of times before nodding his head slowly.

"Okay," he said. "Give them to me. I'll do it."

Kennedy handed Josh the bag and he walked into the other room. Kennedy stood up with her phone in her shaky hands. I knelt down over the girl who had overdosed.

"What have you done, sweetie?" I asked, looking into her eyes. "Through this holy anointing, may the Lord in His love and mercy help you with the grace of the Holy Spirit. May the Lord who frees you from sin save you and raise you."

"Goddamnit, Emma."

I turned to see Ankou standing behind Otomatsu. I looked back at the girl and smiled as she passed. I stood up as Ankou stomped towards me. We were almost nose to nose when he started yelling again.

"Why the fuck would you do that?" he asked, waving his arms around. "I told you to stop that shit. You don't know anything about-"

"She didn't mean to overdose," I said calmly. "The pills Josh got were laced with fentanyl. So not only was her overdose accidental, but her overdose kept her friends from taking it. They would have died too."

"I know that, Emma. If you'd just listen to me-"

"No," I interrupted. "I'm not listening to you anymore."

"You don't get it, do you?" Ankou laughed.

"She didn't want to die!" I yelled. "I'm not messing with free will or anything. She didn't want to kill herself and I made sure her soul was saved, just like it was always meant to-"

The sudden sound of a gunshot from behind made me jump. I turned around in time to see Kennedy's body hit the floor. Josh was standing beside us with a gun in his hand.

"Sorry, Kens," he cried. "I couldn't let you call the cops."

I was frozen in horror as Josh dropped to his knees beside Kennedy.

"Kennedy?" Josh asked quietly. "I- I'm sorry, Kennedy!"

Josh shook Kennedy's shoulders and then backed away from her.

"SHIT!" he sobbed. "WHAT THE FUCK DID I DO?"

Josh quickly held the gun up to his temple.

"No!" I yelled. "Don't!"

He pulled the trigger before I could get another word out.

"Double murder *and* a suicide," Ankou chuckled. "Nice."

"She wasn't the suicide," I breathed.

"Come on, Emma," Otomatsu said. "Let's go."

We selected a new location on our trackers and ended up in Tyler, Texas. There were two cars that were involved in a wreck; one white and one red. The red car ran a red light and hit the driver's side of the white car. The driver of the red car was unconscious. The person in the white car was suffering from internal bleeding. I ran up to the man who was hit. He was holding his stomach while his other arm lay limp; the humerus bone protruding through the skin.

"Emma!" I heard Ankou yell. He walked hurriedly towards me.

"Quit following me!" I snapped at him. "I have a job to do."

"I thought you were supposed to be off somewhere, finding that book."

"It's a scroll," I corrected. "And how do you know we haven't found it already?"

Ankou jerked his head from me to Otomatsu.

"I'll take care of him," Otomatsu said, pointing to the dying man in the car.

"Did you find it?" Ankou asked.

"Maybe," I shrugged.

"Oh, don't be so juvenile. Have you or haven't you found it?"

"We still have to wait on the boat," I said.

"Emma, just answer the question."

"Yes, I found it," I sneered.

"Can I see it?"

"You think we would just carry something like that around with us?"

Ankou paused.

"Did you look at it?" he asked.

"Yeah, but we can't read it," I said. "Apparently it's in *your* language."

"Then how do you know you have the right thing?" Ankou crossed his arms.

"It's the right thing," I narrowed my eyes at him. "Trust me."

"*Trust you?*" Ankou scoffed. "That's rich. That's like me asking you to trust me."

"Not quite. I've never given you a reason not to trust me. You're the one who tried to fuck me over, remember?"

"Which is exactly the reason why I have a hard time trusting you."

"Are you thinking of backing out?" I asked.

"No."

Ankou watched Otomatsu stand next to the dying man. After the silence passed, Ankou shoved his hands into his pants pockets.

"What?" I asked. "What is it?"

"I don't know," Ankou sighed. "I just feel like we're both getting played for some reason."

I looked over at Otomatsu.

"By him?" I pointed. "Hardly. He's trying to help me with this."

"Does he know what you agreed to?"

"No. But if he did, he wouldn't agree to help me."

"I just have this weird feeling about everything," Ankou continued. "Like a huge rug is about to get pulled out from underneath us."

"You just don't like not having complete control over something. Everything will be fine. You're going to help me get Sam out of that sea and then once I know she's safe, I'm yours to do whatever you want."

Ankou pulled his hands out of his pockets and put one of them on my shoulder. Otomatsu noticed immediately and made his way back over to us.

"I very much look forward to that," Ankou smiled.

"Everything okay over here?" Otomatsu asked, purposely standing between us so Ankou had to move his hand away.

"We're fine," I smiled. "We were just discussing a meeting place for when the boat is ready and then Ankou was going."

"Which will be where?" Otomatsu asked.

I looked at Ankou and before I could think of anything to say, he spoke.

"Emma wanted it to be at the exact spot we first met. A bit sentimental, a little bittersweet, a little sadistic. I love it."

I stared at him in shock as he smiled back.

"You know, Ankou," Otomatsu said bitterly, "I don't like demons on a good day. But I *really* dislike you."

Ankou laughed.

"See you back in Missouri, Emma Rose," he winked before disappearing.

I exhaled abruptly, like the wind had been knocked out of me.

"Are you okay?" Otomatsu asked. I nodded. "You know, there's still time to back out."

"I can't do that," I shook my head. "I have to try and save Sam. Even if it doesn't work, at least I'll know I tried."

"You don't owe her that though, Emma. She betrayed you. She got Dumah killed. I know you think she was a little girl who was taken advantage of-"

"She was!" I snapped. "Sure, she messed up. But she deserves to be forgiven. She deserves a second chance."

"But why? Why is this so important to you?"

"You know what?" I sneered. "Just forget it. Give me the scroll."

"What?"

"Give it to me."

Otomatsu reluctantly reached into his satchel. I heard sirens approaching and then saw an ambulance, fire truck, and two police cars pull up to the accident. I saw that a few cars had stopped to help the victims of the wreck and one man was performing CPR on the man who had already passed. Otomatsu held out the scroll and I snatched it from him before putting it in the breast pocket inside my cloak.

"So you're not going through with it now?" he asked.

"Of course I'm still going through with it," I scoffed. "I just don't want you to be there."

"What?"

He sounded hurt.

"And to be honest, I don't want to spend the next week and a half listening to you try to change my mind. So I think we should go our separate ways for now."

"Emma..."

"Sorry," I muttered, looking away.

"No you're not. But that's okay. Be upset with me, or disappointed in me. Take your time. I'll give you the space you need to figure things out. And when you're ready, I'll be waiting for you."

When I turned back to face him, he was gone. A small squeak escaped my throat; a sound so small, but full of instant regret.

I set off for my next mission. I didn't pay much attention to the details of the deaths I witnessed. Over the next several days, they all seemed to blend together into one huge blur. But it didn't matter anymore. Soon, I wouldn't be a death angel any longer. Sam would be saved, and I'd be imprisoned in Hell. Just like I was always supposed to be. I was done running from my fate.

16

I was on my final mission. I had one more death to look over before I'd go to my house, pack some essentials, and then meet up with Ankou and Abaddon to go over last minute details. There was a bombing that left half a dozen people dead in Palestine. It was an area of the world where death angels visited often. A building collapsed in the bombing, trapping a woman and her teenage daughter under the rubble. The daughter was bleeding out from a gash on her thigh. The mother ripped the bottom of her skirt to make a tourniquet, but it was no use. The wound was too wide and the bleeding wasn't slowing down. I sat next to them, in the remains of their home, in their tomb, and waited.

The girl was laying down, her head in her mother's lap, looking up. Every thirty seconds or so, the mother cried out, "We're down here! Please help!"

The girl's eyes fluttered and her mom slapped her cheek.

"Stay with me! Do not die!"

I looked into the girl's eyes and she looked back at me. There was a loud rumble as another bomb detonated somewhere around us. Dust and debris fell and the mother shielded her daughter's head as best as she could. The girl and I could no longer hear the bombs or the cries for help. And then her eyes closed.

"No!" the mother said as the girl went limp. "No, please stay with me!"

She checked the girl's pulse and then began to wail. The hysterical crying went on for five minutes while the woman rocked and hugged her daughter. Finally, she gently laid her down and started looking around.

"You're getting better, I see."

I turned around to see Isla, the red headed angel with the burn scars.

"You knew she was next so you stayed," she smiled.

"I've been getting a little better," I shrugged. "Definitely keeping eye contact."

Isla nodded in approval.

The mother of the dead girl found what she had been looking for. A shard of glass was now in her shaking hands.

"Please take me to my daughter," the woman sobbed. "Please."

"Through this holy anointing, may the Lord in His love and mercy help you with the grace of the Holy Spirit," I said quickly.

The woman ran the piece of glass across both wrists quickly and deeply.

"May the Lord who frees you from sin save you and raise you."

The woman laid down next to her daughter. As her breathing began to slow, her eyes met mine, the crumbling world around us went quiet, and she left us to go to where her daughter was.

"What was that?" Isla asked, bewildered.

"I, uh, found something in Dumah's hut that explained how to save suicides."

"But it doesn't work, does it?"

I nodded slowly. Isla gasped.

"And Dumah was doing it too?"

"Yeah."

"I guess that makes sense, given his background. I'm sorry I was a bit of an eejit when we first met."

"I'm sorry I was such a crappy angel when we met," I chuckled.

Isla and I looked at the mother and daughter, laying side by side. If it weren't for the blood, they'd look like they were peacefully sleeping. Another bomb went off and dust sprinkled their faces, giving them a ghostly appearance. Isla started humming softly. I sat there for a moment, listening to her, and then realized what she was humming. I started singing along with her.

My mother told me
Someday I would buy
Galleys with good oars and
Sails to distant shores.
Stand up on the prow

Noble barque I steer
Steady course to the haven
Hew many foe-men
Hew many foe-men."

I stopped singing and looked at Isla, who was looking at me in amazement.

"Dumah taught me a couple of things," I said shyly.

"Where do you think he learned that song from?" she asked.

We heard screaming outside and Isla let out a long, sad sigh.

"This world is so beautiful," she said. "It's a shame that humans do so many ugly things in it."

"They do a lot of beautiful things too," I replied. "We just rarely get to see those things."

"I just miss the world the way it used to be. Without cars and technology and buildings everywhere you look. It used to be less congested. People had more room and more time to just enjoy life. Now everyone fights with each other and people are practically living on top of one another. They work long hours at jobs they hate and most barely survive off of that. Everyone is tired and unhappy. There's no peace."

"For once, I'm not the most pessimistic person in the room," I said dryly. Isla laughed.

"I look forward to running into you again," she said. "Do you mind if I finish up with this area? There are three more deaths about to happen."

"Go for it," I smiled. "I have somewhere else to be."

"Until next time, Emma," Isla nodded before disappearing.

I looked back at the mother and daughter. There was rapid gunfire nearby and people started screaming again.

"There won't be a next time," I said out loud.

When I arrived at the beach, it seemed darker than usual. It was daytime, but there was a cloudy overcast. The waves were bigger than they normally were and the wind was blowing harder. The feathers of my wings ruffled as I hurriedly made my way to Dumah's old hut. I grabbed vials of holy water, blood grenades, crushed cabbage palm, and the book Dumah had stolen from the Temple of Da'at. I figured I'd give the book to Thalia along with the scroll to return to Quan after we rescued Sam. I only wished that I would be there to apologize to him myself for stealing it. I took a piece of paper and a pen and wrote down a simple apology note before sticking it inside the book.

After I finished gathering everything in a bag, I headed over to my house. I felt bad that Gabe had worked so hard to make it such a nice home for me, and I wouldn't be using it anymore. I entered and stood in the doorway, shocked. The whole living room was filled with all kinds of flowers. There were roses, tulips, zinnias, lilies, daisies, azaleas, dahlias, orchids, daffodils, pansies, bluebells, and petunias. Every single color of the rainbow surrounded me.

"He's been sneaking over here once a week to switch them out for newer ones."

I turned to see Otomatsu at the door,

"Who?" I asked, and then quickly added, "hi."

"Hi," he said softly. "Gabe."

"How has he been able to get over here?"

"Your surprise isn't much of a surprise now."

"The boat?" I asked. He nodded.

"Shit."

"Emma, I've been checking in on things between jobs. Gabe seems to think there are...mutual feelings."

"I've never told him that," I said sharply. "I know he has some little school boy crush on me but I've never done anything to lead him on."

"Emma, you don't have to lie to me. I know you have a crush on him."

"A crush," I snorted. "I'm not a child."

"I know that. I just mean, if he makes you happy, it makes me happy."

"I don't have feelings for him," I lied again.

Otomatsu looked as if he wanted to say something else, but decided not to.

"So when do you go meet Ankou and Abaddon?" he finally said, killing the awkward silence.

"I was actually just about to go get Thalia before heading to the spot we're supposed to meet them at," I shrugged. "I needed to get some things first."

"Are you still mad at me?"

I grunted and looked up at the ceiling.

"I was never mad at you!" I exclaimed. "I've just changed my mind about wanting you there."

"I won't interfere, I promise. I don't want to see you get hurt; that's all."

"I don't want to see *you* get hurt either!"

"I will be fine. I'll keep my distance so they don't think I'm a threat. But still stay close enough in case anything goes wrong."

"Please," I begged. "Just get back to work and wait. If we both stop working for too long, it'll catch their attention. I can't have the archangels get suspicious at all."

Otomatsu nodded slowly.

"Fine. I trust you and Thalia to back out if things seem unsafe."

"Thank you," I said, biting the inside of my cheek.

"And as soon as it's over, I'll meet you back here."

"Okay."

If Otomatsu was around when Ankou tried to take me back to Hell with him, he'd try to stop him. And that might compromise the whole operation with Sam. I just couldn't risk it; even though I wanted Otomatsu with me until the end. He had become like an adoptive father to me. He was the one person I felt safe with and I didn't want to ever be without him. Keeping this part of the plan from him was excruciating because I didn't want to lie to him. But I knew I couldn't tell him. To Otomatsu, the plan was to save Sam, get Abaddon to Maratiel, and free him from Hell. I only hoped that after Ankou took me with him, Otomatsu would still help Abaddon. Abaddon didn't know the side deal Ankou and I had, so there was no reason for Otomatsu to not help him. If I played my cards right, I could help an angel and a demon,

"I have to get going," I said, tilting my head towards the door. "The sooner I get started, the sooner it'll be over with."

Otomatsu reached out and pulled me in tightly.

"Be safe, Emma. Please."

"I will," I said, choking on my words. "I promise."

The hug lasted a few more seconds and then he let me go.

I went to the hotel in Processing and approached Elijah's desk with a cheesy grin on my face.

"Hello, you," he smirked when he saw me. "I kind of miss having you sulking around here."

"Well unfortunately for you and the newly dead, I can't stay long," I said. "Do you know where Thalia is?"

"You mean you're actually actively seeking out Thalia?"

"Yes," I crossed my arms. "I'm not quite as heartless as I used to be. I've changed a lot. I consider Thalia a friend now."

I thought about all of the people who surrounded me who cared for me. Elijah, Thalia, Otomatsu, Gabe, Sekhmet, Baraqiel, Matariel, and even Hutriel were all my friends. They were my family. I smiled as I realized how blessed I was.

"What do you have planned?" Elijah smirked.

"Top secret girl stuff," I winked.

"I'm a virtue, Emma. Sure, I'm stuck behind this desk now, but my divine powers are still very much in tune with others and I can tell something big is happening. You're inspired, excited, and scared."

"Sorry," I said eagerly. "I really can't say at the moment."

"Then I'm afraid I can't tell you where she is," he shrugged.

"Seriously?"

"Information in exchange for information."

We stared at each other until he went back to writing in his book of names.

"Fine!" I gritted my teeth. Elijah stopped writing and looked up at me, smiling.

"She's going to help me save Sam."

"I know. Thalia told me already."

"Elijah-!"

"Sh!" Elijah put a finger up to his mouth quickly. A couple of people looked over at us. Elijah started writing again.

"She's in Hawaii," he said without looking up from his book. "Molokai, specifically."

"Thank you!"

I turned to walk away and then stopped. I looked back at Elijah before running around the side of the desk and hugging him. His arms were pinned under mine but he brought a hand up and patted my shoulder.

"You've always been one of the good ones, Elijah," I said, still holding on. "I hope one day you can get away from this desk and go back to inspiring people. You deserve that."

"Oh," Elijah remarked. "Why, thank you, Emma. I appreciate that."

I let go and backed up.

"See you around, Emma," he smiled.

"Yeah," I said. "See you."

I flew to Molokai to find Thalia, which surprisingly didn't take long. She was watching over a woman who stood in front of a blank canvas. The woman's long, black hair blew in the breeze as she anxiously bounced one knee on the wooden stool she sat on. Thalia gently placed her tiny hands on the woman's shoulder. The woman exhaled slowly, picked up a brush, and dipped it into the blue paint. The brush glided along the white canvas, turning blue with each stroke. A smile appeared on the woman's face, and then on Thalia's. She looked over at me and I waved.

"Emma!" she exclaimed as she flew towards me. "What are you doing here?"

"It's time," I smiled.

"Really?" she asked. "Already?"

I nodded.

"We have the scroll and the boat is done. Whenever you're done here, we're going to go meet Ankou and Abaddon."

"Where's Otomatsu?"

"He's, uh, going to keep working for now. We didn't want the archangels to get suspicious."

"That's a good idea," she smiled.

I looked over at the woman painting.

"Do you need to get back to her?" I asked.

"Oh, no. She's been sitting here for a couple of hours and just started painting."

Thalia walked over to a nearby tree that had red flowers on it. The wind picked up as Thalia shook a couple of the branches. Flower petals carried by the wind landed in the woman's hair and on her arm. She picked one up and smiled. I watched Thalia as she smiled at the painter.

"She does this a lot. She's a very gifted artist but has a really difficult time getting motivated at first. I'll check back in with her once we're done."

"Okay," I said, "let's go."

I held my hand out for Thalia to land on. She held on tightly to my index finger. I closed my eyes and thought about the downtown area of the place I grew up. Then, there was a *whoosh!* We landed on the concrete road, far away from the soft grass of Hawaii. I looked around. Most of the stores that had filled this town were either replaced by newer companies, or boarded up. Today, there were no children running around, no old women sitting at the benches to gossip, and no one selling homemade ice cream. The town hadn't gone downhill, but it was definitely different from the way I remembered it.

"Are you okay?" Thalia asked.

"I'm fine," I lied. "Just weird being back here after all this time."

"It's odd that this is where Ankou wanted to meet you."

"Not at all," I said as I walked to a parking meter. "Because this is the exact spot where we first met."

"Actually," a voice said behind me. "About five feet from where you are."

Ankou and Abaddon were walking towards us.

"No," I said. "This is where it was. Because it happened in front of parking meter #23, which was right in front of the barber shop."

"The barber shop was one over," he pointed. "These are new parking meters."

"That wasn't the barber shop," I scoffed. "That was the seamstress. The barber shop was here."

I pointed to the empty store to my left. Ankou chuckled and walked past me, grabbing my hand as he did so. He centered me in front of the large window of the place he thought had been the barber shop.

"Look up," he said softly.

I looked but didn't see what he was talking about at first. He tilted my chin slightly with his thumb and index finger. The wooden sign that now said, "Paws & Pedis Pet Salon" was covering a faded sign that had been painted on the building. I could just make out the name, "Buster." As in, "Buster's Barber Shop." I glanced at Ankou, who was grinning. I rolled my eyes and smiled.

"I told you, I have no reason to lie to you anymore."

Our eyes locked for a second that seemed to last forever.

"So do you have the scroll or what?" Abaddon interrupted. For a moment, I had forgotten that he and Thalia were with us.

"It's in a safe place," I assured him.

"Your purse?" Ankou asked, pointing to my bag.

"It's not a purse! It's- you know what. I'm not doing this. I will hold onto the scroll until we find Sam, in case you try anything screwy."

"We're not going to try anything," Abaddon assured me.

"Okay, so I have a way to get you two, Thalia, and myself out on the water. But I have no idea how I'm going to get you past Gabe."

"We have an idea," Ankou said. Abaddon nodded.

"What?" Thalia asked.

"Just be sure he's at his hut in about an hour," Abaddon said. "Can you do that?"

"I'll do my best," I said. "And you're sure it'll distract him long enough to get you guys to the shore?"

"Oh, absolutely," Abaddon smiled.

"What about Sekhmet?" Thalia asked.

"This will be a big enough distraction that you won't have to worry about anyone interrupting us."

"But no one will get hurt, right?" I asked.

"Don't worry," Ankou said dryly. "Your boyfriend will be fine."

I scowled at him.

"Time's ticking, folks," Abaddon sighed. "We'll have plenty of time on the boat to deal with a lover's quarrel."

At this, we both glared at Abaddon, who only smirked.

"One hour?" I asked.

"A little less now," Abaddon said.

"Right. Meet you at the shore then."

"That boat better be ready, Emma," Ankou added.

Without answering him, Thalia and I went back to my house. Otomatsu was nowhere to be found. *Good*, I thought. *Stay far, far away from here.*

"No turning back now," Thalia breathed.

"No turning back," I repeated.

I was glad that we had to fly across the sea to the shore on the other side. If we had walked anywhere at the time, my nervousness would certainly have shown in my shaky legs and clenched jaw. Thalia looked extremely focused as she flew beside me. She wasn't her usual, peppy, talkative self. When we landed on the black sand, my stomach did a flip. Tied to the dock was the boat. *My* boat. As we walked to Gabe's, I couldn't help but feel something pulling at me. Telling me to turn back. To call off the whole plan. I stopped walking. Thalia looked back at me and paused.

"What's wrong?" she asked.

"N-nothing," I said, not moving.

"Well, come on. We need to make sure Gabe is around here somewhere."

I picked one foot up and it felt like a boulder. I took one step; then two. Shaking off whatever had been bothering me, I put on a fake smile and called out Gabe's name. When there was no response, I called out again before approaching his front door. I rapped on the door, waited a few seconds, and then grabbed the handle.

"It's locked," I explained.

"Maybe whatever the distraction was is happening already."

I looked around at the dense trees. Everything was still. Thalia flew around the side of the house, and then went up above the tree line. As she came back down, she shook her head.

"I don't see anything," she said.

"Shit," I muttered.

We stood around for some time. The only movement was an occasional breeze that moved the tree branches.

"What if one of us stays here and the other one goes to look for him?" Thalia suggested.

"Yeah, okay. I'll stay here since you're faster."

"Damn right I am!"

I started laughing.

"Thalia! I didn't know you cussed."

"I don't usually, but we are working with demons at the moment. See ya!"

She flew off and my smile quickly disappeared as what she said sank in. *We're working with demons.* But we weren't working with them. Not really. I was using Ankou to save Sam and help Abaddon. I would never work with demons in a way that benefited them. If anything, they were working for *me*. I stared at my bag, wishing the scroll didn't need a demon to translate it.

"Emma?"

I looked up at the path and Gabe was walking towards the house. He had a huge smile on his face. I forced the corners of my mouth upwards, both happy and sad to see him; knowing it might be the last time I see him.

"Hey," I croaked.

"Did you like your surprise?"

"Huh?"

"I wasn't sure which kind was your favorite so I got a little bit of everything."

"Oh, the flowers! Yeah, they're really nice."

Gabe cocked his head to the side.

"What's wrong?"

I think I love you, but I'm about to leave forever to be enslaved by my demon ex-boyfriend who I might still love as well.

"What? Nothing."

"Are you sure?"

"Yeah," I laughed, trying to sound more convincing. "I just sent Thalia off to look for you so I'm just hoping she comes back soon."

Gabe approached me. He placed his hand under my jaw and tilted my face up to his. As he leaned in to kiss me, I wanted to cry. I screamed internally as our lips met and my chest tightened. Gabe's other hand gripped my waist. The kiss seemed to last forever. Just as I was about to pull away, Gabe popped his head up.

"Oh!" he exclaimed. "I almost forgot. Thank you so much for getting another boat. I know losing the other one must have been hard for you. But when Sekhmet said you had another one made so I could come see you, I was so happy."

I gave him another forced grin.

"I named our boat. I hope you don't mind."

"What-"

"EMMA!"

Gabe and I jumped at the sound of Thalia screaming from somewhere in the forest. I pulled my sword out of its sheath as we walked towards the tree line. Finally, Thalia came into view with Sekhmet running beside her.

"What's wrong?" I yelled.

"There's a horde of demons attacking the other shore!" Sekhmet cried.

I looked at Thalia, who gave me a troubling stare.

"Wait right here," Gabe told me.

"We need all the help we can get," Sekhmet explained. "There are hundreds of them."

"What?" I asked.

"It's bad, Emma," Sekhmet continued. "There are runts, wasps, and tanks all charging Matariel's shore. We don't know what's causing them to do it. But we need to get back as soon as possible to help."

"We'll be right behind you guys," I explained. "I'll try and go get Otomatsu real quick."

"Okay, but don't take too long," Sekhmet said as she turned to go. "This is a serious problem."

Gabe kissed me on the cheek.

"Stay safe, okay?" I pleaded.

"You too," he said. "I'd rather you not get involved if it's as bad as she says. But I also know you can protect yourself."

"Gabe!" Sekhmet called from the woods.

"See you in a bit," I said.

Gabe smiled and took off after Sekhmet. Once they were out of sight, Thalia turned to me quickly.

"What the hell, Emma!"

"What! I didn't know that was part of the plan!"

"What if our friends get hurt?"

"Ankou and Abaddon promised no one would."

"Right. And we just trust a pair of elite demons who just released a horde for everyone else to try and fight."

"It'll be okay."

"You don't know that!"

"You're right!" I snapped. "I don't know that. But I am trying my absolute hardest to stay positive. I'm trying to keep faith. Do me a favor and try doing the same."

Thalia scoffed but didn't say anything else. We sat there in unsure silence until Ankou and Abaddon cautiously came into view. Thalia and I both tensed when we saw them. Ankou was wearing a dark blue dress shirt with white pants. He looked as though he were dressed specifically for sailing, which pissed me off. He was doing it to be a smart ass. Abaddon was wearing the usual elite demon suit; this one was a dark gray and black plaid ensemble that made him look like a modern day Sherlock Holmes. Ankou was carrying a small bag, similar to mine.

"What did you do?" I asked sharply.

"Caused a diversion, like I said I would," Ankou replied.

"A horde of demons attacking the other shore?" Thalia questioned.

"They're ordered to just destroy property," Ankou explained. "I had to send a lot of them though. Otherwise the fight would be over too soon and we'd get caught."

"Nobody better get hurt," I threatened. "You promised."

Ankou laughed and started to walk past me. I grabbed his arm.

"I mean it, Ankou."

"We need to get going," he said. "We're wasting time."

Ankou jerked free and kept walking. Thalia slowly flew after him, shaking her head at me. Abaddon put a hand on my shoulder and leaned in.

"Everything will be fine," he said softly. "You said Matariel is the dark angel helping people get out of Hell, right?"

I nodded.

"Good. Ankou told me about his little bargain with you."

My eyes widened.

"Don't worry," he assured me. "You help me, and I promise that you won't have to worry about that."

Abaddon extended his hand out to allow me to lead the way. We all walked in silence to the shore. The water was oddly calm and there was a slight breeze. Ankou led the way to the dock where the boat sat, waiting for us. When the back of the boat came into view, I felt sick to my stomach. Ankou saw it at the same time I did and chuckled.

"Are you serious?" he asked, pointing.

There were three red flowers painted on the stern with the word, "Rose," in the middle of them. Ankou got in and sat down, grinning. Thalia landed on the wooden pier and made herself human-size before stepping onto the boat. As Abaddon and I approached, Ankou stood up and held his hand out to me. Ignoring him, I unsteadily lowered myself in and sat down next to Thalia. After Abaddon seated himself next to Ankou, I untied the boat from the dock and pushed us away. Luckily, Abaddon knew how to sail fairly well, so I let him get us out on the water. I kept one hand on my sword and the other on my bag.

Once we were far enough from Sentencing, the shore no longer in sight, Abaddon let the sails down. The boat bobbed ever so gently on the water's surface. I reluctantly looked over the side into the blue fathoms that held The Restless out of sight.

"How are we going to find Sam?" I asked.

Ankou looked at Abaddon, who pulled something out of the bag sitting between the two of them. It was a broken arrow, only the point and a couple inches of the shaft were left.

"What is it?" Thalia asked.

"It's one of Sam's arrows," I said. Ankou smiled and nodded.

Abaddon started tying a thick string around the head of the arrow.

"What are you going to do with that?" I asked.

"Going fishing," he said.

17

The sun started setting and I couldn't help but to think about Gabe, Sekhmet, Baraqiel, and Matariel. I hoped everyone was okay. There wasn't much talking on the boat as the sky began to darken. I lit the lantern hanging on a wire hook towards the bow. The light glowed softly and Abaddon lifted a hand from behind me to twist the wick adjuster, making it brighter.

"We need all the light we can get," he explained. "I'm going to start translating the scroll while Ankou and you search for Sam."

"What will I be doing?" Thalia asked.

"I need you to make sure none of the Restless get on the boat," Abaddon said. "If you can manipulate mongrels, those stupid things should be a piece of cake."

Thalia glared at him.

"Who put him in charge?" she asked.

"He *is* the oldest being out of the four of us," Ankou smirked. "He's earned the right to boss us around."

"Abaddon is older than you?" I asked. "I thought you said you were the first demon."

Abaddon laughed.

"Is that what he told you?"

"Technically, I was the first human who was turned into a demon," Ankou explained. "But just like the archangels, there are demons who have been around long before humans ever existed."

"And here I was thinking you were some big deal," I said.

"Ankou is a very important, very successful elite demon," Abaddon added. "Well, successful until recently."

Abaddon winked at me, which made me chuckle.

"Still important," Ankou muttered.

"However," Abaddon said, "I still pull rank."

Ankou lowered his head and even though the lighting was poor, I swore I could see him blush in humiliation.

"Scroll?" Abaddon demanded.

I pulled the scroll out of my bag. It suddenly felt heavier than it had before. I handed it to Abaddon, gripping it tightly as he yanked it away. He positioned himself under the light of the lantern and looked it over. His eyes grew wide and he gave me the slightest nod.

"This is definitely it," he breathed.

"And it'll work?" I asked. "I just need to say whatever is on that and it'll get Sam out of here?"

"More or less, yes."

"Thank you, Abaddon," I smiled before lowering my voice. "I'm glad I can help both you and Sam."

Abaddon grinned.

"You are an extraordinary angel, Emma. I'm very happy our paths crossed."

I went to the side of the boat where Ankou was sitting. The string was in the water and the arrow head was deep below the surface. He didn't look at me as I sat down beside him.

"So, not the first demon, huh?" I smirked.

"You don't have to keep bringing it up, Emma."

"What, were you trying to impress me by letting me think you were the first-ever demon?"

"I was the first human who was turned into a demon," Ankou reminded me. "My parents were the first people to exist and I was the first fuck up. That's pretty impressive."

I raised my eyebrows.

"And because of my parents, demons had a reason to leave Hell. Before humans, these creatures with souls and morals, demons spent all of their time in Hell, pouting that they couldn't overthrow God. As long as humans exist, demons have a purpose. *I* have a purpose."

"Yet here you are, helping an angel you hate rescue a little girl you hate. Maybe there's still a little good in you after all."

"Trust me, there's not. You know the only reason I'm doing this is because you swore to spend eternity in Hell with me. Not only do I get to have my way with you, you won't be saving anymore suicides. Maybe there's hope for my reputation yet."

"Oh my god," I laughed. "All of this, just to save your precious ego."

"Will you take this for a bit?" Ankou asked, holding out the string. I cautiously took it from him and watched as he pulled an orange from his bag. He peeled the thick rind away and took a segment off before taking a bite. It made a small popping sound as his teeth bit into it, and I could almost remember what oranges tasted like as the sweet scent filled my nose.

"Want a bite?" he asked, smiling as he wiped juice from his lip.

"No," I said coldly.

"You know," he said softly in my ear, "when I take you back with me, you'll eventually start feeling hungry again. I'll share all the oranges and whatever else you want."

"I don't need to eat," I said. "I'm dead, remember? No need for food."

"That's not the point of Hell, Emma. You don't *need* anything, but you can have whatever you want. Whenever you want."

I backed away to meet his eyes. His free hand touched my thigh while the orange dripped from his other hand. He was so close that I could smell the fruit on his breath. A splash in the water behind us made me jump and Ankou let go of my leg. Thalia stood up quickly and gasped.

"What's wrong?" I said, not moving.

"Sun's gone down," Abaddon sighed and pointed. "We've been spotted."

I squinted at the water. Things that looked like fireflies twinkled back at us. Except they weren't fireflies. They were eyes.

"I gotta tell you, I really hate those things," Ankou muttered. "Creepy fuckers."

"Just be sure not to put any body parts over the side of the boat," Abaddon said, not looking up from what he was writing. "They won't reach up for you unless you get close to the water."

I scooted back a few inches, gripping the string tightly. I glanced at Thalia and gave her an assuring smile. Hours passed and nothing happened, other than the occasional splash from one of the corpses in the water. Ankou and I took turns holding the arrow on the string while Abaddon worked on translating the scroll. Thalia patrolled around the boat, keeping an eye on the Restless.

"What are you thinking about?" Ankou asked suddenly. I sat up straight and looked at him.

"What do you care what I'm thinking?"

"I'm always curious about what non-demons are thinking about. With them, it's easy. Power, destruction, chaos, sex, murder…you know, the usual demon stuff."

I sat for a moment and thought. I looked over my shoulder at Thalia before leaning in closer to whisper.

"I wish I could tell everyone goodbye," I admitted. "I know I couldn't because they'd all try and convince me not to do this. And probably fight you, which would have caused all sorts of drama. And I'd try to tell them I'm doing this on my own, but they wouldn't understand. But still...I wish I could at least tell Otomatsu goodbye. That I'll miss him more than anything, and to thank him for teaching me so much. I'd tell him not to be sad or angry that I'm going, because I wouldn't want him to be. I'd want him to find someone else to spend his time with. I wish I could tell Sekhmet and Barry that I hope this makes up for what happened to Dumah. I'd apologize again for my mistakes and tell them that I did my best to make things right. I wish I could tell Gabe that there's nothing wrong with him and that leaving had nothing to do with how I feel about him. I have always tried so hard to do the right thing. And in doing so, someone either gets hurt or something bad happens. I want to be able to tell everyone that this was me doing something good and taking myself out of the picture before something bad could happen."

"You know, not all of it is on you," Ankou smiled. "After all, I am the one who killed Dumah and Sam. Looking back, I probably didn't have to do that. I guess I was throwing a bit of a tantrum. I didn't get my way for once, and I took it very personally. And you were still human at the time. I was bested by a human. But when you became a death angel and started saving suicides, I really thought I was going to lose my shit. And I fought so hard to say something to you about it, because you didn't even know if it was working for sure. What's weird is Dumah had that prayer for who knows how long, and never once tried it."

"He probably felt like it interfered with free will," I said.

"I don't know," Ankou shook his head. "It's almost as if he got it just for you to find. You were destined to become a death angel. Which is funny because like you, I thought you were just some average, boring girl."

"Well, I guess I proved both of us wrong," I smirked.

"Yeah, you did."

We smiled at each other, holding each other's gaze. Ankou leaned his face in towards mine slowly. Suddenly, there was a tug on the string.

"Oh shit!" I gasped, grabbing it tighter.

I bent over the side of the boat as the string tried to take me with it. Two Restless grabbed my arms and pulled me forward. In an instant, I was under water, the string moving around me in all directions. I quickly wrapped it around my left arm before it jerked me from side to side. As I tried to get to the surface, several more arms grabbed my wings. I looked around and saw empty eye sockets, missing jaws, and exposed brain tissue. The corpses all clawed at me and pulled me further into the darkness. The faint light from the lantern disappeared as my muffled scream came out in violent bubbles around me. I felt more hands grab me and I realized I was going back up. The light above me came into view again. My head broke the water's surface and I let out a huge gasp. Two Restless were trying to lift me out of the water.

"Emma!" I heard Thalia yell.

"Pull her up!" Abaddon commanded.

I was lifted up onto the boat, the string still hooked around my wings and left arm. It tightened as whatever was on the end tried to take off again.

"AHH!" I screamed. "GET IT BEFORE IT RIPS MY ARM OFF!"

Ankou grabbed it with both hands and everyone started pulling me backwards. Thalia ran to the edge of the boat and reached her hands out.

"No!" I yelled.

"It's okay, Emma," she said. "I'm making them go back into the water. They won't get on the boat."

"Did you make them save me?" I asked her.

"They're actually pretty easy to manipulate," she shrugged, "just like the mongrels."

Abaddon and Ankou untangled me and we were able to start reeling the string in. The faintest hint of morning started to make an appearance in the sky. I looked out at the water. Dozens of heads bobbed up and down, eyes fixed on us. But the Restless didn't move.

"The sun is coming up!" Abaddon grunted. "Help, get her up!"

We all grabbed onto the string and yanked back in rhythmic motions. Just as the sky was turning from black to gray, a small figure began to rise to the water's surface. Even when I saw the strands of red hair, I still couldn't believe it was her. Her eyes were closed and she was gripping the broken piece of the arrow tightly against her chest. The skin around her mouth was peeled back, revealing her teeth. Her skin was grayish-blue and clung to the bones of her tiny frame. Abaddon and Ankou leaned over the side of the boat and pulled Sam's body up onto the deck. Suddenly, Sam's eyes opened; two milky white circles looking up at me. Her mouth gaped open and she sat up slowly. Water trickled out of her mouth followed by a horrible, raspy sound.

"Sam?" I breathed.

Abaddon muttered something in a language I didn't understand and Sam went rigid. Her arms went to her sides and her head hit the wooden floor of the boat with a hard knock. She squirmed around as if an invisible rope was tightly wrapped around her.

"We need to move quickly," Abaddon said. "Emma, give me your sword."

"What?"

"Sword! Now!"

I touched the handle with a shaky hand.

"Emma," Thalia said softly. I looked at her and she shook her head.

I paused for a moment, and then slowly pulled the sword out of its sheath. I carefully handed it to Abaddon and felt my stomach drop as soon as it left my grip.

"Ankou?" he ordered.

Ankou held his hand out. Abaddon ran the blade along Ankou's palm and a bright red ribbon of blood appeared.

"Thalia, your turn," Abaddon said.

"No way," Thalia said.

"I just need a little bit of your blood," Abaddon explained. "It'll only hurt a little bit, and it will heal quickly."

"Mine's already starting to close up," Ankou winced.

"Thalia!" I said. "Please!"

Thalia gave me a pleading look, but I didn't budge. Sam was starting to groan as she continued to wiggle on the deck. Thalia's shoulders dropped in defeat and she held her hand out to Abaddon.

"Good," he said as he gave her the small cut. "Okay, Emma is going to hold Sam's mouth open while Thalia and Ankou let about five to ten drops of blood drip into her mouth."

I heard an "ugh" from Thalia and couldn't help but feel the same. I squatted down next to Sam and pinched her chin with one hand while holding her head still with the other. Ankou and Thalia quickly stood over us with their hands hovering above Sam. I heard Abaddon muttering something from behind me but couldn't hear him over the gurgling moans coming from Sam. The cuts on Ankou and Thalia's hands closed up as the last drops of blood fell into Sam's mouth. She went still and quiet.

"Did it work?" I asked, looking at Abaddon, my voice sounding odd.

I stood up and glanced around the boat. There was an iridescent dome around us and the boat, like a barrier.

"What is that?" I asked. My voice didn't have the same echo to it as it did before the dome appeared.

"Nothing can get in or out until we're finished," Abaddon explained, retrieving the scroll and handing it to me.

"You didn't tell me about this," Ankou said.

"I don't need to tell you every little thing. You're lower rank than me. Remember that?"

I glanced from Ankou to Thalia, and then back to Abaddon.

"Emma, I've written down how to pronounce every word correctly. If you read the whole thing, Sam will come back. She might be confused at first, which is why I put the barrier up. I don't want her running off the side of the boat or getting hurt. So as soon as you finish, get ready to help me grab her."

"And- and you're sure this w-will work?" I stammered.

"Yes. Just focus on the words on the scroll."

He took a step back and watched me. Everyone was watching me. I looked down at Sam's still body and then lifted the scroll up to my face.

"Naem. Emoc sah nam fo rouh linaf eht. Meit fo den eht sa ornbre eb liwl nad Astan nad Dgo fo lobod ilicarifasc eht mrof emoc liwl eh."

"Wait!" Ankou shouted and took a step toward me. "Emma, don't!"

Abaddon waved his arm quickly and Ankou fell to his knees, his arms bound to his sides like Sam's. I gasped when I saw his mouth; or at least where his mouth used to be. Instead of lips, there was what looked like a scar from healed stitches. I turned to Abaddon.

"I'm not going to let you be his slave, Emma."

"What?" Thalia asked. "What's he talking about?"

"Emma made a pact with Ankou that if he helped her save Sam, she'd go back to Hell with him for eternity."

"Emma…"

"But I'm not going to let that happen," Abaddon continued. "Finish what the scroll says and I'll take care of Ankou. I won't let him hurt you."

Ankou shook his head violently and muffled screaming came from his throat, although whatever he was trying to say was undetectable. I continued to read.

"Mhi ptos ot bela eb liwl monde orn gelna on nad, Lehl nad Eanehv mrof dame eb lalsh eh. Gineb lalsh Lehl fo meit eht nad lalf liwl nam. Rateh revo ekat nad esa eht mrof ersi liwl eh Esteourudnio fo Oen eht, Oen Nedroh eht ot svemthels veig krad nad thlig nhew."

I finished the inscription and lowered the scroll. No one moved.

"Did you do it correctly?" Abaddon asked, snatching the scroll from me and looking it over.

"I don't know!" I exclaimed. "I read it just like how you wrote it down!"

"Emma…"

I looked at Thalia. Her body began to lift off the boat.

"What are you doing?" I asked.

"I'm not doing anything!" she cried. "Something...doesn't feel right."

"What's happening?" I asked Abaddon.

"It worked," he smiled.

Ankou's body began to levitate as well. Thalia started screaming and her body began to twist. The skin and muscle began to deflate until she almost looked like one of the Restless. Ankou started to scream as well. His mouth was back to normal as he howled in pain. I saw something dark flying at us and then realized it was Otomatsu. As he got closer, I started waving frantically, trying to warn him.

"Watch out!" I yelled.

He hit the barrier and was sent backwards in the air. I watched as he took out his sword and tried striking at the dome. Thalia and Ankou's screams were so loud, I could hardly stand it.

"Stop it!" I said, taking a step towards them. "We need to help them! They're in pain!"

Then, the blade of my sword was at my throat. I tilted my head towards Abaddon slightly.

"No, Emma," he said sharply. "I can't let you. We need them to bring Sam back."

"What!" I shrieked. "No! You never said anything about sacrificing anyone! Thalia's my friend!"

"Oh please," he rolled his eyes. "You can't stand her. I did you a favor by talking Ankou into choosing her. At least it wasn't one of your actual friends."

I looked at Thalia, who wasn't screaming anymore. She was whimpering as her body continued to shrivel.

"That's not true," I cried. "I would never have brought you along if I knew you'd get hurt. You *are* my friend. I'm so sorry!"

Thalia tried to say something, but only a faint exhale came from her as her eyes closed and she went limp.

"You are my friend..."

Her body became a skeleton, and then turned to dust. Ankou had stopped screaming and looked at me with heavy eyes.

"I'm-" Ankou tried speaking and couldn't. "I'm s-"

He gasped as his eyes rolled back.

"I didn't know," I whispered.

And then he was gone.

"Oh my god," I choked. "What have I done?"

Abaddon pointed to Sam. Her skin was plump and her body looked normal again. Her cheeks were rosy and I could make out the freckles on them. Her body started lifting off the deck of the boat, her eyes still closed.

"What's going on?" I asked. "What's happening to her?"

"She's being reborn," Abaddon said in wonderment.

We watched as color came back to Sam's lips and her ragged clothes materialized. Her eyes opened and I gasped. The irises were an icy blue, almost white, with a red ring around the edges. Everything about her looked like Sam except for her eyes.

"Something's not right," I said. "This isn't right."

Sam looked down at us and I felt uneasy.

"Sam?" I whispered.

She slowly grinned a wide, mischievous grin. We locked eyes for what seemed like forever. And then she vanished.

"Where did she go?" I asked.

"She got through the barrier," Abaddon murmured. "Clever little thing."

"WHERE DID SHE GO?" I bellowed.

"It's begun," Abaddon chuckled, putting his hand on his forehead and dropping my sword. There was a loud clang as it landed on the deck. I picked it up quickly and pointed it at him. He started laughing. The barrier around the boat disappeared, and I could hear Otomatsu shouting. He landed next to me and pointed his katana at Abaddon.

"What just happened?" Otomatsu yelled.

Abaddon continued laughing, doubled over and held his stomach. Otomatsu grabbed him by the front of his shirt and shook him violently.

"WHAT IS GOING ON?" he bellowed.

"The end," Abaddon giggled and pointed at me. "And it's all because of her."

18

Everything seemed to be spinning. I couldn't focus on anything around me. The next thing I knew, Abaddon was gone and Otomatsu had me by the shoulders, asking me questions. His voice was somewhere far away though. *What happened? Where's Thalia? Are you okay?* My ears were listening but I couldn't hear. My eyes were looking at him but I couldn't see him. Suddenly, I felt the sharp sting of a slap across my face. I came out of my state of shock, blinking hard.

"EMMA!"

I looked at Otomatsu.

"What happened?"

"I-I'm not sure," I managed to say. "One m-minute they were here and then..."

"Who?"

"Ankou and..."

Thalia, I thought. They were dead. I killed them by bringing Sam back.

"Sam," I whispered.

"Where's Sam?" Otomatsu asked.

"I-I don't know. I don't know."

"What happened to Ankou and Thalia, Emma?"

The weight of his question suffocated me. Tears filled my eyes and I wrapped my arms around myself as I screamed. Lightning cracked across the sky and the boat exploded from the sonic boom I produced. Otomatsu grabbed me from behind and lifted me above the wreckage. Tidal waves crashed around us while Otomatsu flew higher. He started flying towards our shore when I stopped him.

"No!" I cried. "We have to check on everyone in Sentencing!"

"Emma, we need to figure out what's going on!"

"I need to make sure they're okay first," I said. "Please."

Otomatsu looked at me and then sighed before turning around. Lightning and thunder continued to fill the dark sky as we made our way to Sentencing. The rain began to fall as we landed on the black sand.

"Gabe!" I shouted, looking around frantically. "Sekhmet!"

I ran as fast as my feet could carry me. I made my way down the path to where Gabe's house was. All that was left was rubble. The entire home had been destroyed.

"Oh god," I gasped.

"What happened?" Otomatsu asked.

"We were attacked," a voice said from the trees.

We turned and saw Gabe slowly making his way out into the clearing. He had four deep gashes on the side of his head, and there was a bloody hole where his ear used to be. I hurried over to him and lifted my hand to his head.

"Are you-?"

"Did you know?" he asked, backing away.

I froze.

"Did you?" he repeated, more coldly this time. I recoiled as he aggressively took a step towards me.

"I didn't know there was going to be an attack," I said. "I just knew there was going to be a distraction."

"A distraction," Gabe scoffed.

"They promised me no one would get hurt," I said, looking at the side of his head.

"*They promised you?*" he glared at me. "THEY PROMISED YOU!"

I flinched at the sudden yelling.

"Baraqiel and Matariel are dead."

My heart sank.

"What?"

Otomatsu gently placed a hand on my shoulder.

"How?" Otomatsu asked.

"In the attack," Gabe explained. "They were targeting Matariel, and we tried to fight them off. But there were just too many of them. Mongrels, tanks, wasps, and runts all came after him. We didn't stand a chance. Baraqiel lost Matariel again and just sort of went berserker. We didn't find his body until after the horde left. They were fighting us one minute and the next, they just stopped and walked away. As if nothing happened. Sekhmet was injured as well. Lost a leg. I don't know if it'll fully heal or not."

"And...Baraqiel and Matariel?" I croaked.

"Same as Dumah," Gabe said harshly. "They'll be reborn as humans. Except they won't know each other. They won't know that they waited thousands of years to be reunited with each other, only to be torn apart again."

"I can't believe this is happening," I murmured.

"You can't?" Gabe scoffed. "This was all your idea, wasn't it? You knew this was going to happen!"

"No!" I cried. "I swear, I didn't know they were going to attack anyone!"

"Oh really? Because Ah Puch named you personally and said that you were a part of the whole plan. That you specifically named Matariel and Baraqiel as the dark angels who were helping people get out of Hell."

At this, Otomatsu let go of my shoulder.

"I was only trying to help Abaddon!" I pleaded. "He wanted to know how to get out of Hell and I wanted to help him!"

"Abaddon is one of the Princes of Hell!" Gabe snapped. "He, along with Mammon, Asmodeus, and Leviathan came to Hell with Satan after they tried to overthrow God. He's one of the original demons, Emma. He's the overseer of the Abyss. He would never leave Hell."

"I- I didn't know."

"There's a lot you didn't know," Gabe said. "Maybe you should have learned more about the responsibilities you were taking on instead of trying to meet your own selfish needs, and using everyone that cares about you in the process."

"I never meant for anyone to get hurt," I repeated. "You have to know that."

"You weren't trying to hurt me by pretending you had feelings for me?"

"I do have feelings for you," I said coldly. "It's just...complicated. I didn't want to hurt you."

"No, you just screwed me for your own needs. Both literally and figuratively."

"Is that true, Emma?" Otomatsu asked.

"That's actually none of your business," I retorted. "But it was never my intention to lead anyone on."

"That's a lie and you know it," Gabe said.

Before I could respond, he spoke again.

"I want you to leave. And I never want to see you again."

I stood there a moment as Gabe turned to the remains of his home.

"GO!" he shouted.

"Come on," Otomatsu said. "Let's go."

"Will you at least do me one favor?" I asked. "Will you tell Sekhmet that I'm sorry?"

Gabe turned slowly and looked me right in the eye.

"No."

He walked away from us and started sifting through the rubble. I began to say something else, but Otomatsu guided me away from Gabe. We made our way back to the shore solemnly and flew to Processing, hoping to get more information on what was happening. The light rain turned into a heavy downpour and the wind made it difficult for us to fly. We soared high above the crashing waves and as we reached our shore, I noticed the tide was almost to the front door of Dumah's hut. I looked at Otomatsu.

"We can't worry about that right now," he said, trying to sound calm. "Not until we can figure out what's going on."

The rain stopped as we landed in the courtyard outside of the hotel, however, deafening thunder continued to boom overhead. There were several greeters and angels ushering people into lines.

"Please, calmly form three lines and we will get everyone checked in and moved on!" one woman was yelling. She had a smile on her face, but I could tell she was also panicking.

"Everyone, please remain calm!" another man yelled.

"What's going on?" I asked him.

"I'm not really sure," he said in a shaky voice. "We're having thousands of people come in all at once. One of the archangels told us that we're no longer doing processing for anyone and we need to move them to Paradise as quickly as possible."

Otomatsu and I pushed past the crowd of newcomers, trying to get inside the hotel. Elijah was standing at his desk, frantically flipping through the pages of his book. He did a double-take as he saw us approaching.

"Any idea what the bloody hell is going on?" Elijah asked, wide-eyed.

This was the first time I had ever seen him disheveled. His hair, which was normally combed back, was flopping against his sweaty forehead. I stepped closer to the desk and noticed that the book he had been flipping through was sitting on top of two other books. Beside the stack were two more.

"What is happening, Emma?" his voice cracked.

"I don't know," I breathed.

"We came here looking for answers," Otomatsu added.

"Well, you won't get any from me," Elijah said. "I was sitting here, going through names, and all of a sudden, these all appeared!"

I looked to the floor, where he was pointing and gasped. There were stacks of thick books that matched the ones on the desk.

"Are those all-?" I began.

"New arrivals? Yeah. Either just coming in, or about to. Azreal came in not too long ago and told me we're shutting the hotel down. All new arrivals are being processed immediately for Paradise."

"What?" I asked. Elijah nodded. I looked around, noticing for the first time that the lobby was completely empty.

"I'm not really sure what to do at this point. All I know is going through the books and checking people in. No one has told me what's happening, and honestly, I'm frightened."

"It's okay," I reassured him. "We're trying to find someone who knows. Why don't you come with us?"

"And leave this?" Elijah looked around.

"If one of the archangels told you the hotel is done, then there's nothing left for you here," Otomatsu said. "Come on."

Elijah hesitantly stepped away from the desk and nodded.

The three of us walked out of the building and back into the chaos that was outside. I spotted Hannah, who had processed me all those years ago, and tried flagging her down.

"Hannah!" I called. "Hannah!"

She quickly glanced back at me but didn't stop.

"Hannah," I repeated, getting closer to her. Several people were between us, making it hard to talk. "Do you know what's going on?"

"I'm sorry, Emma. I can't talk. I have too many people to take care of."

"Can you at least-?"

A sound that completely drowned out the thunder made everyone, including myself, cover our ears. Several people crouched down and started crying while others held one another, as if preparing for an attack. It sounded like both human and animalistic screams; like it was coming from the mouths of a thousand creatures at once.

"WHAT IS THAT?" I yelled.

"THE SERAPHIM!" Hannah shouted.

"WHY?"

But Hannah had turned away and was lost to the sea of people, trying to find their way. The screaming stopped and Otomatsu grabbed my shoulder.

"We need to go find Quan!" he said. "Someone at the Temple will know what's happening."

The three of us headed toward The Gates and the screaming began again. We all covered our ears and winced as we hurried through the entrance. There were no archangels anywhere. The screaming stopped and I dropped my hands.

Otomatsu drew his katana and proceeded towards the temple with caution.

"What are you doing?" I asked, pointing to the sword.

"I have a really bad feeling."

Elijah and I looked at each other.

"Hannah must have been mistaken," Elijah laughed nervously.

"Why?" I asked.

"She said the sound we keep hearing is the seraphim," he explained. "That can only mean one thing."

"Which is?" I prodded.

"The end times," he answered.

I froze.

"Don't be ridiculous," Otomatsu scoffed. "Aren't there supposed to be trumpets or something like that?"

Elijah frowned as we approached the doors of the temple.

"The screaming of the seraphim *are* the trumpets."

My stomach dropped as Otomatsu pulled on the giant rope. The bell sounded and the three of us stood there in awkward silence. When no one answered, Otomatsu looked at me, shrugged, and pulled on the rope again. The ear-splitting screams started again. I cupped the sides of my head once more and Otomatsu aggressively pushed the doors open. The three of us hurried inside and we shut the door.

"HELLO?" Otomatsu called. "WE TRIED RINGING THE BELL BUT NO ONE ANSWERED!"

It was useless. The screaming was so loud that I could hardly hear Otomatsu's shouting. I looked around. There was no one inside. Books laid open on tables and chairs pushed away, as if a fire alarm went off and everyone evacuated the building in a hurry. The screaming ceased as we made our way through the aisles.

"Where is everyone?" I asked.

"HELLO?" Otomatsu called again. His voice echoed through the vacant building.

"Come on," he said to Elijah and me and started running.

We followed quickly behind him up to Quan's room. There was a soft glow coming from the cracked door.

"Quan?" Otomatsu called gently.

He pushed open the door and I saw Quan cowering by the lit fireplace, crying. When he saw us, his eyes widened and he scooted towards us on his knees.

"What have you done?" he cried with his arms outstretched.

"What?" I asked. "We haven't done anything."

"I never should have let you two in here," he whimpered. "All my fault...all my fault."

"Quan, what is going on?" Otomatsu asked as he sheathed his katana.

"Should have never-"

"QUAN!"

Otomatsu slapped Quan across the face and pulled him up by his shoulders.

"Tell us what's happening!" he demanded, shaking Quan hard.

"The...end."

I gasped. Abaddon had said the same thing right after Sam disappeared. The screaming started again and Otomatsu dropped Quan to cover his ears.

"OH GOD!" Quan wailed. "I'M SO SORRY! I DIDN'T KNOW! I DIDN'T KNOW!"

"IS IT THE SERAPHIM?" I asked him as loudly as I could.

Quan curled up in a ball on the floor and started rocking back and forth, sobbing uncontrollably.

"I DIDN'T KNOW SHE WOULD DO IT! I DIDN'T KNOW! OH PLEASE, GOD, I'M SO SORRY!"

We all just stood there, shielding our ears until the shrieking ended. Quan continued to cry and roll around on the ground. Otomatsu kicked him in the back to make him stop.

"Quan!"

Quan stopped and looked up at us.

"You..." he pointed a finger at me. "This is all your fault!"

"I- I-"

"We were never supposed to let death angels into the temple, and now I know why. A death angel unleashed the Antichrist."

"The *what*?" I asked in disbelief. "I did not! I was trying to save my friend, Sam! I don't even know what happened. I read the scroll to free Sam and then Ankou and Thalia....they shriveled up and..."

"They died!" Quan snapped. "You sacrificed to them to resurrect the Antichrist!"

"Stop calling Sam that!" I yelled.

"That is *not* your friend, Sam," Quan shook his head violently. "She's become something else."

"What the fuck are you talking about?"

"Do you have the scroll?" Quan asked.

The boat.

"Shit."

Otomatsu and Elijah stared at me.

"Emma, where is the scroll?" Quan asked again.

"It was on the boat...when it crashed."

Quan's eyes widened and he balled up on the floor again, sobbing. The screaming started for the fifth time. By that point, we all knew to cover our ears and pause whatever was going on. We waited, still as statues, until it was over.

"Emma," Elijah said, "what exactly did the scroll say?"

"I- I don't know. Abaddon translated it for me, but not really. He just wrote out how to pronounce the language. Otomatsu said that he saw something on the scroll that looked like the Sea of Anathema, so we thought it was the right thing we needed to get Sam out of that water!"

"There is no scroll that just *frees* the Restless from the Sea!" Quan spat. "If you would have just been honest with me when you two came here, instead of getting me drunk and stealing, I would have told you that! There has always been a rule to never let death angels enter the Temple of Da'at, unless they were closely watched. I was never told why, but I heard rumors. Rumors that a death angel would be the one to bring about the end times. I thought it was nonsense. Complete nonsense! An angel would never be the cause of so much pain and destruction! When I first met Dumah, he begged me to let him come in and read. He asked many times, and I told him no. One day, he showed up, asking again. He suggested I stand guard, to make sure he didn't do anything he wasn't supposed to. I finally gave in. I thought he was nice and could be trusted. I had no idea that he would eventually steal from me! And then I met you."

Quan looked at Otomatsu.

"You were so lost and I felt sorry for you. When you swore you would perform exorcisms on demons, I knew you really wanted to do good things. But then you meet her, and look at what she's gotten you into."

There was a pause long enough for Quan to sit back up and sigh.

"I didn't think the rumors were true," Quan said, rubbing his face with his palms. "I thought the archangels were just a bunch of bullies. They've always disliked death angels, but I thought it was all superiority. I never thought it was because they knew."

"You think the archangels knew a death angel would end the world?" Elijah asked. Before I could argue once again that I didn't end the world, Quan answered.

"They're the highest ranked angels. They've been around longer than humans. The archangels saw Lucifer and the other fallen angels descend into Hell. There has never been any doubt in my mind that they know a lot more than the rest of us do. But I thought if they knew how the world would end, they'd try harder to stop it."

"They can't interfere with the divine timeline," Elijah sighed.

I remembered the archangels mentioning the divine timeline when a guardian angel broke through the veil and interacted with a human. All of the times the archangels were rude to me; it wasn't about me, personally. It was about what I was destined to do.

"What have I done?" I uttered.

"You didn't *do* anything!" Otomatsu assured me, although his tone sounded like he was scolding me.

The screaming started a sixth time. I didn't cover my ears. I stood as still as a statue while everyone else groaned and waited for the deafening sound to end. Once it did, I didn't hesitate to ask my question.

"Where are the archangels?"

Quan blinked hard at me.

"Quan!" Otomatsu snapped. "Where are the archangels?"

"Preparing," he mumbled.

"Preparing for what?" Elijah asked.

"To close The Gates."

The three of us looked at each other as Quan started sobbing again. Elijah started to slowly back away from us.

"Emma," he breathed. I looked at him as he shook his head; tears streamed down his cheeks. "If this is all true…I can't stay with you."

I tried to respond, but nothing came out. My mouth only opened and closed silently, like a fish. Elijah reached the door and held onto the wooden frame. He glanced back over his shoulder at me, with a defeated look on his face.

"I'm sorry," I whispered. Elijah nodded.

"Me too," he muttered before disappearing.

Otomatsu put his hand on my shoulder.

"What do you want to do?" he asked. "I'll go wherever you go."

I didn't reply.

"Emma," Otomatsu squeezed my shoulder. I looked at him.

"What do you want to do?"

"We have to find Sam," I blurted. "I need to know for sure."

He nodded slowly before turning to Quan.

"Everything's going to be okay."

"Just please get her out of here," Quan cried.

The screaming started a seventh time, which caused Quan to wail again.

"IT'S HAPPENING!" he screamed. "HELL HAS BEEN UNLEASHED ON EARTH!"

"WE NEED TO GO!" Otomatsu yelled.

"NO!" Quan pleaded. "DON'T GO WITH HER! SAVE YOURSELF BEFORE THEY CLOSE THE GATES!"

Otomatsu grabbed my arm tightly and led me out of the room. The screaming ceased as we made our way through the main floor. I stopped for a moment.

"Emma," Otomatsu urged. "Come on!"

"What if Quan is right," I said. "What if The Gates close and you won't be able to get into Paradise?"

"You don't have to worry about that," he assured me. "Besides, I became a death angel knowing there was no chance of going to Paradise."

Otomatsu winked at me.

"It's not funny!" I scolded. "This sounds really bad."

"Listen, I'm in this with you. I'm not leaving you to deal with, whatever this is, by yourself. I won't make that mistake again."

"I was trying to push you away so you wouldn't get hurt," I explained. "And now I'm worried again that you'll get hurt."

"You don't need to worry about me," he smiled. "I can take care of myself."

"What if things are as bad as Quan says they are?"

"She's a little girl," Otomatsu said. "How dangerous could she be?"

We had no idea what was happening on Earth, or how bad it was. But we were about to find out.

19

In a quiet Missouri town, the residents were just starting their morning as the sunrise lit up the sky with pinks and oranges. A little girl named Maggie, stood in the driveway, staring at all the colors. Her mom, Jillian, sat Maggie's lunchbox on the front passenger seat. It contained vegan nuggets, carrot sticks, hummus, and grapes. Jillian then pulled out her phone to see the calendar notification that had just chimed. It was a reminder that her yoga class had been canceled due to the instructor having a "family emergency." Jillian was an organized woman who didn't like last minute changes. Instead of dropping Maggie off at preschool and heading to yoga, she would need to find something else to occupy her time that morning. *Maybe I could get a pedicure*, she thought. But one thing was certain. Jillian dreaded the weekend. It meant two days of her husband and daughter being home with her. No quiet house. No binge-watching her favorite shows or reading her book. Just constantly cleaning up after them and making food for them. Maggie was still gazing up at the sky when Jillian picked her up.

"Mommy, it looks like the world is on fire."

Her mom smiled tiredly as she buckled Maggie into her seat and agreed that it did indeed look like the world was on fire. Little did they know, as the car started and children's songs played through the speakers, how true that would soon be.

    A few miles down the road from where Maggie was asking her mom about her favorite princess, an elderly couple was sitting at a stoplight. The husband, Dave, was driving his wife, Anne, to her eye doctor appointment. Anne's vision had been getting worse, although Dave's wasn't all that great either. Anne reminded him that after her appointment, they needed to stop by the grocery store to pick up their prescriptions from the pharmacy and then get what she needed to make pot roast the following day. Anne's pot roast was a favorite of Dave's and he had been asking her to make it for weeks. Neither of them noticed that the light had turned green and the car behind honked its horn three times. Dave waved apologetically and went on. Dave admitted he was daydreaming of Anne's pot roast and that "tomorrow can't come sooner."

    In the car behind Dave and Anne was Steve. Steve was having a bad morning. He was running late for work and the "old fucker," as he referred to the driver in front of him, wasn't helping matters. Steve slept through his alarm, so he had to skip showering. He tried wetting and gelling his hair down, but the stubborn cowlick in the back still stood straight up. All he ended up doing was get his work shirt wet and make the cowlick look less fluffy and more like a porcupine quill. Steve started the coffee maker and frantically brushed his teeth. He brushed so hard and fast that he poked his gum with the toothbrush, causing it to bleed. As he made his way back to the kitchen, he heard a dripping sound. When he turned the corner, he saw coffee spilled all over the floor and counter. He had forgotten to put a cup under the spout. Once everything was cleaned up, Steve ran to his car coffeeless, with a wet shirt and a gelled mess of hair. If he went slightly over the speed limit, he'd still have a chance of making it to work on time. That was until he got stuck behind the "old fucker" who didn't even notice the light turning green. And the "old fucker" was driving five miles under the speed limit. He was definitely going to be late. *On the bright side,* Steve thought, *tomorrow is the weekend.*

  Steve's son, Hank, was standing on the high school football field. It was complete bullshit that marching band practice started so early in the morning. Hank supposed it was to beat the mid-August heat. Even so, school started in two weeks and getting to sleep in was one of the benefits of summer vacation. He had to get up earlier than his parents to drive to school for practice. He loved playing the trumpet, but disliked marching band. The school's marching band was mediocre at best, but it was necessary for any chance at a music scholarship. The long term goal was to become a studio musician for famous artists, possibly even going on tour with them. His parents constantly begged him to make a backup plan, but there just wasn't anything else that interested him. Hank was only halfway paying attention to the band director, his trumpet held stiffly in front of his face and the mouthpiece pressed firmly against his lips. But he couldn't help but think about the kiss that had occurred six days prior. Hank's first kiss. He had been invited to a friend's house for a birthday party and although Hank didn't drink, he reluctantly went after his father insisted it would be good for him. He knew his father wanted him to have a similar high school experience that he had. But he'd never be able to. Hank would never be athletic like his father. He would never be a show off like his father. He would never be popular like his father. He would never be straight like his father.

    Across town, at the coffee shop on Main Street, Parker leaned on the counter, thinking about the kiss too. He had been introduced to Hank at his cousin's house party. Hank was about to start his junior year and Parker had graduated the year before. The whole evening, Parker kept wondering how they had gone to the same school and hadn't ever known each other. Parker was confident in who he was, a young pansexual man who was counting down the minutes until he was done with his summer job and headed back to his

West Coast college. Hank, however, was bashful and sweet, and obviously not out. While everyone else had snuck to the backyard to pass a joint around, Parker stayed inside with Hank. For almost a whole hour, they were alone; talking and getting to know each other better. At one point, Parker told a stupid joke that made Hank laugh so hard that he playfully slapped Parker's knee. And for whatever reason, Parker took Hank's hand with his. They stopped laughing and locked eyes. Parker leaned in slowly, giving Hank more than enough time to let go of his hand and back away. Instead, Hank clumsily went in and smacked his face into Parker's. He apologized. Parker hushed him and smiled before kissing him properly.

  The two of them made out until they heard the back door open, followed by giggling and coughing. Each boy moved to opposite sides of the couch as their friends entered the room and started tearing into the various snacks laid out on the coffee table. Throughout the rest of the night, Parker and Hank acted as though nothing had happened. They stole glances every chance they got though. Eventually, Parker stood up and reminded his cousin that he had work in the morning. As it was, he'd only get a few hours of sleep; but he didn't want the night to end. Hank abruptly offered Parker a ride home, blushing at how eager he sounded. No one suspected a thing though, and the drive to Parker's house was as sweet as their time on the couch. They exchanged phone numbers and had been texting all week. Every time Hank's phone lit up, he quickly grabbed it before his parents could see the name on the screen. He was always ready to explain that Parker was a girl he had met at the party, in case they questioned anything. But the week went by without either of them noticing anything different in their son's behavior.

Parker was counting down the minutes until his morning break so he could check his messages. He had made plans to meet Hank after work and find a secluded spot where they could hang out, away from the rest of the world. Parker was crouched behind the counter, about to put the, "Back in 5 minutes" sign on the counter, when the door opened.

"Of course," Parker muttered under his breath.

He stood up quickly, putting on his best "customer service" smile.

"Hey, how's it-?"

It took a moment for Parker to realize what he saw. A little girl, he thought maybe eight years old, slowly shuffled into the cafe, covered in blood. There was a tiny red handprint on the white front door from where she had closed it. The little girl's red hair was matted down with blood, some of it dripping down her cheeks like crimson tears.

"Oh my-! Are you, are you okay, honey?" Parker asked, stepping towards the girl.

"I'm trying..." the girl said hoarsely. She sounded as if she might have a cold.

Parker knelt down in front of her and gently touched her shoulders.

"Are you hurt?" he asked. "Is this your blood?"

"No," the little girl shook her head. "The woman next door...she's a seamstress?"

"Sophie? Y-yes. Oh god, is she okay?"

The girl shook her head again. Parker let go of her shoulders and stood back up. Something about her frightened him. She was a child, but a tiny voice in the back of Parker's mind told him to run. But he was frozen.

"I-I should call 911," he stuttered.

"Yes," the little girl said in her raspy voice. "Let them come. I'm still a little weak, but I can still have some fun before my strength is fully restored."

"What are you talking about?"

"Once my power is fully restored, I'll be able to wipe out whole city blocks at a time. But for now, taking you all out one by one will do."

"You all?"

The little girl, who Parker thought looked so sweet despite being covered in blood, slowly looked up at him and smiled.

"Humans," she hissed.

The girl lunged her hands into Parker's abdomen. He didn't have time to scream; all that came out was a gasp. Her fingers dug around inside of him while blood spurted from his mouth. Intestines and other organs rolled out and splattered on the floor, landing between his feet. The last thing Parker saw before he died was his heart being ripped from his body. His phone vibrated in his pocket, blood slowly seeping through his jeans and onto its screen. Hank was texting him, asking how his morning was going.

    Parker's body slumped to the floor and continued to bleed out while the little girl rubbed his heart against her cheeks. It was still warm, and felt smooth and wet on her face. She giggled as the heart tickled her nose slightly. The little girl looked down at the dead body and gruesome pile of organs and dropped the heart. It made a dull splatting sound as it landed on the floor. She kicked the dead boy in the ribs and the body made an abrupt sound of passing gas, followed by a foul stench. The girl giggled again and looked into his lifeless eyes.

    "Oh my god, you're shitting yourself!" she laughed in her raspy voice. "If someone discovers your body, they're going to know your pants are full of shit!"

    The girl's laughing abruptly stopped and she grimaced at the terrified look that was still on the boy's face.

"You're all so fucking pathetic," she said before spitting on him. The saliva smacked right onto Parker's forehead. "All you care about is your technology and all of the ridiculous, materialistic bullshit humans have made. You were given everything you ever needed. God gave you everything. And I'm here to take it all away, because none of you deserve it."

With all of her force, the girl stomped Parker's face; her blood-soaked purple tennis shoes crushed his head in. The stars on her shoes lit up at the force of her foot hitting Parker's head. She gasped at the outcome and slowly lifted her foot out of the mess. There was no way to tell what was a nose or lips anymore. Bits of white jaw bone and teeth poked through the mangled tissue. The girl raised both hands up to her mouth and laughed again.

"I'm becoming stronger," she smiled into her cupped hands.

Then, she made her way through the back door and into the kitchen. Loaves of bread and muffins sat wrapped on the countertop next to a gas stove. Next to the stove was a commercial deep fryer filled with oil. There were metal baskets hanging on a rack above it, and the oil was a brownish color. The little girl shuffled over to the fryer and turned the temperature all the way up. She gave one nod of approval and walked out of the kitchen. Before she reached the dead body again, the door opened and a middle aged woman in a business suit walked into the cafe, looking down at her phone. Her stilettos clacked against the tile in beat with her long, red fingernails tapping on her phone screen. The girl froze and waited for the woman to glance up.

"Hey, Parker," she sighed. "I'll have my usual, unless you're out of soy milk. If you're out of soy milk, I'll just have a cold brew, but with very little ice."

When there was no response, the woman finally looked up. Parker, and Parker's insides, were strewn all over the tiled floor. Blood almost reached the woman's stilettos and she quickly scurried backwards, banging the back of her head against the door.

"OH MY GOD!"

She raised her cell phone with shaking hands and dialed, gagging at the gruesome scene in front of her.

"911, what's your emergency?" the dispatcher answered.

"There's so much blood everywhere!" the woman said through her rapid breathing. "Oh my god, someone has been hurt badly. I think he's dead!"

"Who's dead, ma'am?" the dispatcher asked in his calm, reassuring voice.

She didn't respond at first, only made a series of sharp, squeaking noises, as if she's being choked.

"Ma'am?" the dispatcher asked again. "Is someone hurt?"

The woman looked at the girl, who just stood there with her hands behind her back and her toes pointed inward.

"There-there's a little girl," the woman said. "She's covered in blood."

"Is she hurt?" he asked.

"N-no," the woman stuttered. "She's...smiling at me."

"Tell them to come," the little girl smirked. "Tell them that they need to send everyone now."

"You need to send the police," the woman shuttered as tears ran down her face. "You need to send everyone now."

"Ma'am, I need you to stay on the phone until the police arrive, okay?"

The little girl shook her head slowly at the woman and smiled again.

"I don't think I'm going to be able to do that," the woman cried.

"Why is that?" he asked.

There was no response.

"Ma'am? Why can't you stay on the phone with me?"

The little girl gently took the woman's phone with her left hand and held it up to her ear.

With her right hand, she ran a chef's knife across the woman's throat.

"She can't stay on the phone because I just slit her throat," the little girl said hoarsely.

"Who–"

Blood poured onto the woman's business suit as she sank to the floor, one hand firmly pressed against the laceration. An alarm went off as smoke began to seep into the room. The woman clawed at the little girl's legs weakly before falling over. The dispatcher was still trying to talk when the girl dropped the phone into the pool of blood at her feet. The woman had stopped moving and her eyes rolled back. The little girl walked around the woman's body and went through the door as something in the kitchen exploded.

A husband and wife, both in their early 20s, were jogging through town for their morning run. The wife, Priscilla, had taken a pregnancy test before they left the house, and it was positive. Her husband, Mike, had recently convinced her that they should stop trying to conceive. They had been trying for a baby for two years and he didn't want to go through any more disappointment. He didn't want to see *her* go through any more disappointment. So, they booked a two week vacation in France and gave up on the idea of children. She was thinking all morning about how she was going to tell him the news, afraid of how he'd respond.

"Hold on, Mike, I have to tie my shoe," she panted.

As Priscilla bent down to work on her shoe laces, Mike took the moment to stretch and check his watch. They had already run almost two miles. Mike looked over at the cafe and daydreamed of eating muffins, chocolate croissants, and danishes. Priscilla had them both on a strict diet that involved zero sugar, alcohol, and gluten. He couldn't remember the last time he had a beer and the thought made his mouth water. She had also made him swear off masterbating, and scheduled sex for specific nights of the month, when she was at her most fertile. However, as much as Mike wanted to make his wife happy, he couldn't oblige. Every month, when Priscilla would get her period, Mike spent every chance he'd get jerking off. He felt guilty every time he'd throw away the tissues and clear his internet history, thinking it was somehow his fault they weren't getting pregnant. But the next month would come around and as soon as Priscilla would cry into her pillow, Mike knew he'd sneak off after she fell asleep to search, "amateur college girls."

As Priscilla tied her shoe, Mike watched her breasts jiggle in her sports bra. He noticed how great they looked from this angle and imagined her giving him head, right there in broad daylight. He realized he was starting to get hard thinking about it and quickly shook off the thought.

"You wanna grab a little something from the cafe?" he asked as Priscilla stood up. "I would literally kill for a banana nut muffin."

"I thought we weren't going to break our diet until we were on vacation," Priscilla said. "Would you rather waste the money and calories on a stale American muffin, or wait until we can have pain au chocolat in Paris?"

Mike grunted and wrapped his arms around Priscilla's waist.

"I'm just ready to eat whatever I want, whenever I want," he grinned as he squeezed her butt cheek.

"Mike!" she exclaimed and giggled.

"I'm looking forward to everything," he said softly. "No more stressing over baby stuff. It's going to be just the two of us, enjoying each other's time, and doing whatever we want."

Priscilla pulled away from Mike and adjusted the waistband of her leggings.

"What?" he asked.

"Mike-"

Priscilla stopped talking and just stared.

"What's wrong?"

"Oh my god!"

Priscilla started running towards the cafe. Mike could see a child, a little girl, and it looked like she was covered in blood. He chased after Priscilla and saw that the door of the cafe was open slightly.

"Honey, is everything okay?" Priscilla asked as they got closer.

Mike looked at the bottom of the door and saw a hand with fingernails painted red sticking out, making the door unable to latch shut. He could smell smoke and grabbed Priscilla's shoulder.

"Something's wrong," Mike said as sirens grew closer.

"What do you mean?" Priscilla turned to ask him. "This little girl needs our help."

"You're pregnant," the little girl said, reaching her hands out towards Priscilla's stomach.

Priscilla gasped and grabbed her belly.

"How-?"

"I can hear its heartbeat," the girl smiled. "It would have eventually been a girl. Too bad you two won't ever meet her."

"What is she talking about?" Mike asked.

"He doesn't want a baby," the girl grinned. "He wants it to be just the two of you. He wants to eat junk food and fuck you just for the fun of it, and not because it's a chore."

Mike and Priscilla looked at each other, both stunned, as five police cars pulled up in front of the cafe. The little girl ran to the officers, crying and screaming, "HELP ME! HE HAS A KNIFE!"

"FREEZE!" one of the officers yelled as several of them pointed their guns at Mike.

"I didn't do anything!" Mike hollered.

"You're making a mistake!" Priscilla cried. "We just got here and it looks like-"

As she took a step forward, the police officers jutted their guns out at them again.

"I SAID FREEZE, GOD DAMMIT!" the officer repeated. "PUT YOUR HANDS UP WHERE WE CAN SEE THEM!"

Priscilla slowly put her shaking hands up above her head, but Mike took another step forward.

"He killed a man and a lady inside," the little girl cried. "He has a knife!"

"SHOW US YOUR HANDS!" the officer screamed. "NOW!"

Mike lifted his hands and the knife the little girl had used to slit the business woman's throat was now gripped in his left palm. Looking up at it, Mike gasped and dropped it. He wiped his bloody hand on his shirt and began trembling.

"I swear, I didn't do anything!" Mike pleaded as tears streamed down his face and he took another step.

"IF YOU TAKE ANOTHER STEP, WE *WILL* OPEN FIRE!"

"I'm not doing it," Mike sobbed. "I'm trying to stand still but my feet- I can't control-"

The gunfire was deafening as Mike's body was hit multiple times. Priscilla screamed and crouched down, covering her ears. The police officers looked around at each other, confused. They didn't notice the huge smile on the little girl's face as they pointed their guns at each other. One of them started praying silently as urine ran down his pant leg. A moment later, every officer fired his or her gun, and then dropped to the ground. Priscilla was still curled up, crying hysterically, when the girl walked over to her. She looked up as the girl raised her hand slowly; her thumb pointed to the sky and her index finger pointed at Priscilla.

"Bang," the little girl muttered.

Priscilla's head whipped backwards and blood sprayed out of the back. She fell to the ground with a small hole in her forehead. There was another explosion from inside the building and the glass windows shattered. Smoke poured out of the cafe as more people gathered around to see what had happened. There were screams of terror and someone started dry heaving at the sight. The little girl, still covered in blood, skipped through the horrified crowd. She pointed to a woman and watched as she doubled over, clutching her chest and gasping. The little girl then pointed two fingers at two men who were coming over to help the officers. They stopped suddenly, looked at each other, and then started beating each other relentlessly.

The two men were punching and clawing at each other like animals, paying no attention to the woman lying on the ground having a heart attack.

One of the men punched the other one so hard, his nose bent in an unnatural direction. The second man punched the first in the mouth; a few teeth flew out and bounced across the pavement. The man with the broken nose lost his balance and fell to the ground. The other man got behind him, stepped on his back, and grabbed a handful of hair. As he pulled the other man's head back, his scalp started ripping, revealing the skull. The man with the broken nose screamed and reached for one of the dead police officer's guns on the ground. He shot the man who had ripped his scalp. He then brought the gun up to his temple and pulled the trigger.

  The little girl continued to skip through the town as more people showed up; either to find where the smoke was coming, why there was screaming, or just because they were being drawn to her. She started humming a song and nodded her head towards the bystanders along with the beat. One by one, their heads exploded like popped water balloons. Smoke filled the sky as the fire spread to other buildings on Main Street. The little girl skipped up to a puddle of blood by one of the headless bodies and splashed in it, as any child would do on a rainy day. She was getting much stronger. It was time.

  She walked up to the highway, away from the chaos and gore of the little downtown area. Cars were going about their business, unaware of what was happening just a few miles away. Dave and his wife, Anne, were in one of the cars, coming back from the eye doctor's. They were discussing the grim news that Anne's sight was getting significantly worse, when the little girl walked out onto the highway. Anne screamed as Dave swerved the car, barely missing the girl, and side-swiped the car next to them. Dan over-corrected the steering and the car skidded to the other side of the road. Once they hit the grass, the car flipped twice and landed on its roof. Dave was knocked unconscious and Anne suffered a broken arm and hip. As she dangled upside down, crying, the little girl walked through the cars who had screeched to a halt. She lifted a hand towards Dave and Anne's car and then clenched her fist. The car slowly compacted around them, crushing them as her fist tightened. As the little girl opened her hand back up, the car burst into flames. She then waved her arm to the left, causing the cars on the highway to slide in the same direction. She did the same to the cars on her right before walking to the center of the road. The little girl knelt down on the ground and placed both palms on the asphalt. There was a rumbling sound and the ground started trembling. People abandoned their cars and started running away as the seraphim's screaming began.

"The trumpets have sounded," she said quietly. "Earth is ours."

The concrete started splitting and the ground opened up right in front of the little girl. She knew there were already hundreds of demons on Earth already, but there were still many more in Hell. She would make sure they knew that Earth was now theirs for the taking. Demons started ascending from Hell, and everything was thrown into utter chaos. People were being eaten alive and torn in half. There were people being set on fire while others were unable to breathe, suffocating to death. The little girl started skipping again, pleased by the destruction around her.

She made her way back through town until she came to a daycare building. She stood in front of the building for a moment, thinking of all the gruesome ways she was going to kill the children inside.

"Sam?" a voice said softly from behind her.

The little girl slowly turned around and faced two death angels, both armed with swords. The man had his katana pointed straight at her. The young woman beside him held onto hers, the blade glowing from the flames that engulfed it, but she had it lowered.

20

"Ah, the one who freed me," she grinned.

"Do you know who I am?" I asked. "It's me, Emma."

"I have flashes of Sam's memories. And of Ankou's. And of Thalia's. Of God and Satan. I am both. I am neither. I am Nihil. I am Omnia. I am Finis."

I looked at Otomatsu.

"'Nothing,' 'everything,' and 'the end,'" he translated.

"Okay, well for the sake of making things easier," I said, "I'm going to stick with Sam because you still look very much like Sam."

"Emma," Otomatsu sighed, "we're too late. Look."

He pointed at my wrist and I held my tracker up. There were dying people showing up everywhere around us. I zoomed out on the map, showing the entire state. Then, the entire country. And then the world. The red dots were spreading so fast, most of the map was turning red. I looked back up at Sam, who was smiling.

"Sam, please don't do this," I begged. "I know you're still in there somewhere and the *real* Sam would never want to hurt anyone."

"Did you forget that I was the one working with your demon boyfriend?" she laughed. "Sam was a horrible angel."

Her voice didn't sound like Sam's. It was like several voices in one and she sounded a little raspy.

"She was manipulated by demons!"

"She was weak!" *Sam* spat. "No one forced her to betray God! She knew her decisions could end up leading to Hell overthrowing Earth and the coming of the Antichrist. However, she never considered *she* would become the Antichrist."

"No," I breathed.

"And *you*," she smiled at me, "you were the one who set the whole thing in motion."

"No! I didn't do anything!"

"Oh but you did, Emma. You read the scroll. You sacrificed an angel and a demon and created little ol' me!"

I couldn't believe it. She was confirming the thing I had feared ever since I read the scroll. From the very beginning, something had felt wrong about the whole thing. But I had told myself that it was because Ankou was involved. I was so blinded by all of my conflicting feelings about him, that I didn't see Abaddon sneak right in to betray us both.

"Yes," *Sam* smiled as she read my thoughts. "Abaddon was behind it all. He has been since the beginning of time. It's always been Abaddon."

"You called?"

I turned around and saw Abaddon standing behind us.

"I can't believe you did this to me," I said to Abaddon. "To Ankou and Thalia!"

"You did it willingly," Abaddon crossed his arms. "You should have done more research before handing over that scroll."

"I thought I could trust you!"

"Oh my god, Emma, how many times is it going to take for you to finally get it through that thick head of yours? You can't trust anyone!"

"You said you needed my help."

"And Ankou told you his name was Alastor and that he loved you."

"You betrayed him too. You got a fellow demon killed."

"You think, for one second, that I gave a shit about Ankou?" Abaddon scoffed. "I was banished from Paradise with Satan and I've been biding my time until I could fulfill my destiny. I was always meant to be the one to bring upon the end of the world. I just needed the damn scroll. You see, the prophecy is that an angel and a demon would end human kind, and that they would need to sacrifice another angel and demon in order to do it. You and I did all of this."

Abaddon raised his hands and spun slowly in place.

"So is this where you try to kill us?" I asked.

Abaddon and *Sam* laughed.

"Why on God's green Earth would we want to kill you?" *Sam* questioned. "You're my second favorite being after Abaddon here. Kill you, no. No, I won't be doing that. I want you to stick around and watch the show."

She turned to Otomatsu.

"You on the other hand...you're the asshole who's been exorcising demons. I would take great pleasure in killing you."

Otomatsu and I held our swords high in defense.

"Oh please," she chuckled and waved her hand. Our swords disappeared into thin air.

"Do you honestly think there is anything you can do to stop me?" she continued. "I'm the Antichrist. This is my domain now. I'm unstoppable."

"That's it!" I whispered to Otomatsu. "We need to head back to Processing, *now*!"

Without hesitation, Otomatsu and I teleported back to Processing. If we thought it was hectic before, it was a hundred times worse when we returned. People were running around, panicked, and there were no greeters or booths where new arrivals usually signed in. We pushed through the crowd, trying to make our way towards The Gates, but there were so many people, it was hard to get to.

"We need to find one of the archangels!" I said loudly.

"Emma, we need to get inside where it's safe."

"We have to stop her! We have to stop her before-!"

Otomatsu put a hand on my shoulder. I looked back at him.

"Come on, Otomatsu!" I pleaded. "We have to do something!"

"Emma, there's nothing we can do," Otomatsu said somberly. "It's over. All we can do now is ask for forgiveness and hope we will be allowed into Paradise finally."

"No!" I pulled away from him. "How can you say that? How can you just give up like that? Give up on *me* like that?"

"I have never given up on you," he said, gently brushing my cheek with the back of his hand. "I care about you more than anyone else. You truly are a great person who has only wanted to see the best in others. But enough is enough. I'm not angry at you at all for this, but this is the end. You tried so hard to make things right, and in the process became a better death angel. But you need to let it go now."

"No!" I repeated. "I'm not giving up just because you want to!"

I pushed harder through the crowd and made my way up closer to the entrance of The Gates. I could see Michael and Barachiel on the other side as the other archangels were trying to usher people through the opening.

"Michael! Barachiel!" I shouted and waved. They saw me and hesitated before coming over. I could see Barachiel lean over and whisper something to Michael.

"Hey," Michael said gloomily as Otomatsu caught up to me.

"Where's Jesus?" I asked.

"What?" all three of them asked.

"Michael, something's happened," I said.

"I know, Emma."

"I'm so sorry," I turned to Barachiel. "Ankou..."

"I know," Barachiel said. "It's okay. It was all part of the plan."

"And so were you," Michael smiled weakly.

"How can you two say that?" I scoffed. "Thousands of people are being tortured and are dying! We can fix this!"

"No, Emma," Barachiel shook his head. "This was always supposed to happen. But don't be sad. All of these people get to start an eternity in Paradise. No more sickness or hunger-"

"Most of these people would have lived long, healthy lives!" I snapped. "And now they don't get that!"

"They get something much better than a life on Earth, Emma," Michael sighed.

"Where's Jesus?" I repeated.

"At God's side," Michael said. "Where else would he be?"

"Um, on Earth fighting the Antichrist?"

Michael and Barachiel looked at each other.

"What?" I asked.

"Emma," Michael started.

"What! You're an archangel! Just go get him!"

"Emma," Otomatsu said. "I think he's trying to tell you that he's not coming."

"That's bullshit!" I barked. "Everyone knows that Jesus comes back to Earth to fight the Antichrist!"

Barachiel shook his head and looked down at the ground.

"Who's going to save everyone left on Earth?" I asked.

"Emma, they are saved," Michael smiled. "The others...well, they were never going to Paradise to begin with."

I watched dozens of people enter through The Gates. Men, women, and children were all smiling as they entered Paradise. The panic-induced crowd back at the beginning was completely different than the group I was watching. Once they realized where they were going, everyone seemed so much more relaxed and excited. Then, I saw Isla and another female death angel. I watched as they made their way towards the entrance, both with huge smiles on their faces. Isla eventually saw me and Otomatsu and waved enthusiastically. I waved back and turned to the archangels.

"So the death angels *do* get to go to Paradise?" Otomatsu asked.

"Um, of course," Barachiel said, his eyes shifting to Michael.

"Can you excuse us for one moment?" Otomatsu smiled. The archangels both nodded.

Otomatsu ushered me away from the fence and leaned in close to me.

"Emma, we can go to Paradise," he grinned.

"I was given that choice not that long ago and I didn't want it," I frowned.

"But a lot of us death angels weren't given the choice. We've spent our afterlives thinking we'd never get into Paradise."

I looked at him and knew what he was saying without saying it.

"You want to go," I said finally.

"I want you to go with me," Otomatsu explained. "You could see your family again."

"It's not real, Otomatsu! It's just your own distorted version of Paradise. It's not reality."

"Reality is distorted now anyways, now that demons are running Earth," he shrugged. "We can finally rest, Emma."

"But we won't be together," I said, tears filling my eyes.

"You'll be in my Paradise and I'll be in yours," he smiled. "I will always be with you."

Otomatsu held his hand out to me. I stood there, thinking about how I had spent years, chasing Ankou, thinking of ways to kill him. Thinking of Dumah and how I'd bring him back. Thinking of Sam and how I'd end up rescuing her somehow. Up until recently, I had wasted my time as an angel. I had finally started to like and accept my role. And it was all thanks to Otomatsu. The silver lining to all of this was that I had him. I took his hand and gripped it tightly.

"It's okay," he said softly. "We'll do this together."

"Together," I smiled.

We followed the crowd to the entrance. There were about twenty people in front of us. I could see Isla and the other death angel on the other side of The Gates, almost to the stairway leading up. I was going to Paradise. I'd be with Otomatsu, my parents, and my brother. There would be no more worries. But there would be plenty of zebras and ice cream.

"You ready?" Otomatsu asked as we inched closer. I nodded.

The group in front of us went in and I hesitated.

"It's okay," Otomatsu squeezed my hand three times. "I'll step forward first, and then you follow."

I nodded as he walked forward. He went through the entrance and there was a strong pull on my arm.

"Ow!" I recoiled my arm.

Otomatsu stood on the other side and rubbed his arm.

"Come on, Emma," he said as people pushed past me.

I stepped forward and it was like walking into a wall; only there wasn't anything in front of me except Otomatsu.

"Emma?"

"I can't get in!" I panicked, trying to push through the invisible barrier.

"Hey!" he called. "Michael! Barachiel!"

The archangels came over, weaving in and out of people. The looks on their faces told me everything I needed to know.

"I can't go, can I?" I asked.

Otomatsu looked at them.

"Emma, I am so sorry," Michael sighed. "Unfortunately, there have to be consequences for what you've done."

"No," Otomatsu said. My heart sank.

"It's okay," I lied. "I'll be fine. You go ahead."

"Emma, I don't want to go without you. I can't leave you."

"We'll be together soon," I smiled. "I'll be in your Paradise, remember? I'll always be with you."

"NO!"

Tears ran down his face as people continued to push past us.

"Go," I nodded, fighting back my own tears. "I'll see you soon."

Michael put his hands on Otomatsu's shoulders and gently led him away. Barachiel gave me a nod and then followed after them. I watched them move further and further away from me. As they reached the bottom step, Otomatsu turned one last time to look at me. I gave him my best fake smile and waved. He didn't return the wave, or the smile, and turned to start walking up the stairs. I stayed there for a while as more and more people entered. A small part of me kept hoping that the archangels would change their minds and come back for me. But they never did.

Eventually, I left Processing and went back to Earth. I chose to go to New York to see how things looked in a big city. Almost everywhere I turned, there were demons running rampant and people screaming. Cars were left abandoned in the middle of streets and buildings were on fire. I looked down at my wrist and noticed the screen on the tracker was black. I took it off and tapped it a couple of times. When it still did nothing, I dropped it on the pavement in front of the Ambassador Theatre. I had always dreamed of someday seeing a Broadway show. Even after I died, I could have seen some. But I wasted so much time plotting my revenge against Ankou. A large poster above the front door displaying the current show was burning. It tilted slightly before crashing to the ground.

I walked down the road until I came across a woman in dirty clothes kneeling on the ground. Her filthy hands were pressed together in front of her face and her eyes were closed. She was praying in the middle of the apocalypse. As I got closer, I could hear what she was saying.

"Please, Lord, take me away from all of this pain and suffering. I don't belong here. I know I did some bad things in my life but I promise that if you save me, I will spend eternity worshiping you and repenting. Please don't leave me behind. Please let me go be with you."

I kneeled down in front of her and gently placed my hands on hers. She jumped at my touch and opened her eyes. As soon as she saw me, she fell backwards and shimmied away on her elbows.

"Please don't hurt me!" she pleaded, shielding her face with her arm.

"I promise, I'm not here to hurt you," I said.

"You-you can see me?"

The homeless woman lowered her arm slowly and looked at me.

"Yes. Are you an angel?"

I nodded.

"Have you come to stop this?" she asked.

"I can't," I muttered.

"Oh," she said grimly. "So...this is it, huh? The end times?"

"I'm afraid so."

"I always read that the people who were saved went straight to Heaven when the end times started. I'm not in Heaven."

"I don't think that's exactly how it's going to happen," I explained. "I think people are going to be here until they die; I don't think anyone is going to just vanish into thin air."

"I see," she nodded.

She sat for a moment, thinking and looking around. Then, she stood up, walked over to a pile of trash and grabbed a glass jar from one of the ripped bags. She smashed the end of the jar on the pavement.

"Don't!" I said frantically.

"I'm not staying here, waiting to be torn to shreds by demons," she cried.

"You won't go to Heaven if you kill yourself."

She hung her head and chuckled.

"Of course," she shook her head. "I've spent the last five years living on the streets, begging for money and stealing whatever I could get my hands on, for drugs. I moved to New York to become someone and all I did was get addicted to heroin. What a waste."

She laughed to herself again and dropped the broken jar.

"I guess there's probably enough drug dealers around to at least enjoy that for a little bit longer. Well, thanks anyways."

Suddenly, a horde of ten wasps came around the corner. The woman saw them at the same time I did and screamed. I got in front of her and grabbed a blood grenade from my belt.

"Run!" I shouted to her. "Get somewhere safe!"

I threw the grenade and it exploded on impact, blasting seven of the wasps. The three remaining stopped and looked at me.

"Come on!" I growled.

They let out screeches and ran at me. I grabbed a vial of holy water but as I held it up, the wasps ran right past me. I turned in time to see that the woman was still standing there.

"NO!" I yelled. "RUN!"

She stayed frozen as they reached her. She screamed as they mauled her, ripping at her flesh. I ran over and threw the holy water at them. Their hard exoskeletons were unphased by it. I picked up a large piece of cement and threw it as hard as I could.

"STOP IT!" I screamed.

The sonic boom from my voice made them stop clawing at the woman and run off. I bent down next to her and lifted her head.

"I told you to run," I said. "Why didn't you run?"

"Maybe-" she choked. "It's better-"

I held my hand against the large gash on her stomach. When I looked back at her face, the world went quiet and her body went limp. I laid her down gently and looked around.

If only I still had my sword, I thought. *I might have been able to protect her.*

I heard a clanging sound behind me and I was surprised to see Dumah's sword, *my* sword, laying on the ground. I carefully picked it up and glanced around. The sword looked as beautiful as ever. I looked up at the sky and smirked.

"Thank you," I said.

I sheathed the blade and thought about where to go next. And then it came to me.

"Maddi."

I teleported to her nursing home in Washington D.C. and hoped I wasn't too late. Although the city was under attack, it seemed to be mostly in the area closest to the Capitol. When I got to her room, Maddi was sound asleep, completely unaware of the world falling apart around her. I sat down on the edge of her bed and she stirred a little. I fidgeted with the handle of my sword.

"Everything about me was so painfully average when I was alive. When I died, I knew I hadn't done anything to leave my mark on the world. I thought I had a chance to be someone special. And I tried really, really hard in the end."

My voice cracked as a lump formed in my throat.

"You went on to do some pretty amazing things," I continued. "You lived a full, wonderful life. You made the world a better place. And I destroyed it."

A hand reached out and touched my thigh gingerly.

"You always sold yourself short, you know that?" Maddi said softly.

I looked at her and smiled.

"Hey, Maddi."

"Hey, Emma. You sure look different now."

"Yeah," I laughed. "I became a death angel."

"Bad ass," she smiled. "So, are you here for me?"

"Sort of. I'm going to stay with you until it's time."

A loud explosion outside made us both jump.

"Sounds like it won't be too much longer," Maddi sighed.

"Yeah. I'm sorry."

"Quit apologizing so much. No one likes a Debbie Downer, especially when they're about to die."

"I wish you had more time," I said.

"I don't! I've been ready for a while now. I'm tired of being stuck in a body that's slowly shutting down, with a mind that doesn't let me recognize my own children sometimes."

There was another explosion and the sky outside Maddi's window lit up yellow and orange.

"Do you mind closing the curtains?" she asked.

I nodded and got up as she tried to sit herself up in bed.

"You seem pretty alert today," I said.

"I have good days and bad. I'd rather end on a good day."

I heard people somewhere from inside the building screaming.

"Emma," Maddi said, taking my hand in hers. "Thank you for everything."

"What do you mean?" I asked.

"For being the first person to accept me for who I am."

"Whitney loved you too."

"I know, but Whitney always loved Whitney more. She put her own needs above everything else. You made sure everyone else was happy and having a good time. I was struggling so much with my identity and you made me feel like there wasn't anything wrong with me."

"That's because there *wasn't* anything wrong with you," I said.

"My own parents didn't think so."

"Well they were idiots. You were the best thing about them."

Maddi smiled, and then looked seriously at me.

"I almost killed myself after the conversion therapy camp."

"I know."

"I didn't because of you."

"Well I hope you didn't because of *you* also."

"But you gave me hope. I figured if one person could accept me as much as you did, surely there were others out there that would. And I'm so glad you gave me that hope. Otherwise, I would have never met my Cece."

I squeezed her hand.

"Am I going to Heaven?" Maddi asked. "I know I wasn't that much of a believer after everything that happened to me."

"That's the beautiful thing, Maddi. You can give up on God, but God never gives up on you. And yes, you're going to Heaven."

"Will Cece be there?"

"She'll be waiting for you with open arms."

Maddi beamed and then closed her eyes.

"I'm tired, Emma. I need to rest for just a moment."

"That's okay."

"Promise you won't go anywhere."

"I'm not leaving your side."

"When I wake up, tell me all about being a death angel."

"Okay."

I heard footsteps approaching and looked towards the doorway. Ah Puch stood there, looking just as shocked to see me as I was to see him.

"Emma?" he asked.

I put my finger up to my lips and nodded towards Maddi, who was fast asleep. Ah Puch took a step inside the room and I stood up to get between the two of them.

"Turn around and walk out that door now," I whispered. "You can do whatever you want to everyone in this building, but leave this one alone."

"Friend of yours?"

"My best friend."

Ah Puch glanced at Maddi and then back at me.

"Fine," he waved a hand at me. "It's the least I can do for you. After all, you gave us all of this."

I narrowed my eyes.

"Well, have fun with your old friend. See you around."

"Wait," I choked.

Ah Puch paused.

"Can I ask for a favor?"

"Anything for you, Emma."

"Could you..."

I looked at Maddi.

"C-could you-"

"Kill your friend?"

"As painlessly as possible. She doesn't deserve to be here."

"She won't feel a thing."

"Promise me."

"I swear."

I sat back down on the bed and took Maddi's hand in mine. Ah Puch got closer to her, picking up a pillow that had been on her armchair. I turned away, gripping her hand tightly. She curled her fingers around my palm and breathed heavily in her sleep. A moment later, her grip loosened and her breathing stopped. I slowly turned around. Ah Puch was no longer in the room, the pillow was back on the chair, and Maddi had passed. Her mouth was slightly opened and she looked like she was still sleeping. I started sobbing uncontrollably and hugged her still body.

"I hope I'm in your Paradise with you," I cried. "I love you so much."

I kissed her cheek and fixed her hair. Next, I placed her hands across her stomach and covered her up with the blanket. Then, I put the wedding photo of her and Cecilia on the bed next to her and turned the bedside table lamp off.

I walked out of the nursing home and followed the sounds of screaming, not able to take my mind off of Ah Puch killing Maddi. I continued going in the direction a crowd was running away from. I knew I was getting close to a demon when the only people around me were dead ones.

Mangled bodies laid in piles of flesh and gore. The ground was wet with blood and I stepped into a puddle of it. I shuddered as I shook off my boot. A drop of something hit my cheek. I wiped at it with my finger. It was blood. Drops splattered onto the pavement like rain and I ran under the awning of a nearby building. Then, the naked upper half of a man fell from the sky and hit the ground with a loud squish.

"Come out, come out, wherever you arrre!" a voice called from above. "I can hear you scurrying around down there!"

I glanced up as the lower half of the man fell. I took a step back as the bare buttocks and legs landed inches from me.

"Ah, I know you!" I heard.

The demon landed, his huge, bat-like wings folding behind him. His skin was purplish-blue and he had giant antlers on top of his head. His face resembled a boar, complete with tusks sticking out of his mouth. His hands were massive in comparison to the rest of his body, enormous claws at the end of each finger.

"You're Emma!" he continued. "The death angel who did all of this!"

"And you are?" I asked.

"Sonneillon," he bowed dramatically. "Pleasure to meet you."

"I need a favor," I said abruptly.

"Uh, sure. What did you have in mind?"

"I need you to kill me."

"What?" Sonneillon laughed. "You're joking."

"Not at all, actually."

He thought for a moment.

"Why?"

"Because I don't want to spend eternity here."

He paused again and scratched the hair on his chin.

"You're trying to get into Paradise."

I nodded.

"Why would I want to help you do that?"

"I gave you all of this. Eventually, all of the humans on Earth will be dead. They'll be in Heaven or Hell. Demons won't have a need for Earth anymore. So it'll just be me. I'll be completely alone."

"And what if you don't go to Paradise?" he asked. "What if you end up *down there*, with us?"

He pointed down and gasped playfully.

"Would you risk being in Hell with demons forever?"

"It's not ideal but at the very least I wouldn't be alone," I shrugged.

Sonneillon walked towards me, his claws reaching out.

"Are you sure about this?"

"Never been more sure of anything in my existence," I muttered. "Just do it."

Sonneillon approached me, grabbed my shoulder, and lifted me above himself. He pulled my left leg and right arm. Nothing happened. He tried again, grunting as he pulled harder.

"Is this some sort of joke?" he asked, looking up at me.

"I wish it was," I sighed.

Sonneillon inhaled and then tried pulling on me once more, letting out a roar of frustration. He sat me down hard enough that I fell back on my butt.

"Hey!" I said, although it didn't hurt.

"Well, it looks like you're stuck here," Sonneillon snorted in irritation and walked away. "Thanks for wasting my time."

"Yeah, thanks for nothing," I called out.

21

I needed to clear my mind and come up with a plan, so I decided to head to the beach where Otomatsu and I first met. As I got closer to shore, I could hear what sounded like crying. *Great*, I thought. My beach had been taken over. My feet hit the sand and I looked around in the dark. I could see movement up on the rocks. I climbed up to get a closer look, thinking that maybe it was an animal. But as I came up to the ledge, I could see there were two figures. Abaddon and a female demon were having aggressive sex. Abaddon was kneeling behind her, and she was on all fours. Both of them were completely naked and Abaddon had a hand cupping one of her breasts and one tightly around her neck. Her squealing was getting progressively louder until it turned into screams.

"DO YOU TWO MIND?" I yelled. They stopped and looked at me.

"Oh hey, Emma," Abaddon smiled. "You know, I noticed you and that other death angel came here often and I can see why! It's absolutely beautiful here."

"Leave," I said fiercely. "Now."

The woman laughed and slowly got to her feet.

"Aw man," Abaddon sighed and sat back on his bare bottom.

The naked woman walked over to me, placing her hand out.

"Emma, I've heard so much about you. I'm Lilith."

"Oh," I said, not taking her hand. She dropped it and frowned.

"Hm, not very friendly, huh?" she pouted.

"I want...you two to leave," I repeated. "You have the entire planet to fuck up and turn into a second Hell. Just give me this one place."

Lilith leaned close enough to me, her cheek brushing mine.

"No," she whispered.

I shoved her backwards and she lunged at me, screaming.

"You angel bitch!"

I let her grab me by the throat and pin me down on the ground. She squeezed with all her might, but it wasn't doing anything to me. In a fit of rage, she started clawing at my face.

"Abaddon!" she shrieked. "What's happening!"

I could see his face through her arms flailing around my head. He looked just as surprised as I was. Finally, he pulled Lilith off of me. I sat up and saw that she was panting.

"What the fuck is this?" Lilith asked.

"I- I'm not sure," I smirked. "But it seems that demons can't hurt me anymore. Even elites like you two."

Abaddon walked over to the pile of clothes on the rocks and pulled a dagger out. He charged at me and I braced myself, closing my eyes. The dagger made contact, digging into my stomach. I opened my eyes and looked from my stomach up to Abaddon. He grimaced as he twisted the blade around. I smiled back.

"Nothing," I shrugged.

He pulled the dagger out, looked at it, and then looked at me.

"Come on, Lilith," Abaddon said. "Let's go."

Abaddon pulled his pants on and smiled at me.

"I'll tell you what," he said. "I'll give you enough time to say goodbye to your beach, but we'll be back."

"And we'll bring friends the next time too!" Lilith added as she pulled a sheer dress on. "The next time you see this place, it'll be the biggest demon orgy you've ever fucking seen!"

I pulled my sword out and set it ablaze. Lilith let out a laugh.

"Do you know how to use that blade, little girl?"

"You wanna come back over here and find out?" I snarled.

Lilith took a step towards me and Abaddon grabbed her arm.

"Just let it go," Abaddon said.

"Get your hand off of me!" she pulled away violently and charged me.

I swung my sword with all of my might as Lilith reached me and I sliced right through her neck. Her head flew off and landed on the rock right before her body crumpled in a heap. Abaddon blinked at me, in shock, quickly grabbed the rest of his clothes, and then disappeared. I went to sit down just as the first light of morning was beginning to spread across the sky. There was an unknown fluid on the rock where the two demons had been.

"Ugh!" I recoiled.

I stormed back down to the shore. They were going to take my beach just to spite me. There was absolutely nothing left for me on Earth. I started walking along the shoreline, with no destination in mind. It wasn't until I reached Mombasa, Kenya a few days later that I realized I was halfway out of Africa. Occasionally, the terrain would get too difficult to walk on and I'd have to fly to get around it, but I always stuck to the shore. I saw less and less humans, but didn't see nearly as many demons as I thought I would. On the thirty-ninth day, I reached the Gulf of Aden and passed into Yemen and Saudi Arabia by the Red Sea.

As I walked, I watched the sun set over the water. It surprised me how different sunrises and sunsets looked in different parts of the world. I was contemplating this when I came across a loggerhead sea turtle washed up on the beach, tangled in a net. I hurried over to see if it was breathing and flipped it over onto its stomach. It was still alive, but just barely. I drew my sword and started carefully cutting the net away from its neck and flippers. Once I had it freed, it just laid there. I had been too late and it was too weak to move. The tide came up higher, gently splashing water against the turtle's face.

"MOVE!" I yelled abruptly. "Please!"

It didn't react to my yelling.

"Please..."

I waited for any sign that it was all right. Finally, the turtle moved its head ever so slightly. I gasped.

"You're alive!"

I quickly took my cloak and boots off, and pushed my shirt sleeves up. I got behind it and pulled up. I dragged it awkwardly down to the water. It immediately started drinking.

"I'll try and find you something to eat!"

I got into the water waist-high and looked around for any type of plant. Eventually I found some seagrass and grabbed handfuls of it. I took it over to the sea turtle and held the grass in front of its face. It looked at the grass for a moment before stretching its head forward to take a bite.

"Yes!" I said excitedly. "That's good! Keep eating!"

The turtle ate all of the grass I had, so I went back for more. When I returned, the turtle was slowly inching into the water more.

"Wait!" I said. "You're still weak. You might not make it if you try to swim!"

But it paddled forward, further into the water, and swam away. I watched it disappear into the deep ocean and I was once again left alone. I hung my head and headed back to the beach. I sat and watched as the sky went from orange to dark blue, contemplating my life and afterlife. I thought about how every person I had ever cared about was in Paradise. Thinking about it should have made me feel better, but it didn't. I wanted so badly to focus on being happy for everyone, but a part of me was stuck on being envious. On the third day of sitting on the beach, I was interrupted by sobbing.

"Please, help me!"

I looked around to see where the sound was coming from. Eventually, a man stumbled onto the beach. He was alone and his white shirt was covered in blood. His arms were flailing around as he continued to call out for help. I waved both arms at him, but he didn't seem to notice me. I got up and made my way to him, wondering if I had somehow become invisible to humans again. As I got closer to him, I noticed that both of his eyes had been gouged out and both ears cut off. There was swollen green and red skin around the ear canal, and pus was running from the wounds.

"Sir?" I said softly. He didn't respond to my voice.

"Please!" he shouted hoarsely again. "Please, someone!"

I noticed the streaks and rashes forming on his cheeks and neck. He had severe blood poisoning. I stood still, watching him stagger down to the shoreline. As soon as the water hit his blistered bare feet, he stopped calling out. He slowly waded into the water, and then swam out into the sea. I moved back up to the taller rocks to get a better look at what the man was doing. I saw him swim further out and then float for a minute.

"Through this holy anointing-" I said softly.

I thought about Ankou stopping me from saving the woman in the garage. The one who was killing herself and her baby. The man in the water had his sight and hearing taken by a demon. But why? Had he done something to deserve it? I didn't finish. Instead, I concentrated hard on his soul. Who was he? What had he been like? And then I saw everything he had done. All of the men he had killed and the terrible things he had done to their wives.

I watched the man float for a bit longer before going under the surface. He didn't come back up. He chose to drown himself before being punished any longer. He had no idea what awaited him though. I was done saving suicides. Ankou had been right all along. And then, an idea came to me. A terrible, awful idea. But one that I hoped would somehow get me into Paradise.

"I can't do this," I said out loud. "I don't want to do this. And I can't even die!"

I looked at my sword laying on the tangled net.

No, I thought. *I can't be killed. But maybe there's another way.*

I took a deep breath and propped myself up on my knees.

"God, forgive me for what I'm about to do."

The wind picked up and sprayed my body with saltwater. The night sky was black above the ocean. I turned my sword around, holding it by the blade, and sat the handle end against the sand. The tip of the blade was aimed right at my chest.

"Through this holy anointing, may the Lord in His love and mercy help you with the grace of the Holy Spirit."

My voice was surprisingly calm and my hands were steady as I continued.

"May the Lord who frees you from sin save you and raise you."

I closed my eyes and pushed my body into the sword as hard as I could. But I felt nothing. I looked down. The blade was through me. I pulled it in deeper, to the point where the handle was against my chest. I couldn't feel anything. I slowly pulled the sword out and there were no marks on my body, no blood, just a small rip in the fabric of my shirt.

"What the hell?"

I got up, sheathed my sword, and looked up at the sky.

"WHYYY?!" I screamed. "WHY ARE YOU DOING THIS TO ME? I DIDN'T WANT ANY OF THIS TO HAPPEN! I DIDN'T WANT IT TO BE ME!"

Nothing happened.

"ANSWER ME!"

I buried my face into my hands and wept.

"I'm alone," I croaked. "I'm all alone."

No, you're not.

My head shot up at once and I looked around. There was no one there.

"H-hello?"

Nothing.

I chuckled to myself, and then jumped at the sound of my own laughter; a sound I hadn't heard in quite some time.

"I'm losing my mind," I shook my head.

No, you're not, I heard again. I whipped around, drawing my sword.

"Who's there?" I asked loudly. "Show yourself!"

I can't do that.

"Why not?"

Because I am everywhere.

I recognized the voice. It was my voice! In my head but somehow out loud at the same time. And it wasn't like when I thought about something. I wasn't in control of this voice.

"Who-who are you?"

I am who you called for. I am who I am. El. Yahweh. Allah. Alpha and Omega.

"God?" I asked, my voice barely above a whisper.

No answer.

"Why do you sound like me?"

I use your voice to speak to you because it is the voice you hear more than any other. It is familiar.

"So...why are you talking to me now?"

You called. I answered.

"I think I've called for you before and never received an answer."

Are you sure about that? Or were you not listening for the answer?

"Oh please," I scoffed. "Don't pull that cryptic shit with me."

Suddenly, lightning struck the ground about twenty feet away from me. The light blinded me and the crash was deafening. I covered my ears and crouched down. Then, the wind picked up and I looked out to the sea. A wall of water grew and grew, hundreds of feet above the surface. It suddenly came down and towards me. I raised my hands to shield myself, but the water didn't hit me.

I watched the water back up slowly into the sea and the wind died down until everything was calm again.

"S-sorry," I muttered.

Do not test me.

"Sorry!" I repeated.

Emma, I know you are carrying a heavy load.

I scoffed again and continued walking.

I'm sorry.

"So did you know I would be the one?"

Yes.

"Have you known since I was human?"

No.

"Even though you're all-knowing?"

It's more complicated than that.

"Well, it seems like I have plenty of time to learn. Try me."

Everything is already laid out. From beginning to end. I put the pieces on the board but I don't move them. I know what is going to happen before it happens, but I don't know the details of how it will happen.

"That doesn't sound like all-knowing."

I told you, it's complicated. I knew it would be a death angel who ended humanity. It wasn't until you chose to become one that I saw it would be you.

"But why even end humanity? You created all of this. Why let them all die? You're also all-powerful."

Just because I can, doesn't mean I should.

"Yeah, like curing cancer," I said sarcastically.

Men have the potential to cure cancer. They'd rather be rich and keep people sick. I don't create murderers or drug addicts. People do that. Some illnesses come from poor choices. Cancer isn't something I created. At some point someone's cells formed differently. That person had a child and that DNA was passed on. I don't want to see humans suffer. I don't want them to hurt. But unfortunately, pain is part of the human experience. You can't appreciate joy without experiencing sadness first. That's where I went wrong, I suppose. I should have made humans more like a lot of the animals I created. Without empathy and passion and love.

"There are animals who experience love," I argued.

They experience companionship. It's different. But I wanted to give humans the gift of feeling what I feel. Love. Excitement. Disappointed. Nervousness. Relief. Calmness. Boredom. Disgust. Fear. Loneliness.

I peeked my head up.

Oh yes, I feel loneliness too. Why do you think I chose to create all of this?

"Because you can?"

Because I wanted to. Humans started off just like animals. It was more of a companionship. But when I created Adam and Eve and gave them souls, they became more like me. I was naive though. I had hoped humans would be good, and stay good, if they didn't know right from wrong. But then I realized, the only way they could be good is if they knew bad existed.

"What do you mean?" I asked.

I asked Satan to tempt them, to see if they would make the right decision. They didn't. Neither did their sons, Ankou and Cain. I really wanted humans to be good, without forcing them to be. But I let them make their own choices and over thousands of years, things never got any better. In fact, I think they only got worse.

"But because of demons tempting them! Humans wouldn't be so bad if evil forces weren't constantly pushing them in the wrong direction!"

Children learn right from wrong at an early age. They know what hurts themselves and others. But they still grow up and make poor choices. I knew this day would come. Humans overall have become so self-absorbed that there's no correcting it. The planet is sick from all of the waste and chemicals humans have created. The air is polluted. The oceans are dying. Animals are being hunted just for sport. That's not why I put them here. And all of the weapons and drugs humans have created to kill each other. I created an entire universe full of endless galaxies. And to see this planet, my creation, being destroyed by another one of my creations... It's too much. So, we made a pact to end things.

"Who?"

Satan and me.

"What! So you just gave up on humans?"

Believe me, I didn't want to. But I'd rather see millions enter Paradise now, than wait longer and see things get even worse.

"So it was a mutual decision that things would just end now, and you two would collect whoever was left?"

More or less.

"And you used me to do it?"

Someone had to.

"Well, I wish it wasn't me."

That's what Jesus said too.

"Except he was the hero of the story. I'm the villain."

You're not the villain. You're more of an anti-hero. You're not bad, Emma. The choices you've made have always been with good intentions.

"So then why not let me into Paradise? If you know I'm a good person, why not let me finally rest and be at peace? I did what I was meant to do!"

Your journey is not over yet.

"What is left for me to do? I unleashed the Antichrist. The world is ending. By the way, what will happen to Sam- or, what used to be Sam?"

All of the demons will eventually return to Hell. The Antichrist will roam the world alone.

"Just like you've left me here all alone."

You're not alone.

"Yes, I am!"

No, you're not.

I sighed.

"I know I'm not alone because you're always with me. But that's not what I meant."

That's not what I meant either.

"Well then, what did you mean?"

Silence.

"Hello?"

Nothing. I stopped walking.

"Please don't do this to me now!" I panicked. "I have so many more questions!"

I began to fly upwards.

"Please, God!" I cried as I went higher.

"Don't do this to me! Don't leave me all alone!"

I slowly lowered myself back to the ground and glanced over at my boots and cloak. I noticed something sticking out of one of the inner pockets. I inhaled sharply, realizing what it was, and pulled Eduardo's note out. I had completely forgotten about it. It was crumpled and stained, but I was still able to make out what it said:

Dearest Emma,

I want to start off by thanking you. I know you've carried so much guilt about my death, but please don't. I was given a second chance at life! I wasn't happy as a death angel, if you couldn't already tell. One of my favorite pieces of literature is "Ligeia" by Edgar Allen Poe. There is a poem in the story titled, "The Conqueror Worm." It's about a play where humans are caught in an endless cycle of fear and suffering. Angels, who make up the audience, watch in shock and horror, helpless to defend them. The poem is about mortality and inevitable death. There's nothing we can do to intervene because humanity is on its own. The only true way to end fear and suffering is through death, The Conqueror Worm. My soul needs rest, Emma. I was more than ready to go to Paradise when I died again. I wouldn't have had my amazing life if it wasn't for you. I wouldn't get to spend eternity in Paradise with my loved ones if it wasn't for you. I always saw potential in you, Emma. Your drive to always do what is best for others is what makes you the perfect candidate to become a death angel. I'm glad I was able to remember you as Dumah, but see how far you've come as Eduardo. I'm very proud of you. And that doesn't mean you're not going to mess up and make mistakes along the way. But if I know you, and I do, you're going to find a way to make things right. I have faith in you.

Best regards,
Eduardo Reyes

P.S. You are the Conqueror Worm.

I finished the letter, folded it carefully, and slipped it back into its pocket.

I paused and thought about what God had said.

My journey wasn't over yet.

I'm not alone.

"Hey, Emma!"

I turned and looked up at the grassy hill. Sekhmet, Hutriel, Gabe, and two other dark angels I didn't recognize were standing there, looking at me. A sixth person came into view, wearing all black. I gasped as soon as Otomatsu's eyes met mine. He started running towards me as I stood there in shock. Even as he squeezed me and spun me around, I couldn't quite believe he was there.

"I found you," he said, still hugging me. "I found you."

"How-?" I started as I looked up at him. "You went through the Gates and up the stairs. You're supposed to be in Paradise."

"I couldn't leave you."

As tears filled my eyes, I whispered, "I'm not alone."

Otomatsu put his arm around me and we walked up the hill to the others. Gabe looked everywhere but at me. Sekhmet limped over to me and hugged me.

"I'm so sorry," I whispered.

"Shh, it's okay," she replied.

Sekhmet smiled at me before turning to the others.

"Emma, this is Ananiel and Zihrun. And you already know Hutriel."

Hutriel waved. I noticed she was carrying Otomatsu's satchel.

"It's nice to meet you both," I said. They both nodded.

Hutriel handed Otomatsu his satchel back.

"What's that?" I asked.

"Stopped by your hut before Processing was completely locked down," he explained. "Grabbed a few essentials."

"So what do you say?" Sekhmet smiled. "Wanna help us kick some demon ass?"

Epilogue

The Antichrist had decided to go by her former name, Sam. She knew it would disturb the death angel that had brought about the end of the world, and that put a smile on her face. The first few months of Hell being unleashed on Earth had been full of death and destruction. Demons wiped out millions of humans, although there were still some in hiding. Abaddon, Astaroth, Ah Puch, Lamashtu, and the newly made elite, Heimlich, made up the Realm Council, whose sole purpose was to recruit human souls to become new demons.

The Antichrist sat in the oval office of the White House, listening to her Realm Council laughing and celebrating over their victory. Ah Puch and Astaroth were smoking cigars and making crude jokes about former American presidents. Heimlich passionately recounted his days as a human, when he had been an important part of another invasion; Lamashtu listened in admiration. Abaddon sat across the room, watching everyone, but watching Sam with particular intensity. Something was obviously troubling her.

Abaddon got up and crossed the room, softly placing a hand on Heimlich's back as he passed him. Heimlich returned an enthusiastic slap on Abaddon's arm and continued his storytelling. Once he was on the other side of the desk, he knelt down next to Sam. She didn't look at him as she continued to watch her inner circle commemorate.

"Is everything okay?" Abaddon asked softly. "You've been very quiet since we got here."

Sam sat back in her chair, her small feet dangling inches off the ground. She rested her elbow on the arm of the chair and sat her chin on top of her fist.

"I feel a change," Sam said pensively.

"Well, of course you do," Abaddon chuckled. "Hell has overthrown Earth. We made God and all of his angels retreat to Paradise."

"It's not that," Sam said. "I feel like things aren't over for us with the angels."

"You don't mean Emma?" Abaddon smirked.

"She can't be killed," Sam stood up, catching the attention of the entire room. "That means, no matter how many demons I make, or how many of them are here on Earth, there will always be an angel among us. A part of God's kingdom in my realm."

"What could she possibly do to be any kind of threat to us?" Astaroth asked.

"As long as she's here, Earth isn't completely mine."

Sam looked down at her blood-stained purple tennis shoes. One of the laces was becoming loose. She bent down, re-tied her shoe, and as she stood back up, she smiled.

"I think I'd like to have a playdate with an old friend."

Author's Notes

Content warning: This fictional piece of literature may contain content disturbing or offensive to some readers. This is not my intent. It is simply a work of fiction that started with a nightmare I had in 2019 and has since then become this whole fantasy world I've created. This book contains material for readers who are sensitive to self harm/suicide, dark religious themes, violence and death, blood and gore, and addiction. Please note that it is not the author's intent to cause distress to any reader, but if you find any of these subjects triggering, please take note and proceed with caution. Remember to practice self-care before, during, and after reading. For more information, please go to: www.vanessakramerauthor.com

*If you or someone you know is in crisis and needs immediate help, Call or text 988 to connect with the 988 Suicide & Crisis Lifeline . The Lifeline provides 24-hour, confidential support to anyone in suicidal crisis or emotional distress.

Thank you to my family and friends for their ongoing support, and to my street team, my BookNess Monsters, for everything they do.

Made in the USA
Columbia, SC
17 May 2025